The Snow Path to Dingle

Other books by the international award-winning author,
Nancy Blanton

The Prince of Glencurragh

The Earl in Black Armor

When Starlings Fly as One

Brand Yourself Royally in 8 Simple Steps:
Harness the Secrets of Kings and Queens
for a Personal Brand that Rules

The Curious Adventure of Roodle Jones

Heaven on the Half Shell:
The Story of the Northwest's Love Affair with the Oyster

The Snow Path to Dingle

A Novel of Ireland

NANCY BLANTON

EDB

Ellys-Daughtrey Books
Fernandina Beach, Florida

THE SNOW PATH TO DINGLE

Previously publishes as Sharavogue
A Novel of Ireland and the West Indies

Second Edition

The first edition of this book was published in November, 2012. The second edition includes a list of other books by the author, maps related to the story, and additional end matter (i.e. book club questions and sample text from the prequel, The Prince of Glencurragh).

ISBN:978-1-7335928-4-0

Printed in the United States of America

Ellys-Daughtrey Books, date: 09/23/2022
Fernandina Beach, FL
ellys-daughtrey.blogspot.com

Cover design by Ellys-Daughtrey Books.

For Karl, in gratitude for our many amazing adventures.

Acknowledgements

The story of Elvy came to me in a simple phrase so compelling it woke me from a deep sleep and set me on a course that even now continues. The phrase, the snow path to dingle, refused to be ignored and I had to find out what it meant and where it led. It became my working title and inspired me for years until the book was completed. I'm grateful for that phrase and the lesson it taught me, that gifts can come from the most unexpected places, and the joy is in the discovery.

For their constant support and encouragement during this journey, I first thank my husband Karl who weathered all my ups and downs, thrills and disappointments, and feigned interest when I described the latest historical tidbit I'd uncovered. I thank my mother Virginia who raved over some initial chapters and at least knew I had finished the book before we lost her.

Thanks to my father Edward who would be proud, I know, for even though at one point I told him I didn't think I could write anymore, he insisted I would write again when I was ready. Thank you Daddy, for believing.

My sister Daphne and my best friend Marilyn maintained their enthusiasm no matter how much time passed, and Marilyn's father Joe read every word and made a point of telling me everything he liked about the story before we lost him too. I also thank my sister Gayle and my nieces Rachel and Kelly; and Jean Gordon who has supported me like an angel for twenty-six years, who is just as comforting long-distance as if she stood right beside me, and who continues to teach me about unconditional love.

I am also grateful to my fellow writers, dear friends from work, and my friends through the Association for Women In Communications, all of whom helped me whether overtly or just by being who they are: Pam Abbey, Dusti Blood, Peter Bernhardt, Wendy Dore, Marilyn Farrell, David Gordon, Lorraine Howell, Jane Kilburn, JoAnne Lee, Elaine Long, Elaine

Marklund, Colleen McPoland, Michele Morgan, Anne and Richard Muller, Trish Murphy, Chris Nardine, Michael Neff, Karen Nims, Sandra Noel, Katie Nowlin, Mayo Ochiltree, Marlys St Laurent, Mick Shultz, Rob Walgren and Beth Whitman.

And one last comment on behalf of all authors, and especially independents: thank you to all the readers who are willing to look beyond the New York Times bestsellers to find wondrous stories, who buy books instead of borrow, and who share their enjoyment in reviews, social media comments, and recommendations. Authors work years to create and perfect their books, usually with many sacrifices and out-of-pocket expenses. Your comments, recommendations and support help keep us going.

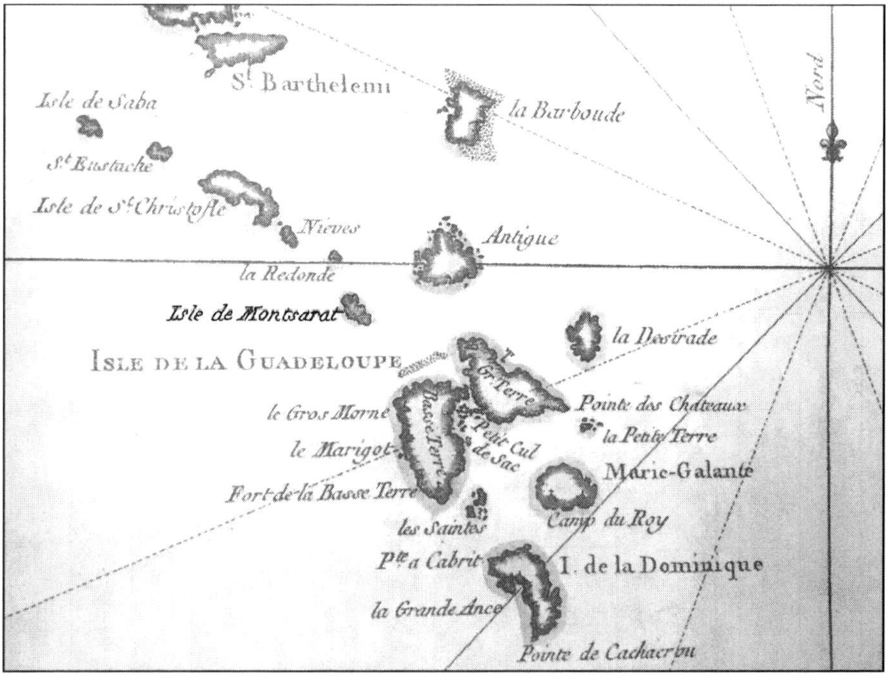

Location of the island, Montserrat, in the West Indies.

Ireland

ULSTER
CONNACHT
Dublin
Galway
LEINSTER
Wexford
MUNSTER
Dingle
Youghal
Skebreen

1

River of Hope
December 1649
Province of Munster, Ireland

This is a righteous judgment of God upon these barbarous wretches who have imbrued their hands in so much innocent blood...

~ Oliver Cromwell, 1649

From the beginning, all I had ever wanted was to live my destiny. I was the daughter of a great warrior, born to be a leader of my people and defender of my country. I was not a liar. I was not a killer, and hardly an assassin. It is only by the cruelest of circumstances that I was thus transformed. I had just turned fifteen years of age—too young to question whether my choices would be my own, and too foolish to realize the world turned on its own relentless path with little regard for a red-haired orphan girl. I was safe. I had hope. And then, just before dusk on a bleak December day, a traveler arrived on a thick black horse.

A cold blast of wind caused me to shudder the moment he entered our dank little tavern, tucked as it was off the roadway amongst the junipers beneath a great Scots pine. I felt a rare chill seize the back of my neck, but my mind was distracted by Uncle Aengus's shouting. He did so frequently and I knew I should not let anger command my behavior, but I had no one about me with a reasoned head to tell me how to do things otherwise. Uncle Aengus was nothing but a child in men's clothing, and any of the villagers would describe him so. He was twenty years my senior and yet we argued like siblings. Though I'd just finished scrubbing every table and every tankard, and cleaning up after our meal, he set me about cleaning the tavern hearth. I allowed my bitterness to swell and rule my tongue. I spewed out a worthy string of curses on his life for him thinking I'd have my sore hands in the filth again, and mind you I'd learned some fine curses from the wives of our steadfast customers.

"Die, Aengus O'Daly, and make a puddin' for the crows!" I cried. But Aengus pinched the fat of my arm with such a fury I fast conceded, grabbed my pail with as much clatter as I could muster, and set to the task.

"And make quick of it Elvy, or ye'll be dumping the ashes after dark and you know it's a fearsome danger. When you're done, set a good hot fire for the lads."

"It's the dark I should fear, is it? And never mind the raging storm a-comin'?" I flicked my tongue at him as he turned his back to me. Elvy was not my true name, and though I had grown accustomed to it I still resented it when I was angry. My own mother called me Ailbhe before a fever took her away from us—it is a strong Irish name meaning white, noble and bright, and I knew she intended me for the pure and high life my grandfathers had ordained. My mother descended from Gerald FitzGerald, the 15th Earl of Desmond, and I was proud to have grown tall and lanky as she and her forebears had been. I was daughter of a warrior on my father's side from the powerful clan of Burke, and like them I was strong and quick. My ancestors were kings owning great tracts of land sweeping across the province of Munster. My given name should have been revered in every household. But our lands and houses had been taken by the English decades before my birth. And it was not my noble name that was known throughout our village, but the soft and loving sound uttered from my father's lips. Elvy was the only name Uncle Aengus would call me, except urchin when he wished to raise my hackles.

The twinkle in the eyes of our few customers meant our quarrel had provided entertainment, and so for a brief wisp of a moment I was glad when the traveler's arrival drew the attention off me.

Aengus's tavern was the first structure just west of the old bridge that crossed the River Ilen. Though the local gentlemen were our mainstay, we gladly welcomed the coins from parched folk crossing the river off the Cork road. I glanced up, brushing an unruly copper curl from my eyes, and returned to my work until the sight of him registered like a whip's lash to my brow. I dropped my pail to the stone hearth, spilling the ashes I'd just collected on the dirt floor I'd just swept.

With the tails of his black cloak dripping mud and the hood pulled over his brow, he could have been the Devil himself, risen up from the bog. He collapsed on a rough-hewn bench like wet sack of bones and upset a full tankard of ale. I might have cursed him as well for the mess he'd made, had he not looked up with the vacant eyes of a man who has foreseen his own end. Those eyes sent a shiver up my spine and caused the voices to hush and the old village men to stare, their ales half drunk and their mouths gaping. I pulled the rough-spun hem of my skirt close around my ankles and watched the color drain from Aengus's face until his jowls turned stone gray.

We had seen this man before, passing through Skebreen from Youghal, and Aengus knew him as Malcolm. His appearance surely heralded disaster, for word had come already that the English General Oliver Cromwell had chosen Youghal to establish his winter quarters. Malcolm needed say nothing of the general's terrible progress from Drogheda in northeast, where the great Irish rebellion had begun, to Wexford in the southeast, for the news had preceded him in morbid detail with entire villages slain, women and children cut down like weeds and left to die in blood-sodden ditches. In Wexford, just a few days ride away, two thousand souls had been lost and the destruction was so horrific it prevented even the army from camping there. And so, the brutal general had pushed farther west on the rocky coast road toward Munster, toward Cork, seeking every last rebel even where there be none. In Skebreen we had all prayed Cromwell would tire of his crusade before marching any farther.

Malcolm opened his lips to speak but no sound came, his voice lost in a fierce constriction, and the old men waited until at last his sound eked out as high as a woman's: "He comes!" He raised an arm and pointed a bony finger toward each of us in turn, twisting slightly as if he himself was the instrument of death selecting the next soul to take. "I bring news of Oliver Cromwell and his filthy cavalry. They ride this way, sure as you breathe, and his fleet, heavy with cannon, sails beside him. He rides from Kinsale to Desmond Castle, and from there southwest. In my own village, the magistrate fell at his feet, snivelin' like an idiot and pleading for our lives to be spared. But that be not enough for this monster. His work be not done until he sees a river of blood. Now he presses his deadly boot upon our very throats, so I've come with a warning. You must all collect your families and leave here and make haste! Join me now and head deep into the wilds of Kerry where the butcher dare not follow. What say you, Aengus O'Daly, my old friend? Will ye go?"

Aengus looked as if he'd seen a spirit pass before him, his mouth hanging open for the flies, his fine graying hair in long strings about his face. Tall and narrow as the pines he was, but bending to the winds like a willow. As my guardian since I was seven years old, he protected me fierce, like a big brother who'd dare any soul to touch his sister. He looked at me with his sad brown eyes, then down at his battered old shoes and I knew his answer. Had my father been with us, he'd have raised his sword already. But Da was in his grave, and all the able young lads who might defend the village had joined rebel bands to the north or pirate ships to the west.

Aengus was no warrior. In his whole life, he'd not been more than a stone's throw from our village, and I'd never seen him lift more than a thumb to kill a flea. The little windowless tavern with its drafty door and leaking thatch offered little comfort, and yet I wondered did he fear leaving more than he feared to stay. He shook his head, an autumn leaf barely turned by the wind.

"Should I go, what's here will be burnt sure as we breathe. And should they come, they'll be wantin' the drink and not the man. I'll serve 'em what I have and may be spared."

"Ye're daft!" Malcolm cried. "Cromwell spares nothing but his own and those who can bring him profit. He leads a path of murder and destruction so bloody few survive to tell the tale."

A fragile silence filled the tavern until old Mr. Fitzgibbon stood and and his rumpled brown cloak hung in folds from his shoulders to his shins. He scratched his white-bearded chin with the tip of his pipe. No one knew Mr. Fitzgibbon's exact age, but his craggy face and bent stance suggested years beyond anyone else in the village, and he seemed to know the history of the earth and all its wisdom. "'Tis the land that draws Cromwell. He's fresh out of a civil war and cares to know what's here for the taking to reward his best men. Mayhap he's not in a killing mood after all the bloodshed that has been, though I'd not lay a wager on it.

"Anaways, do not fool yourself into believing Kerry offers escape. Are you forgetting the battles fought by the Earl of Desmond nearly seventy years gone now? And after that the bloody massacre at Smerwick on Ireland's farthest edge? You'll find no refuge west of here if it's where the English wish to go. I say, pray you with fervor this madman will pass us by. We've no rebel camp and hardly an establishment suitable for a general's rest. Insignificance may be our brightest hope."

I whispered a prayer to my beloved St. Brendan for protection.

He alone I trusted, who had sailed west from our island in a tiny leather boat, and returned years later to prove that indeed Heaven exists and is magnificent beyond anyone's dreams. If he could return safely from such a daring voyage into the unknown, he could lift the curse that now befell our little village.

But I could not prevent the whisper of doubt that found my ear, nor the heavy weight of dread filling my chest as I remembered the omen I had seen the last eventide: a setting sun with a blood-red circle around it and a stroke cleaving it in two. I could not read its meaning then, and I dared not ask Uncle Aengus for he would either swoon or panic, but I was sure it warned of a danger. If it foretold something terrible for Skebreen, naught could be done now. I scooped the spilled ashes back into my pail and uncovered the banked coals with the tip of a willow branch as my father had taught me. In my mind I could see his blue eyes, bright and challenging as my own, and hear his voice as clear as if he crouched beside me. "Is it honor ye value, daughter," he would ask, "or will ye be takin' defeat?"

Since he'd first lifted me screaming from my mother's arms, he had filled my head with centuries of chieftains and warriors defending a great kingdom. With each telling he breathed the fire into my belly. Honor or defeat—both always there for the choosing, and it was no true warrior of our blood who would choose the latter. "To choose honor is to choose life," he would say, "even if it brings death." And then he would laugh out loud at the irony. Would Da find it honorable to wait for Cromwell's coming and hope we'd be ignored? Or to flee to the wilds where we might not be followed? Or would he see defeat? My belly began to burn as the smoking coals found new life, and I sucked in a quick breath.

"The bridge!" The words escaped my lips before I'd even thought them. Mr. Fitzgibbon's head snapped around and he gave me a curious stare.

"What say you, girl?"

"The bridge, sir. The little stone bridge crossing the river Ilen. 'Tis the only thing leading him right to us. What if we could tear it down, and him pass right by?"

The others stared at me now, and Aengus stood hard as a stone, glaring fierce as if to make me disappear. He always preferred me to stay quiet and unnoticed when the customers were in, the better to protect my maidenhead, and always he was disappointed for I could not hold my tongue. Mr. Fitzgibbon stepped away from his bench, his whiskers twitching and his lips moving without words.

"Ye cannot hide a bridge, lass," Mr. McSherry said as if placating a dull child, and shrill laughter erupted from his brother Sean. Always together in their farming frocks, the McSherrys never had a fresh idea between them. But old Mr. Fitzgibbon stepped closer, one of his frail legs trembling, and found the strength of his voice that had guided our little village for decades.

"Hold now, gentlemen," the elder said. "To be sure, our Elvy's an impulsive little sprite, but in fact she may have something there for us to consider."

There was grumbling across the room as if we'd just raised the price of ale. "It's insanity, man. Ye cannot remove a bridge once it's built!" Mr. McSherry argued. "And do I needs bother to mention you're takin' strategic advice from a flame-haired fop of a barmaid who's still with the hips of a boy and always believin' she's some kind of a princess?"

The men of the tavern knew me as well as their own children and grandchildren, including the most tender places to cast their barbs and get a rise. I stood, as tall as I could manage, ash-blackened fists on my hips. "A fop, am I? And here ye are, a bunch of gossipers carrying on with your feeble tales," I hissed, "whilst our lads and lands are to be attacked by this vicious, killing enemy! How can you sit so, drinking your ale and blatherin' as if it's just the lord of the manor having a bad case of the gout? I'm far more a princess than you are a man, for at least I'm looking to solve our troubles and not just fume about them!"

But Mr. Fitzgibbon silenced me with a wave of his hand. His eyes had turned bright as the stars and he straightened his back, standing taller than ever I'd seen him, then he cast his smoldering pipe at our feet. Its sparks died quickly as they settled. Another omen, I was sure, but there was my weakness with omens. Would our troubles be extinguished? Or our village? My mother would have known the answer instantly, but I could not read the meanings until circumstances made them obvious. I could not read them in time to change the future.

"Insanity? No." Mr. Fitzgibbon said, and then paused for emphasis. "Genius is what it is." At this the others erupted into arguments in every corner of the tavern and lasting well into the night. I stayed in the shadows by the hearth as they raged, but in the end no one could pose an alternative that could stand up against Mr. Fitzgibbon's wise counsel and worldly experience. He persuaded them with his gentle, unyielding tongue, and then commanded them. "Go now, gentlemen, and come back on the morrow's dawn, your wives, your sons and your daughters with you. The old folk, too. If each takes a stone, the bridge will fall in the wink of a cat's eye. Bring buckets and axes, an ox and a plow horse if you've got them. When you go home after, bring in the livestock for the warmth, as we'll have no hearth fires until the threat of Cromwell is gone. You can maybe hide a bridge, gentlemen, but ye canna hide a village with the peat smoke rising above the trees.

"And when the bridge is gone," the old man added, "our boys will hide along the riverbank to let us know when Cromwell's band has passed us by. Elvy, have your shoes on and your shawl about your shoulders. Being your idea, you'll lead us all to our task."

I felt the prideful spirits soaring in my head. Genius, Mr. Fitzgibbon had called me. We would dismantle a bridge that had existed before any of us were born. We would save the village from Cromwell, and I—*but a girl*—would lead the way. And then I felt the spirits of the dead rise against me for daring to scatter ashes after dark. Aengus warned me it would anger them and now they planned their revenge as they swarmed around me, their tiny needles pricking and digging sharp points into the back of my neck. Fear, plain and simple, that a brilliant idea one instant could lead to disaster the next.

By the songs of the first bird the following morning, I dressed and pulled my mother's green shawl around my shoulders. It was old, nubby and threadbare, but still green as the leaves in spring, and it was the only thing I had left that had been hers. It offered little warmth but it was a great comfort, as if my mother's arms were about me as I marched toward the Ilen, with Aengus beside me muttering all the way. The night's storm had passed but the ground was puddled and muddy, and above me the clouds seemed thin and bruised. Along the river's edge everyone in the village had gathered, nearly three score of us, shivering with cold anticipation.

The Ilen took no notice. Coming south to us from the Mullaghmesha mountain, she lay in bronze repose with her misty veil close at her surface. She was the very river who nourished every fox and sparrow from above Bantry and all the way out to sea at Baltimore. At Skebreen she turned west abruptly as if she'd simply changed her mind, and then south again as if to wrap a gentle arm about us. Sometimes flowing narrow and peaceful, she was our meandering ribbon of sweet dark nectar yielding trout in the spring and salmon in summer. With the winter rains she swelled at her seams, as anxious and irritable as a new mother; and, yes, wasn't the earth at her flanks the most fertile? At her narrow waist, the old bridge linked north to south, and was skirted in splendid green ivy to entice prosperous travelers. It had always been our open door to the world, bringing trade, supplies, news and letters from our kin and country. But now it was the gaping hole that exposed the village to dangers we'd heard of but did not wish to know.

With the bridge away, the Ilen could rush and flow to her heart's content without its shadow to cloud her waters. She would be our protector, our moat against a siege. I stood on the riverbank, and Mr. Fitzgibbon handed me an ax.

"Be thankful our bridge is old and many of her stones brittle, child, to make the task easier."

"Mr. Fitzgibbon," I whispered, my cold hands shaking. "What if it doesn't work? What if Cromwell comes anyway?"

He leaned closer. "So it may happen, Elvy. No one's to know in advance, but we all love a clever trick, don't we? If it fails, at least we've had a bit of hope while we're waiting. Nothing conquers fear like activity. Now, strike the first blow where you think it'll do the most good."

I took a deep breath and exhaled slowly. I knew nothing of bridges, only that an army with its horses and supply wagons would need its center to cross. This bridge was plenty sturdy with its stone supports and wooden planks. I imagined some sweaty worker scappling the stone into the proper shape with a crude toothed chisel, then stopping for his dinner of peas, bread, cheese, and beer. And the architect, his back aching and a candle dripping as he drew the lines and calculated the number of stones each section would require. Had he supervised each hour of construction, nodding approval or scolding the worker for mistakes? Had he paced the riverbank as the last stone was placed, then puffed out his chest with pride? And had the worker and the architect both boasted to their friends of their accomplishment, so small and yet so wondrous? And would these men now turn in their graves as a tavern maid began its destruction?

If I continued to think of them I could not do the task before me. I focused instead on the clear banks of the river. By removing the bridge we were only restoring the Ilen to her to her natural state. I stepped to the middle of the bridge, aiming my ax over the side at the narrow stones that pressed together to form the arch. I swung, and a chip fell away like the broken tooth of a scrapper's smile. The others cheered and quickly formed lines across the top of the ancient structure, some along the riverbank, sweating and pounding, the old men heaving large stones with their strong hands and backs or filling the buckets with smaller stones and passing them to the women singing their courage along the bluff. I stood on the riverbank with the men, believing for a while I was one of them, chipping away at the bridge's foundation, rolling away the stones I could not lift, my shoes sinking into the muddy ground. We cheered again when the center of the arch splashed down to the river's deep bottom, and once more when they sent the planks floating like little barges heading south to Baltimore. We forgot our hunger and worked with greater purpose as the chill December wind whisked around our legs. My shoulders ached and my fingers were raw and bleeding, but slowly the bridge began to lose its shape, like an anthill being moved grain by grain to higher ground.

When darkness settled, the children slept together beneath the trees, and yet we labored under the very silver stars where childish wishes had been begged through the ages. By dawn the youngest lads were artfully placing branches along the Cork road to disguise any trace of what had been, and were ferried back to safety in a fishermen's small curragh.

Four days we waited, with no word nor sight of any travelers. At night Aengus and I huddled together, no fire nor livestock to warm us. Had Cromwell come and passed us by? Had our plan succeeded? By the fifth day I could stand it no longer. I followed the ditch behind the tavern down to the bank where the bridge had been. Kevin Harrington, just ten years old, was our sentry crouched in the brush behind a mossy boulder.

He gave me that crooked smile I'd known since he was old enough to walk and his mother let me play with him when they came to the village square. I gave him a nod, then hid beneath a rhododendron to watch for myself. In mid-afternoon the clop of a horse startled me. The rider wore a dung-colored tunic that blended with the browns of the forest behind him. He rode past us along the river, then slowed and continued a bit farther. On a rise just beyond us he stopped, turned in his saddle, and lifted his broad-brimmed hat to look about. My heart pounded a tribal beat until I thought for sure it would explode and I'd die right there. I could not breathe. My palms sweated, clenching the branches of the bush like the hawk clutches the throat of a dying rat. Please let him ride on. *Please* let my little scheme be the saving of our village.

The scout rode over the hill. I exhaled slowly and looked up at Kevin's wide eyes. He stared back, his Adam's apple jumping as he swallowed, but still we waited, unable to move from our posts until we knew for sure we were safe. I had started to crawl from my spot when I heard the pounding hooves again. The rider returned fast, his horse kicking up thick clods of dirt. He pulled up short where the branches had been laid, and walked his horse eastward, looking from side to side of the riverbank. I dared in my heart to believe for just one second that our ruse had worked but knew already the lie was to myself. He mounted again and spurred his horse back to where other soldiers would be waiting. Foolish girl! Foolish village, for listening to such a foolish girl! In what seemed like only minutes we heard the harrowing thunder of a hundred or more horses coming for us all.

The ground beneath me trembled as if the earth itself might split, and the poor hiding bush came alive in my hands, trembling with the fear of it. When the soldiers came around the bend there was no end to them, dark and heavy as if forged of iron, crashing through the bare branches, leaving nothing God-given to hinder their progress.

At the lead they were two abreast and six deep, huge men on black horses, breastplates gleaming in the afternoon light. Large brimmed helmets shaded their eyes and their stiff white collars. They ruled their horses with thick armored gloves and clutched the hilts of enormous swords under wide leather straps. Turned cuffs of their heavy boots rose well above their knees, as if so deep into the muck they would venture to stamp out the life of a rebel. Behind them came others dressed in leather tunics and red sashes, some with broad hats adorned with feather plumes.

Then came the musketeers in their red coats, with heavy matchlock muskets and bandoliers, and the pikemen with their tall helmets and long terrible pikes. And behind these men, but leading a swarm of others, came the one on a copper horse gleaming with armor. Fearing nothing, this rider wore no helmet or breastplate. It was clear he could only be our enemy, General Oliver Cromwell himself.

His white-plumed black hat was grander than any other and shaded all but the sparse hair over his frowning lips. The stiff points of his long collar rested on a massive leather tunic, as rigid as his back with the shoulder coverings extended beyond his width to make him look broader of chest. A wide red sash sliced from shoulder to hip, ending at the bright sheath that housed his sword. The soldiers parted as he rode forward and joined his scout. The two men dismounted just where our lads had placed cut branches to camouflage our work. The scout removed one of them, and I felt my stomach twist against my spine.

Cromwell looked down, then along the wintered banks to the east and west. He removed his hat, giving me the first glimpse of his eyes, as black and flat as a long-dead salmon, and his broad and bulbous nose giving his face the dull arrogance of a bull.

A wind came down the river and lifted the locks of his light hair like tiny serpents roused from their sleep. He glared at the stone where Kevin crouched. *Be still,* I prayed, and do not betray us. But our young Kevin could bear no scrutiny and he bolted, his arms and legs flailing wildly and crashing off through the woods toward the village.

Cromwell shouted. "Four of you, after that mongrel. Bring him before me alive. And do not make long my wait!" The soldiers spurred their horses and plunged into the river after poor Kevin. The flowing river that I thought would protect us seemed no impediment at all. I begged that the horses might drown, but they showed no fear of the water and their riders used the currents to their favor. In minutes they were scaling the bluff on our side of the river, the water sluicing from their flanks as they crashed into the woods before I could but take a second breath. I clung to my little bush, knowing Kevin would lead the soldiers like an arrow into the heart of the village with none prepared for their coming. I had to get a warning to Aengus. But which direction could I take and not be seen? I considered the options too long, paralyzed by my own fear.

Before I could run I felt the sharp sting of a blade between my shoulders and a hand squeezing my ankle like a vise. The black-haired karroge—a filthy cockroach with dirt-smeared face and rotten teeth—grabbed my skirt waist and heaved me to my feet.

"Tall for such a young one." He lifted a lock of my hair and sniffed it, then tugged my hem to get a look at my leg. I jerked away. "Filthy little savage. I'd have ye myself were it not more fun to see the general squeeze the lifeblood out of ye. Let's go see the man, ye nasty urchin!" There was that name again, and it set me to squealing and squirming to get free, but the soldier grabbed my arm so hard I thought sure it was broken.

Stinking of sweat, dirt, ale and horse, he jerked me up against his vile chest and pushed me through the brush toward his mount. He lifted me to his saddle like a sack of barley and plunged back across the river. I screamed, fearing the current, but it was far less threatening than what awaited me on the opposite bank. The soldier nearly crushed my ribs as the horse heaved up the bluff and through the brush. At the top beside the road, he shoved me from his horse and I dropped to the ground in a heap, my face but a whisper from the general's square-toed, muddied boots.

2

Escape from Skebreen

We come to break the power of a company of lawless rebels.

~ Oliver Cromwell

I lifted my chin slowly, fearing at any moment a dagger would pierce my back or a sword would take my head. My heart hammered within my breast as I saw the red sash, the broad belt at his waist securing the dagger and sword I so feared, and then the heavy forbidding tunic. I swear by St. Brendan's head I'll never know what courage made me do it, but I curled my fists and looked defiantly to Cromwell's pock-marked face, framed by thin locks of greasy brown hair. He pursed his lips into a black line, his mouth seeming too small for a man of such terrible reputation and the whiskers too fine for a man's beard or to hide the fat wart that jutted from beneath his lower lip. His long nose was reddened and swollen from the cold, making him look as if he'd drunk too much ale.

My terror turned to anger, my thoughts flooded with contempt. Was this the terrible monster sent in by the English to crush our brave rebellion? Whose men breached Drogheda's walls like vermin, cutting down a thousand townspeople and attacking even a church where men sought refuge, firing the wooden pews beneath the steeple and roasting the men hiding there like rabbits on a spit? Was this the officer who ordered decimation, that every tenth Irish soldier was to be killed, and the rest banished to slavery on some faraway island? And was he the same criminal who descended on poor Wexford with ten thousand foot soldiers and cavalry, his ships bobbing in the harbor like mad dogs straining at their ropes, and then slaughtered two thousand townspeople though they begged to surrender? And whose men so greedily plundered and trashed every house until nothing but ruin remained?

Over his left brow and squeezing through the lashes beneath one heavy-lidded eye, two more warts grew large, brown, and hideous. He looked down on me and I felt a shudder run from the base of my spine to my scalp: his pupils were not black as they had seemed from across the river, but gray as a foggy dusk, no light coming from behind, nor even so much as a glimmer from some depth of his spirit he might seldom tap. His gaze was as soulless as the Devil's own, that scanned the world and all that lay before him, measuring everything for its level of obstruction or potential value. A human life—an Irish life—meant no more to him than a bucket of spoiled meat.

Whatever his goal, any obstacle would surely fall quickly and violently, and anything of value would likely know a worse fate in his hands. His upper lip curled in horrid distaste. "Who causes me such consternation and impedes on my army's progress?" he shouted. "What has become of the bridge that here belongs?"

"I…" It was all I could get out, as if my terror had wrapped a cord around my throat. If only in that moment I could have drawn enough strength to holler the curses I knew so well, or at the very least to spit upon his cruel, destructive boot. But my tongue was dry, my voice sealed, my body shivering in the dirt.

He rolled his gaze skyward. "God help this little fool to speak," he said, and then turned his attention beyond me, at the river bank across the divide. "Who will explain to me!" he bellowed. "Where is the stone bridge that my army now requires?"

Then another soldier splashed from the river and over the bluff with Kevin squirming against his hold. He dropped the boy beside me, wet and weak as a sack of fish. Kevin's face was streaked with tears, his breeches torn and soaking, his shins sluicing blood.

Shouts echoed from across the river. I stole a quick glance over my shoulder. The villagers had been roused by the commotion, and those who could came running. My heart leapt with joy that they might somehow save us, and in the next instant my stomach cringed with fear that Cromwell's men would cut them all down where they stood. The cold river rushed between us, indifferent.

Aengus was there on his knees with old Mr. Fitzgibbon standing beside him, gripping his shoulder. I could hear the huff of air through the general's nose as he breathed a hard fury while the villagers gathered. When he seemed satisfied with his audience, Cromwell burst forth once again.

"Where...is...the...bridge?" He spoke loudly and deliberately, as if to slow children. Mr. Gould must have been selected as the spokesman, for he stepped forward, his round face reddened, his tattered doublet straining against his middle-aged potbelly. He answered, his choirboy voice even higher than usual, yet he surprised me with his bravery.

"Begging your pardon, my lord general, sir. A fierce and violent storm was through just a fortnight past and washed the bridge away. A terrible thing, sir. We've not had the time or the means to rebuild it."

Cromwell looked down at Kevin and me. His lips parted, revealing a sharp, crooked tooth more prominent than the others. He set his stance a bit wider until his stinking boot was just a hand's width from my skirts.

"Washed away, you say? And yet no stones lay about. Am I to suppose the river is washed clean of them? It would be a forceful storm, one would say, to carry off stones of such weight and proportion."

"Indeed, a howling storm, sir. Yes, it is so. But the heavy stones, ye know, sunk down to the bottom, never to rise again." Mr. Gould called out, his pudgy hands clasped over his floppy wool hat and his voice barely carrying across the rippling waters.

The last of the four soldiers appeared near the place on the riverbank where the villagers had gathered. He lifted above him a forgotten wooden pail still jammed with small, squared stones that had once helped form the bridge's arch. A firestorm burst within my rib cage as I realized the damage done.

Cromwell bowed his head, closed his eyes and inhaled deeply. I felt suddenly weak, as if he sucked the very air from the lungs of all who were near. "This bridge has been *dismantled*," he shouted. "And you have lied to an agent who carries out the business of England. Who dares to destroy the property of my countrymen?" His voice was not deep as one might expect from a death monger such as he, but it vibrated with the power of a mighty iron pike that stabbed deeply into a ground well cultivated by terror. "Who dares such destruction? Are these the offenders cowering before me?"

His answer was none but a boy's cry into his mother's skirts. Then I heard the short gasps from Kevin, gone into a great panic. My mind cast about frantically for some answer and means of escape or some hint of what Cromwell might do next. Would he have his men kill us all? Would he hang our heads from the eaves of our houses, or on pikes along the road as a warning to others? Would he set a great fire and burn us until our last screams curdled and hushed? I dared to look up at his horrible face once more, and from Kevin's lips escaped a high, infant's cry so piercing it broke something in the air that surrounded us. As if summoned from the caverns of hell, the blood filled Cromwell's cheeks until they blazed purple and crimson. He drew his sword in one fluid motion and brought it down with such swiftness I could hear its wind and the thud and crunch of his hateful slash through Kevin's collarbone. Hot blood splattered my cheeks and arms, and for a second Kevin's body jerked in the dirt at the feet of his killer. Then he toppled, his head falling against my hand and his blood spraying a gruesome arc from my skirt to Cromwell's boot.

Time stopped, as if the sun and moon in horror and protest refused to journey farther. I watched as a fine mist of blood settled like a soft, pink dew to the ground. Then a gasp of breath awoke my ears and I heard the screaming from far behind me, from men and women alike, and the shouting, and the rustle of the horses, the creak of leather and ring and clatter of armor and sword, and then running, the thunderous shake of the ground. Before me Cromwell still gripped the bloodstained sword, his face seized in a grimace so horrible only a great demon could wear it, and in those flat gray eyes I saw the fires of joy released. I jerked my hand from beneath Kevin's head and rose to my feet without thinking, and then I was screaming as if to shatter the stars.

"Murderer! Slime! May the Heavens strike you down and make the grave your bed, or give me strength to kill you myself! By my father's soul, you shall *die in agony* for what you have done. I shall be Ireland, and Ireland shall have her revenge!"

He gaped down at me and I bolted before Cromwell or any of his soldiers could move, running hard as ever I had, darting off the path and into the woods, away from the river, away from the soldiers, no thought but to escape. There was no time to plan, no time to feel. There was only the stampede of my heart, the image of Kevin's head, the blood spurting, the sound of his last frantic breath, the chilling eyes of Cromwell.

"Capture her!" Cromwell roared from the river's edge. "Let her lips speak defiance from the tip of a pike."

I flitted from bush to fern to tree as a sparrow, darting this way and that to escape the soldiers crashing through behind me. And though I ran

I could still hear the general's bellowing.

"This work is *treason* against England. You will rebuild this bridge and I will cross it on the morrow, or by the breath of God I will reconstruct it myself from your brainless skulls!"

Amid the screams were the thunderous pounding hooves ripping through the underbrush and the splashing of horses into the Ilen as soldiers tore after the terrified villagers. The fire within me exploded in great red blasts and I saw Cromwell's horrid face in every direction I turned, the bright crimson blood staining the ground where I fled, the pleading eyes of poor Kevin and great dark birds swooping down to strip the flesh from his bones. I ran like a wild horse from the bridle, faster until the way got so thick I could only crawl, and I hurled myself into the muskrat havens with the ferns and vines tearing at my arms, skirt, and hair. I kept going until I reached the old castle wall: a Burke Castle, my family's castle, a ruin of stones abandoned by the English nearly a century before. But for England my castle would stand, and I would sit on its throne as princess. If only it remained, I would call on every kingdom in the land and from its sturdy walls we would hail down on Cromwell's army and *destroy it.*

I lost my footing, tumbled into a patch of pea vines and rolled down a slope until a tree root broke my fall. Then I clambered in amongst the dead leaves, vines and ivy, seeking the safety of the faerie thorn tree that had once guarded the door, and now only the broken hearth stone and the mud-brick rubble that once had been my father's house.

I tucked my knees to my chin, so much had I grown since last I'd hid there. I hushed my breathing, pulled the shawl over my head and tried to calm my fluttering heart so I could decide what to do. The bridge must have taken weeks to erect, and the villagers would never be able to rebuild it in a day. Cromwell would kill all of them and suffer not for it. He would decorate our village with the grimacing faces of all those I had known and loved since my birth. I might have preferred that fate for them over rebuilding a bridge for such a devil, but the thought of death for them or for myself sent a pain deep into my heart. I wanted to live. I wanted to do what my father had dreamed. I wanted to take back the castle and all the Burke lands, to be the princess, and yes even the queen he said I was born to be. And most of all I wanted to see that dirty, murdering, hateful Cromwell bleed his last drop of blood at my feet, to avenge every death that had come at his command and see him die in agony. It dawned on me that my curse to Cromwell was not just another one pulled from the library of curses at my command. This one was rooted in my gut and in my throat, more real than any curse I had ever spoken.

I could not go on in life as a simple peasant girl and forget what this man had done as I trembled at his feet. I now realized what I was truly born to do. I was not to sit as a princess on a throne. I was instead an avenging angel, a warrior girl like Joan of Arc. Cromwell must die at my hand. Cromwell, and by his blood, all of England who would oppress my people and me. Yes—this would be my life's work. I would kill Cromwell and have him looking me in the face as it happened. I would take a stone from our village bridge and shove it into his mouth as he did protest, and then I'd bury my dagger gleefully and deeply into his cold, black heart! I had no thought of how I would do it, or from what resources I could draw to oppose such a powerful foe. Yet I knew with absolute certainty this was my one true destiny. I could have continued for days feeding on the great strength of righteous anger, but I heard the voices of soldiers. I coiled tightly and held my breath, praying for the camouflage the leaves and vines could provide.

The soldiers crashed through the woods, hacking from left to right and stabbing into the brush with their swords. From the hilltop where I had fallen, I heard the scrape of metal against the old castle's stone. Heavy boots crushed the ferns and twigs above me. I pressed my freezing hands between my thighs.

"She's passed here, where the vines are bent and crushed. She'll not be far at least." The voice was thick and gruff like the voices of the old men at Aengus's tavern.

"We've searched the entire hill. She's not to be found," said another voice, lighter and perhaps younger.

A voice farther off called out, sharp and high, the words precise. "The child is gone, and damned we'll all be should we kill her. It's not the proper work of a good soldier. We must return and tell the general she's dispatched."

"And have her turn up again?" the gruff one said. "And have the villagers gossipin' that Cromwell's army is so wretched even a young wench can escape? If we'll be damned in time for her head, better that than to hang from Cromwell's noose this day for our failure. Keep searching."

I heard the rustling and cracking of the twigs and undergrowth as they moved along a southward path leading back to Skebreen. Thanks be to St. Brendan's grace, somehow they had passed me by. But, my village! What harm would they do there? What horrors? They clearly meant to kill me and allow no escape, and they would torture anyone to learn my whereabouts. From my fetal pose I prayed our townspeople would scatter into the hills and never be found by Cromwell's men. But I knew Aengus would not go unless he was forced. Had he not said as much? I could not abandon him. I had to find a way past the soldiers to save Aengus myself.

When the chatter of birds returned and I was certain the way was clear, I crawled free of the vines, but not along the path I had come that now bore the marks of the soldiers' boots. Instead I took the opposite direction along a secret path I had not used in years, that I knew as well as the wolf knows the way to her lair. Though it was grown thick with vines I could still see the faint line of it and recognized its' jags and rises from all the times my father had led me through them. And at the end of it lay the Ilen. If the bridge at Skebreen marked her waist, then this section was her breast, wider across and shallower, the current not yet picking up speed, with two tiny islands of moss, tree, vine and root interrupting the water's flow. And just at the place where the Ilen curved back toward the southwest to make her mad dash to the sea, a muddy crag with a thick stand of ferns hid my means of escape: a tiny, leaky curragh, a boat made by my father's hand with skins stretched tight across frail wooden ribs, her insides once coated thick with tar and her outsides greased against the water. I heaved the little craft out of its hiding place and turned it over on the mud.

Rotted in places, the grease long washed away, my little vessel had no oar to guide it. I could only hope my bare hands would propel me at least well enough to get from island to island, with a moment's rest at each to bail the water that would surely flood its floor. I climbed in and pushed hard, and the little craft teetered so that I feared it would capsize and drown me at once, but then it steadied. From its low bow I paddled with a wild fury but in minutes felt my knees wet as my skirt soaked up the river water. I fought for just a few feet more until the bow bumped the moss of the first island. I grabbed at rock and root to pull past, and then onward toward the next little island. The journey had opened a hole in the skins big enough to put my hand through, and water now pumped into the curragh. I splashed and pulled with my arms toward the next island and then jumped out, slipped on the moss and fell on my belly. Before I could grab hold of it my little curragh was beyond my reach, sinking down until I could see only the smallest crescent of the bow as the river claimed it.

Now I was on an island, with no boat to ferry me nor raft of wood to float me. Twilight was settling and the trees and stones were beginning to gray and lose their fine bright edges. Were I to wait, I would be safe here from the soldiers and wolves, but would more likely die of the cold and hunger with no assurance that help would come with the dawn. In the village, torches would be lit, the soldiers shouting at those who ran in terror before them. If captured, they would be murdered or forced to work through the night piecing back together the bridge that I, the genius, had suggested we tear apart.

But there was no time for regret while Aengus was my goal. If I could get back across this last span of river undetected, I could hide in the ditch where I'd always dumped the ashes and try to get to Aengus to come away with me before the soldiers found him. I had to get across.

It was then I remembered a rare scorcher of a day when I was just a babe, and my father brought me to the river's edge to cool my feet. I had squirmed and wriggled away from his hold and then tumbled head-first into the water. Something caused me to turn on my back and it felt as if a hand from the depths reached up to hold me there, floating like a leaf. When my frightened Da grabbed me I was laughing, and he said sure I was part fish. I could make it to the river bank if I stayed on my back, my arms would be my oars, and if I trusted the hand beneath me I would not drown.

I sat at first on the island's edge and eased myself into the cold water, cringing as it chilled my belly. Then I turned and pressed my back into it, pushing with my legs, reaching and pulling with my arms until the building current took a liking to the folds of my skirt. This was not the hand I had counted on. I pulled harder with my arms and kicked, the tiny island growing more distant and then the edges of the bank just out of reach. A curling eddy seemed to draw me near and then push me away until my hand touched a tangle of roots, a lifeline that I seized to pull myself to the bank. I crawled out sopping and shivering, but from there I did not rest and did not look back. I ran for the village and for Aengus.

The torches burned as I had imagined, black smoke rising and violent shadows casting about like spirits and goblins, yet the village was oddly quiet. I crept on my hands and knees through the refuse and filth of the ditch behind our tavern, raising my head only to be certain the tavern still stood before me and no soldiers were near. But clouds had moved in, blinding even the stars. Before I could rise I was slammed hard into the dirt bottom, my face buried in ash as if a tree had fallen upon me, and a hand held my jaw and grasped my mouth that I could not scream. I squirmed for my life, managing to kick something hard that held me down.

"Och, lass, will ye always be bruisin' me shins with each trouble that befalls ye?" Aengus whispered hard and harsh, his lips just behind my ear, and I quit my squirming except to grab a handful of any part of his clothing just to hold onto him.

"Were they here? Did they come for you?"

"Hush now, Elvy. Stay with me, just behind. They're takin' the others to the riverside to start 'em to their task, but sure as foul weather they'll be back with their weapons and their killing ways. We must hurry."

I followed Aengus into the deserted tavern, and we hid behind the bar, wedged so hard together I could feel the bones of his ribs up against mine. I could not see his face but felt his breathing into the hair atop my head. His voice sounded muffled and strained.

"I feared for all these years something' would come to take ye from me. I never expected anything such as we have here, but there's nothing for it. Cromwell's men have camped all along the Cork road, with guards posted around the village through the night. They've orders to capture you for your hanging and let no one else escape. He dies who harbors you. Ye must get away, lass, and fast."

"No, we must go, Aengus!" I tried to jerk around, but he held me fast in our tight quarters.

"Hear me now, lass. I canna go, and I won't. But if ye do not go, they'll kill ye before my eyes or kill every villager on their way to find ye. Mayhap they'll kill us all for the fun of it and save ye for the last. Any way ye look at it, ye've become the target and there's doom."

The tears filled my eyes now, for it's truth that's hardest to hear, even though I knew it already. The English soldiers were prepared for our village to be next victim in their murdering spree. With my curse against Cromwell and my escape, I'd only made their justification easy.

"Mr. Fitzgibbon and I have come up with a plan, but ye must follow it exactly. D'ye hear me now? We'll tell the soldiers that in fact it was your father who masterminded the whole bridge idea, and has gone off on a pirate ship. We'll say in your fear ye've taken one o' Lord Condon's horses and headed east to find yer Da, back toward Cobh harbor. It should throw 'em off track long enough."

"Stolen a horse!" I cried. "They'll kill me for that alone!" I turned as best I could, but it was too dark to see Aengus's familiar brown eyes. I saw clear enough the rag wrapped around his head and padded at his jaw.

I reached up to touch it, but he jerked his head back.

"What is it? Did the soldiers..."

"Nay, not the soldiers. I had a pain and was up to the manor house fer a cure. Sure Cromwell will go there once he's remembered it, but they've not been there yet. Lord Condon has no love for the general, and it's himself we'll be countin' on, havin' his acquaintances to help a young lass in need." Aengus looked the better fool with his head wrapped in a kerchief, but he was serious as any father sending a child alone into the wilds. He reached into his shirt and pulled out a folded paper. "Ye'll take this and guard it carefully. It's a letter of introduction."

"What help is a letter? I can barely read myself!"

"Listen now. Ye'll leave tonight. Stay off the road, but follow it northwest, past Bantry and to Kenmare. Travel so as not to be seen. It's three days if ye keep movin' steady, so find a good ruin or cover in the woods to sleep. At the fork just past Kenmare ye turn left. Go southwest, lass, into Kerry. Ye'll be in the O'Sullivan stronghold, and Lord Condon's cousin will see you to a merchant ship."

"A ship? For all that's rooted in Ireland's soil, Aengus! Why would I wish to board a ship?"

"Because ye canna stay, lass! Ye'll head fer the Leeward Islands, the West Indies. Travelers tell of an Irish colony there, with lands and wealth. Find it and ye'll be safe until Cromwell and his dirty hordes have left us."

I felt a growing pain in my gut, as if the men and women who at that moment were building a bridge over the Ilen instead were tiny specters within me, hacking and stabbing with their pikes and knives. And beneath that I felt something slowly bubbling forth in my veins, something that had festered and simmered, hot and dark and terrible, and now rose up like the first boil of a great black stew. Tears began to well and spill down my cheeks.

"Aengus, I cannot take a ship from here. I cannot go! Cromwell will destroy everything. We have to kill him. I have to kill him!"

"If ye stay, we'll all be dead by morning. D'ye hear? Do I needs explain again?"

I had no better plan to offer, though my jaw tightened and my teeth clenched. "No, Aengus. Tell me the rest."

"All right then. When you arrive in the islands, take the letter to the governor. O'Sullivan will tell ye how to find him. See that the governor reads the letter personally. It asks that ye be housed safely until we can bring ye home again. The man owes a debt to our Lord Condon."

Only then did it dawn on me why he wore the kerchief. "Aengus, did you sell your own teeth to Lord Condon for this letter? Is that it?"

He shoved the letter at me. "Take it now! I'll not have ye an ocean away from me without some assurance for your safety, will I?" He pushed my back and we crawled from our hiding space. He thrust a rolled blanket into my hands. "Take this as well. There's enough food inside to see ye fer a day or two. When the time is right, ye'll come home. I dunna know how ye got here to me. I prayed ye'd find a way and ye made it safe, so now ye must leave the same way and never let them catch ye. Now off with ye!"

By all the gold in the faeries' caves, I could not believe my Aengus was trembling and his face wet with tears. I touched his cheek and felt them warm on my fingertips. All at once something shifted and I knew he was right, and I had no choice but to go.

"Aengus, I never dreamed such a thing would happen to send me away. I know what you've done for me. Don't you ever doubt that I'll be home again. I'll see my own dagger through the heart of Cromwell, and when I come home to Skebreen it'll be to a grand celebration, and you standing beside me."

I shoved the letter into my skirt pocket, hugged the blanket to my chest and ran out the tavern as fast as I could to get well away, into the woods heading west. I knew now what the omen from the evening before had foretold. The red circle around the sun had been Kevin's bloody death, and the line cleaving the sun in two was my separation from Aengus. I feared it might be forever. A cold rain splattered my cheeks as I reached a dark bend turning north.

3

Under the Faerie Thorn

The Irish have never had any great kindness from the English.

~ Christopher Codrington, 1632

Within the cold, thick walls of a castle ruin I burrowed among the fallen stones and ghostly shadows, pulling the thin blanket over my head in hopes the wolves and soldiers would not discover me. The biscuits Aengus had packed were dry and hard, but I ate both of them even though I would have nothing for my breakfast. The crunch of the crust was satisfying somehow as I pondered my plight.

It was well, my leaving Skebreen, and the only choice that offered a future, but now I felt the aloneness in a way I never had before. I had known loss, and the terrible disconnectedness of being orphaned. With Aengus at least I had found belonging. I had wondered why my parents, who were strong and powerful in the world, had died while I who was without purpose lived. Now as if a fresh candle was lit I knew my purpose, but in the same instant I had lost my belonging. If killing Cromwell was to be my life's mission, I longed for the blood relations who sustained my mother. I craved the brotherhood of wild rebellion my warrior father had known. His voice filled my head as if he crouched beside me.

"Before the English come, t'would ha' been a castle hearth with a cracklin' fire where ye'd be warmin' yer bones."

I pulled my mother's shawl tight around me as the night grew colder, and let his words give me company. How I missed his wiry whiskers and his stories by the hearth. When he was done there'd be tears streaming down my cheeks. "Why can't we go to the castle now, Da?" I would beg. "If I am really a princess, why can't I live as one?"

He just shook his head. "Because the English drew a map, labeled it all with English names and English titles, and them havin' no concern at all for those of us livin' on the land hundreds of years. Do ye have a deed, they'd ask. Well now, we'd never had the need for such a thing. Land was passed down from father to son or daughter without a deed required. So the English drew up their own deeds and sent in their army to cast us out, as if we were breakin' the law just by livin'."

My father's anger had smoldered as mine did now. All his life he had itched for rebellion. The night the Barry brothers came for him, I knew he would go. It was January 1642. Thomas Barry told him, scraping the last of the soup from our old iron pot, "A plan is forged, and we'll need every man, every sword, every pistol and musket."

His brother Seamus leaned in closer to hear. "A dozen or more horses graze a field up by Rathbarry Castle, just what's needed for our lads going into the fight. The gathering's to be on the hill just above. We'll take the horses at dawn, and if our arms be enough, the castle as well."

"Wait!" Seamus jumped to his feet. He jerked open the cottage door letting a cold burst of air stoke the fire to a frenzy, retrieved something dark from a pack on his horse and returned. He pressed this thing against Da's shoulder. I remembered the orange glow from the firelight that haloed Da's head, and the intermingling pattern of gray and blood red in the fabric.

"Faolán," Seamus said. "It's yer own father's cloak from his last skirmish, saved by my own father after all these years."

"Ye must be with us," Thomas whispered. "It be the first strike for these parts. There'll not be another chance the like of it."

My father's hand rose from his knee and closed around the folds of the cloak. He exhaled slowly and breathed back in, his shoulders lifting. Then he stood, fists on his hips, the cloak falling over him as if it had always been his to wear. "By the cross o' Christ, the Father has given us this day. Let us not be wastin' it. Elvy, fetch me that!" He pointed toward the door where his sword lay sheathed beneath the rushes. I lifted it as best I could, for it was longer than me and surely as heavy. I dragged it toward him until he nodded.

"There'll come a day, lass, when ye'll wield a sword as well as any Burke, and there'll be no pity for them that come against ye." He adjusted his woolens and fastened the cloak about his shoulders with a great knot, hard as a stone. I felt a chill sear through my insides and settle into my gut, my heart fluttering like a bird in a fox jaw.

"I'll go now, lass, to stand for all that went before us—what was took from us long ago and what belongs to us even now. Wait for my return as always, and when ye see me eyes ye'll know we've won. Ye'll be the princess ye were born to be, not scratchin' out your living' from the dirt."

He pressed a thumb to my cheeks and wiped the wet away. "Here now, lass. Ye're a princess, castle or no. And what becomes of a princess?"

"She becomes a queen," I uttered through trembling lips.

"And the rest. What does a queen do? Say it to me now."

"Come faerie, come banshee, come soldier with sword, she holds her head high, and rules with her word."

"Exactly so."

I watched him fasten his broadsword to the horse they had brought for him. I heard the bitter snap of leather reins across his palm. Like the tide that rushes in and then drains away, the Barrys were gone and my father with them. Only Sean looked back as they rode into the night, my father leading the way.

Aengus had come for me three days later. He banged on the door but I refused to answer. He pushed on the door and I pushed back as well as I could until he shoved his battered shoe into the doorjamb. When he saw my face he stepped away and collapsed on the stepping stones, screeching louder than a raven and wailing out my father's name. *Da's name*. Faolán. The fiercest of any wolf. I opened the door wide and crouched beside him, pulling the dirty hand from his tear-streaked face.

"Yer Da has fallen, lass," Aengus said. "He is our great hero, and a curse of all curses on the English what kilt him." A shaft of silver light pierced the clouds where the gold of the sun had been only a little while before. The leaves in the trees stilled and all the birds fell away. There were words in my chest wanting to burst forth, and a great pain in my throat choking everything back. A terrible heat rose from my chest to my throat and cheeks, climbing beneath my skin like a vine, threatening to burst open. When I realized I still grasped Aengus's hand, I shoved it back and kicked my bare foot against his side as hard as my tender young muscles could allow until I heard his cry of pain with delighted ears. The lock on my throat was freed. I gasped a great breath released the most fearsome scream I had ever mustered.

"You lie, Aengus O'Daly. Be gone!" I hollered. By the time he lifted his head, I was under the protection of the faerie thorn tree that grew by our door, a heavy stone in my hand ready for the throwing.

Aengus rose to his knees, peered at me with startled blue eyes and shook his head slowly, long hair drooping like the ears of a hound. "Here now, lass, ye canna be livin' here alone, can ye? Yer Da would want me lookin' after ye, so. Come now."

"Come closer so I'll knock your eye out with this stone, and closer still the faerie thorn will shred you sure!"

Aengus scratched his head, peering through the branches and searching for an opening. I knew I was safe, for Aengus would never tempt the faeries. Anyone who cut or harmed a faerie thorn was in for misfortune himself. Some who'd been pricked by the thorns had seen their arms fall off right in front of them. Aengus had told me so. He raised a trembling hand in my direction but let it fall back to his side.

"Elvy, you're but a wee child, no mam to keep ye warm, no da to keep ye safe. Ye must come with me, or I'll never know another night's sleep worryin' fer ye so."

Though I loved Aengus, I took a deep breath and hurled my rock as hard as I could against his shin. He let out a grand yelp and hopped around on one foot while holding the other up behind his arse. His free arm flailed in the air as he carried on.

"Jaysus, lass, I should've known ye had a fair aim like yer Da." He hopped around a few minutes more, grumbling harsh to himself. Still holding his leg, he looked down the hill toward the village. The first firelights could be seen clear down to Mr. McSherry's place near the tavern.

He straightened, tugged his frayed shirt sleeves over his wrists and crossed his arms, looking up at the darkening sky. "Ye know, lass, I realize you've got grievous much to be considerin', and it's a fine location ye've selected. I might've chosen it myself were I in yer position." He shook his head. "'Tis cold even now, and likely to freeze as the night comes o'er us. I think it's time I was seein' to a good warm fire down at the tavern. Might put a bit o' meat in my soup as well, for extra nourishment against the chill. I'll jus' be leavin' ye to your thoughts and ye can come out when yer ready."

I heard him clod off along the stones and swore I would never come out. But before long I could smell the sweet, dark smoke from the turf fires in the village. I hugged tighter against the gnarly trunk, trying hard to smell only the thin bark and the rich earth. I slept, and when I woke I was shivering and could no longer feel my feet. I looked about cautiously and crawled from beneath the tree, and then from the darkness a great hand swooped down and caught me around the chest. I released my best piercing scream, but was caught in an iron grip. Aengus had been waiting in the brush all along.

"Thought ye were the only one with a trick or two up yer sleeve? I'll be gatherin' what's yours to take with us, but like it or not, Elvy, it's with me you're goin' to go."

Sometimes I pretended Da was there among the men in the tavern and I was comforted. But sometimes, when the talk turned to rebellion, the black stew in my belly burned anew. Now as I traveled it came forth to a roiling boil and I counted all my losses. Into that angry, bubbling cauldron I fed a richer meat than any hare or hen—my hatred for Oliver Cromwell—and then in fitful dreams I let that stew simmer and thicken.

By dawn I was on the road to Kenmare, narrow and rocky but not heavily traveled. Though I longed to beg a ride from a passing wagon I hid myself away, knowing my tangled hair and blood-stained clothes told a tale well beyond a night's shelter in the woods. I feared raising questions among strangers whose loyalties I did not know. Hunger churned within me and then subsided as I forced myself forward. Just ahead there was a low hill. I reckoned this was where the path would divide, as Aengus had said, and I must turn toward Kerry. I moved with full intention.

From the top of a rise looking down over Kenmare River; the wind foretold a cutting change in weather. I tied my shawl about my head and neck and draped the blanket over my shoulders. With a sudden shiver I appraised the paths that beckoned in each direction.

4

The Snow Path to Dingle

This, indeed, is a country well worth fighting for.

~ Cromwell at Tipperary

Behind me the ragged path sloped back toward the forest and the damp ridges and troughs I had just traveled. To my left was the way to Lord Condon's cousin and Kerry, the path green with winter rye and veering gently down the hill over soft moss and rounded pebble, and continuing to the south and west. This was the path I must follow, taking me safely and swiftly to the O'Sullivans and the remote villages on the rocky coast. I would feel at home there, and I knew they would protect me. Yet it was close. Several days' walk for me would be but two days' ride for the soldiers.

If Mr. Fitzgibbon was right, the soldiers could easily seal off the peninsula so that any rebels, me included, would find no escape. Could I make it to a ship before they came for me? And if I did, would I have the courage to board it and leave Ireland's shores? I braced my teeth as a gust of wind swept my face. To my right was a steep incline with dark, jutting rocks, slick and muddy.

I could see to the top where a rare white snow dusted the stones and the path, blurring the edges and bleeding into the gray sky behind. This path would lead me to the north and west, toward the lands of O'Donoghue, FitzGerald, FitzMaurice, and O'Conor. These were the lands the English considered barren and uncivilized—of hard ground and harsh weather, not nearly as productive as lands in the south. People scraped out what living they could herding goats or taking to the sea. Many turned to other means, like the traveling bands of wood-kerns stealing English cattle or robbing fancy English carriages that dared to pass along forest-shrouded roads. Farther west, the rocky fingers of Dingle peninsula stretched into the sea, favoring the crustiest fishermen and offering tight, craggy coves to hide the swift vessels of rebels stalking English ships. Why could I not travel freely among those clans, telling of Cromwell's stark brutality, raising my own army of fierce and brutish soldiers who needed no armor to advertise their powers? Such an army would frighten the skin from the bones of Cromwell's soldiers and make our vengeance swift.

The shape and form of that path caused my blood to flow a little faster, but I turned away. I must follow Aengus's instruction if I would survive. I turned toward Kerry, and yet my feet made no move. I peered down at my dirty shoes and the cold pebbles like tiny islands glistening in the black mud. If I reached Kerry safely and took a merchant ship to the West Indies, how far would I be from my home, and how long before I could return?

I had not seen a merchant ship except at great distance, and had never set foot aboard one. What if I was lost in a storm and drowned like some of our poor fishermen? Or sold as a slave to the Spanish? Even if I did arrive at these islands, I might never get to the governor and then might never return home again. My hands trembled as the idea terrified me as much as Cromwell's soldiers.

The letter was stiff and reassuring in my skirt pocket as I dared another glance at the snow path, and when the cold wind touched my face again it was as if a stone wall formed behind me and beside me, immovable and insurmountable. I knew in my bones I would not go south to Kerry. I could not leave Ireland on a faint hope of one day returning. What honor rested in this choice? How could I be sure that I would fulfill my destiny from such a remote place? I must stay, reclaim my land, and with my own bare hands flay any Englishman who stood against me. I belonged on Irish soil, closer to home, closer to Aengus—and closer to my enemy, whose death I would plan every minute until I could make it so. I whispered a prayer to St. Brendan the adventurer for protection, and then an apology to Uncle Aengus. With a deep and sure breath, I set my shoes on the rocks going north, and started up the path.

I felt a stinging wind, colder with each step I climbed as if to test my resolve. By the first steep crest my lips and chin were growing numb. My shoulders shivered no matter how I clutched the blanket around them. My fingers felt bloodless and brittle as twigs. I rounded a curve near a rock ledge, picking my way through some stones that cut through the path. I heard a strange scuffling sound and then a hard blow to my ribs knocked the breath from my lungs. The hard ground rose toward my face and I tumbled like a log down a slick patch of moss, coming to rest only when my shoulder and hip slammed against a boulder beneath a great rock shelf. A man fell beside me, clapped a firm hand over my mouth and dragged me well into the cold, dark space. I could not scream and scarcely breathed, believing he meant to kill me. But then a terrible thunder shook the ground above us. I watched with horror as huge black horses flew over the ground above the shelf, splattering icy mud into our faces and splitting the air like lightning as they hit the turf, carrying English soldiers forward and away. I flinched with every sound, but the man held me firm allowing no cry to escape. The soldiers passed over us like vultures flying low, and I smelled them, ten or more, befouling the air with their soot, sweat, and manure.

My stomach curled as if to heave, and I struggled against the man who held me. My skin begged to escape, and my mind wished only to rush among those soldiers and stab them mightily with the sharpest blade ever honed, to see their heads on pikes and parade before them, showing the blood that streaked my peasant's skirt. But the horses thundered down the hill, and as their sounds distanced I kicked, squirmed, and throttled my captor to get away.

Suddenly he released me and I scrambled and turned to get a look at him. In the tumble my shawl had slipped away and my hair had fallen all around my face. I swept it back roughly and saw the waistcoat first, pale blue with shiny buttons, draped with a gray cloak of fine wool, now muddied down one side. No hat covered his chestnut hair, cropped short so that his angular face looked all the more so with its long, thin nose. His eyes were blue as the sea over ivory sand in a cove where no wave broke. A jagged scar marked his left cheekbone, suggesting he'd been in a scrap or two. But his brows were finely shaped and his lips generous. A wily lock of hair curled under the pad of his lobe, and I was entangled there. My cheeks flamed with the surprise of it. No boy had ever caused such stir in me before, and this as quickly and jarringly as a slap. His lips cocked to one side in a grin so disarming I shouted, letting anger cover for my embarrassment.

"Why did you knock me down? Just look at my skirt now!" I tugged and straightened, suddenly reminded of the dark bloodstains at the hem. When I looked up, I knew he'd seen them.

"Apologies, my lady, for the rude greeting, but I did indeed think it best to remove you from the path of galloping horses. I presumed it was me the soldiers hunted"—his voice smooth as a silkie's back but tainted with hint of Scot—"but now I wonder, was it you instead? They've never hunted me with quite such fervor."

"Soldiers do not hunt me," I lied. "I'm merely a traveler on my way to visit kin."

"Of course," he nodded. "And I am a wealthy lord on my way to collect my inheritance."

I stood up, intending to brush the dirt from my backside, realizing instead it was mud. My blanket lay behind me, torn and useless, soaked through in a puddle. I wiped my soiled hands on a mossy rock and sighed in exasperation.

"Where are you bound to visit these relatives?" he asked.

I lowered my lashes quickly lest he read my thoughts. "Galway," I said, recalling some place names I'd heard in the tavern. "And perhaps north from there, to Clew Bay. I'm sure I've some relatives up that way as well."

"Ah, pirates are they?" He raised a brow, creasing the fair skin above it.

"Certainly not! I myself am a princess, descended from one of the greatest clans of all Ireland. We are Burkes."

"Well met, Mademoiselle Burke. And I am a Stuart of Scotland, most fortunate to be in such company." He bowed grandly. "I'm traveling that way myself. In fact, I know the shortest and safest route. Might I accompany you, in case more soldiers would threaten your journey?"

"Not if you continue to insult me."

"Please forgive me, my lady. I meant no harm. It's only that Clew Bay is known for its pirates, and they are lauded for the harassment they impose on English shipping. It's no insult in these parts to be of their blood."

He still wore the smirk, and I trusted him not at all but remained a bit shaken, both by the flight of the soldiers and by the unfamiliar feelings I was experiencing. I would be glad for his company—any company—and he had made clear his feelings toward the English. "Join me if you will, then," I said in my haughtiest voice. "But first I must have the reason the soldiers hunt you."

"You first," he said quickly. "Begging your pardon, of course, but you are the one with blood on her skirts."

My jaw must have dropped to my collar bone, but I snapped back.

"Do you insult me again? How dare..."

"Not at all. I'm only asking," he replied smoothly. "Perhaps you're in danger and I can come to your aid if needs be. I am quite a skilled swordsman, though at present I lack a sword. Still, I do offer some protection as I believe I've already demonstrated."

He stood beside me now, taller and as thin, his stubble just beginning to curl into a beard. It had been some time since he'd last shaved, but his face was no dirtier than my own. The closer he moved the more my skin tingled and I thought I should run, but then he pulled a small package from his cloak. He glanced at me from the corner of his eye and opened the white linen slowly, placing it on a flat rock beside us. His hands were fine, not gnarled and stained like those of most men I had known, but the tip of his right index finger was missing down to the first joint, most likely cut off in some kind of a fight. Within the handkerchief he revealed chunks of white cheese and little English biscuits. My own hand betrayed me and darted out. He caught it and squeezed until I jerked it away.

"Provisions of Cheshire cheese and biscuit, compliments of a drowsy English officer. I'm happy to share, but usually I must know my friends better before inviting them to dine. What's your name, my lady?" He released my hand and I rubbed my palms against my skirt, so ashamed I was unable to meet his eyes.

"Elvy," I said softly, and then wished I'd said Ailbhe instead.

"Elvy Burke, is it? Well then. It is my honor. I am Kade McEown, at your service." He bowed low but kept an eye on me all the while.

"I thought you said you were a Stuart!"

"I thought you said you were a princess."

"I am!"

"And I am noble as well. Related to the king himself from a long line of meandering heritage. Shall we sit down to enjoy our feast? Och, no—the mud. We'll stand then."

He doled out the food sparingly, though he gave me more than he kept for himself. I ate wildly, barely tasting as I consumed. I could not help it, so tired and hungry and scared was I that the tears began to stream down my cheeks. Then, for the gift of English biscuits, my youthful weakness got the better of me and I risked everything. He listened intently as I poured out my tale of Cromwell, the bridge, poor Kevin Harrington, and the murdering soldiers. I even confessed my intention to kill Cromwell myself and become Ireland's hero. His blue eyes seemed sincere and kind, but at this last, he cocked his head to one side.

"That's quite an endeavor for one so young and alone. Tell me then, Elvy Burke. If we were to round the next bend and come across the great general sleeping by the roadside, what would you do?"

I was warmed to my story by now, my defenses fell away and I hesitated not a bit. "In these hills it would be easy to find a rock as sturdy as a cannonball, and I would hurl it to his head with perfect marksmanship. Mind you, the blow would not kill him, only render him helpless while I strung him from a tree—maybe like that one just there." I pointed down the hill to a tall one with branches reaching out like the arms of a skeleton. He nodded his approval.

"And I'd not hang him by the neck as he's done so many Irish men and women, but from his heels as you'd hang a boar or a stag to dress. When he woke from his sleep he'd find me there before him, singing one of my father's favorite ballads, my sharpest blade in hand, carving away the skin from his head to the soles of his stinking feet—just like the old women of the deep forest did centuries before I was born. And when he'd no skin left, save for the lids of his eyes, I'd lay the bloody blade before him that he might contemplate the tool of his destruction as he slowly died from the bleeding, the birds and the insects tearing at him, and the sun of the day cooking him dry."

Kade's face drained of color. "May I never be your enemy, Elvy, for your hate bubbles forth like a poison."

I couldn't help but smile with the pride of it, and my heart pounded with passion. It was the first time I had spoken my story out loud, and I liked the feel and sound of it. One day it would not be a story; it would be legend. And then it was his turn to tell. "And what of you?" I asked.

"What's that?" He lifted his brow again, and his crooked grin returned causing the scar on his cheek to crinkle. I focused there, knowing already when I looked into his eyes I had difficulty looking away.

"You've not told me why the soldiers are chasing you."

He pulled a coin from his pocket, flipped it into the air, caught it, and flipped it again. "I think it's safe to say, you're the soldiers' quarry and not me. But fair is fair, especially among outlaws." He stood beside me, flipped the coin high into the air, then stepped forward just in time to land it on top of his head. He picked it off and laid it in my palm. "This, my lady, is the tool of my wealth and jewel of my destruction."

The coin was gold, thin as a wafer and marked on one side with a bare-chested angel, his wings spread wide, his sword ready. I had never seen anything more beautiful in the carving and the color, and liked the way the fine metal shined and warmed in my hand. I returned it reluctantly, and he flipped it so quickly I had to jerk away or be hit on the nose. He held out both palms to show they were empty, then stuck out his tongue where the coin lay glowing in the dimming twilight. He spat it into his palm again and dropped it back into his pocket.

"You're a magician then?"

"Of sorts."

"And this is why they chase you?"

"It's a bit more complex than mere magic. There are circles among the English court, and indeed in palaces and manors from Dresden to Dublin, who believe a chemistry exists that can change silver into gold. And because gold lasts forever, not only can this chemistry be the key to enormous wealth, it may in fact be the key to immortality. These people believe very strongly that if they use this gold to discover a magic potion and then drink of it, they will never grow old. Like the gold, they will live forever."

"And you have such a chemistry?" I grew more curious as he talked, catching a glint from the corner of his eye.

"It's not chemistry that I have, actually. It's the illusion of it."

"I don't know what that means."

He picked up a pebble and placed it in my palm. "Suppose this was a coin of silver. Suppose I told you I could cook it over a low fire, and with my own secret alchemy I could turn to your silver into gold. Would you do it? Would you give me your coin?"

"Of course! It's only a pebble."

"Suppose you were the princess in your castle, your banquet hall full of courtiers each with their silver coins, eager to see them magically transformed, eager to wake up instantly richer—with you as their entertainer and benefactor. Would you give them this opportunity?

"Only if I was certain it truly worked. I'd not want them all to be disappointed."

Kade nodded. "But supposed you wanted to believe it so badly that you'd allowed someone to convince you it was true, and suppose…"

"Kade!" I was blushing full force now. Not only was I in the company of the handsomest of men, but also of a masterful thief. I was astounded.

"An entire banquet hall full of people? Really? You took their money? And how did you escape?"

"It was most unfortunate, fair princess. I was just about to take my leave in the hour before dawn when the lord of the castle, so excited he was unable to sleep, decided to check on my progress. He came upon me in the courtyard, and though I did make my apologies for not staying until breakfast, he sent his wolfhound after me. In the chase I took a terrible fall and lost the coins in a cow pasture. I escaped with just a mark."

He showed me a torn stocking and the scabbed ankle wound from a dog bite. "It's a lucky wound, for the hound was right mighty. I'm afraid it was all quite embarrassing to the lord, and he is anxious to see me hang." Now it was Kade who was red-faced.

"So," I attempted to mimic his smirk. "It is well then, for us both to travel north."

His grin returned. "It is well. Come. We will put some distance between us and this place where the soldiers crossed. In time we'll find shelter for a rest. It's a long trek ahead through Killarney. The town will be infested with English, but there's an abbey that will feed us. Then I know a safe route to follow."

I was beginning to trust him, though I hadn't much choice. The higher the path climbed, the thicker the fog and the colder the air. Soon we were enshrouded by mist and darkness, feeling our way along cleared ground and cut rocks. I clutched the hem of his cloak to keep from tripping. We spoke little, but after a while he turned to me, pointing to a rise where a dolmen was barely visible against the blue-black sky. It was formed of huge stones on all sides and the largest on top like a slant-roofed shack.

"A grand shelter should there be rain, snow, or wind, and we'll sleep."

"But...it's a tomb!" I cried.

"Aye, and ancient. Wouldn't your Irish ancestors proudly cover your head for the night to see you on your way? Come."

I balked. "The bones of the dead still rest there. Spirits will come for us. They'll be angry, and could swallow us into the hills!"

"There are no bones. Here, I'll show you." He climbed, and I released his cloak and fell a few steps behind. I could barely see his shape as he crouched to enter an opening between the rocks. He slipped in easily, then turned to face me. "Do you see? Grave robbers have been here before us. It's why the rock has been moved, allowing us to enter. There's a fine bed of tall grass. If it frightens you, think of a spirit who'd protect you rather than harm. Call that one and you'll be safe as a babe. Come!"

I bent down, then jolted right back up. It occurred to me, not only was I considering sleeping on a grave where the dead might reach up and take me, but also beside a man who I knew not at all. Aengus would be sputtering like a madman if he knew, and if truth be told that gave the idea a certain appeal.

"So," Kade knelt on the grass. "I see the hesitating and sure I know why. It's not just about the spirits, is it? You are about to bed down with someone you think is a fugitive and a thief."

I said nothing, but my face might have revealed my misgivings.

"Well, then, know this first, that I am not a thief. An illusionist is the better term. And second, know that you're not alone in your risk, for I bed down with a fierce princess who has blood on her skirts and contemplates a vicious murder. 'Tis I who faces the greater danger."

He had his point. In the growing darkness I could not see it, but I knew the grin was there. I crouched by the opening, trying to see him better. The wind swept behind me, chilling my skin as if my shawl was only gossamer.

"We've a long road ahead," he coaxed. "At least share the warmth of my cloak."

"Fair enough." My heart was pounding against my ribs for the fear and excitement of it, and there was no denying the draw of a warm place to rest. I crawled in beside him. Except for Aengus, I'd never been so close to a man or boy before. His scent was like earth and wood—solid and familiar. He swept his cloak over us and we lay as one, our clothes the only barrier between us.

"There now." He slid an arm about my waist and pressed his lips against my ear. "We are like husband and wife, aye?" His hips pressed against mine, and my skin prickled with goose pimples. A growing hardness in his breeches felt hot against my backside. "Would you like to know the pleasures of man and wife? The comforts and delights of skin against skin, without all these encumbrances? It would be fair warmer besides."

He squirmed against me and I liked the feel of it, a tingling along my neck that I had never felt before and a warm ache between my thighs that grew with each press of his hips against mine. Though we were strangers, there was nothing to keep us from exploring the secrets of man and wife, no one ever to know but ourselves. The more he moved against me the more I longed for his touch and a taste of the forbidden. His hand moved over my breast and squeezed. I gasped, but he caught it and covered my mouth with his lips, warm and wet, his tongue entering me in a way that made me long to feel his heat deep within my womb. I turned to him.

The howl of a wolf split the air around us, and Kade sat up too quickly, banging his forehead against the stone. He fell back again, but the howl returned, close, perhaps in the woods just a few long strides from our shelter. "If they come for us we are trapped," he whispered. He pulled a small dagger from his cloak and held it before him. "Sit up, your back against the stone. If they come through the opening, I'll slit the first one's throat and he'll block the way against the others."

He sat beside me, his dagger at ready. We heard the howl twice more and dared not speak another word to each other lest we draw the wolves to us. Then came a long silence, and after that, the soft, even sound of his breathing. To calm my heart I did as he'd suggested. I thought of my mother's spirit watching over me and keeping me safe. I rested my head on Kade's shoulder. Compared to the previous night since I'd left Skebreen, I slept like a cat in the sun.

In the early dawn I heard the soft sound of water against stone, like someone filling a basin. It was a pleasing sound and I began to stir, remembering vaguely where I was. I turned toward Kade. His eyes were wide. He pressed a finger to his lips and held me still. We listened until the water stopped, and then I heard a hideous belch and the heavy thrashing of boots through the brush. I wanted to bolt from the dolmen, but Kade held me until we heard the steps no more. He wrapped his cloak around me.

"Wait here," he said, crawling toward the opening. I followed right behind him, his cloak tight about my shoulders. We crept through the brush as silently as possible toward a precipice and a great boulder at its edge. I crouched behind Kade, and we peered over. There was the broad back of an English soldier who had relieved himself against our shelter. He picked his way down a steep, rocky path toward a camp that spread out before us nearly as far as we could see, twenty tents or more, and scores of horses beyond.

The smoke from their breakfast fires was just beginning to curl over the trees. We backed away slowly, crept past the dolmen and back across the path, down the opposite slope, and then into the woods. When we were well beyond view of the dolmen, Kade fell to his knees in the underbrush, his head bowed low and strange utterings coming fast and desperate from his lips. I waited, but he continued on until I had to kneel down beside him.

The sky was growing lighter, and in the brush nearby a hare stopped to eye us suspiciously, then darted away in a flash. Kade lifted his head and ceased his utterings only at the disturbance of my grumbling stomach. He stood up and peered straight ahead into the deeper forest. I could not swear it by the dim light, but I believe his eyes were rimmed with tears.

"May God love his angels and saints," Kade said softly, "but still find room in Heaven for his outlaws. Come, Elvy. We dare not follow the path."

5

The Delivery

Come Fairies, take me out of this dull world, for I would ride with you upon the wind and dance upon the mountains like a flame!

—William Butler Yeats

Through the thickest part of the forest we moved toward Killarney. Kade measured our progress from the hilltops or by climbing high in the trees where he might get a view of our distance. "Traffic grows heavy the farther north we go," he said. "We'd be nearly to town by now if we could use the road, but by the morrow's eve we'll find shelter and a meal."

In some places our cover gave way to the rock and heather, and we had naught but Kade's gray cloak to conceal us. Englishmen and soldiers were everywhere, for Killarney was a vital crossroads. They had taken the grounds of the monastery for their camp, so we had to find our way around them without stopping for food.

By now I trusted Kade fully, for I followed his lead without question on a rugged path too narrow for a wagon and suitable only for mule or stag. We foraged what we could from the land around us and kept moving until my toes were blistered and I winced at every new step. Well past dark we found refuge in the root hole of a fallen tree. We went to sleep hungry, and when we woke we realized we were on the outskirts of another small village. From among the brush we stared down on the clustered rooftops. Kade shook his head slowly.

"We have reached Castlemaine, but I think we're done in, lass. Your feet will carry you no further without tending, and we'll be needing real food and shelter if we're to continue on this course. We must risk going into the village."

"What if soldiers are hidden there? News of our crimes may have traveled, especially if a reward has been offered." I was anxious, having seen so many soldiers the day before.

"People would turn us in for a mouthful of bread, so a reward is not our concern." Kade shrugged, and his jaw moved side to side as he ground his teeth. There had to be a way to avoid discovery.

"What about your coin? Can we not use it to buy our food and our safe passage?"

Kade smirked. "How many gold coins do you think these villagers see? Nay, it would only raise questions and draw the soldiers to us. Worse, we would never reap the coin's true value. Best to hold it for a better purpose."

Just then his eyes changed, and the beginnings of that grin creased his cheek. He pointed toward a cottage set off from the others, its stone chimney crumbling and without smoke. A tiny old woman came out, her white hair puffing from beneath a small gray cap, her spectacles thick as the sole of Cromwell's boot. She dumped a pot of rubbish into a ditch, then hobbled slowly back inside.

"I have an idea," Kade said. "If I'm successful we'll have supper, but you must climb this tree and stay well out of sight. Do you promise?"

I did. I was so hungry I was willing to do almost anything. I climbed while he scurried around collecting twigs and branches from the forest floor. It was difficult to know on whose land we trespassed, but landowners in general did not take kindly to peasants stealing their wood. I held my tongue. With his arms full he approached the cottage. The door opened a crack and then was thrown wide. The tiny woman reached for Kade's sleeve and dragged him inside, shutting the door behind him.

I waited. I truly waited as long as I possibly could. But there was no Kade coming out of the cottage and no sign of smoke from the chimney. And more's the pity for my legs were cramping, tucked as I was in the crook of a tree. What had become of him I could barely guess. Was the old woman a witch? A conjuror? Had she brought up the faeries and even now they were carving him up for their supper? I climbed down from my perch and hid behind some brush nearer the cabin but still had no sign of Kade. I should have stayed back, but the waiting was more than I could bear. Soon it overpowered every bit of promise, and I marched right up to the cottage door, banging on it with my fist.

"Kade! Kade, come out!" I shouted as sure the whole village could hear, and me so concerned over Kade and crazed with hunger I forgot we were in hiding. I withdrew my hand quickly, as if I could rescind the sound of an echo. Then came the squealing resistance of a tired old hinge; the door opened just wide enough for a beak of a nose to poke through, and then a bit wider. Before me an old man with a bald crown and white fringe of hair peeped out and blinked. His tiny blue eyes stared past me, and his cracked lips began to tremble as he drew the door full open.

"Who is there?" the old man croaked.

The woman came up behind him, her glasses so smudged with soot she was nearly as blind as her husband. "Peadar!" came her weak, scratchy whine. "Have ye...Dear lad, have ye brought home a wife?"

I peered into the tiny, dark cottage until I saw Kade standing, still holding the scavenged wood while the little lady hugged him tightly, weeping and wailing as if he'd come from the dead. Kade's eyes pleaded. For an instant I was bewildered, but seeing him so unnerved touched something within me and I burst into action. I gave the old man a smart peck on his cheek and pushed past him to peel the old woman's arms away from Kade.

"Peadar, ye must give the poor woman room to breathe!" I scolded him. "She's had quite a start. Here now, dear, a chair fer ye. Peadar, have ye not set their fire? Do ye want 'em to freeze from the cold?"

His senses returned, Kade started to work at the hearth. I held the woman's frail hand as she wept. The old man remained by the door, thin silver streams marking his cheeks and tears dripping from his pointy chin.

"Ye're a blessed gift from God," he said. "We thought we were never to see our grandson again, and now we're blessed with the two o' ye. Please tell us yer name, dear."

"It is Elvy!" Kade called over his shoulder. "She's going to be a princess."

"So she is, so she is," the old fellow responded, and the woman began her wailing all over again. Kade smiled at me with an eyebrow raised and his lovely grin at full force. I smiled back. Now we were both liars and thieves, making fools of this poor old couple that had mistaken us and at any moment might come to their senses. I knew it was wrong, but cold and hunger sent all shame and reason from my head. I couldn't be sure when I'd have food again, and already my feet were throbbing in gratitude for a warm place to rest. I prayed silently with every breath, St. Brendan, please forgive us.

As the first flames crackled in the hearth, the old man felt his way to a bench so rickety I feared it would not hold him. His knees creaked as he slowly lowered himself to sit. Kade knelt beside him on the dirt floor, and the old man nodded and gave out a rattled sigh.

"When ye marched off fer Dublin with the other lads," he said, his voice shaking, "we feared we'd ne'er see ye again. It's been nearly two year and we'd not heard. With yer mam and da gone, sure we thought it our fate to wait until death come. Our pot is cold and we were lookin' at the last of our oats. It was to be our dyin' meal. Now here ye are. D'ye know, ye've saved us and we've got new life, isn't it so, Cliona? Now it's to be our celebration feast with Peadar and his young bride home!"

The old woman responded with another wave of racking cries. "Och, I must get me senses about me. Yes, me babes! Ye must eat after all yer travels. A feast to welcome ye home again."

With the fire beginning to blaze, Cliona handed me a threadbare quilt to spread over her wooden table and squeezed my hand. "Mustn't have the pot and table sharing secrets, eh? Nor curses either. It's the barrier between the two."

To the pot over the fire she added a fistful of dried peas scraped from the bottom of a jar. She pulled a last piece of dry brown bread from her tiny cupboard and placed it on the table while the porridge began to boil. "It's only widow's porridge," she remarked. "Not a lamb's tail nor a bird's breast to make it hearty. But our Peadar will remedy that on the morrow! Aye, Peadar? A little meat fer us, eh?"

"We'll see about it," Kade said.

The old man picked up a stick and began chipping at it with a small kitchen knife. His breathing grew loud and wheezy. "Arrah," he said, nodding, "we'll be hearin' all about yer adventures in Dublin, lad, but let's save it fer later, eh? First, ye must be knowin' the English constable was through nigh a fortnight ago, isn't it so, Cliona?"

The old woman said nothing, so neither did I. After a silence, Kade said, "Aye?"

"Aye," the old man returned. "Gave a knock at every door in the village, so everyone had to feed him. Greedy old goat, he is."

"It's so," Kade said.

"He come lookin' fer ye, Peadar. Said yer name clear as church bells to every soul. Wanted to know when ye'd be home again."

Kade was silent.

"Wants to collect what's owed, says he."

"Does he now." Kade stood and poked at the fire, keeping the flames hot under the pot and keeping his responses short so that even I could not hear the tinge of his accent.

"His very words. I told him ye'd gone to war like all the young lads, gone to defend the English in Dublin Castle. Were he to know ye fought with the rebels, then we'd not have fared as well. I told the man, Dublin still in English hands and all that, ye should have made it home to us long ago. We feared ye were many months dead, is what I told him."

"Well then, there's no lie to that. It was exactly so until ye've seen me this day."

The old man sat still as a statue, and we listened to him breathe.

"Go on, then, Murchadh!" Cliona urged.

The old man blinked and shook his head. "Constable says he'll be back. Says he means to collect what's owed and will keep comin' till his purse is satisfied. I gave him down the banks in as fierce a tone as I could muster, but he'd not hear a word of it. Says next visit he'll no' be so friendly."

"And when's your man due then?" Kade asked, still keeping the fire well contained and trying to appear disinterested, though we both knew a visit from the constable would mean death to us.

The old man concentrated his efforts on the stick in his hand, a-carving away at it. Cliona fetched a big wooden spoon and stirred the porridge until a light steam rose. We waited for Murchadh to continue until my patience was so thin I had to stop myself from shaking him about, and then he wheezed a rattled breath.

"'Morrow, I 'spect. Or the next day. Soon."

Cliona piped up. "I warned ye Peadar, ye should not ha' gambled with him. He's a cheat sure as we all breathe, and not one to forgive e'en the slightest debt. He'll hound us all till ye're found, will he, or turn us out from our home."

"I've naught to give 'im," Kade said, and poked another stick into the fire.

Murchadh stopped his carving. "S'true enough, lad. None have in these parts." Then he leaned toward Kade and spoke very low, as if to keep Cliona and me from hearing, though we heard every word clear as day. "Mind, there's yet the delivery to be made."

"The delivery," Kade repeated.

"Aye, lad. It's where ye left it, no? There's money to be had from it, and more now I'd dare say, with times as they are and things harder to come by. All this time I ne'er breathed a word of it to a soul. I'd ha' starved first."

"And near enough to it," Cliona added.

"Hmm. The delivery," Kade repeated. He was stalling, hoping the old man would reveal a bit more before his own ignorance was obvious. He scratched his chin and looked toward the tattered roof as if considering his options. Murchadh cleared his throat roughly and poked his curved, bony fingers in my direction.

"It be a wise thing, lad. Sure ye had certain plans fer it and all, but ye've a young wife, mebbe a bairn on the way. 'S no time to be hangin' on to such what can do ye good."

Kade nodded. "I'm sure it's the truth, sir; that it is." I wondered what he was thinking, looking deep into the fire as he was. Whatever the delivery might be, we'd be smart to have our porridge and be gone before our ruse was discovered or the constable came. I hoped to see a ripple or two of his grin that had grown so familiar, but his face had gone plain as a puddle.

"Ah! Now there's a good lad. Marriage changes everything, doesn't it Elvy?" Cliona said. I nodded and smiled as sweetly as I could. She patted my knee.

"But," Kade said abruptly, "I'll not stay and pay him or he'll ne'er leave us be. If he thinks me dead, let him continue so. If he still won't leave you be, you'll pay him half."

"Half?" The old man reared back until I thought he was near falling over. His white brows arched high, and his unseeing eyes cast about for a place to land. "But, lad, he'll not go fer it!"

The grin was shining now, brilliant as a breastplate. Whoever Peadar might have been, Kade was taking over. "Tell him I'm dead and pay half what I owe. Tell him ye had to sell all my belongin's and some o' yer own, but ye could not live knowin' such a debt stained our family's reputation."

"There's no lie there as well," Cliona sniffed and looked down at the floor. The pot was bubbling furiously now, and a good scent filled the cottage. Cliona gave the porridge another stir. "Here's how it will be," she said. "We'll tell him ye died a great hero, 'twas your own sword what defended Dublin, and the whole village is the better fer havin' known ye. We'll make him feel it's a privilege to have even half."

"There's a dinger." Kade said, with a quick point of a finger. "Let him walk away feelin' his is the better part o' the bargain! He's sure to leave ye be then, and if he won't I'll come back as a ghost and scare the life out of him."

The old man's hands were shaking with the excitement of it. He turned toward me. "Tell me now, child. Did any o' the villagers see ye comin' through today? Anyone who knows ye're with us now?"

"We come in from the forest. We never saw a soul," I said.

"Thanks be to God!" The old man slapped his knee with surprising energy. "We'll make our story hold. After supper ye'll load the wagon, lad. The mule is weak, but still good fer the trip. Yer bride can gather enough straw from the field to cover. Ye can hide beneath it as we pass through the village and none will be the wiser. We'll be off with the mornin's first light."

"Ye know the way then, sir?" Kade asked.

"Peadar! The mule himself knows, for there's but one road. It's two days ride nay matter how ye journey, but there's few we'll meet on the way who'll be over interested in a tired old couple, and the weather's chill but it's fine. We'll be back in half a fortnight." He leaned close to Kade. "I've heard there's work to be had in those parts as well, lad, down on the wharf. I think if ye decided to stay, ye may settle down fer startin' a new family. Cliona and me would come join ye one day."

"'Tis a lovely plan," Kade said. I was growing excited at the idea. We'd be heading toward the sea, and have a wagon to take us two days farther in our journey, two days closer to the clans that would shelter us and stand to fight against Cromwell once again. The old couple offered us the perfect disguise.

When the porridge was ready I put the pot on the table, and Cliona served it up on two wooden trenchers. Kade and I shared one, though she gave us each a wooden spoon. Our supper was small but tasted like Heaven itself and warmed my bones after so many days in the wilds. We finished quickly, partly from hunger but also for knowing there was work to be done before we could rest.

While Murchadh waited in the cottage, Cliona led the way down a narrow path behind it to the steep edge of a small hill. There she pulled the brush away, exposing a cave dug into the hillside. She turned to us with a broad smile showing a few brown-stained teeth. "Must be sixty jugs or more remainin', lad. It's not what it was, but still a small fortune."

The cave was broad enough for a dozen head of sheep to sleep all tucked in together. Kade and I could have spent a warm, sheltered night there had we known of it. But along its walls and stacked in every direction were hogshead barrels of wine and fat earthenware whisky jugs as familiar to me as Aengus's face.

"It's the spirits," I blurted, for wasn't it Aengus who had stores of his own just like these back at the shebeen, selling drinks to the lads for his living and dodging the constable's demand for a share.

"Warms me heart just to see 'em, Peadar. I never asked how ye come by 'em and ne'er will, fer it's pleased I am that ye did. The lot will fetch a fine price fer us when we need it most. We've not much light left to the day. Best get to loadin'." Cliona pointed to an old wagon that seemed to be rotting beneath a tree. "That'll do ye well."

Kade brought the battered old contraption over, and we began lifting the heavy jugs. I could see why they had not sold the spirits themselves, for I could not imagine their weakened old arms being able to lift them. The wagon groaned with each bit of new weight. Cliona stood by watching, a faint smile creasing her wrinkled cheeks.

"Mind ye, keep a good trench in the middle, so ye and yer bride have a place to lay when we ride through the village," she said. We loaded every last jug until my back was aching and dark had fallen around us.

"We must go back in now. No time fer yer stories tonight, Peadar, fer we need our rest. Dawn will come in a wink, and we'll need to be off afore it." Cliona tapped Kade's shoulder.

"Right as right, by the winds that carve the peaks o' the Slieve Mish," Kade said. With each sentence he was sounding more like them.

We bedded down on the floor near the fire and I treasured the crackle of each dying ember. We must have fallen asleep quickly, for I remember scant little until Cliona was shaking us awake before dawn. Outside it was cold and gray, with only a hint of yellow drawing its thin line at the horizon. From a shed behind the house, Cliona led a tired old mule at the end of a frayed rope. Kade hitched him up and brought the wagon around to collect Murchadh, and Cliona brought me the old quilt from the table.

"Put this o'er ye, then cover o'er thick with straw. Ye'll be well hid and not have the neighbors askin' questions."

We did as she said, and Kade and I lay together so close I could feel his breath against my cheek. Cliona held the reins and Murchadh gave a whistle. The wagon lurched forward with a great screech. We bumped and clattered down the low hill through the village without a single soul hailing us. After a while I was sure the village was far behind us, for Murchadh called out.

"Peadar," said he. "Will ye not sing us a song, lad, to set us right for our journey?"

"Och, it's a splendid idea. Ye know how I love to hear ye sing, dear," Cliona said. I stiffened and turned to Kade, shaking my head. We'd be found out for sure when Kade's voice did not match the beloved Peadar's. Kade gave me a wink.

"Sure I'm a bit rusty, sir, for I've not brought forth a tune at all these many months past."

"And rusty are my ears fer the want of it, lad," Murchadh countered.

Kade shrugged. There was no help for it. We'd have to work with the consequences as they came. He pulled me closer until his lips pressed my ear. "They'll like this one," he whispered, and I realized despite the danger he *wanted* to sing. I prayed in my heart his arrogance would not be the death of us. He began then, rich and soft as if he'd fallen to earth from an angel's choir:

The song that I'm going to sing,
I hope it will give you content,
Concerning a silly old man,
That was going to pay his rent.

And on he went, about a farmer who was overtaken by a robber. The farmer, who had hidden the rent money in his saddle, cast it over a hedge and bade the thief go after it. Then the farmer took the robber's horse and escaped. When he arrived at his landlord's house to pay his rent he discovered the thief's fortune.

He open'd this rogue's portmantle,
It was glorious to behold;
There were three hundred pounds in silver,
And three hundred pounds in gold.

Cliona laughed like a child, and Murchadh said, "Ah, me boy, ye're as fine as ever, not a speck o' rust to be heard. Rest now, fer we've a long day ahead."

Tired and sore, we stayed a night at a tiny old inn. Cliona paid our bill with a portion of spirits, begging the pardon of the innkeeper and crying as she parted with it, as if it were the last bit she had on the earth.

We were off again early the next morning, over roads even more stony and rough than before. I peered up from the hay once as a grand tower castle came into view, standing four storeys high on a promontory with the sea shining behind it and the salt-scented air stinging my nostrils. The wagon jolted suddenly as Cliona steered off the road and tucked the wagon behind a large growth of gorse and brambles. I lifted my head but Murchadh pressed me down. I heard horses at a slow canter and men shouting orders.

"'Tis Old King Minard's Castle," Cliona said. "We mustn't be seen or they'll fall upon us. Word is that Lord Hussey of Castlegregory plans to use the castle for defense against Cromwell's soldiers, should they come this far west."

"Proud though it be," Kade said, "Cromwell's soldiers travel with cannons. They'll knock the castle down like kindlin'."

Murchadh only grunted in response. When the soldiers passed, Cliona guided the wagon back to the roadway.

"We're near Trabeg now, and Dingle town just beyond," she said. "Not to see the likes o' them rascals in these parts annahow." We bumped and wobbled slowly up a hill and down the other side.

My belly began to churn, and I faced Kade on those hard boards. "We're at the shore!" I whispered. "We should have turned north by now. The soldiers will find us if we don't turn north."

But Kade shook his head. "We cannot leave them now, with such a heavy burden. We'll be done soon enough and on our way."

I pushed away from him. "Do you mean to steal it all then, Kade?" I didn't want to believe he would steal from a poor old couple; but he was a thief after all, and we had traveled far into our deception. He shook his head.

"I mean to help them, is all. I might take a small portion in payment, but no more. Mebbe just enough to buy a horse for our travels. Trust me now and try to sleep. It makes it easier to bear the jolting."

Another bump and the cargo seemed to shift, the weight of it pressing against my legs. Though it felt as if the faeries danced in my belly, I drifted into a broken sleep until I heard the call of a seagull and smelled the freshening air of the changing tide. I thought I must be dreaming I was near Skebreen until I felt a firm hand wrap my ankle and jerk me solidly, so hard I thought my leg might pop from my hip. I landed in the mud behind the wagon and screeched out, "Kaaaaaade!" But he was already being carried away, a dark burly man on either side of him holding him high beneath his arms, his thin legs kicking wildly to no avail.

I felt an arm swing around my waist, and though I screeched and squirmed, the arm was thick and greasy and lifted my feet well off the ground. I was carried after Kade so swiftly I barely had time to look over my shoulder. I caught the last glimpse of Murchadh, standing beside the wagon. He wasn't blind at all, for he was counting out coin.

More men lifted the jugs and hogsheads we had loaded and carried them away. Cliona wiped a tear from her cheek and smiled broadly, waving a hearty good-bye as if we were dear relations heading off on holiday.

When I turned to see where I was going, the wide sea spread out before me with the gulls soaring overhead and a dark smuggler's ship bobbing just beyond the waves, her three masts reaching for the sky like the oath-taking fingers of a great black skeleton. The name *Jackdaw* was painted crudely across the stern, and men on the beach loaded boats to carry the spirits and other goods to be stowed and shipped away. I squirmed all the mightier as I realized what had happened and why the old couple had been so joyful to see us; but the greasy arm jerked tighter so I could barely breathe, and my heart pounded so fiercely it might burst right through my chest. We had been sold. *Sold*. We were being loaded on boats like sheep for the market, and now St. Brendan alone knew where our journey would take us and how, if at all, we would survive.

I looked back and saw in the distance another promontory with a domed center; it could only be Dun Sian, the fort of the fairies, and I knew within their ancient palace they wept.

6

Across the Threatening Sea

I found my self a stranger in my own country, and therefore resolved to lay hold on the first opportunity that might convoy me to any other part of the World, how far distant soever...

~ Richard Ligon, 1647

The greasy brute hustled me aboard ship, his boots slamming down on the wooden planks as if he were a great giant tromping over a tiny mortal village. I squirmed and kicked, thinking my height would give me advantage; but his arms, seasoned by years of sea labor, were like iron and my struggles were for naught. Helpless as a rag doll, I looked back at the dirty foam that washed the black shore, smelled the rotting fish and the heavy saltiness of decaying seaweed. My skin bristled against cold ocean spray, and my stomach threatened to heave forth what little it contained.

He set me down and pushed me amidships, where a man equally brutish threatened several cowering souls with the barrel of his black pistol. I spotted Kade among them. He grinned slightly, but I thought I saw a tremble to it. Tears sprung to my eyes. How would we escape now? How were we to reach the clans in the north? I searched for a way out in every direction, seeing only the dark sides of the ship, the slimy deck, the foul crewmen all about, and the endless, mysterious sea just beyond. My heart pounded wildly and I could not calm it. Cold enveloped me as if the blood had left my body. I found my way to Kade's side just as my knees gave way. He caught me before I fell to the deck in a heap.

"Hold up there, lass," said he.

I pulled myself straight and tried to get my feet beneath me, though my ankles felt like they had no bones. I whispered, "How can we get away, Kade? We must get away!"

"Shush, ye." the gun-waving brute hollered. He stepped closer until the hollow of the barrel was sneezing distance from my nose. "We've no need fer whimperin' here! We'll see how the sharks like it if ye try my patience further."

"Whimperin'," said I. As if a flame had been rekindled, my lungs sucked in the air and hate gave me strength. "I'll not have the likes of you telling me I'm whimperin'. You've ne'er had a clean hand or a kind thought in your life, and by the bowels of the earth I'll..."

"All's well here, sir," Kade stepped in front of me, still gripping my wrist but putting a good distance between the sailor and me. "All is quiet and well."

The man glared over Kade's shoulder at me but backed off. "So it be, so it remain." he said gruffly. Kade turned, and a ball of sweat dropped from his temple to his jaw. He squeezed my wrist tightly and came so close I thought he would kiss me. Instead he pressed his lips to my ear.

"Hold up now, Elvy. You face a danger as great as when Cromwell's sword was poised above your head. These men have nothing to lose and value only the coin. There'll be no getting away if they think you're more trouble than you're worth. Keep your head about you. We've come far. We'll find our way through this as well."

I looked down at my battered shoes and fumed. "How could that Murchadh and Cliona do this to us!"

"Do what to us, Elvy? Outsmart us? For want of a meal we lowered our guard and so lost a gamble. The game is not over."

I turned away in frustration just as a coil of rope landed at my feet. "*Cast off,*" a man shouted, and the men on the deck sprang to action, shouting commands from fore and aft, until the dark ship began to creak and roll, moving slowly away from the shore, helped by the outgoing tide. I glanced at the other captives beside us, nearly a dozen young men, women and children, each looking as ragged and bewildered as we. A pain seized deep in my gut, as if someone had grabbed my innards, squeezed them into his fist, and then wrenched downward. An older woman behind me vomited on the deck and the foul stench reached my nostrils. The fine hairs of my arms stood up as if alert now to a danger beyond imagining.

"We'll all be worth some coin in the slave trade, if that's where we're destined," Kade whispered. "Will it be south to serve the pashas on the Barbary Coast? East to the deserts where they wear robes and speak in strange tongues? Or across the vast ocean west, to the new plantations that need a constant supply of labor? Virginia or the West Indies. The sooner we know, the better for planning our escape."

A young man behind us stepped closer, his lips quivering and his breath stinking of a night's revelry that had cost him his freedom. "Sure he's not goin' to sell us south! Slaves there are given only foul water and black bread that even the dogs won't eat! I've heard they work men 'ere they drop, then beat 'em till they rise and work again. Some are shackled to a ship fer years and die wi' their hands still fastened on the oars."

A shudder ran up my spine and the back of my neck. The fist in my gut now grasped a dull knife, sawing away at my deepest, most tender flesh. A cool wind whisked my forehead of a sudden, and I remembered the crisp letter in my skirt that promised something better: respect, solace, hope. "West, dear Kade. Hope west."

The seagulls screeched overhead, and heavy footsteps crossed the deck toward us. Crewmen stepped aside to make a path, and through it came a man of strange build, short in stature and nearly as broad as he was tall. His hair was pure white and tied with a leather thong like the English officers. He surveyed us with eyes black and calculating. With the stubby fingers of one hand he tugged at the fine white whiskers on his jowls, and with the other hand he rubbed his broad belly the way a woman strokes her babe a-kicking in the womb—the very sight of which caused me to erupt with nervous laughter and I had to cover my mouth to hide it.

"This be yer cap'n here," the pistol-wielding brute shouted. "Cap'n Gerald Cocke."

"Cock! He's a cock!" I blurted and giggled out loud. I couldn't help myself. I was scared beyond my wits, and here he was, strutting across the deck with his belly thrust out like a banty rooster. My nerves were ablaze, and though I was certain of the danger we were facing, I seemed to have no control. The crewman raised his gun and my breath caught in my throat. Kade's fingernails dug into my arm until there was blood coming.

The captain approached, stirring so many emotions in my veins I knew not whether I could soar like a bird over his head or collapse like a jellyfish at his feet. As it was I simply shook, and still the nervous giggle waited just beneath the surface to betray me.

I had not realized until this moment that my hair hung free, dancing wildly about my face and neck and drawing unwanted attention. The captain took a curl between his fingers and lifted it as if to check what might lie beneath, and then he hooked it and jerked my head toward his. A quick shriek escaped my throat.

"Impertinence," he said in a high, nasal tone, "is trait usually quite intolerable, but sometimes translating into inventiveness in the bed chamber. Shall we see which it will be for you, little one, or would I tire of you too quickly and toss my profit overboard?"

Little? I'm taller than you, my throat begged to say, but Kade now had a fierce pinch digging into the small of my back and I held my tongue. The captain came even closer, as did his odor: of spiced food, heavy wine, tobacco, sweat, and some kind of flowery perfume that I suspected traced back to a brothel. Kade suddenly moved away from me and leaned against the ship's gunnel. He cleared his throat loudly and distracted the captain.

"Arrah, I'd no' mess wi' that 'un, if I were you, Cap'n," Kade said with a strong Scots accent that seemed to suit his purpose. He rubbed a finger under his nose and gave the captain a knowing glare. I started toward him, but he turned a shoulder to me.

"How's 'at, lad?" the captain said.

"Beggin' yer pardon, sir," Kade brushed the dust from his shoulder as if he was some kind of gentleman. "As I know she's a fine one to look at, and tender-young. That flamin' hair made her a standout for the lads. Still, I seen the lad she was with before, sir. It's a pity, too. Strappin' fella that he was. The world's gone dark fer him now, ye know, and he's as mad as he is blind."

"Ye're lyin'." The captain glared at Kade, who scratched roughly at the back of his head and frowned.

"Well, the truth of it, sir, is there were also the sores. Wasn't that they were runnin' so bad as couldn't be rightly bandaged. 'Twas the stench, sir. Could set a man off his meal, beggin' yer pardon."

"Ye're lyin'! Get ye aft and away from me business." The captain stepped toward me, but Kade came and stood beside me. He grinned wider than I'd ever seen, showing his teeth for all to see. He shook his head at the captain.

"Have yer fate then, sir! Enjoy! It's clear neither I nor God can stand in yer way. But there is one other thing ye'd be knowin' afore ye went in."

"By God's own wind, lad. What is it now?"

Kade stepped toward the captain, and they were shoulder to shoulder, Kade whispering to him as the captain stared right at me. The captain gave him a hard shove and came for me. I was sure I'd pinch his head off myself if he moved just a hair's breadth closer, but then he slowed. I saw his eyes widen a bit and the firm set of his mouth falter. He looked down at the hem of my skirt and the bloodstain that remained, then grabbed my shoulder and spun me around. He hesitated for a bit and then burst into uproarious laughter, with all the crew on deck joining in.

"Ach!" said he, "I believe the man's right, ye're a poxy wench and a bloody mess o' one at that!" He released me, giving me a slight shove backward. "Keep yer distance from me and my men while ye're on me ship, lass, and if ye don't die before we reach the Leewards, I'll try not to cast ye overboard! I'm cheated by yer price, but I'll be getting some value out of ye if it's only to grind ye up fer fish meal."

My cheeks burned at the insult, but I tugged my skirt to get a look at what he'd seen. The back of it was stained clear through with my own blood, and from my seat right down past my knees. My courses! They had made their grand entrance into my life, and I was the last to know. I glared at Kade, who peered at me white-faced and hollow-eyed. The captain left me standing there, with all the dirty faces of his crew staring as if I were a dripping cut of raw meat.

I ran past Kade and across the deck. No one tried to stop me, for there was no escaping now that the ship was away. I found stairs and stumbled down as fast as I could to get free of those predatory eyes and find something clean to wear among the captain's cargo.

Below the main deck was the orlop, with sleeping quarters for the crew and the cook's galley. Two young men stowing victuals paid me no mind. With the sparse light filtering through vents in the hull, I found a ladder into the shadows of the cargo hold. A mixture of smells assaulted me, from rotting wood and pungent salt to soured ale and urine. The ship rocked and I stumbled against great barrels of ale. I squeezed past them, as well as the jars of whiskey and casks of stolen wine. There were crates of corks and tinware; bottles of oil; hogsheads of flour, dried peas; there were barrels of rosin, pitch, and tar; powder and shot; chests of pottery and dirty sacks of coal.

I pressed deeper toward the bow and found four great chests, each stuffed full with bolts of cloth. In one I found light cloth for men's shirts, and I ripped into it for a clean yard. Hiding behind the chests, I stripped off my skirt and cleaned myself up as best I could. I found a bucket next to a coil of rope and relieved myself into it. Urine was the only solution I'd have to clean my skirt. I'd have to soak for a while until the blood came free. There would be another stain, and the skirt would have a stench to it when it dried, but there was no help for it.

I held the skirt in my hand, and then the captain's words came back to me clear as when he first spoke them, though I hadn't then heeded: Leewards. It was the same word Aengus had used. *We were heading west to the Indies.*

I pulled Aengus's letter from the pocket and smoothed its rumpled corners. Thank St. Brendan and all his ancestors for my dear sweet Aengus. He just might have saved everything. Already I was imagining presenting my letter to the governor, his astonishment at realizing who I was, being led to my well-appointed room in the manor house and given fine clothes to wear, and then being accommodated on the finest ship sailing back to Ireland.

Loud voices from the orlop stirred me back to my situation. I tucked the letter deep beneath the shirt cloth for safekeeping in the chest while I tended to my skirt, and wrapped the torn cloth well about my privates and secured at my waist. That's when the pain began to set in. I'd felt it before, but I thought it was the fear and rough treatment that wrenched my belly. Now I knew it for what it was and crouched low, rubbing my ache. I knew pain was all a part of the cycle—the older girls in my village had complained of it—but I hadn't expected it to be so keen, like a sword thrust in and then twisted. I held myself, wondering how long it would last, and then a smile came to my lips. At least I could now call myself a woman, no longer just a girl. I had proof now that I could be a wife, I could bear children.

It occurred to me that motherhood did not couple well with intentions for murder. Still I took some satisfaction from knowing I was full and completely formed, able to carry on my bloodline if destiny should spare my life. There might still be a chance for me to regain our ancestral lands, and then I and my children after me would wear the regal mantle of our heritage. Ah, and if I were blessed with children, I would not die young as my own mother had done, and Da. I would live as long as Cliona and Murchadh—and be just as wily.

But these imaginings kindled other thoughts. How could I present my letter of introduction as a true princess to the governor of the Leewards, but look like a grubby servant wearing a stained and stinking skirt? I'd have to replace it somehow before I met him. I quickly searched among the chests for finished clothing or another suitable cloth. The best I could find was a pale blue linen nearly the color of Kade's waistcoat and I wrapped a section of it well about me. There were footsteps on the ladder into the hold, and then a noise even closer. I slipped behind the chest again, hoping the open lid would not bring the intruder right to me.

"Elvy?" Kade's voice called.

"I'm here," I said, relieved that it was he, and popped up so I'd be seen.

He came close and knelt beside the chest, grinning.

"All's well, so?"

"All's well? All's well?" Though I had recognized the positives of my situation, I was not about to share them with Kade. Not after what he'd done to me on the deck. And, it was partly his fault we were captives. Had we escaped the old couple and headed north as I had pleaded, we would be safe now. "We're prisoners aboard a ship taking us far from our intended route, my courses are upon me causing me grievous pain, and you've gone to embarrassing me so before the captain and the whole crew. What must they think of me?"

"Does it matter, if they leave you be? I had to act quickly to keep the captain from you. And besides, you provided the solution yourself. Are you not grateful I found a way to use it to advantage?"

I sighed heavily, hoping to release some of the gripping pain along with my breath. "Advantage," I repeated, and shook my head slowly.

"The captain knows your affliction. It means to him you're healthy and ripe. If he can keep you unsoiled on this journey you'll fetch the highest price for him in the slave market. It's to your advantage and his that the crew think you diseased."

I faced him squarely. "Slave market?" It was one thing to know we'd been sold as slaves, and yet another to consider the true consequences that awaited us. I shuddered.

"Heed now." Kade grasped my shoulder and gave a gentle shake. "Things are always changing and opportunities come in their own time. We need only be patient and alert to them so we might act quickly. Secure that cloth about you and let us return to the deck before we lose all sight of home."

Home. I followed him back up the ladder. The crew already had settled into the routine duties, and the deck had gone quiet but for the seagulls overhead. I listened to them, wishing I could be one of them. Until I found myself aboard the *Jackdaw* I was driven onward by my fear, by Aengus's warnings, and by the sheer excitement of escape from Cromwell's soldiers. When I met Kade, the excitement only intensified and it was as if we were on this grand adventure together, our deceit of the soldiers bringing me great delight.

But when I saw before me a vast and threatening expanse of ocean and behind me the green-topped cliffs of the Dingle shore, a panic truly set in that made my earlier fears seem frivolous. The seagulls' cries became piercing shrieks, while beneath my feet the wet boards creaked and groaned in protest. The cold wind whipped my hair across my face as a punishment, and beneath my skin an army marched over my shoulders and up my arms, breached the ramparts of my rib cage, and entered my chest to lay a brutal siege on my heart, though it did fight back like a warrior beating wildly on a drum. I ran toward the stern and slammed my hips against the gunnel, believing for one mad instant that I might hurl my body into the sea, grasp at the gray shores of home, and it would take me back, *it would take me back*. But the shore was slipping farther and farther away. Something pulled at me and held me there until my choice—if ever I had one—was far beyond my reach.

When I turned it was Kade who held the folds of my makeshift skirt, as if he had seen my madness and would keep me from it. He looked into my eyes for one sweet instant, and then he seemed taken by his own madness. Sharply he yanked me aside and took my place at the gunnel where he vomited loudly and violently into the sea. Crewmen roared with laughter and hurled their insults. Kade returned his finest grin, smeared as it was with puke.

The siege on Kade's stomach continued that day and all the night, and through the entire time the ship sailed its southward course to Madeira, where the captain took on fresh fruit, salted fish, water and more wine. We were refused leave from the ship and were locked below, but gradually the tumult in Kade's gut began to ease. I nursed him with ale and boiled biscuits from the ship's galley, and by the time we sailed again he was on his feet.

From Madeira we sailed south to Cape Verde, where the captain took on salt, wood, more water, and provisions. We were at anchor four days. The captain made sure Kade and I were separated at night, but during the day I spent my time on the upper deck dozing, brooding, and sometimes just staring at the lights that played across the cresting waves.

Kade spent his time improving his reputation with the burly men of the crew, playing his coin tricks and telling bawdy stories of the courtiers and English gentry across Ireland. Kade believed a relationship with the smugglers could be the key to our survival when we reached our destination, but I kept a wary distance, still feeling the burn of their lustful gazes.

From Cape Verde the currents pushed southwest. The captain harnessed every breeze and gust to gather speed, but then the wind left us. The ship stilled in the water like a duck sleeping on a pond. Without the wind came a heat as I had never known, so oppressive it was troubling to lift an arm above my head. Though it still be winter, every soul aboard sought the main deck for air and there sought any unclaimed speck of shade. I found a spot toward the bow but well clear of the head. Kade soon plopped down beside me.

"And what is it that takes your attention, gazing out to sea as if there were angels dancing on it?" Kade asked. He smelled of salt, the sweat beads gathering across his brow and upper lip and dampening his hair.

"I was thinking of St. Brendan and wondering did he come this way. There are tales of him and his crew getting stuck, going to an island to celebrate Easter, and finding themselves resting on the back of a great sea beast. We could come upon one of the islands he found, with the white marble palaces and a feast ready for eating. It's St. Brendan himself who protects us and guides our ship."

"You believe so?"

"Of course it's so. It's why we are heading to the Leewards and nowhere else. St. Brendan has always protected me."

"It's a fortunate thing, though methinks he may have missed a few occasions to step in. As it is, you might mention to him that if we two are on the same path, you may be a degree or so off course. 'Tis the Devil himself who's guiding me."

"Kade! You mustn't say such things! You'll only draw more trouble."

"Ah now, Elvy. I found my entry on the Devil's list many years ago, and it'll require more than a nod from St. Brendan to wipe it away."

I looked away, not wanting to meet his eyes just then. He was likely right. His thieving ways were not going to recommend him to Heaven.

I myself would be a murderer once my destiny played out, but I would be relieving the world of a horrible menace and hoped to be welcomed into Heaven because of it. Could Kade be equally redeemed? Before I could speak of it, he fished his gold coin from his pocket and began to flip it from palm to palm and weave it through his fingers as quickly as a lizard curling over and under some twigs.

"I've wondered, Elvy," said he. "Why is it you pray to St. Brendan? Why not to God?"

The answer was perfectly obvious, but I remembered Kade's fervent prayers in the woods. He was a Scot, likely a Protestant of the old ways—ways that were not for me. Our small and unimportant village had escaped many of the demands of the churchmen, who eagerly accepted the supplications from Aengus's kegs of ale. I had stitched together my own patchwork of a religion from the times I spent beneath the faerie tree and among the trees in the wood, from Aengus's superstitions, and from stories I'd heard in the tavern.

"God is in the churches, is he not?"

"So they say." Kade nodded.

"Churches are run by priests and the like. Churches are for religion, and religion is why men fight wars."

"Religion and land and wealth," Kade agreed.

"Land and wealth in the name of religion. Cromwell marches through Ireland with his crushing Protestant army, but it's truly only to take the land away from the Irish and the Catholics. If it was to rescue the English settlers and stop the rebellion, why did he wait eight years to come?"

"Fair enough," said he.

"St. Brendan represents freedom, not laws and rules and greed. St. Brendan sailed the sea just as we do now. He brought back beautiful stories that made people happy and gave them hope. I know St. Brendan hears me when I pray."

"Well then, lass, you must have a fine counselor to recommend you to God himself. Would you put in a good word for me? It can hardly hurt."

"That I will." We sat in silence a few moments, hearing only the ocean's gentle lapping at the ship's waterline. But then there was more I needed to know.

"Kade?"

"Yes, princess?" He grinned at me, but I ignored it.

"Why did you become a thief?"

The grin faded. "I did not *become* a thief. I was named so by my own father."

I was astonished. "What father would do such a thing to his own son? Why would he?"

Kade frowned and looked out to the horizon. "Because I borrowed his horse to visit a young lady hardly a day's ride from our home. Upon my return he responded with such a fury I've never ventured to see his face again. He called me a thief and cast me out, so I set out to show him precisely a thief's appearance, that he never can mistake it. If ever I see the sodding bastard again, I'll be wearing silk and velvet and my purse will be fat to the point of bursting. Then he'll know a thief and will wish he knew him better."

His grin turned to a stiff, faint smile with a hardened jaw. I looked at his fraying shirt, his growth of beard, and the deck of the ship where we and the other captives waited for the wind to take us. St. Brendan had his tasks before him if Kade were to return home in finery.

"I'll pray for us all," I promised.

Kade smiled and shook his head. "I doubt your St. Brendan traveled as far as we're going, lass. It'll be new ground for him as well."

"How far will it be to the Leewards, Kade?

"I cannot say the distance, but it will be two weeks more before we see land, and likely days after that before we reach port."

"Two weeks more to endure. The water supply runs low, and there are but a few beer casks left. My teeth are beginning to hurt and I long for something to eat besides hard biscuit. If it is so very far, why do merchants like Captain Cocke go there?"

"Ah, have you not heard about the West Indies? All the trading nations want their toehold there. The Spanish have plundered gold beyond anyone's wildest imagination from the lands thereabouts. Piracy is rampant, but also there is land ripe for colonization. For those who might trade in indigo, tobacco, or cotton, the Indies seem ideal, for the plantations know no winter and the growing season never ends. In such a place a man might establish himself, particularly if he lacks opportunities at home. He can make his fortune trading with English and Dutch merchants, and have adventures of which he'd not dreamed."

"Is it so? Are men growing rich?"

"I've heard some have made vast fortunes. But indigo is a slow and stinking business, and the tobacco lacks the quality found in the leaves from the Virginia colonies. Instead, some are setting their sights on sugar. Every rich merchant and noble in Europe demands it and will pay handsomely for it. The Dutch have had a lock on the trade from Brazil, but planters have made a success of it in an island called Barbados. If it takes hold in the other islands as well, there are enormous profits to be made."

"Sugar! But sugar can be had already, only it costs six times as much as honey. Why would so many pay so dearly?"

"I imagine it tastes the sweeter to the nobles for allowing them to have what the masses cannot, or it is that the fine white powder suits the eye and the finer tastes. I dare say, Elvy, it would grace your table were you a princess reigning in your castle. If the island plantations can produce a great supply, English traders could rule the world's sugar market—and eventually rule the Indies. Problem is, the plantations require a lot of labor, and more's the profit if the labor is free."

He gave me a long, meaningful look and combed his fingers through sweat-soaked hair. He stood, looking across the ship as if someone had called his name, and then I saw his hair lift gently from his forehead as if an invisible hand brushed it away. There were shrill cries from the men in the masts above us, and the ship came about to capture the new-found wind.

7

Teeth of the Indies

Suerly the Journye is great, and further by 1000 miles than I ever supposed itt to be.

~ Sir Henry Colt, 1631

We sailed endlessly on, in which time I'd repaired my clothing and completely healed my blistered feet. But discomfort aboard the ship made sleep elusive, our food was growing poor, water was in short supply and I was exceedingly restless, pacing the ship's deck that with each passing day seemed smaller and more crowded. I grew irritable and anxious to be free of the curious, hungry looks from the crew. I wondered what lay ahead and was further annoyed by Kade's apparent lack of concern.

"I thought you told me when we sailed from Madeira it was but two weeks' passage to the Indies. It has been that and as much again, yet we sail on. Will we ever see land, Kade? Have we passed the islands by?"

"They lie ahead yet. The captain has chosen a route to avoid being taken by pirates."

I raised an eyebrow. "Is it so, then? And when were you chosen to become the captain's confidant?"

He looked away, and a realization spilled over me like water over a smooth stone. "I'll be tarred and feathered, Kade McEown, if you didn't say the opposite but a day past—that the captain's safest route was fast and true, straight to the closest port. You've really no hint of where we are, have you?" I jumped to my feet and pressed toward him until we were nose to nose. He stepped back a bit, but I could see the beginnings of a grin come to his lips. Sheepish, some folk call it, and I wonder where they got the term, for I'd never seen a poor sheep look as gleefully sinful.

We heard a rustling and a grunt just above us as a crewman hoisted himself among the ropes and climbed spider-like to the top of the mast, joining another who waited there.

"*Land ho*," the first one shouted. There were cheers from everyone on the deck and hands clapped together in excitement. My skin prickled.

"*Land ho*," confirmed the second man.

Kade nodded, the light in his eyes flickering. "Isn't it as I told you? The islands lie ahead."

I gave his forearm a fierce pinch, and we moved forward to make way for the sudden scramble and clatter of activity, the young fellows in their hurry slipping on the slick deck, the older ones cackling, resting on their elbows, and calling the younger ones fools or worse. I squinted across the water and could just define a dark form on the horizon, hardly distinguishable from a storm cloud. A knot of similar size did form in my gut, and my scalp began to itch. What lay ahead for us now I could hardly even wonder, except that tangled in the experience lay our every single hope.

"What island is it, Kade?"

"Barbados, I expect. Carlisle Bay at Bridgetown. It is the farthest east and is the first port of call. The Leewards lay a few days' sail beyond."

I did not care to imagine further sailing. I willed the tiny island closer to me with each passing breath. I wanted to feel my feet upon firm earth, to smell the very dirt beneath me, to lean my back against the solid trunk of a tree and know no sway or roll. I longed for green vines, for the cool roughness of a gray rock and its solid thud when I hurled it. I longed for new faces and no more of the captain, his crew and the other sad captives. I longed for old faces, too: the stalk neck and childlike eyes of Aengus, the ruddy cheeks of all the men I had known my whole life. And I longed for the sweet scruffy beard of my father rubbing against my cheek.

"There's a good day's sailing before we'll come into port. I'll wager we'll be in on the morning's tide," Kade said.

"I must prepare myself to meet the governor." I stumbled below deck, fighting back the tears.

The wind stayed with us through the night, and by morning the dark island loomed large, with gentle green slopes, rock-studded shores, and white sand beaches. The turquoise waters surrounded us, stroking and slapping the hull by turns. Finned sea creatures began to surface and play at our flanks, and as the crewmen's clatter and hustle climbed, so fell the captives into the prickly silence of fear and anticipation. The captain provided a bucket of seawater for us to wash, and I took full advantage, wanting to look as well as possible upon arrival. We sat in the sun to dry and I worked my fingers through the knots in my hair while the men stowed unneeded lines and gear to make way for cargo unloading. Seabirds swooped and screamed overhead, demanding a share of anything though there was no food to be had. Kade sat beside me on the deck, opened his palm and displayed six small coins.

"It's my winnings from the crew. A mighty fortune," he told me. "Or at least enough for a meal or two."

I nodded, having no interest in food as my stomach churned, the verdant hills drawing nearer.

"Hide this away." Kade handed me his gold coin with the archangel.

"Keep it safe while I have others to work with. It will be most valuable to us once we get to wherever they're taking us."

I tucked the coin against my breast and pulled my bodice tighter. Another ship approached from the west, a bit farther off than we. In the harbor there were probably twenty more, and we could now see movement on the shore. The air was so delicious I could nearly faint from drawing in deep breaths of salt, soil, wood smoke, and a thousand other enticing fragrances I could not yet identify.

"Kade." I clasped my hands so they did not shake. "Talk to me. Tell me a story, for I can barely endure this waiting."

He considered me and grinned full force, the blue of his eyes sparkling brighter than the sea. "I've just the tale for you, fair princess, since you've a fierce interest in destiny. It comes from centuries past, from the time of Robert the Bruce, King of Scotland. You know of him?"

"I do! My father used to tell of him."

He nodded and I listened, hearing first the slicing of the ship's hull through the waves. Kade gazed toward the island, his face smooth as a boy's.

"It was the beginning of our family's fortune, for my ancestor was a poor relation to the Bruce and fought with his army against the English even as the Irish rebels fight today. Robert's younger brother Edward wished to match Robert's success in Scotland by crowning himself king of all Ireland. He negotiated with the Irish, who agreed that if Edward could succeed where they had failed and cast the English out, they would gladly name him king.

"Edward amassed a huge army of Scots and Irish warriors fighting shoulder to shoulder, and a fine set of lads they were, but the English were not to be taken easily. Edward sent to Robert for help, and Robert responded, landing with reinforcements in the south."

"Kinsale?" I asked, grateful for the distraction.

"Likely it was Cobh, but I couldna say for sure. Now, Edward liked to face his enemy head-on, but Robert was more of a strategist. Robert forged an alliance with an Irish king from the west, and together they planned a surprise attack on the English."

"And your ancestor was among them?"

"Patience now, I'm getting to it. Skirmishes raged all across the land and warriors were everywhere, sometimes as spies, sometimes as mercenaries seeking fortune on their own. My ancestor John Stuart was scout and protector for King Robert, and right mighty he was about it. While the Scots and Irish soldiers marched to position, John scoured the hills for spies. In the steepest hills near Cashel he came upon an encampment, and at the very crest its leader lay fast asleep among the rocks.

"Bright English armor told of the man's great wealth and importance. Without delay our man John did slay this fellow surely, and presented the severed head to the Bruce. To demonstrate Scottish power, Robert immediately sent the head to the English lord general at Dublin Castle. For his bravery, John was lavishly rewarded with lands and cattle in Scotland, and without delay he headed home to claim it."

My jaw dropped as if I'd lost the muscle in it, and I felt as though a pike had skewered the length of my spine. My gut twisted while Kade's eyes glowed with a long-nurtured pride. I jumped to my feet, my hands curling into fists. This man before me, this very man I had spent weeks with as my partner and companion, was descended from the one devil-coward who had murdered my own ancestor, in fact his own ally. I felt at once that black poison anger shoot into my throat and burn through to my eyes, my tongue, my heart, and my very fingertips.

"Bravery, you say? To slay a man as he sleeps? But for *your* ancestor I'd even now be in my own castle. 'Twas *my* family's ruin from which yours profited. King Conor of the Burkes formed an alliance with Robert the Bruce. 'Twas *he* who took his men to higher ground, preparing to swoop down upon the English flank like a hawk. 'Twas *he* who wore the English armor as the spoils of his great victories and was murdered for it as he slumbered among the rocks!"

Kade now looked bewildered, his brow furrowed, eyes squinting as he slowly shook his head. "No, John slew his enemy, and all the land knows of it! It was a most fortunate encounter."

"All the land knows of it? By the jowls of St. Brendan, *you bet* we do."

He turned his back to me and focused on the sea, his lips moving but no sound coming out. He searched for an excuse, I dare say, smug to himself and probably formulating the next lie to be told. I don't know what came over me, except that I would have no more of it. My blood surged hot and fierce as a bonfire. I ran at him with all my fury and hit him just below the blades of his shoulders. He toppled forward and I fell to the deck with the force of my own momentum. As if the earth had slowed its movement, I saw Kade's feet rise out from under him, and like a bucket of slop from the galley he flipped over the gunnel and into the sea with a great white splash. I scrambled to my feet and leaned over the rail where he had stood.

"Och!" said I, with no one there to hear me. "It must be six fathoms down. God willing, you broke your rigid neck."

But just then I saw a brown head surface, looking like a piece of driftwood and me thinking the driftwood had the greater value. He lifted his face, and where I had hoped to see anger or at least surprise I saw bewilderment, which quickly faded away as the corner of his mouth curled up. Had I a drop less sense I'd have jumped to the water after him just to strangle him. I heaved myself against the gunnel and shouted down to him. "The devil and sixpence go with you, and you'll want neither company nor money! May you melt off the earth like snow off a ditch!"

I turned from the sight of him and marched toward the bow.

The *Jackdaw* pulled closer to the harbor and the busy crewmen had taken no notice, but I could not prevent myself from one backward glance. As his luck would have it, the full sails of a second ship approached the harbor behind us. Kade began to swim in the ship's direction.

"I hope they save you just to skin you alive and have you for supper!" I shouted, but by then I could no longer see him. Good riddance was all I could think. I was certain my ancestors looked down on me with pride and gratitude for the justice done. But we were arriving in the harbor and soon the captain would set his anchor. I could not concern myself with Kade further.

I rushed below decks to the hold, to gather my letter from its hiding place among the fabrics before the trunks were taken to shore. In the hold the crewmen already were working, and the trunks of fabric were not where I had left them. I tore through the hold, searching every corner without success. I pushed past the crewmen, who laughed and tugged at my skirt.

"Settle ye down on me lap, lass, and I'll show ye just what ye're lookin' fer!" one of them said, and the others laughed uproariously. I jerked my skirt away and clambered up to the main deck, only to find the trunks of fabric stacked and waiting to be off-loaded. I threw myself upon the nearest one and struggled with the latch until one of the grimy thugs grabbed my shoulders and threw me off.

"These are not fer the likes of ye, and ye'll not be deprivin' us of our profits with yer touchin' all the finery! Get off!" the crewmen shouted.

"DIE and give the crows a puddin'." I screamed at him with such a fury I know not what else I said. But a second crewmen grabbed me about the waist, hoisted me over his shoulder, and then cast me to the deck, where I landed hard, bruising my arm. I was held there by another until the ship dropped anchor, and then I could only watch in horror as the trunks were loaded one by one aboard a pinnace, and the pinnace cast off toward the island. I screamed and struggled so fiercely the crewman sought a rope to bind me hand and waist beneath the galley stair. I wept uncontrollably as cargo was off-loaded, as crewmen disappeared from the ship, as several other captives were sent below. I could think of nothing but my letter. Without it I had no more to recommend me than any of the other captives. How would I get free and return to Ireland? How would I escape the labors that awaited the others so that I could achieve my destiny? I simply had to retrieve the letter.

My only hope was to follow the trunks once I was taken to the island. When a crewman finally freed me from the ropes, I ran to the deck for a glimpse of them. It was only then I realized every pinnace was gone. I looked toward the lush greenery of the island, with its gentle peaks and sunlight glinting like gold off the blue-green waves.

"When do they come to retrieve us?" I asked a crewman.

He released a curious laugh. "Relax, lass, and find yer space below. Ye'll not be stoppin' here. The cap'n has his buyer to see on Montserrat."

"Montserrat?"

"Aye, but four days sail from here. Barbados be greedy fer the finer things, but Montserrat be more needful fer labor. Ye'll fetch a higher price."

A burn traveled up my spine and down again, spreading into my core and oozing among my organs like melting lard. And then the lard began to cook my stomach until the very meat of it was popping like bacon.

"No!" I shouted, and "NO!" My screaming spattered forth as if from some unknown source, and I could not stop until the crewman returned me to my bindings in the galley and shoved a rag into my mouth.

I cried until my throat lost all sound and until my eyes had no more water. I was so defeated I thought my heart would cease its steady, hollow beat. By nightfall the crewmen removed my bindings, but I was exhausted and without an alternative, so I stayed in my hole beneath the stair.

By eventide the next day we sailed, and as I stared out over the dark waters, a dread began to build in me that I had not felt since the day I saw the sun divided and learned of my father's passing. I was more alone now than ever I had been. Aengus's letter was gone. My only friend Kade was gone. I was an ocean's crossing from my home and my people, without money or belongings, and I was being taken to a distant island where I would be sold like livestock. And after that? I knew not what to expect.

The dread rooted in me, thick and gnarled, writhing and twisting and squeezing out all my spaces until my stomach felt hard and small as an acorn. I closed my eyes and there came the vision of a black rod of iron, unbending and threatening, its tip red hot and moving steadily toward me. My blood responded, pumping in my neck and hands and pounding its drum in my head. Then in a flash of light something changed, and the iron rod was a sword in my father's powerful grip. I saw his eyes, fierce as a great wolf on the attack, and then the hand became my own, the fingers white with the strain of holding such a weapon, but holding it fast. I opened my eyes to the dark waters around me, but the night's first stars revealed their glory as a flock of seabirds fluttered overhead seeking their roost. One bird left the others, dipping its wing and arcing back toward its own singular course.

It was an omen. I must prevail. I would prevail. I would learn what I had to, suffer how I might, but I would find my way out of my predicament. I would get the help I needed to fulfill my destiny, however long it would take, whatever sacrifices were demanded of me. "And by St. Brendan's bollocks I will strike down anyone who gets in my way!" I whispered.

Just then I felt the heat of Kade's coin against my breast and pressed my fingers there. I had forgotten Kade had given it to me for safe keeping. The thief has lost his tool, I thought, half-smiling. At least I still had that. I must keep it safe no matter what happened. It might be the only thing that one day brings me home.

On the dawn of the fourth day I paced the deck impatiently, knowing the day of arrival had come. With a fiery glare I defied any of the crewmen who dared to interrupt my path. Seven other captives huddled below deck awaiting their fate, but I was near the bow when the stubby hand of Captain Cocke grasped my shoulder and pressed me down.

"Still yourself, lass. What's all your concern fer annaways? Ye've but exchanged one barren island fer another." His laugh sounded like the cackle of geese, renewing my contempt for him. I looked the direction of his fat pointed finger. Montserrat came into view, and I watched it approach, knowing at once how it got its name. Jutting out of the sea like a jawbone with sharp, serrated teeth, it promised to devour alive all who ventured to its shores.

"Christopher Columbus named her Montserrat, after a holy mountain somewhere in Spain. The imbecilic Spanish pig without imagination names one useless rock fer another. But this one is crawlin' with Irish, sent south from St. Christopher's island just beyond, nearly a score of years past. Mayhap ye'll find some kinfolk, or mate with a slave and birth a passel o' brown-spotted babes."

He laughed again, turned like a top and tottered away, leaving me to stare at the dreadful mountain, the deep black trenches running down its sides, and the high serpentine cliffs undulating along the shore. A stone castle prison with spiked iron gates would seem a pleasant home by comparison.

8

Sharavogue

For as we passed along near the shore, the Plantations appeared to us one above the other; like several stories in stately buildings...

~ Richard Ligon, 1657

My dread coiled deeper, its soft blind tendril seeking out the last tiny cavity I had withheld. When I saw white forms on the hillsides, I thought the island might yet hold that one bit of comfort I sought. Sheep were familiar and safe. Sheep were like home. But as the *Jackdaw* slipped into the harbor, disgust gave my dread a sharper tip. They were not sheep, but goats. Goats! The Devil's offspring with their yellow teeth, crazy slit eyes, and tight little horns. Goats that would sooner butt you and trample you in their excrement than give you milk. I was descending into hell itself, and realized Kade had been right: St. Brendan had not ventured so far or he would have warned of such a vile place.

Captain Cocke called for the anchor and the crew set about their duties. The captives and some of the cargo were loaded into pinnaces and rowed to shore. I climbed down a rope ladder until I was pulled into the boat, and then I turned to face the island. At last, the cool spray of the tumbling surf touched my face. I let the wind lift my hair and cool my scalp. Would it be the only taste of freedom I would know?

When the pinnace's bow scraped the sand, I climbed gratefully into the shallows with the others, relieved to feel the sand beneath my feet and between my toes, even though it was unstable and shifted beneath me. The farther up the shore I moved, the more solid my footing and the more hope

I gained. The town buildings rising just above our landing looked weathered but sturdy, offering a vision of hope. I might now speak with someone who knew a way out or could guide me to the governor for an audience. As if I were free to do so, I started toward them, but one of the ship's crew grabbed my arm and jerked me backward.

"Filthy dog. Leave me be." I snapped. He merely laughed and heeded the captain's order to line us all up near a rock pile on the shore. The captain stood before us, meeting no one's eye but checking the little marks he'd made in a small journal. One of the captives collapsed, and another pulled her back to her feet and held her there. The sun was white hot above our heads, and the water lapped just inches from our feet.

I took in the salt smell mixed with earth and wood and rotting fish, and then all of it was overpowered by the wafting scent of fresh bread baking. I grew mad with want; my acorn stomach rippled back to life and cramped for the desire of it. I looked toward the town but saw no fires burning, no clear place where a baker might lovingly pat his flour into loaves for the oven. But the aroma was there, strong and sweet. My dry mouth suddenly oozed. Just then we heard the clop of hooves and the rumble of a wagon rounding a bend and coming toward us, pulled by a single gray plow horse.

"Strip off yer clothes!" Captain Cocke shouted. "We've no decent market if we hide the goods beneath such tattered fabric, have we? Off with it, every stitch."

Two of the crewmen raised their pistols, shoving us together. Slowly we began to remove those precious threads that held the last of our dignity. We huddled, taking comfort and cover from each other's bodies, and we wept, every one of us, as the captain circled us and scribbled the attributes of our flesh into his book. The crewmen ripped the clothing away as we unfastened and removed it, and tossed it into a struggling seaweed fire. Though the air grew hot, we shivered. Though the sun warmed our shoulders, it only emphasized our exposure. I swept my hair forward to cover my breasts and clutched my thin bodice against them, concealing Kade's gold coin within my fist.

I peered over my shoulder at the two men approaching in the wagon. One wore a brown tunic and was burly like my father had been, but with fine light hair. The other was tall and dark-haired, his lace cuffs pushed back toward his elbows, his brocade doublet unfastened. He wore voluminous knee breeches and stockings tinged yellow. He jumped from the wagon before it came to a stop and his brown ankle boots dug into the sand.

When he shook hands with the captain. I thought he must be English, and he confirmed so as soon as he spoke. The sound sent a spiral of fear up the back of my neck to sting the tops of my ears.

"It is a long wait for an impatient man, Captain Cocke, but I'm pleased at last you've arrived. And how was your crossing?"

The captain cleared his throat and gestured back toward the *Jackdaw*. "The time of year is not best, Master Wingfield. The winter winds are unpredictable, but my ship remains true and I trust her with my life."

"Ah, and so you must, Captain." He looked at the tangle of our naked bodies, each of us trying in vain to cover ourselves and retain some level of modesty.

He nodded. "I'll have a look now, and have our business done straight away, sir. I'm sure you have news to deliver, and your men are anxious for a rest at the tavern."

"LINE UP." The captain voiced a high pitch, sending a chill up my spine as the crewmen shoved us into a ragged, sopping, weeping line. I felt dirty, and at the same time as vulnerable as a newborn with nothing to protect me, nothing to hide me nor distinguish me, nothing but flesh and bone to stand for all I had believed myself to be. I was stripped in every way, shivering, aware of the eyes that traveled my flanks, and now came the tall English planter inspecting each of us as if he were examining horse flesh or cattle.

He squeezed the shoulder of the young boy, then touched the jaw of a woman next, and examined her front teeth. He squeezed the calf muscle of the tall fellow and tested the muscles across his shoulder blades by pinching their thickness. When he came to me, my breath caught in my throat. I trembled, as cold as if I stood on an icy mountaintop. I kept my gaze down, as if by looking at no one, no one could look at me. But he stood before me and waited, breathing softly through his nose. In that moment I thought he bore a measure of kindness, and my only hope was to beg for his mercy. I raised my eyes to his waist level and started to speak.

"Hut-tut," the captain said, raising his hand before my face. A crewman suddenly jerked the bodice from my grasp, and the gold coin dropped from my hand. I felt it brush between my breasts and slip against my belly before it fell like an anchor to the sand at my feet. I dared not look up or down but simply shifted my feet in hopes to cover it and no one notice its existence. My throat closed on my breath, my last hope grounded.

The Englishman stepped closer, examining my hair and my face. He stood toe to toe with me and placed his hands on my bare hips. I flinched at the familiarity, but he held me fast. My cheeks blushed hotter than I'd ever felt before. I had to turn my chin up to do so, but I glared straight into his cool gray eyes, my meanest, most regal glare, not knowing at the time that such defiance was a hanging offense. There was whiskey on his breath and stubble on his jaw. His dark hair was wild about his crown and ears, and though there were deep lines and dark circles about his eyes, I saw a glint of humor there as well. His hands lingered a little longer, and then slipped down the sides of my thighs and calves, coming to a rest as he examined my feet. When he rose again to eye level his wide mouth turned up at one corner, then he stepped back. He circled me slowly and so near I could not move nor breathe.

"What is her age, Cocke?"

"Seventeen, sir, nigh eighteen, and untouched. Pure as a spring flower, on my honor."

"Well, that's a dubious oath, to be sure, but I'll give you a well done, Captain," he said. "Indeed, you've managed to answer my requirements with these offerings, though the bodies are thin and weak. I'll take them all, but we must adjust the price accordingly."

"My Lord, I assure you they traveled like paying passengers and lack but a meal and a night's rest on solid ground to restore them."

The Englishman grunted loudly and turned toward the ship. Suddenly the wind changed, and I caught the stench of dead fish and something else more dreadful and putrid. Dizziness swept over me, and I thought I would vomit from it. The sailor behind me pushed me forward.

"Steady on!" he growled. "Catchin' a whiff o' the woad, sir. That's all."

"Yes," the Englishman nodded. "It's from the indigo vats on the south side, well distant from Plymouth, but the wind works against us today. It will pass. Now then, Cocke, let us conclude our business. Where is my back?"

The captain hesitated. I thought perhaps he was pretending not to have heard the Englishman, though that would have been impossible unless he were deaf.

"My *back*, Captain. You promised me a good strong back to give me labor. I'll see the man now."

"I'm afraid, sir, I..."

"What is it, Captain? Spit it out! Where is the laborer you promised?"

The captain bowed his head and shook it slowly, side to side. "I did have a fine specimen aboard for you, sir. He escaped, I do swear it. And to his own demise. He was on my deck as sure as the rest of these, and just as we reached Barbados, in an instant as if God's own hand descended, he was struck away."

A blood red fury washed the Englishman's face as quick as a hawk strikes its prey. He grabbed the captain's collar and hoisted him against a pile of ballast stones. "You'd best be lying to me, old man! I've waited long for what I ordered—far and away too long. The need has only grown while you've been sailing your worm-infested ship, and here I wait still, the harvest upon me. Where is he? You sold him to another?"

The captain looked skyward, scratching his jowls cautiously, buying time. It had to be Kade of whom they spoke. Had he remained with us, Kade would have been the strongest and most able-bodied of the captives. My pushing Kade overboard had compromised the captain's position with the English planter. I blessed St. Brendan and all Heaven's angels the captain knew not what I had done.

"I did not even know he were overboard until I saw naught but a severed leg floatin' in our wake," Cocke said gravely. "It was the sharks what took him, sir, and I expect not long after he hit the waves. He tried to escape, and what a horrid bloody death it was fer his trouble. Terrible. Terrible. Perhaps he was not so bright a fellow as he appeared, and it's a small mercy he's gone, sir. Violent, but quick."

The captain was lying, sure I knew it. Had I not seen Kade swimming away from us as if half fish himself, a ship within a few strokes of ours and Barbados just a bit farther beyond? But the captain was convincing, even a small tear forming at the corner of his eye, such that I began questioning my own eyes. Had I turned away too soon, before the tragedy struck? I'd lost sight of him quickly. Had I kilt him then, by shoving him off? His poor leg shredded away as the captain said, by the jagged teeth of a shark? I was sick from hunger already and now it left me, replaced by dread and guilt. Was I a murderess before I'd intended? Had I shoved Kade to a hideous death by a sea monster? My knees weakened. Like the other woman before me, I collapsed right there on the sand, but a heap of naked flesh.

It was a time before someone grabbed my arm and pulled me back to my feet. My sight went from cloudy to clear and back again; then I was lifted and the wagon creaked beneath my weight.

"Captain, I'll not be taking such a tale for an excuse. By God, I had your word, and now you would have me believe you would cross the sea with but one able man for my fields? And him lost? You'd best find the man here among the palmettos before nightfall. I'll take these slaves to the plantation now, but I'll be back and carrying the biggest pistol my father ever owned so that I may see you staring down its barrel. If you don't produce the man, I'll be blasting a valley through your God-forsaken skull."

I felt the others crowd into the wagon around me and heard the horse shake his ears. The wagon heaved as the Englishman found the jump seat.

Leather snapped against the horse's backside and we lurched forward. Overhead the sun beamed strong and seabirds shrieked their indignation. It was no worse than my own, for in addition to my faintness I now felt chills rippling up my back and along my arms. Plantation, he had said. We were to be slaves on a plantation. The wagon bumped along a poor road climbing a hill, and I raised my head just long enough to see the slanted rooftops of the town slipping away behind us. Kade's coin was somewhere in the sand, and though I struggled I was powerless to retrieve it. Though I willed my body to kick, thrust out my arms and legs and run back, these appendages did not move but lay helpless and limp on the boards. Then my mind, tried to its' limit, gave out as well and all went black.

After a time the halt of the wagon woke me, and I was able to lift my head enough to peer over the boards. A crude wooden sign hung on a brick fencepost, the letters burned deep and black into the wood: SHARAVOGUE. My fear was reawakened, for I knew well enough the word's meaning from the Irish *searbhóg*—a bitter place. We were on the cleared flat of a hillside, thick forest above and below. I looked toward the sea, shimmering beneath the midmorning sun, but there was no ship in view, nor any town, and the road closed in behind us and was no road at all.

9

The Big House

The servants have the worser lives, for they are put to very hard labor, ill lodging, and their diet very slight.

~ Richard Ligon, 1657

We were pulled from the wagon and set to the ground. I looked behind me and saw a great yard of dirt and sparse, sunbaked grass, crude wooden outbuildings, and a shell and gravel path leading to a great house at the far edge of the yard. The ground floor was built of rough stone with large, deep window openings covered by broad shutters. The upper floor was of wood, with glass windows that reflected the white peaks of the distant windswept waves.

The house was not beautiful by any measure but fearsome by great strides, and behind it loomed the mountain steep and jagged at its peak, choked at its foothills by forbidding forest and vines. The Englishman bounded over two stone steps, through heavy carved doors of rust-colored wood, and into a dark corridor.

The dread in my stomach suddenly awakened, only worsening as I inhaled the perfume of tropical flowers and the sticky-sweet scent of overripe and rotting fruits. The intense heat of day bore down upon our heads.

I pushed past the others and ran into a thick stand of bushes nearby, my stomach heaving. As I recovered I heard harsh laughter and believed they laughed at me, but when I emerged from the bushes sweating and weaker still, I realized the great bustle all around the yard. The laughter came from three tall boys with coal-black skin who jostled each other as they carried fat, leafy bundles to a wooden shed, while two others rolled barrels down the hill toward the gate. Another pushed a wobbly wooden cart and beyond him yet another watered a team of oxen.

There were women, dark skinned and light, carrying woven baskets and kindling wood across the yard. Two of them sang as they worked the rows of a vegetable garden beside the house, some of them with children clinging to their legs, while goats and dogs and cackling chickens roamed freely.

The light-haired, burly fellow led us through the middle of this activity, straight toward the big house. Still in our nakedness, we were allowed to sit on a patch of grass until a dark girl brought us a single gourd of ale to pass. The taste was like honey and slaked my parched throat. I drank gratefully and then we huddled together and waited, too tired and afraid even to speak, while the sun baked our shoulders. At times the sweet scent of verbena wafted around us, breaking through the heavy smoke of a constant wood fire nearby.

I saw the plow horse unhitched from the wagon and taken away, and when I looked toward the sea beyond I understood why it no longer would be needed. Cutting through the whitecaps below our hill, the *Jackdaw's* sails were fully raised to swiftly increase the distance between the captain and the master's pistol. And though it was the ship that had held me captive and brought me to the island, the sight of it leaving made me feel more desolate.

When the sun had moved behind us, the wind changed and blue-gray clouds began to gather overhead. A tall, thin man approached wearing a sand-colored homespun robe that hung to his shins. His legs were like sticks, lacking the bulge of muscle, and his skin was not black but brown like the high branches of the trees back home in Ireland. But he was not of Ireland. His hair was cropped close to his skull and grew in the tight curls of black lamb's wool. His eyes were tar-black, and his face held no humor or kindness. He grasped a horsewhip in one hand and a broad-brimmed straw hat in the other. At his hips he wore a dark leather belt and a long curved knife in place of a sword. When he spoke we all listened hard, for we dared not beg him to repeat.

"I be Mr. Drax. Not slave or servant, I am schooled and named for de finest plantation of de gret island Barbados. I be brought here as de paid overseer of Lord Tempest Wingfield's sugar plantation. I mek sure you be assigned good work, and dat your work be done. I am to be obeyed. I punish you when work be not finish. Speak to de others about de rules here, for dere be many. Do not break dem. On de morrow you work, and by night you fix your own place of rest at de slave village. For tonight, by de master's gret mercy, you will be clothed and allowed to sleep at de master's shelter."

He left us, and in a few moments a girl came. Her pale yellow shift hung like a sack from her bony shoulders to her shins. Her bare feet were dark on top, but white of skin, dust and sand on bottom. Her skin was darker than Mr. Drax's and smooth as still water. Her nose and cheeks were broad and her ears almost pointed at the tips, holding back the thin black braids that fell in a hundred strings down her back. She peered at us through black eyes hooded by thick, shiny lids. She did not speak, but waved us into the house and gestured for us to sit on the broad wooden planks.

Before us a wide staircase of polished wood led to the upper floor, where double doors with gleaming brass handles were closed against us. Bright lanterns at the sides of the stairway sent shadows dancing up the risers and cast greater darkness to the corridors on either side of us, where only occasionally did a narrow wooden doorway interrupt the solid lines of stone. Above our heads an open railing ran the length of the walk, where someone might lean to speak to one of us below.

The girl brought gourds of drink that were passed, and then a basket of a thin dry bread that we quickly emptied, leaving not a crumb. Next she brought a thin gruel of broth that we consumed just as greedily. We ate in silence, forgetting our nakedness at least for a while as the wind howled around the corners of the house like a famished wolf searching for a way in to his prey. And then the girl gestured for us to follow her back outside where Mr. Drax waited.

"Come you now, I take you to de master's shelter. On de morn' we rise early." And off he went down the path as rain began to fall in heavy splatters on the stones. I started to follow, but the girl grasped my elbow and pulled me back inside, shutting the door on my view of the others.

For a moment I feared I would be the first to feel the sting of Mr. Drax's horsewhip, but she led me to a bed chamber on the ground floor. The room was dark inside, its black shutters closed against the rain. The wind ripped through the slats, though they held fast. The girl lit a candle on a cabinet top. It flickered wildly, but allowed me to see a wash basin and a spindly wooden chair. Against the opposite wall a narrow bed had clean white sheets and a blue woolen blanket. My heart leapt! And then followed my mind. I had never had a room to myself in all my life, and here it was within the very walls of the manor house.

For certain the master had recognized me for the princess I was, and now I would be treated accordingly. If only my father could see it, that by some wondrous mistake justice had been served. Cromwell himself had run me out of Ireland, away from my claim and my heritage, only to deliver me to it on the other side of the ocean. But I could not rejoice just yet, for I was unsure what was coming next.

The girl seemed to have no voice, for she gestured toward the basin, a small chunk of yellow soap and the towel that rested beside it, and then to a filmy white dressing gown that hung on a hook behind the door. I nodded and she left me alone. As tired and frightened as I felt, I could not prevent the smile that crossed my lips. I was to have a room and a servant then. It would be as my father had promised: someone to prepare my bed, and in the morning bring me fresh clean clothes and a breakfast of fruits and sweets.

The blood rushed into my head, and I had to steady myself. I pressed my hand against the wall behind the washbasin and dipped the other into the cool water. I inhaled the jasmine scent of the soap. The girl smiled and backed away. I began to wash vigorously, caring not that I might remove the skin's surface that protects from disease, for the feel of soap against my skin was delicious pleasure after all the filth of the *Jackdaw*. I sunk my hands in and splashed my face, scrubbed the back of my neck and rubbed it with the towel, and then I lost myself completely to it, to the cool water and soap foam against my stomach, my breasts and arms, my thighs and privy parts, and even my toes. The water was darkened when I was through, but I didn't care. I prayed it would be the last time in my life that I would be so dirty. I slipped the dressing gown over my head, feeling the fine fabric settle delightfully over my still-damp skin.

The girl removed my basin and towel; then she placed the spindly chair in the middle of the floor and gestured for me to sit. With a wide-tooth comb she began the task of untangling and smoothing my hair. I closed my eyes and let her work. Had anyone in my life ever done such a thing for me? My mam, when I was just a child? If she had, the memory was lost to me, for I would always wish to recall the pleasure of hands smoothing the curls from my brow, working away the knots that went beyond my hair and into my neck and shoulders. Though sometimes she pulled and ravaged my scalp, I gave not a cry for I would do nothing that might cause her to stop her welcomed work. She took her time, stopping to show me a long, curly lock that she had smoothed to silk, then smiled and began again.

She tapped my shoulder when she was done, and I stood as she left me alone. My hair hung in soft waves, blanketing my back right down to my waist. My scalp tingled, and I allowed the pleasure and fatigue to settle into my bones. Then I fixed on the bed, beckoning from across the room in the flickering light, its linens swaying slightly from the wind. I sat on it, feeling the sheets against my palms and the softness of the bedding beneath me. I waited not a second longer before slipping in, pushing my toes deep into my soft cocoon. I lay my head down and closed my eyes just to chisel deep into my mind what it felt like to sleep in a real bed. It was where I belonged, and I intended to sleep in a bed ever after.

I must have drifted into dreaming, for when I awoke the wind had calmed and the rain splattered against the shutters. I heard footsteps on the floor above me, and words, or rather grumbling and shouting. It seemed to stop, then returned even louder with banging and breaking of glass. So quickly had I adopted my role of royalty in this bed chamber, I thought there was a bit of nerve for the man to be awakening me with his carrying on, and told myself I'd speak with him come morning.

Then a distant thunder sounded nearer and the voices sharpened. Was the master arguing with someone? It seemed a terrible disagreement, I sat up in the bed clutching the sheet to my chin. Footsteps pounded until the very walls around me shuddered. Something clattered to the floor. A door slammed. Footsteps on the stairs fell so heavily the house itself seemed to expand and contract like the heaving lungs of a giant. And then they were gone. Thunder exploded over the rooftop. A gust of wind ripped through my shutters and doused the tiny nub of my candle with its own wax. The door to my room burst open.

My chest seized so that I could barely breathe, but the blood still pounded in my ears. I could see nothing in the darkness. I assured myself it was only the wind, but I felt a chill down my spine as if a cold splash of rain had found its mark there. Lightning cracked like a whip through the stormy sky and lit the walls. The master was standing by the door, his hair wild like a wolf's mane, his eyes like glass and his face as white and shadowy as a skull. I tried to scream, but I was frozen in the darkness and terrified to move. Where could I go? He blocked the door. And as darkness returned my panic grew.

I heard the creak and groan of the spindly chair beneath his weight, and the gurgle as he drank from a bottle. He set the bottle on the floor and belched, and the little chair creaked once more before it collapsed beneath him in a great pop and clatter.

"*God's WOUNDS*," he roared, and a string of oaths and curses followed, nearly drowning out the raucous lightning when it struck again. In the light he stood like a giant amidst the broken wood, hurling pieces of it against the wall.

"Stop it. *Get out*," I shouted in my arrogance, furious that he had interrupted my dreamful sleep with his drunkenness. I had seen enough of it at Aengus's shebeen to know it was mostly blustering and little substance, but had never considered the danger to myself of a drunken and angry man. My eyes began to adjust to the darkness, enough so that I saw him turn his attention from the chair to me. The hairs on my arms bristled in warning. He stepped closer.

"What did you say?"

"Enough of your curses. Get out! Let me sleep."

"You little fool, I will..." He stopped, and I heard only the rain pounding and splattering on the surfaces all around us. And then he began to laugh, loud and high like a boy who has gladly killed his first bird. He sat on the bed next to me, and when I tried to push him away he grabbed my wrists and pushed me back on the bed. His face hovered over mine, and I smelled the whiskey on his breath and the sweat that soaked his shirt and dripped from his chin to my neck. "You will sleep soon enough. Our business comes first, and if you do not please me you'll sleep with the crabs and the lizards."

I squirmed, but he held my arms fast. "You'll not..." I tried to argue, but he clasped one hand over my lips until I stilled.

"You'll do as I say," he whispered, "for it's how you'll find your freedom. That's what you want, isn't it? Fight me and I'll double your indenture or sell you to the brothel for the sailors."

The rain came down even harder, and I lost my courage. I began to cry and was furious with myself for it, but there was no help. "I'm no slave, I'm a...princess..." I managed to utter between my sobs, and felt like an idiot as it left my lips. Sure he heard me, for he laughed into my face, the stench of liquor so strong it made me gag.

"You're a princess and I am king of all England," said he, and he jerked back the sheet that covered me. "Pretend you are my queen and please me well."

He slipped his hand under my gown and touched my breasts, my belly, my thighs; and then he found the private place between them.

"There now."

I squirmed to be free of him, terrified of what would come next, but his hold was strong. With one hand he pressed my chest, securing me to the bed, and with the other hand he worked at the fastenings of his breeches, his fingers fumbling. He freed himself to his satisfaction and then settled his hips over mine, working my legs apart with his knees.

"There now." He pressed and rubbed against me. I held my breath for as long as I could and tried to lay as still as possible, just as a wild animal feigns death to discourage its predators. I turned away and felt his sweat drop to my chin and cheek.

"Help me now! Please me, as I demand!" He grunted into my ear. If it would have freed me of him sooner I would gladly have obliged, but truly I had no inkling what to do. I'd only heard of the deed in the tavern and never once had seen it done. But I tried, for fear of drawing his anger even more. I fumbled at the breeches still clinging to his hips. I forced myself to move my hand down his belly and towards his private parts, but just as I touched a patch of hair I was frightened and recoiled.

He shoved my hand aside and pressed against me yet again, slamming his hips against mine, and then forcing my thighs so wide I felt a scorching pain. He slammed his hips against me again and again until I felt bruised, but when at last he stopped his thrusting and fell upon me as heavy as stone, it was only the skin that was savaged and raw, and the muscle bruised against the edges of bone. A violent movement, an act not completed. I felt no deep penetration. He heaved a great sigh.

"Idiot!" he shouted. "Fool!" This time he was not addressing me. He pushed away and stood far from the bed, kicking the splintered wood that had been the chair until it scattered around the room like rats scrambling for a hole. "*God be cursed* if I be not a man." He grabbed the bottle from the cabinet and drank deeply, then dashed the bottle to a thousand pieces against the wall.

For a moment he did not move, and I held my breath for fear of starting things up all over, but then I couldn't manage it longer and slowly exhaled as silently as I could. In the faint light that came in through the shutters I saw his shoulders settle. He turned, and though I could not see the direction of his gaze, I felt its heat clearly upon me. He came to the bed again and sat beside me. Could he not hear my heart flailing? My breath coming in short, terrified gasps? Could he not see my body trembling so much as to shake the bed itself? He touched my cheek with the pad of his thumb.

"Your complexion is fine, lass. Not delicate like a lily, for that could never suit you. Soft, but resilient, more like a wild orchid. Yes, that's more to the root of it. An orchid brightly colored and exotic in its beauty, appearing to be fragile and yet surviving the most inhospitable circumstance. Elusive for any fool who might seek it, and poison I dare say, for he who will pluck at its' stem." He looked at me a moment longer, then thundered from the room, slamming the door behind him and leaving the shards of glass where they lay.

In the chamber above he raged on, shouting his oaths, stomping about, crashing and banging the furniture, and sometimes falling into silence. I tried pulling the pillow over my head, wishing only to sleep but knowing it was hopeless under such tirades. I shivered beneath the sheet, my feet and hands as cold as if I'd held them in the sea, my body waiting for the moment he would burst through the door and try me once again.

Before long I heard footsteps and the click of the latch. Chills shot up my spine and across my shoulders, and I almost cried out, but it was the girl this time, come to light the candle. She brought a straw broom and swept away the glass that my feet would not be cut. She brought clothes and tugged the drawstrings of my gown so I understood she wanted me to dress. She helped me into the shift, its fabric unpleasant after the soft weave of the gown. Over the shift I fastened a dark skirt more coarse than the shift, and then a simple bodice over the top. She gave me a crude pair of cowhide shoes, and my hair remained uncovered and unbound.

She led me from the chamber, down a dark hall, and behind the house to the kitchen. A fire blazed in the side yard, and an old man silently poked at the searing coals. The girl led me away to a covered walkway smelling of smoke, sweat and urine, where others snored loudly in fishing net hammocks that had been strung from the rafters. She placed my hand firmly on an empty one and walked away.

I understood immediately. I had been tried, and now I was discarded. The chills I had felt before and the dread I thought I had expelled now found solid purchase in the pit of my gut.

10

The Indenture

If a boyler get any part into the scalding sugar, it sticks like Glew, or Birdlime, and 'tis hard to save either Limb or Life.

~ Edward Littleton, 1689

I slept not, wondering if at any minute someone else might come for me, or the girl might take me back where the master could finish what he'd started. My legs and thighs still ached, and my gut twisted in torment. As companions to my nagging fears, tiny insects set about with a constant hum to assault my eyes, my scalp, my ankles and my ears with their hot-cinder stings. Cockroaches skittered on the stones beneath us and twice climbed down the ropes to entangle in my hair.

"They dinna bite so much, ne'er mind. It's yer sweet-smellin' soap what attracts 'em," a man said in the darkness.

"That'll wear off in time, so stop yer fidgetin'," hissed a woman. "At least ye be not on the ground where they all but carry ye off. Hush now."

I longed for the white-sheeted comfort of my princess chamber and wondered if others had been through what I had with the master. Did they know for what purpose I'd been held behind, and did they now believe I'd been tried and cast out?

For the fact that the rape was not completed, I was grateful. To think of the man so close to me, so violent, so urgent to take me in ways I'd never known, caused bumps to arise along my arms and my heart to race as if it was happening all over. I could feel again the roughness of his hands against my thighs and the heat of his wretched, drunken breath at my neck.

And yet, fierce and terrible as he was, there was tenderness in the way he had touched my cheek. If he had succeeded as he'd tried, would he have allowed me to stay? Though I knew not yet the true nature of the deed, I believe I might have paid that price. I did know the great store men set in their ability to bed a woman, and how they loved to boast of it in the taverns. The women did not seem that much the worse for it. Should the master call for me again, would I try harder to please him? Or, because he had failed, would he hate the sight of me? I would know soon enough.

The silent girl came for us before sunrise. I felt bedraggled, sore and unrested, but more than willing to leave the torturous hammock. She led us to the front of the big house, where we ate dry bread and small chunks of cheese and passed the gourd. Afterwards we were lined up in front of one of the outbuildings—the milling house, someone called it—and soon a writing table and chair were placed before us. We stood, waiting until the dawn yellowed the horizon. Then the master came from the big house, a stack of papers in his hand. His hair was combed straight back and fastened with a black ribbon, and his doublet was buttoned and neat. The chair creaked but a little when he sat, positioning the papers on the table before him and looking them over one by one. He gestured to a balding, narrow-shouldered man who'd been on the *Jackda*w. The man stepped up to the table.

A woman whispered behind me. "Doona look him eye to eye, sure ye'll be hangin' from a tree by noontide. Impudence, they call it, just fer facin' up to 'em."

Words were spoken across the table, though I could not hear well enough to understand. The man walked away toward the yard, and then another was summoned, and another, each one leaving the table with a shred of paper in hand, until I looked about me and no others were left.

My turn had arrived. My skin prickled and my stomach threatened to heave the small bits of bread I'd been able to swallow, but I was more than a little curious about the paper and even more so about the man who was giving it out.

I stepped closer to the table. Though I wanted to, I dared not meet his eyes. Instead I focused on his writing hand, the long fingers gripping the quill, the fine dark hairs on the back of his hand, the clean nails holding steady as he dipped the quill into the inkwell, the fist tightening as he cursed over a splatter.

"What is your name?" he asked, not looking up. His voice was stern but not angry.

"Ailbhe," I answered.

"Alva?"

"Elvy!" I said, suddenly wanting to hear him speak it as my father had. A fly buzzed about his head as if suggesting what to write, then flitted off to the yard. The hand hovered over the paper only briefly and then began in tiny scratches and large sweeping curves to write down some language.

When the master finished the top half to his satisfaction, he glanced up. I saw his cool gray eyes for the smallest instant and quickly looked away. The were without light, serious and red-rimmed, and beneath them were bruise-like shadows of sleepless nights. I should have hated those eyes, but I had seen the like of them before in the villagers of Skebreen the very night I left them. They had witnessed horrors never dreamed and seen the darkest places where flowers once had bloomed. They were eyes without hope.

"The bottom here is your portion," the master said. He wrote again, muttering as he did, reading from the top of the page and copying to the bottom. He set the quill in its holder and scattered sand across the paper, then carefully tore the page across its middle, making sure the tear was as jagged as the mountain tops.

"See there, your indenture. The two indented pieces fit perfectly together, and the words of contract on both halves are the same, so that there be no mistake over the terms if misunderstanding should arise. Know that on Montserrat our indentures are strictly enforced. If escape is your plan, rest assured you'll be shot, hanged or returned to me, in which case your indenture will be doubled."

He looked me up and down. I felt it more than saw it, as if his very hands rested on my hips again, and not his eyes. But then he sniffed once, pushed the bottom half of the paper toward me, and looked away as if toward the next slave or servant he would call, though there were no more waiting. I realized then what had passed between us was forgotten and what he felt toward me was nothing more than indifference.

"Seven years," said he, "starting today. Make your way to the boiling house, there where the smoke rises, to learn your chores. It is harvest time and we must work night and day. Do not be a nuisance to me or you'll find yourself in the cane fields sure enough."

My hands trembled as I took the paper and my mind raged. *Seven years.* The man was a fool if he thought so. Matters awaited me, like the bloody, lifeless body of Oliver Cromwell. I had no time for the tasks this man would set me about. A part of my nature demanded to reach out and slap him—fury fueled by the indignities of the night before—but a wiser part stayed that hand. I had much careful navigating to do if I would find audience with the governor. The master knew him, I was sure. I would have to bide my time and stay out of trouble until my perfect opportunity arose.

I turned away and followed a pebbled path to the boiling house, tucking an indenture contract I could not read into a skirt I did not even own. The wind had calmed, and smoke closed in about me as I neared the structure. I could hear the greedy crackle of fire and the high timbre of cut logs tossed against each other to feed it. Where I entered there were no doors, and along one side the wall was open, naught but wooden posts at intervals to support the thatched roof. A crude brick furnace ran nearly the length of the building. Beneath its surface the fires burned, heating four large copper kettles that hung above. Smoke rose in heavy streams seeking freedom through vents in the roof. Black-skinned boys fed sticks and logs into the fires, and when their skinny arms were emptied, they ran back to the woodpile for more. Workers of black, brown, and white labored all about, carrying earthen pots and jugs, filling gourds of water, chopping more wood for the pile.

At the center of it all stood a black man of such size I had never seen before, his waist nearly as narrow as my own but his shoulders surely four times as broad, the muscles tight and well-formed, the sweat dripping in rivulets down his back. He held a large spoon-like skimmer in one hand. Suddenly he dropped it, raised his arms on either side of his head, and screeched out at such a pitch it pained my ears and sent some of the workers scattering. I started to approach him, and he seemed to sense it so, for he turned with such a deliberate violence my breath caught in my chest and my instincts commanded me to shrink to the size of a pea, though I could not. In his eyes burned such a fury as the fires from hell must hold, and it paralyzed me there as he dropped to his knees and splashed a massive hand into a waiting bucket of water. He bared his teeth in a horrid snarl the fiercest wolves might wish to master. Then the fury banked, and slowly he lifted his dripping hand and examined it.

I heard the rustle of skirts and a strange click from behind me. An old, dark-skinned woman approached, her rough-hewn cane tapping the sides of posts and pots as she crossed the distance to the man. She was broad of hip and breast, and wrapped about her head was a scarf as blue as the crystal sea that surrounded the island. She took the man's hand gently, held it to her cheek, and then led him behind her out of the building and into the sunlight. But for the fires still crackling in the furnace, all was silent and no one moved, but watched the woman's every gesture. She sat on the chopping block. The man knelt before her and set his injured hand in her lap. She pulled a tiny pouch from her skirt, raised it before her eyes, and reared back her head until all I could see of her face was her rounded chin and thick lips that moved rapidly as she whispered to the sky. Her chin tilted down again and she opened the pouch, speaking now to the man whose head was bowed before her. She withdrew a pinch of something and smoothed it across the man's wound. In the sunlight it glistened like oil. She touched his head and both stood, something peculiar passing between them, though no more words were spoken. Then I heard the master's voice behind me.

"Thank you, Badu."

The old woman only nodded and turned towards the woods behind.

"Are you fit, Maestro?" the master asked.

The huge black man stretched his hands high into the air and flexed the smooth muscles of his shoulders. Between those hands he might easily have crushed the master's head if he chose, but he dropped his arms and nodded. The master pulled a flask from a vest pocket and handed it to Maestro, who took a long drink. It was then that I noticed the white splotches peppering Maestro's hands and wrists, scars from wounds delivered by the boiling concoction he tended. He nodded silently and returned to his station at the furnace.

"His buckets!" the master shouted at me. "Refill his buckets with cool water and make haste. Can you not see his need?" He turned and left the boiling house, and the activity that had stopped started up as before. I grasped a bucket and found water in the rain barrels under the eaves, then refilled another and placed them just behind Maestro. I stepped back and looked about, wondering what else might be expected.

Maestro used but one hand to work the skimmer, keeping the injured one at his side. He stood before the largest copper kettle. To a pan beside him he skimmed the brownish-yellow froth from his boiling brew. The scent of it was strange, mingling with the heavy wood smoke. At times it smelled sweet, not like honey but heavier, like the raw nectar of a flower many times multiplied. At times it smelled of the earth, slightly salty and rich with things decayed and things not yet sprung from their seed. And then I could pick out something else, like the smell of spoilt meat—sweet and still resembling the thing of its source but tainted by time. Maestro set the skimmer down and picked up the large ladle. He began to move his brew to the next largest kettle, while the boys fed the fire below. The liquid poured from the ladle, a dark reddish-brown, and I believed for one horrid moment it was the blood of goats or calves.

Then, through the open wall I saw beyond Maestro to the source of his mixture. Three men worked at a mill drawn by two oxen. One led the oxen on a track encircling a small framed mill house, pulling a long wooden arm that turned the works for a mechanism at the center of the structure. The other two men fed plant stalks into it so that they went in one side whole and came out the other side flattened and shredded. Juice pressed from the stalks flowed into a pan beneath and then downhill along a makeshift trough to a cistern. Others worked at the cistern, filling the buckets that supplied Maestro's kettles. At the finishing end of Maestro's boiling line, they placed another cistern where his darkest brew could cool.

One of the slave men beckoned me to help carry buckets of raw juice. As I turned I heard a great commotion; something crashed, and water splashed across the back of my skirt. A cry from the bowels of hell itself burst forth, slamming my heart against my bones. I had set the buckets too close, and Maestro had fallen over one of them onto his back. I ran to him, but he shoved me away with such force that I fell a fathom away from him at least, landing hard on my hip and elbow. He seemed unhurt, struggling to his feet, but his face was lined like a frightful mask and he was coming toward me.

"She be away, man." Mr. Drax said to Maestro, and held up the palm of his hand. "She go to de curin' house and not be a trouble to you. Go back now." Mr. Drax stepped around me as I straightened my skirt and got to my knees. He faced me, and from behind him I saw Maestro issue a hateful glare, then turn back toward the furnace.

"You fail now, your first day," Mr. Drax scolded. "And you have harm de boiler. He be important to de master. Don't want to fail again," he said, squeezing my arm. He helped me to stand, only to drag me from the boiling house and across the yard behind it to the curing house. Outside the curing house were the hogsheads of Maestro's brew, which now resembled heavy, wet sand. Stacks of earthen pots leaned haphazardly against the outer walls.

"You plug de pot so nothin' do escape." Mr. Drax demonstrated, forcing a cork into a hole in the pot's bottom. "Den pack dis mixture in full." He scooped the brown muck into the pot with a wooden spoon and packed it down with the spoon's flattened back. "When your pots be full, into de house dey go, and sit on de pans for two days. Den you pull out de corks and let dem drip. Someone come for de pans after."

He led me inside the curing house, where a straw fire burned in the center, cradled in stone, and all around it pots were arranged on large earthen trays. The day was growing warmer, and by midmorning the air was hotter than the worst summer day I'd ever experienced back home. But in that house the heat took me as if someone had tossed a heavy blanket over my head and stifled my breath.

"Keep de fires warm and de doors closed," Mr. Drax warned. "De air mus' be dry for de curin'. Each day we set de pots. Dey stay for thirty days, so never mix today's pots with de ones from de day or de week before. See de markings." He pointed to the rims of the dripping trays, each marked in charcoal with the date the pots were set.

My temples dripped with sweat, and I gladly followed Mr. Drax back outside to feel a light breeze on my brow. "You keep de fire burnin' night and day, and you pack and set thirty pots a day. I come back and count each day. Meet your numbers, or dey be doubled and you work until you do."

He turned away and left me there. Two women worked nearby, packing their own sets of pots. They watched me, and one spoke to the other in a language I'd never heard. The second woman laughed.

"He come and go like a spirit," the first one said to me. "An evil spirit." She smiled, revealing empty spaces where teeth had once been, and spat on the ground.

I sat by my pots and watched the women work. The tasks seemed easy enough, and they were far older than me. I felt sure if they could finish thirty pots in a day, I could finish ten more.

When the sun was high, we stopped for a meal of beans and a soft yellow fruit called plantain. We tended the fire every time we finished more pots and carried them into the curing house. I worked until my fingers were sore and my arms and shoulders ached, but by sundown I had set only seventeen pots.

When Mr. Drax returned, he counted each pot carefully and shook his head. "You fail again."

"I started later than the others, when I came over from the boiling house and..." I tried to explain.

"Yes, de boilin' house. If I let you go with so much failure, tomorrow all de others think dey have no need to meet dey quota. If de master angry and want someone's head on a pike, better it be yours dan mine. You stay. You work." He turned again and left me, walking slowly from the curing house to the big house. Dusk already had settled across the yard. The smoke of the cook fires rose up from the slave village. I felt my stomach cramp with hunger, and watched the dark figures drift away from the yard for the night. I drew the next pot toward me, feeling the rough edges against my raw fingers, and the sting of hot tears on my cheeks.

11

The Procession

"They believe a Resurrection, and that they shall go into their own Country again, and have their youth renewed."

~ Richard Ligon, 1657

A gull's cry awakened me. I lay in the dirt beside the curing house, my hand still wrapped around the wooden spoon handle and three pots left to fill. The slave women stood over me scowling. Whether it was pity they felt, or a desire to deprive Mr. Drax the pleasure of disciplining me, I'll never know, but they sat me up and one of them fastened my hair with a string of braided grasses while the other quickly packed the last pots, so that when Mr. Drax arrived he found the three of us preparing for the new day's toil. He eyed me curiously, his instincts perhaps whispering to him that something was amiss.

"De quota be met, now to begin again." He gave the women a stern look and then descended the hill toward the fields, one hand resting on the hilt of the long curved bill for cutting the cane and the other gripping a tightly coiled leather whip. I had no care to know the pain that came from the end of it.

I exhaled my relief, but there was no time for thoughts of escape or destiny, or even for the hunger that dug its claws deep into my stomach and gnawed around all of my edges. I had missed what little breakfast might have been had but dared not fail again at my tasks. I could be sent to the fields. I had never labored so before, and though I was tall I was likely too weak to carry the great bundles of cane I saw the men stacking by the mill. The hunger made my hands tremble and I felt dizzy each time I stood to carry the pots into the curing house. And the sun, bright and glorious as it was, bore down upon our heads with such intensity I thought my neck would cook like a piece of pork fat and snap into pieces. Still I had to succeed no matter the struggle. Here I would suffer, but in the cane fields I feared I would die.

Hoping desperately to learn from the slave women, I watched their strong brown arms, their silent concentration, working together in fluid motion and me the stone in their track. When I stumbled into the curing house and nearly broke one of their neatly packed pots, they shook their heads angrily. I knew if I did not meet my quota again, they would not help me. I dug with my spoon and packed the heavy, gritty mixture while flies tormented my eyes and ears. By the time the others left for their cook fires, Mr. Drax stood before me, his dark stick legs accusing me enough without the assistance of eyes or mouth. I was half-finished with the pot I held, and one more left to go. He glared down upon my head even as he pushed a piece of the crackly bread into my sticky, dirty hand.

"Time now to go. Time to find your home place, to make your bed and sleep. Dis be not your place now. On de morrow you be on de field gang."

Heat surged in my chest and up into my neck as if my own blood wanted to boil over and flow out of my eyes and mouth. I wanted to bawl like a baby, and the need formed a hard, bitter knot in my throat. I had worked so hard, until my back ached and my fingers bled, but even with the help of the others I had failed yet again. If Mr. Drax saw my cheeks flush he showed no sign, and I refused to show him a single tear. He pointed to the north and a narrow path where I'd seen many others go after a day's work. "Take your ration from de kitchen, and find your quarters at de end ob de path."

I indulged myself with a last longing look toward the big house and my private chamber. I had to get back to it somehow, and to the master who could lead me to the governor. I had to get out of this place and home again. For now I saw no options. I chewed the tasteless bread greedily and all too soon it was gone.

In the kitchen yard, a fire blazed beneath a huge black kettle. Slaves and servants lined up for their rations. When my turn came, it was a trencher of beans, yams, and another hunk of the bread. I sat down in the yard and ate it all with my unwashed fingers, swiping up the juices. If I noticed the taste I cannot say, for my hunger demanded food of any kind and allowed no time for the savoring. The fullness of my belly was a welcome luxury I'd nearly forgotten. What I needed next was a place to rest, to hide like the small dog that avoids the larger ones so they might not see the vulnerability, confusion, anger, and fear working its way to my surface. I followed the path to the slave village.

It was far worse than I had imagined. Small, low huts were fashioned from reeds, scrap wood, tree bark, palm thatch, and cane trash, all arranged in haphazard patterns. Smoke from the cook fires grayed the air all about me, and those tending the fires did not so much as glance at me as I passed. I recognized the narrow-shouldered man from the *Jackdaw* and ran to him. Sure he must have seen my desperation as if it were written in stripes across my face. He nodded, glancing over his shoulder at the others as if to help me would bring disfavor.

"Most folk patch a hut together from what they can find, but the master builds a few. There be an empty one yon." He spoke softly and tipped his head to the left. I looked in that direction to a small reed hut with a palm thatch roof and no door. "Someone passed away. You can snatch it up before another comes to claim it."

I crawled inside the hut, barely large enough for me to lay in without my feet sticking out the opening and naught but a few clumps of straw for a bed, but it gave me the cover I needed. I thought I would fall to sleep the moment I laid down my head; but instead in the waning dusk I saw a tiny web spun across a corner, and even tinier flies hanging helplessly, their wings made useless by gossamer. I saw no spider but knew as surely as the flies that it was coming. I turned away and peered through the spaces of the reeds, watching the darkness close in and hearing sounds all about me from things I could not see: footsteps, cries, snores, voices, broken sticks, animals, predators. I imagined a hundred jumping spiders and my insides their trapeze. I stared up at the thatch that was my roof, and the warm night became cold all about me. I was alone, truly and fully, with no one within half the earth's distance who knew me or cared for me. Even my trusted St. Brendan felt well beyond my reach.

I thought of the night in the dolmen. It seemed as if years had passed since Kade and I had crawled beneath that solid stone roof. Though danger was about, Kade had been beside me and his warm cloak across my shoulders. I had never felt afraid with Kade there. Then the hard knot in my throat broke free, and I began to quake and shudder, my tears flowing like a river and my sobs silent like the dead.

I must have slept for a while but awoke to strange sounds, as if wolves were howling, only higher pitched. I drew myself into a ball, fearing some kind of wild animal, and then through the reeds I saw fire flickering in orange and gold, and black silhouettes moving around them. The shapes were coming closer, until a group of people, eight or ten, crouched at my very doorway. One held a torch. The largest among them I recognized as Maestro. He carried a woman's body and laid it down in front of my hut. I realized with a start that the woman must be the one who had lived where I now lay. Her lifeless hands were clasped and fastened at her chest. I drew in even tighter, sure they did not know I was there, and I feared what they might do if I disturbed them.

I recognized the old woman Badu by the shape of her turban, and the silent girl from the big house stood beside her. The group formed a circle about the body and began to sing. Each person in turn sang a part in words I could not recognize. When one man seemed to falter, Badu reached across the circle and slapped him, then he corrected himself and the song continued. I barely breathed, trying hard to remain unnoticed though I shivered uncontrollably. The song traveled around the group three times, and then Badu stepped away. The others followed her, and Maestro lifted the body. The group formed a single line moving like an eel among the kelp, and Badu led them back toward the yard. I should have stayed quiet in my hut. I should have gone to sleep, knowing what awaited me the following day, but these were secret proceedings and I had to know what they were about. As helpless as I was, I thought any knowledge could bring me benefit. I followed, staying several paces behind Maestro and keeping to the brush.

The procession passed the big house and then turned down the hill and out the front gate where I had seen "Sharavogue" on the wooden sign. The path dipped into a valley just north of the road and through a thick stand of trees, the waning moon shedding just enough light to see the way forward. I followed, keeping the torch in my view until I could see a pond reflecting the flame. Around it the trees rustled and an owl voiced a warning. Maestro set the body down by the still water. Badu crouched, slowly removed her apron and sopped it in the pond water. The other women followed, sopping aprons or cloths, whatever they seemed to have. I moved a little closer in the brush, hoping to hear any words that were spoken.

Badu wrung her apron so that the water dripped slowly and evenly over the dead woman's face and breasts, while the others did so over her stomach, arms, and legs. Then with these cloths they washed the body gently. Some of the women wept, but Badu had no tears, and Maestro stood apart from them as if his job was done. Badu muttered constantly, and when she raised the apron above her head, her voice boomed across the little pond like the wild cry of an eagle. She jumped to her feet and turned around and around, the still-wet cloth held above her head and sending out silver droplets as she whirled. "Let me loose, let me loose," she shouted to the sky, until she seemed to stumble, dizzy from her turns, and fell against a bush. The others reached for her, but she steadied herself and then knelt at the dead woman's head, placing her palm across the face.

"It be done. She be free, and now we go," Badu said. Maestro lifted the body again and led the way, with Badu and the silent girl just behind him. I crouched low as they passed, but then heard them stop. I dared to lift my eyes enough to see what had happened.

Badu stood beside the bush where I hid. Her gaze penetrated into mine, the light from the torch dancing in bright reflection. A chill ran up my spine as cold as a quick winter frost. Though she spoke no words, I heard her as if she whispered into my ear: I know you are here. You do not belong, and I will not forget. The silent girl stopped also, but she stared at the ground and never glanced toward me until Badu began to walk again. I remained hidden as they all passed but dared not let them get too far ahead lest I be lost alone in the wood. The procession continued on, but I climbed into my hut that already I claimed as my haven. I curled into a ball on the clumps of straw, hugging my knees to my chest.

Badu had seen me, hiding and watching something secret, something forbidden. What consequence might that bring, I wondered, as exhaustion began to claim my bones. Could it be any worse than the wrath of Cromwell, or the whip that awaited me at dawn?

12

On the Field Gang

The Devel was in the English-man, that he makes every thing work; he makes the Negro work, the Horse work, the Ass work, the Wood work, the Water work, and the Winde work.

~ A slave saying

At the sound of an eerie, mournful trumpeting I peered through the reeds of my hut. Possibly some strange bird roosted near. But I saw only Mr. Drax standing alone in the midst of the slave village, using a seashell like a herald's horn. Maestro appeared on the path almost immediately and headed toward the yard. Others began to stir about. I pulled the straw from my hair and retied it with the braid, climbing out of my hut to relieve myself in the woods. When I returned, Mr. Drax was waiting.

"De A-gang be already in de field. You join de B-gang in de yard straightaway. Work behind de A-gang, a-haulin' away de cane and clearin' away de cane trash. Move now," said he, and headed up the path, his curved bill and horsewhip at his belt and his walking stick scraping the pebbles as he passed.

I hurried after him, realizing there would be no breakfast until later. I struggled to keep up with his long strides as the stitching in my left shoe gave way and the side of my foot met sand and rock. In the yard, four men and three women waited. Mr. Drax passed them without a word, and they all fell in step behind me. We crossed the same ground Badu had crossed the night before but turned left toward the big house instead of right toward the gate. I glanced there anyway. Where were Badu and the silent girl this morning, and what had their midnight ritual had been about?

In the distance behind the big house, the A-gang worked under a morning sun burning steadily through the mist. They moved in a dark, relentless line against the endless green cane, each body set apart from the next just enough for their bills to slice the air and cut through the tall stalks, leaving behind the piles of their destruction and our day's work: slaves' work.

Mr. Drax glared at each of us in turn and led us along the path toward the working field. In minutes my shift was damp with sweat and my exposed foot throbbed. He set me at the end of a second line, binding the cane into bundles for the men to carry back to the yard. As they passed, the women cleared the leaves and stems that had been stripped away—the cane trash—and piled it along the edges of the field to be collected by yet another gang who would burn it in other fields to control the rats.

"Ayaaah!" the A-gang leader bellowed, and the line of workers advanced against the next row of cane, the sharp bills arcing down with a swish, a whack, and a bright flash. His broad black back glistened with sweat beneath the ragged brim of a straw hat, and the wind swept the green and yellow stalks waving and undulating for row after row before him. "Ayaaah," he cried again, and the hard cane rods, bright as a popinjay, fell at their feet.

I measured lengths of heavy twine from my shoulder to the earth and laid them across a flat rock for another slave to cut. We hung the lengths of twine from our necks until the bundles were brought forward, then pulled them out to secure each bundle firmly with big, tight knots. I was suited to this work, for my fingers were long, thin, and fairly deft at the knotting, but my hands grew sore after the first few bundles, rubbing against the coarse twine. The sun baked the air until it stung my face and seared my lungs. After a few hours I could barely lift my arms but dared not slow for fear of Mr. Drax, who paced along the field's edge tapping his leather whip against his thigh.

Behind him high on the hill, just a silhouette against the brightness, the master sat on his horse. He was bare-headed but the firm posture of his head and shoulders defined him, and his tall mount stood alert and proud. I stared for a moment, feeling the sweat trickle down my temple and between my breasts. What did he think about, this man who had tried to take me and then discarded me when he failed? Why did he watch us work? Then a pile of cane was dumped at my feet and I began binding it as I felt bound. My head throbbed in the incessant heat. Then there came relief as the silent girl arrived.

She balanced a large basket of bread on her head and led a small brown mule at the end of a rope with large gourds of water strapped across its back. I dropped what I was doing and ran toward her, then I stopped. Did the others do the same? Was I safe? I turned and saw that behind me they came steadily, if not as swiftly, wiping brows with dirt-smeared hands.

"Thank you," I said as the silent girl offered me the first ladle of water. I brought it gratefully to my lips, and then a savage pain ripped deep into the flesh of my ankle. I dropped the ladle into the dirt, its water filling a parched wheel rut, and dropped to my knees beside it. I thought a mad dog had attacked me with a fierce snap, parting the skin. But there was no dog. I looked up, and the silent girl backed away. Mr. Drax stood beside me, whip in his hand. Hot blood dripped down into my damaged shoe.

"De water for de A-gang, what do de mos' work. What dey leab behind, if any, den go to de B-gang. You stand aside and you wait." He coiled the whip slowly, watching me, then kicked my hip. "Get to de side and make way." He pointed back toward the field.

I crawled to the side of the path and pulled my knees close to my chest, watching the others approach. My ankle stung and swelled, and blood seeped freely from my wound out the open hole in my shoe, coloring the ground. I turned away, smarting from the wound but more so from the rebuke. I removed the shoe and used sand to clean away the trail of drying blood from my foot. I found long leaves in the cane trash near me and wrapped my ankle with them, if for nothing else than to keep the flies away. For good measure I wrapped my sore foot as well. Then I simply waited, tucking my ankle beneath my skirt to shield it from the belligerent sun.

The others crossed the tall grass to gather around the mule and formed a jagged line as the silent girl served them water one by one. They slurped the cool drink from the ladle, and then she handed each a section of bread. One of the men must have struggled against his hunger, and yet it won out, for he took a round of bread from her basket as she served another. He gnawed into it like a starving animal stripping flesh from a kill. I heard a loud crack as if a branch of a tree had fallen, and the man dropped to his knees as I had done. He cried out, a sound of anguish and fury. A gash across his back and shoulder gleamed white and then red, the blood oozing from the slashed skin.

Mr. Drax used his bill to force the man away from the others and made him kneel in the dirt facing the cane field. He spoke a few words to the man, not allowing him to turn or respond. Then the overseer stepped back. He removed his hat and bowed his head, chin on his chest. The workers were deathly silent, nor did a single bird cry or a gust of wind dare to rustle the cane. Mr. Drax seemed to be praying, his lips at times pressed together and at other times moving rapidly and fervently, mouthing words with careful passion. The others waited, and then as Mr. Drax raised his chin one of the women fell to her knees weeping. Mr. Drax turned his head from side to side, unfurled his whip, and with a quick snap of his arm made a second crack across the man's back. As wicked as it was, the sound was not so piercing as the perceived pain that I now recognized, and I flinched as if it was my own back being scourged.

The man did not cry out this time but held his tongue even as the third and fourth crack flayed his skin. I shut my eyes and held my hands to my ears, for I could bear no more of it. When I dared to peer between my lashes, one of the other slaves led the whipped man back to the field, Mr. Drax but a few paces behind them.

As the others followed, the silent girl brought me a full ladle of water and a hunk of bread. I took them gratefully, and she smiled, revealing even white teeth and eyes both dark and calm, though rimmed with tears. On the hill behind her I searched for the master, but he was gone.

That night I crawled into my tiny hut, grateful for every reed that gave me solitude and closed the others out. My head ached from the constant sun, my nose and the backs of my hands were blistered from exposure, and my throbbing ankle attracted tiny black flies that I shooed away until I could no longer care. Did the whipped man ache and sting and swat away the flies, and did he struggle for comfort and rest? Just then, as I was dropping off to sleep, I heard a gentle tapping on the reeds. In the deepening twilight I saw the silent girl crouched at my door, and behind her stood Badu, her turban unmistakable against the blue-black sky. The silent girl reached toward me, offering something: a soft green leaf folded into a square. I opened it, but in the waning light I could not see anything there. The silent girl extended her leg, showing me an ankle like my injured one, and rubbed a thumb along her skin where mine was cut. She'd brought me an ointment for my wound. I could not help it when my tears began to fall; my need for a kindness ambushed me and ruined my defenses. She smiled, her bright teeth as comforting and welcome as the stars that had shined above my faerie thorn so long ago.

In the days ahead our work grew even harder. The sea wind died away and the heat was relentless. Tiny gnats worried my ears and eyes. My shoulders ached and my fingers turned raw and cracked, and yet Mr. Drax hollered commands like snaps of the whip, urging greater and greater speed. The A-gang worked as if to fight back the sun, and before them the cane grew thicker and tougher, the dead leaves and trash falling behind them in heaps up to my knees.

One day when the sun was at its zenith, we came upon a sweet-sick stench so powerful my hand instinctively shielded my nose and my insides threatened to bring forth. The gang stopped, and Mr. Drax moved in to investigate the trouble. We could see the shape of a cow laying in the field, butchered and rotting, its entrails drawn out in many directions where animals had tugged and pulled. Flies swarmed above it, black and angry at our disturbance, and the stink settled over us, dense as a fog. When Mr. Drax lifted a section of entrails with the end of his walking stick, small rodents darted from beneath the carcass, and the stench exploded with a newfound force, hitting us in repulsive waves. Cold sweat burst forth on my forehead and I choked on my own breath. My stomach heaved. The next thing I remember is the smell of a horse, and I opened my eyes to see the dark hooves of the master's steed just an arm's length from my head.

"Bouccans be de mos' likely ones do it, suh," Mr. Drax was saying. "Come up here in dey ships to steal food. She be missin' two day now, and some say dey see a ship move in by night. If it be de Caribs, dey do a cleaner job ob de butcherin' and hardly leave a trace."

"No." I heard the master's voice. "The Carib tribes are not in the area now. They've moved their camps farther north. I'm sure it was as you say. I shall speak to the governor about it. In the meantime, have the B-gang clear away the remains and the A-gang continue harvesting. We'll need to set a night watch on the cattle for a while."

"Yessir," Mr. Drax said.

"Now, what of the girl?"

"She be not fit for de fields, Master Wingfield. Nor de boilin' house, nor de curin' house. She be not much use at all, only trouble. You mus' sell her." Mr. Drax picked up a fist full of dirt from the ground before him and rubbed his hands together. Most of the dirt showered to his feet, but he tossed a bit of it toward me and started to turn.

"No," Master Wingfield said. "She's not to be sold."

"Master Wingfield," Mr. Drax protested. "She be a hindrance to de harvest. You show her a leniency, she be a bad example to de other workers."

The horse stamped the ground, anxious to run. I felt its vibrations where my fingertips touched the earth, but the pain in my head was so monstrous I could not muster the strength to move. The master's voice came to me, a thin echo on a fine wind.

"Put her to work at the laundry. No, on second thought, she might do better in the cassava house. I'll have Timothee come for her in the wagon."

I had no idea what cassava was, but as it offered escape from the fields I loved the sound of it already. I knew not what lay in store for me next, but I heard two things that made me forget my nausea and begin to restore my strength. That I would not be sold again as a slave was the first thing. No matter how low I found myself, I feared to go through that degrading experience again, and face the possibility of finding myself in conditions even more wretched. And second, I had heard the word *governor*. The master would *speak* to him. Somehow through the master I would get to him as well.

13

The Cassava House

This root, before it come to be eaten, suffers a strange conversion; for, being absolute poison when 'tis gathered, by good ordering, comes to be wholesome and nourishing.

~ Richard Ligon, 1657

Strong hands lifted me from the ground, laid me on the flat boards of a wagon, and took me to the big house, so it was the kitchen I saw when at last I could raise my head.

"It's the heat what's taken her down. And I'd not be surprised if they all drop in the field on such a day." The cook was tall and horse-faced, her body pear-shaped and imposing. Her eyes were darkest brown, as honest as the richest earth. She complained bitterly and pressed a pewter tankard of ale to my lips, her fingers warm and firm on my chin. As soon as I could walk she sent me to my hut and would hear no protestations. I fell asleep in the humid darkness and did not rise before dawn the following day, when Mr. Drax called for me.

"Follow," he snapped. I crawled weakly from my haven and followed him across the main yard to a small, open structure furnished with several large wooden bowls, iron griddles, and a cook fire. Strange webbed cones made from woven palm leaves hung from the roof nearly to the floor, weighted at the bottom with stones larger than my fist. A crude ladder at the back gave access to the roof.

"You be no good for anathin' so far. Because de baker woman die, de mastuh sen' you here. Don' expec' you will do any better," he said. "You make de cassaba bread now. I show you one time. You make de bread, or you fail again and de master see you mus' be sold." He shook his head, pressing his lips together and widening his eyes so that I could see the red veins against the white. "It make no difference to me what you do, but do not be wastin' my time."

From a large basket he picked up a twisted brown root and broke it open, showing me the hard, white meat inside. "Cassaba grow wild on de island, and de women dig for it, but dey also hab it in de kitchen garden, de big plant wi' de green and yellow leaves. You dig de root jus' so." He gestured toward several rough baskets for collecting roots. "Eat de root jus' as you find it, it make you sick from de poison. Skip a single step in how I show you, it make eberyone sick." He glared at me so long I wished to squirm away from him; then he began to work.

He showed me how to peel and grate the root into a pulpy mass, then pack it into coarse linen bags. The bags went into the woven cones, and the stone at the bottom helped squeeze out the tainted juice. What remained was a damp, clumpy meal.

"Let de poison drain away, den let de spirit dry up. What you hab left be good meal for de bread." As Mr. Drax directed, I spread the drained meal in the large bowls to dry, then pounded the meal with a wooden mallet, adding a bit of salt.

"Get de cook fire hot now, den press de meal flat into de hoop in a big cake, de way you see it when you eat it. Make sure it hol' together. You don' be firm, de bread crumble away," he said. "Cook one side, den de other, den toss de bread onto de roof to dry in de sun. Do not burn it, or I fin' your mistakes where you hide dem and show de master it be time for you to go, straightaway.

"When I come back, if de bread be not baked and de gangs have none to eat, Master Wingfield see what mus' be done."

I watched Mr. Drax leave for the fields. How I wished I had a nice smooth stone from my dooryard in Skebreen to hurl right smartly at his head! I looked about at my new task as the pinkish morning light washed the little cassava house and warmed my determination to confound Mr. Drax. Something about the place appealed to me, and I believed I could make it mine. I would pretend I was preparing food for Aengus's customers in the shebeen. I could never disappoint Mr. Gould or Mr. McSherry, did they ask me for a bite to eat along with their ale or their spirits. In the same way I would not let down Maestro, the silent girl, Badu, or the man who had rescued me from the field. My bread would be good, and I would show them all.

And yet, as I set about my task my hands trembled and my thoughts wavered. What if Mr. Drax had told me wrong or left out an important step so that the bread would be poisoned? What if my bread tasted sour and people could not eat it? What if I was unable to get it all done and some had to go hungry? The consequences of failure fueled an anxiety nearly as powerful as my determination, surging within the muscles of my shoulders as I worked, and burning in my belly. I gritted my teeth against it, willing myself not to cry though I felt the force of a storm bearing down behind my eyes and in my throat.

A body can sustain strong emotion for only a brief time, and then it builds to such intensity one must either release it or explode from within. I had held so much within me even from the first time I had heard of Cromwell's coming to Skebreen, and nothing but fearsome events had followed. Since coming to the Indies I had faced loss and humiliation besides. I was so frightened and awestruck by the master, with each step he took my heart pounded harder than a battle drum. With Mr. Drax, my anger and fear rode hard on the same fierce horse.

If I could just scream my lungs out I might feel relief, but that would only cause the other slaves to think me mad, call me a witch or possessed by a demon. They could hang me or chop me to pieces with their bills. The master might sell me off before I could get to the governor, or lock me away with no hope of ever returning home again. Without that hope I knew I would lose any sanity left to me. I had to find my own way of relieving this unbearable tension.

A melody came to me as I crouched in the little wooden house, pressing dried meal into firm white disks: a faintly remembered lullaby the women of my village used to sing in Old Irish to comfort their babes to sleep. I began softly at first, just to see if I could remember the full of it.

Ay-nee-nee, Ay-nee-nee, Kod-ah-lee-gee, Kod-ah-lee-gee

I gave my voice greater strength as I put muscle into grating fresh root to a lumpy meal.

Ay-nee-nee, Ay-nee-nee, Kod-ah-lee-gee, Kod-ah-lee-gee

And as I put the meal to drain, squeezing out the sour-smelling poison, I sang from the depths of my stomach, feeling the power in my throat and lungs.

Kush-on Khlee Amwee, Kush-on Khlee Amwee!

The louder I sang, the more the ship's ropes that bound my heart loosened their knots, my chest expanding until I could breathe more fully, the stronger my breath with which to sing. And so I did, until the cauldron in my belly took its leave. And louder still, that I might pound and sift and salt my bread and make my griddle hot.

Ay-nee-nee, Ay-nee-nee, Kod-ah-lee-gee, Kod-ah-lee-gee

I heard a scuffle, and then a man stood before me, short and solid, his hair in the narrow fringe of a monk. His blue eyes blazed and his cherub face purpled, the blood in his cheeks and lips sure to burst through the flesh. Pudgy hands trembled before me. "My lady!" He shouted.

I stopped, startled and fearing he might snort like a bull and run me through. He gasped twice to catch his own breath, coughed, and in doing so allowed his face to regain some natural color.

"My lady," he repeated, sounding much like a French sailor who had shouted orders aboard the *Jackdaw*. "I have seen the most magnificent of all cathedrals, heard voices of angels within them, echoing een the halls with such exqueesite sound as to bring tears to my eyes and cause my heart to break—choirboys singing with such clarity and sweetness eet has stolen away my breath and removed all bitterness from my soul. But your sound," he gasped once more and shook his hands before my eyes, "your caterwauling een such gibberish ees an abomination of great proportion, made even more so by what my heart and ears long for een this wretched, heathen place!"

I smiled graciously, for I'd not met the man and would have him recognize the manners of a princess. I knew what caterwauling meant, but I'd not heard the word 'abomination' and thought he meant to compliment me. I bowed my head.

Ay-nee-nee, Ay-nee-nee...

"My lady! No!" He grasped his head as if to keep his skull from cracking, and then I understood his meaning more clearly.

"You are not pleased, then?"

"Pleased! I cannot even discern what gushes from your lips! Ees eet song?"

"It is an old Irish lullaby. It means 'Little bird, little bird, go to sleep, go to sleep.'"

The monk dropped his hands and shook his round head. "Well then, leetle bird, I wish you would follow your own instructions! Eef even a single bird on this island had hoped to slumber, you have set mean spikes een his nest. Eef you continue, I shall be forced to tell the overseer you are disrupting my work." His stood with short legs planted wide apart, hands on hips, head down, and breath heavy, as if working to release his own intense emotion.

I was not so offended that I did not want someone to talk to, and as he didn't turn away, so I thought mayhap he wished the same. "What work is that, sir?"

He raised his eyes, which had calmed to the color of a robin's egg, and pointed down the hill. "The distillery," he responded, then straightened up and squared his shoulders. "Performing the great alchemy of turning molasses into rumbullion, or rum, or some will call eet kill-devil, but such a name ees never to fit my product, which ees smooth as amber silk."

I considered the implications and summed them up fairly quickly. "The master would not want such work disrupted, isn't it so?"

"Quite right, my lady." He nodded proudly. "He ees anxious to see his casks full."

I offered my gracious smile once more, hoping to disarm him just a bit. I jutted my chin at him, for my hands remained soaked in cassava juice. "Then, I offer a bargain. Teach me things, and I will not sing."

He raised his arms and reared back as if I'd cast a bucket of cold water upon him. "Teach you? And what ees eet you would learn?"

"You are a monk. An educated man. Teach me about the vast earth that I might understand where we sit upon it. Teach me about this plantation and this 'wretched' island that I might better navigate it whilst I am here. And teach me about the government and how I might gain introduction to the governor."

His face shot red. "Pah! The governor? My lady, did you not understand your circumstance? We are indentured servants, only one hair's breadth above a slave. You'll never gain audience with the governor, and any other education would be wasted on you. Eef you do not perish from disease or starvation before the month ees out, your highest hope een this lifetime ees to be elevated to the scullery."

I stood, so he could measure my full and regal stature, and looked down on his bald crown. "I will not perish. I will be what I was born to be. I have a purpose in this life, and when I return to Ireland I will fulfill it. If you teach me, you will be rewarded when my birthright is restored."

His nose began to redden, and then he came forth with a loud guffaw so appalling I prepared to slap him, but held back.

"Look about you, child! Every slave from Africa ees a prince, a king, a high priestess! But this ees not Africa, nor Ireland. Here we are slaves until we escape or die. Be grateful eet ees for Tempest Wingfield you work, and not any other. Here at least we are fed and retain a few shreds of our dignity."

I did not want to hear of what he spoke. I only knew I needed his help if I was to find my way to the governor. He shook his head slowly and began to turn away.

Ay-nee-nee, Ay-nee-nee . . .

He jerked back around. "Please!"

"Teach me."

His shoulders fell and a quick breath escaped him. He slowly refilled his lungs and gazed up at the clouds scudding high in the clear sky above us. "Heavenly Father," he whispered, "what have you brought me now?"

He looked into my eyes and a gentle smile began to form on his lips. "Your name, leetle bird?"

"Elvy. From Skebreen."

"Of course. Elvy from Skebreen. I am Timothee, from de Brest, the great French port. Elvy, I accept you as my student, and the Father alone knows why. Only hold your infernal singing until we've learned a bit on that as well. When you've set your bread een the sun and you are ready to begin, you'll find me just down the hill."

I did not venture there the first day, nor the second or the third. I had to best my task in both quantity and quality, to be sure Mr. Drax would feel confidence. It also was not wise to work too quickly. If he thought me idle he might send me to the rat gang that burned the rodent-infested fields, at best a miserable occupation and at worst truly dangerous.

But on the fourth day I worked as if someone held a hot poker to my back, so anxious was I to begin my lessons with Timothee. I pressed the cassava meal into its form in the hot griddle. When it set, I flipped it carefully to cook the other side to a nice golden brown and then tossed the flat cake onto the roof of the shack to dry in the sun. Then I began again. I had twenty more bread cakes to make before I could call my work done. When the last one was set to dry I stepped back to look at it, pleased with my accomplishment. From the fields anyone could see my well-shaped bread drying on the rooftop. I prayed to St. Brendan Mr. Drax would recognize the evidence and not come to check on me. I wiped my hands on my skirt and hurried down the hill to the distillery, the excitement of rebellion singing beneath my skin.

I'd not seen the rum house before, tucked as it was into a stand of trees so much like Aengus's shebeen had been, but it was just a short and well-worn path away from the boiling house. There were several large vats with woven palmetto coverings situated in front of a small wooden house, its sides weathered and gray. Timothee was chopping wood in front of the familiar-looking pot still. He nodded toward me, and then toward the rum house.

"Eet ees built of red cedar, child. The master reserves red cedar for things of importance. Come. I will show you."

I followed him. The house had no windows, but from the open door I had light enough to see the hogsheads, bottles and earthenware jugs stacked all about. In one corner was a crude bed, and beside it a candle, a book, and a pair of spectacles.

"The master wants me always here," he gestured toward the bedding, "to discourage thieves. He doesn't want his slaves drinking rum, for eet makes them crazy or puts them to sleep. Only on Saturdays does he grant them a small portion."

"And do you make a lot of rum?"

"I am fully employed the year around. Right now, and each year from January to May, eet ees harvest time and I am busiest."

"But whoever heard of harvest in winter!"

"You *are* a leetle bird, aren't you! There ees no winter here, child. Our island sits upon the earth's belly, and here eet ees always warm and things will always grow. All eet takes ees time. When sugar cane ees harvested, you simply plant a piece of the stalk in the earth and eet will sprout anew."

"It cannot be!"

"Eet ees so. Then the harvested cane ees put through a roller mill drawn by oxen."

"Yes, I've seen them. The mill looks as if you could be drawn into it and crushed if you get so much as a finger caught in the works."

"It ees work only for the strongest man, and many have suffered, but the master puts men there who are skilled. As the mill work ees done, the sweet juice squeezed from the cane ees captured in a cistern and boiled in great copper kettles. You have seen the boiling house, no?"

I nodded, not wanting to recall the painful incident.

"The boiled juice ees tempered with lime so that eet will granulate, and then this mixture ees set een pots to drain. You have seen these pots as well?"

"I have," I assured him, my hands aching with the memory.

"Ah, yes, well then. This ees when my work ees set een motion. What drains from these pots ees molasses—the elixir from which rum ees made. I blend my own special ingredients, allow the mixture to ferment for one week, and then een the pot still eet ees condensed and transformed."

"Just look at all these casks and jugs! The master must be a fool drunkard then," I declared.

Timothee looked toward the big house and shook his head slowly. "When ships bring fresh supplies, Master Wingfield drinks Madeira wine and brandy, but there are times child, when he drinks for weeks and I do not see him except that he sends his maid for a jug. At other times he does not drink at all but walks the perimeter of his lands over and over, scowling all the while. And when the other planters join him for supper, they stay until dawn, drinking and thundering through the night. His relationship with drink ees curious, indeed. But never think for an instant that the master ees a fool. His vision and intellect would dazzle most men. I believe eet ees this intellect which battles so fervently with his desires."

I looked toward the boiling house where the smoke continuously billowed, and at all the outbuildings huddled around it. "Desires?" I said. "What would be his desires? He has everything. He is the master himself."

"Ah, now you are asking me to describe a man's heart. What troubles him I can only speculate, but his desires are deep and their solution elusive. As for the nature of them, I must leave that for him to share eef ever so he chooses."

Timothee turned west to gauge the angle of the sun. "I must tend the still. Go now, before you are missed."

I returned the next afternoon after finishing my breads, anxious to continue with my new teacher. Timothee was waiting. "Follow me," he said, and led me down a narrow path through the woods behind the distillery. We climbed a steep rise thick with green shrubs and vines, and then angled back down again until we had a fine view of Plymouth town just below us.

"The path continues on. Slaves take the route on Sundays, when they can take things they have made to sell or trade with other planters' slaves. Eet ees a different sort of slave market, no?"

The afternoon sun glinted off the haphazard shingle rooftops, the painted and unpainted storefronts and the narrow alleys scratched out between them. Beyond the rooftops the harbor where I had first arrived was calm and glittering in the waning light. Except for the climate, it wasn't so much different from the towns and villages in Ireland, and instantly I longed to be in Skebreen again, collecting coin from the townsmen and listening to the old men, idle as a piper's little finger, gossiping as if they knew the secrets of all the world. What would they say if they saw me now, halfway across the globe in slave's clothing and still scorning them? How I missed them.

"You mustn't feel alone here, leetle bird," Timothee said as if he had read the thoughts on my face. "We are all far from home, but someday you will find comfort een hearing your native tongue. There are taverns where the Irish go, and some hold plantations of their own. Eet will not change your circumstance to know them, for even the Irishman depends on slave labor to make his profit, and no planter will interfere with the policies of another. I only thought eet might please you to know they are here."

I turned to Timothee, confused. "If they were not brought as slaves, how did they get here?"

He shrugged and pulled a long green leaf from an exotic-looking plant. "Some came first to Barbados on the promise of land and opportunity. For a time there was land to be had there, but quickly eet was taken over by the English and King Charles's audacious grants. The smaller ones were bought out or taken over by the larger. When news came that there was land available on Montserrat, many Irish boarded ships at once to come and claim what they could. Some were fairly successful, and others either died or returned to Barbados. Some Irish arrived from St. Christopher about seven years ago, sent by the English who banished the Catholics from their tiny realm. Those who remain and survive here are a hearty, gritty sort."

I felt the blood begin to burn within my veins, my desire was so strong to bolt down the slope to the town and find every one of them. "We are kin! We are Irish, tortured every one by our desire to have back the land that was taken from us!"

"Ah," Timothee nodded, a half-smile touching his lips. "Ees this your purpose then? To find new land?"

"I will find land, but it is not new and it is not here. My destiny is set in Ireland." I gazed toward the sparkling sea in the distance. "When the time comes I will sail to England first, kill the dirty murdering Cromwell who forced me away. Then I will go home to my father's land and rebuild the castle and the kingdom that was meant for me."

"Um-hmm. You will find on this island quite a queue of those who would see Cromwell dead. We'll talk of that some other time. For now, I would hear more about this castle. I myself have dreams of a great castle far away. Tell me, Elvy."

I felt my cheeks warming, for I had not truly allowed myself to speak of my castle dreams since my father told his grand stories about them years ago. How could I, when back home I would have been teased without mercy? But always they were there, etched into my memory deep and fine, glowing with the light of good peat fire, and as I spoke I found they had sprouted new growth like a seed beneath the soil.

"My castle will sit on a hillside where villagers at great distance will see it gleaming," I began, "its walls strong and thick, and especially on dark, cold nights people will see the warm fire glow from its windows and be comforted. The gates will be heavy black iron, opening wide to welcome my kinsmen and closing hard against the English and any others who might threaten us. Inside the castle will have a great room with a fireplace so grand a team of horses could stand within it, and there will be enormous fires to warm everyone from my village who comes to dine with me. Beside the fireplace my bard will sing of my heroic deeds. I will dance in velvet slippers across a clean stone floor, and dance all night if it be my pleasure. And when I am tired, I will climb a spiral stair made of white alabaster, and at the top a window, as wide as I am tall will overlook my cattle and sheep, and I'll watch my dogs playing in the high grass. And I will go to sleep in a great feather bed with soft, warm coverings and attendants all around to make sure my comforts are met. And at each dawn when I wake, they will brush and braid my hair and bring me sweet treats for my breakfast. My days will be spent making sure my people are fed, the castle stores full, the grounds safe and beautiful with fragrant flowers, and the stables and fields abundant with horses, cattle and sheep."

Timothee stared out to sea as I finished. I tugged his sleeve. "What do you think of it?"

He turned away so that I could not see his eyes. "A lovely dream, and you must hold fast to eet. See eet whenever your eyes show you something ugly or sad. That's what dreams are for, leetle bird. To lift us from circumstance and carry us to comfort and safety. Remember always this: what you desire ees your gift from God. The word itself een the Latin means 'from the father.' Never allow someone to tell you eet ees wrong. Go now, or you'll be late."

"But I want to know your dream first. Please, will you tell me?"

He turned back to face me, his soft eyes moist. "My dream ees not of where I have been, but where I have never been. I would sail as far from here as the winds would take me, set my feet upon the soil of an ancient continent. I have heard there is a castle of exotic shape and color, and I will learn all there ees to know from the masters of the earliest religions who live there, whose fingers touch the very cord that binds them to the great spirit. That ees what would lift me, and that would satisfy my starving soul, and that would be the sweet of my every morning. I know my destiny as clearly as you know yours, Elvy, for I dreamt eet when I was just a boy, and eet has remained vivid all these years. I must seek out the greatest of all spiritual leaders in that mysterious far east, and when I find him I will know, for his connection to God will be stronger and broader than a great iron staircase, and I will set my foot upon eet. My journey had just begun when I was diverted here."

"But what do you mean? What happened?"

"I was on a ship just such as yours, leetle bird, headed for the Orient on a mission to discover new secrets of a spiritual nature and bring back my studies to my brothers in France. And then, after weeks aboard ship, the young deckhand so disturbed me and taunted me with his incessant and obscene sea chanties, I did knock him down and pound him about the face and shoulders. Such a fool I was, I did not know he was the captain's nephew. The captain could have hanged me, but his fear of God stopped him. Instead he rightly stripped me of my robes and sold me cheaply. Eet was my good fortune to be purchased by Master Wingfield, but eet makes me no less a captive and a slave than any other soul whose feet touch this blot upon the earth."

"But you are still a holy man, even without robes, is it not so? The master must be very brave indeed if he would enslave a holy man."

Timothee shook his head sadly. "Eet ees not the master who holds me, child. I am here because I did not demonstrate the ways of St. Francis. Our great teacher asked that those of us who are missionaries to the world be not quarrelsome and use not words for disputes. He asked that we never criticize but be gentle, peaceful, and humble. I diverted myself by my own wretched behavior with that boy aboard the ship, and then again with you just days ago when you were singing. And even more, by my selfishness. I should want only to give and to serve others, and yet I selfishly seek my own spiritual experience."

"But…you seek it to share with others. Isn't that unselfish?"

"God in Heaven knows my heart. I will remain here until I have mastered what must be learned. I will know when eet has happened, and Master Wingfield cannot free me until that knowledge ees revealed."

I stared at him, and then a blast from Mr. Drax's horn heeled us from this talk.

"He ees already een the yard with the gangs," Timothee said. "Again I have been selfish! Telling you these things and making you late. Hurry now, Elvy. Gather your bread for their supper or you'll be whipped."

14

The Irish of Montserrat

Every herring must hang by its own gill.

~ 17th century English saying

A stranger place there could not be, where men are bound without chains: the master by his own tortured heart and Timothee by his failings. Did so fine a thread bind others? My own bindings could not be seen but they were real enough, else I would find myself already in England with my blade through Cromwell's heart. Sea and circumstance held me, but I felt a new hope growing within my breast, and I swore soon I would navigate them both.

I had to have more time with Timothee, for every day I saw him I understood something more and my steps grew sturdier on the ground beneath me. What I needed was time, freedom from my endless tasks in the cassava house, to sit beside Timothee and explore the distances of his knowledge. Mayhap I should have been more curious about the science and religion he had so deeply absorbed, but my youthful eyes could see only as far as the distant rooftops. Sure as a salmon hooked in a stream, my fascination had been snagged just beyond the thresholds of Plymouth's taverns. I wanted to know all about the Irish.

Had I not been snatched from my intended path back in Ireland? Jerked rudely from my plan to head north along the west coast and gather the clans' support? If truly there were so many Irish on Montserrat, why could we not organize just as we would have done in Connacht? We would take for our own the merchant ships that came to call, outfit them as warships, and turn them around for a noble mission and journey back home.

The vision of it passed around my mind like a sweet-scented mist, settling in the low places where it would not burn away. But days passed, and then weeks, that I did not lay eyes on Timothee or Plymouth. After my tardiness Mr. Drax punished me by increasing my quota of bread. He became more watchful and critical if my breads weren't firm enough or the edges evenly browned. I had to climb the ladder to the rooftop several times each day so he would see me from the field and would not come to check on me or lay down greater penalties.

At night I fell exhausted into my hut and yet slept fitfully, dreaming of Aengus's scruffy hair and stalk neck, and the wizened eyes of old Mr. Fitzgibbon; of English soldiers in armor or in broad hats; of blood splattering my skirt and the toe of Cromwell's boot. At times I woke, trembling and sweating, and sleep escaped me until dawn.

It was in these dark, wakeful hours that I devised a plan. In one morning before dawn I could shred enough cassava for two days' bread and set it to drain of its poisons. The following day I could start my cook fires first thing, be done with my breads by noontide, and still have enough cassava meal for the following day's breads. I'd have hours free until evening to spend with Timothee at the rum house.

Or perhaps I could steal even further away. I could follow the hillside path as far as it would take me, to the very streets of Plymouth itself! To the taverns. To my countrymen.

Once this plan expressed itself fully in my head, sleep became a bothersome need I did not wish to satisfy, for it robbed me of time. That night I dozed only lightly, and in the midnight hours when no one was about, I crept silently along the path toward the yard and my cassava house. A cool wind chilled my legs and shoulders, and I had no candle to light my work, but these were minor annoyances as I focused only on my goal. By moonlight and starlight I peeled the roots and grated the meal, wrapping it and pressing out the juice, then setting it to dry. By dawn I began my cook fire, and my hands worked so swiftly that by midday I had made enough bread cakes to meet my quota and more.

As those disks dried I began more peeling and grating. Though my arms were tired, my fingers worked with a new energy and felt no pain. I worked until I had enough meal for the following day's quota, wrapped the meal, hung it in the cones and secured the heavy stone at the bottom. By midafternoon, and at the risk of being missed by Mr. Drax, I was beside Timothee again.

"Tell me more about the Irish of Montserrat," I demanded, my hands trembling with excitement.

He regarded me carefully, as if deciding whether or not I could be trusted. "You are an impetuous leetle bird, Elvy. You must not fan the flames of your dreams with things that will only get you burned."

"Please, Timothee. I must know of my people. You would want the same, wouldn't you? If they were French?"

"I'm not so sure. But eef they were Orientals..." He regarded me once more but seemed to come to terms with it. He nodded and gestured toward a green patch of grass where I could sit, and handed me a scrub brush. "Idleness ees the enemy of the soul. We'll clean the casks as we speak."

The casks were small, and we scrubbed them only with sand and water so nothing but the wood could taint the flavor of the rum.

"Now then," Timothee began. "You wish to know who are these Irish? The names may be familiar, for many come from the province of Munster. We have Collins, Barry, Driscoll, and Ryan; Fingen, Cormack, Callahan, and O'Sullivan."

"O'Sullivan!" I stopped my scrubbing and stared at him. "It were the O'Sullivans, my uncle's relations, I was to meet when I...I turned north and I...Go on, please, Timothee." I bowed my head, for the blood seared my cheeks. Was it the same clan, and might I have ended up just as well had I gone to them, as Aengus had instructed me in the first place? Might one of them be a rich planter, with the means to send me home?

"Most of them are small tobacco farmers, some better off than others depending on the quality of their land. Eet ees still the English who own the largest and best properties. The governor had the best parcel of all. And, since you've a keen interest een the governor, there ees a story to tell. From your village een Ireland, do you know the name of Briskett? Anthony Briskett?"

"I do not."

"Well, my dear, I suppose you would not, for he'd been gone from Ireland for many years by the time you were born. He was the colonizer and governor of our leetle island. A hard, driven man, he was true Irish at heart but descended from a wily and well-connected Italian merchant. He dreamed of creating a prosperous settlement here and found success even from the beginning. He started by bringing een Irish to plant tobacco. The English believed the Irish were slow and slovenly, but Master

Briskett proved they would work harder than any eef they saw a future in eet. He also found that the tobacco leaf grown here was of higher quality than from any of the other island settlements, and some said better than from Ralegh's colony in Virginia. He maintained the reputation by allowing sale only by the leaf, not by the roll where other planters might wrap the poorer quality within the finer. The planters negotiated good prices and turned decent profits, eef not fortunes. Governor Briskett also brought in goats, for they were best at keeping the edges of the fields cleared, especially around the sloping ground and the ghauts—the deep crevices where rain washes down from the mountain and vines grow thick as your arm."

"Goats!" I shook my head and grimaced. "I do hate them so!"

"And I suppose you think they are eager to win your affections?"

I turned away, scrubbing all the harder and packing sand beneath my nails. "But what of the governor? Where is he to be found?"

"I'm getting to that, leetle bird. Do you wish to learn or not?"

"I do."

"All right then; do not interrupt. Governor Briskett set things so the tobacco crops were but eighteen months from seed to cured leaf, and then whisked away by Dutch traders to the best markets. Tobacco ees the primary export of Montserrat, though a couple of planters produce indigo. But that process has a horrid odor. You can smell eet near the harbor. There ees money to be made in the dyes, but few want to live with the stench."

I nodded, remembering the putrid scent that had washed over us at the slave market.

"Eet ees only Master Wingfield who has ventured into sugar, where there are greater profits to be had, but the investment ees high. He went to St. Christopher to learn the process. Governor Briskett warned him away from such a gamble, but then passed away last year and did not live to see what the master has accomplished."

"The governor is…dead?" I asked, horrified. I had just learned of him and now he was dead?

"Eet ees so. He was a good man, but an old man. And the sadness ees that he left behind a young widow and a son just a bit younger than you. But do not deespair. She ees soon to remarry, a prosperous Dutchman. And her own brother has been appointed the new governor—an Irish protestant, Roger Osborne."

My heart leapt. "He is also Irish! I will speak to him and he will surely send me home." I could not sit a second longer. I was on my feet next to Timothee, tugging at the back of his tunic for more.

"I know leetle about him. The master will be dining with him soon, and you'll see him. But be warned, he ees gentry and not likely to concern himself with the wants of a slave or servant, Irish or no. Now sit back down and listen. You will never get home eef you leap before you look at what crevices lie before you."

I sat, tucking my legs up under my skirt to hold them, though they begged to leap and to run. "Go on, please."

"There is another Irishman of whom you may wish to hear. Will I tell you about Master Wingfield?"

"The master? He is Irish? Oh yes!" I nodded vigorously. My fascination with the master was now of a strength to overshadow even the governor.

"His father descended from English who had owned properties een Ireland for hundreds of years, but he was Catholic and had taken an Irish wife. For this the Protestants claimed he was no better than a barbarous Irish clansman and should be banished from the earth. Een about 1634 they gained the political power to take away old Master Wingfield's estate. Without ceremony, he and his family—and many other Catholic families—were put on a ship for the Virginia colony. What an agonizing trip eet must have been, to leave so much of their lives behind! But once they reached Virginia, the Protestant colonists also turned them away. They had to sail on to the Indies and Montserrat, where they heard they would be welcomed. Our master was just a lad then, about your age, when his father cleared the land for this plantation."

"Fifteen?" I was startled. The master was brought on a ship same as I, and though he was not a slave, the location was not of his choice.

"His mother died of a fever within a year of their coming, and his sorrowful father died nearly a decade past, in 1641."

"And the master has been alone? With no wife? No children?"

"Ah, here's where, we must understand, much of his struggle resides."

"What do you mean? Did he have a wife?"

"Nay, child, he had a fever. And such was the fever no remedy could be found to break eet. All on the island believed he would die and leave his estate for the taking. Like wolves they salivated and paced, calling on the demons to worsen his disease. For many days and nights he screamed out his delusions, sweated and burned, his form reduced to a skeleton, barely alive. He lingered there at the edge of Heaven for many days. Eet was Badu, and only Badu, who managed to save him. No one knows what potions or conjuring her task required, for you can be sure there were but a few on this wretched island who prayed for him. But heal him she did. His fever left him forever scarred, and in ways that tear a man from his foundations."

"Why? What do you mean?"

"Mind, eet ees a great confidence I give you now, so hold your tongue. He ees as a barren woman, never to conceive a child."

I stared at him, suddenly fearful that he knew of my episode with the master, as if he had been in the room with us and had seen what was started and not completed. "No!" I struck out. "It cannot be! How would you know such a thing?"

Timothee smiled. "Eet ees not uncommon, leetle bird, for a man who loves his spirits to bare his soul plainly to the man who makes them."

I thought of Aengus, who knew the secrets of most every man in Skebreen, and I knew Timothee spoke the truth.

"And more than that, dear; even the master has times when he seeks a connection to God. I tell you now only because you stand in the balance between loving the man and hating him. I pray you understand him and respect him, for he ees of a finer cloth than any other planter on the island and worthy of reverence."

I considered Timothee. "Then tell me, why does he not set you free?"

Timothee's face darkened. His eyes widened for an instant and then grew sad. Blood rushed into his cheeks in jagged streaks, as if a hand had slapped him and left behind its ruby impression. It struck me too, and I felt as if I had said something so hurtful to him he could hardly bear it.

"I told you," he said softly. "The master does not hold me. Did you not hear just then, my prideful ways? My boastings of the master's confidences? I am my own captive, and yet I refuse to learn. Leave me now! The more I speak to you, the more I reveal my own shortcomings and the deeper grows my despair."

"Timothee!" I cried, but he turned away and left me sitting alone on our patch of grass. He went into his dark rum house and closed the door.

I finished the cask I had been scrubbing and set it aside for him, then hurried back up the hill to the cassava house to collect my breads before Mr. Drax called after me. They were there as I had left them, drying on the rooftop, and my baskets waited to be filled. But a chill seized my spine as if I might face a whipping anyway, for the extra cassava I had spent hours grating, and had so carefully wrapped and hung up to drain, was gone.

15

A Gift from Badu

For what can poor people do, that are without Letters and Numbers, which is the soul of all business that is acted by Mortals, upon the Globe of this World.

~ Richard Ligon, 1657

I searched behind the cassava house, and all the ground and bushes around it. I went to the kitchen at the big house to see if the cook had taken it, but the linen-wrapped meal was not there. Had Mr. Drax come to check on me and taken the meal to cause me to fail in my work? I climbed the ladder to the rooftop and saw Mr. Drax far away, calling in the gangs from the cane fields. He would not have done such a thing even if he had wanted to. Someone else had stolen it. But who? Why?

I was frightened, and not a little bit mad. I stomped back down the hill to the rum house. "Timothee!"

He was still in the house but stepped out quickly. "What ees eet, child? Are you hurt?"

"Someone has stolen my cassava meal."

He came closer and looked me over. "Your breads for the day's supper? They are gone?"

"No," I shook my head. "My breads are as I left them. It is the meal I had grated for tomorrow and set to drain. It is all gone."

"But why did you prepare the meal today for the breads you would cook tomorrow?"

I looked away. "I…I worked extra hard so I'd have time to be with you." I had not wanted to share my secret plan with him. He would never approve. I could feel the heat of his gaze on me and could see the deep frown on his face without even looking.

"Someone has stolen your meal, and this ees a very bad thing, Elvy. Listen to me. You wish to go to Plymouth, and this I see as eef it ees scribbled across your face een black ink. But you must not go alone. Go on Sunday with the others and stay away from the taverns, where you will find only trouble. And never, never go at night. There are terrors on the path beyond your imagination."

I managed a glance at his face. "What kinds of terrors?"

A gasp escaped his lips, and he came toward me and grabbed my shoulder. "I knew I had said too much! You must not go. There are terrors een the lowlands. Unspeakable terrors. Not the least of them ees that eef you are seen you will be arrested or hanged as a runaway. Trust my words, you *must not go*."

"All right, Timothee, I will not go," I said, but I knew I meant only for that night. "What about my stolen meal?"

"Do not put temptation een someone's path. Eef you do, then the sin ees your own as much as the thief's." He stopped, swallowed deeply, and looked up to the heavens. "Father, forgive me. I went too far," he said softly, and then settled a fierce gaze on me. "Gather your breads for supper, and on the morrow follow only the instructions you were given by Mr. Drax and do not vary." He turned and went back into the darkness of the rum house. I was as annoyed with him then as I'd been with Aengus when he stopped me from dumping the ashes at night. What was it men so feared in the darkness? Of all the horrors I'd experienced so far in my life, the worst had taken place in the broad light of day.

That night I slept fitfully and dreamed I'd been about to board a ship sailing for Ireland when it pulled up planks and sailed without me. I woke hours before dawn, restless and angry. How could I remain there in my tiny hut when there were Irish near who should know of my presence and help me with my plans? How could I wait, day after day, when every ship that reached the harbor could be the one to take me home?

I rose and returned to the cassava house and set about my work. There was no shortage of cassava to be had, for it was harvested all year long. I pulled more roots, peeled, and grated until the sunrise blinded my eyes. By the time I began my cook fire, I had wrapped cones of dripping cassava all about me, and the air was thick with the sour odor. I cooked until my wrists hurt and set my breads to dry, though the morning skies were dismal gray. I went to Timothee, my trusted friend, even while knowing in my heart I planned to betray his advice that very night and take the forbidden path to Plymouth. I was sorry to deceive him, but I felt I had no choice. Is it not the mark of a true princess who can wear the face of diplomacy while rigging her ships for war?

"Tell me about the governor's sister," I asked, steering him away from any talk that might meddle with my intentions or force me to lie.

"Mrs. Briskett ees a good woman, from what I know of her. Eet ees always a brave woman who ees willing to leave her homeland and relations to colonize a new land. She has survived for years when many others who came here have not. I have never seen her, but I do suspect she ees strong and wise."

"I should like to meet her. I could make a good handmaiden to her..."

"And thereby secure her gratitude and your passage home. I suppose eet ees possible, but suppose as well you would earn every hour of your passage."

"What do you mean?"

"Never mind. Eet ees not well for me to be so cynical. But again I must warn you, leetle bird. Beware you do not leave the gilded cage that holds you for one far less hospitable."

"We are slaves, Timothee! There is not much gilding to be found in that," I spat back.

I left Timothee and packed up my breads for supper. With each step I imagined how I would leave my hut at dark and find the path Timothee had showed me. It wouldn't take long to reach the town, I was sure, and I had no fear of what I might see. If it was such a dangerous journey, why was the path so well worn? No, I would go to Plymouth and enter an Irish tavern just as the ale was flowing most heavily. I would be welcomed; they would ask about my arrival on the island, and I'd tell my tale of Cromwell's cruelty in Skebreen. And then my imaginings were ruined: I was faced once more by the empty pegs where I had hung my meal to drain. Stolen *again*. I raced back down the hill to Timothee, but he offered no sympathy.

"I warned you not to do eet, leetle bird."

"But what should I do? Who would steal on the plantation, when we are given our bread each day?"

He would not look at me. "Eet ees something to sell or trade. Go and see Badu. She will know what to do. Leave me now."

I was disappointed that he showed no more concern. If thieves were about, we might be in danger. Did he not consider that? And what kind of potion or ointment could Badu offer that would keep a thief away?

The idea of going to a woman of magical powers stirred my belly. It was not that far removed from the stories I'd heard as a child, of little children venturing into the woods only to be eaten by witches. I had matured enough to know those were just tales used by parents to keep their children from wandering away, but not so much that I could keep from shaking as I approached her wooden cabin.

It backed up to the thickest part of the woods some distance from the other huts, and was finer than the others, with real board walls and shingle roof, and a stone stoop in front of the door. Several flat stepping-stones led to the house, lined on either side with herbs that had tiny white blossoms. Earthen pots held black soil with yellow-green leaves sprouting at their centers. A vine of honeysuckle gave out its heady fragrance.

Before curiosity could dispel my fear, I heard the creak of the wooden latch, and Badu stood before me, her body blocking the opening and her turban bright and imposing. She glared silently with round, black eyes until I found the courage to speak.

"I...I've come for help, Badu. My name is Elvy. Timothee said that I should come."

Badu only nodded. She did not speak more but seemed to be waiting for something. I realized I should have brought her a gift or an offering of some kind in exchange for what I would ask. Why had Timothee not told me so?

"I have nothing to offer you," I said, "but I will bring you something you will like if you help me now."

"Hmmph. A bargainer. And so you are. Come in and den we see what you will do."

Badu stepped away, revealing the wondrous interior behind her. Candles flickered, though night had not yet fallen. How I longed for the light of a candle! A golden glow painted the bundled herbs that hung from the wood-plank walls. Seed pods and leaves shaped like severed hands hung from the joists, casting strange shadows. She closed the door behind me and sat down on a large three-legged stool, the only seat in the house. In one corner was a narrow bed with a wooden frame, and in the center of the house, a kitchen work table. All about her across the floor, against the wall, tucked into corners, and crowded together on the table were the gifts presented by others who had come to her for help. All the more I felt the gnawing regret for my omission.

On a shelf behind her were the things she treasured most, for they were lovingly arranged: colorful stones, wood carvings, baskets woven of twigs and grass, and in the center the larger half of a broken earthenware saucer delicately painted with the forms of birds in flight.

"And so," Badu said, halting my inventory. "Here be a troublesome child with a great passion. And now your cassaba meal be stolen."

I collapsed on my knees before her. "You know?" I could hardly believe what I had just heard, but she dismissed my question with a wave of her hand.

"I..." I stopped to clear my throat, for my fear was now getting the better of me. "I worked hard, Badu, to prepare my meal for the next day. But twice now it has been stolen. I fear I will be punished for it. Timothee said I should ask you what to do."

She examined me slowly, from my tattered shoes to my grass-bound hair, and settled her gaze intently on my eyes. She was searching deeply for some sort of truth, but also there was wisdom beyond my reckoning in the dark, soulful brown eyes. "Dere is much you say, and much more you do not say."

I felt a rush of heat to my cheeks and a chill seized my legs. I had to squeeze my knees together that my legs would not tremble. She nodded.

"You mus' do what calls to you, for each thing has its purpose," Badu said. She closed her eyes halfway and appeared to be deep in thought. Then she began to mutter, and I waited silently. Moments passed, and she continued until I thought it best for me to leave, but then she stopped and nodded until her chin nearly touched her chest. "We mus' put a stop to de stealin'. Come with me."

A well-worn path disappeared into the dark canopy behind the house. I followed her down the path into the forest. Darkness was settling and colors faded into the blacks and silvers of dusk, but I followed until she stopped where a vine hung heavy with leaves and white flowers closed to the night. She selected four sections of it and roughly pulled them free. She turned to me.

"Take dese pieces of overlooker vine. Place one at each corner ob de cassaba house. Lay dem out on de ground a few paces away, so when someone pass dey see it. Overlooker will keep thieves out ob de garden, and keep thieves out ob de cassaba."

The vines felt cold in my hand, and Badu glared down on me. "Thank you," I said.

"Go now. And remember your promise for what is owed."

I returned to my hut and kept the vines near me. I hoped in my heart they would work. I was disappointed I couldn't go to Plymouth that night, but I knew I must not go unless my work was done. I slept fitfully until the early morning hours, when I returned to the cassava house to start my chores again. I grated and grated the meal until my hands felt as if they'd been squeezed in a vice. I set the cassava to drain and grated twice as much for the following day. By midmorning I had cooked my breads from the first batch and set the second batch to dry. Then I did as Badu had instructed. I placed a section of overlooker vine a few paces from each corner of the cassava house. I went down the hill to Timothee.

I sat down to help him fill jugs with rum and seal the tops with wax. He did not speak for a while but continued working. When the last jug was sealed, he turned to me.

"Badu has helped you?"

I nodded. "She gave me a vine, supposed to keep thieves away."

"Did she now." He shook his head. "You must not go, leetle bird."

"B...Badu said everything has its purpose." I answered too quickly.

Timothee dropped his chin and closed his eyes. "Eet does not mean that everything ees right." A veil of difference now fell between us, and I would learn no more from him in the afternoon.

I climbed the hill to check on my cassava, and it was as I had left it, the grated meal draining from the pegs. The vines had worked. Or had they? How could I be sure? Mayhap my thief was a wily lad and would have me thinking he was gone when sure he was not. I glanced down the hill at Mr. Drax coming in from the fields. I dared not go to Plymouth until I was sure. I left the cassava hanging overnight. The next day it remained, so I cooked my breads but was not yet convinced. On the third day I was a believer: the cassava hung true once again. I owed a debt to Badu for whatever magic had held the thieves away. For now it was time to put my plan in motion. I would escape on the morrow to Plymouth.

16

Down to Plymouth

At night the giant crabs would crawl out of the woods to feed, the noise of their claws rattling together in the darkness bringing a chill of terror to even the stoutest heart.

~ Henry Whistler, 1654

Through the night I tossed around like a beetle on its back. Excitement flooded my veins, and it was all I could do to stay within my hut and wait. Even yet, I was at the cassava house well before dawn, making my breads and wondering: how would I choose my time to leave and my absence not be noticed? It soon came clear enough, as if St. Brendan sent down the angels to light my way.

When the midday sun seared the rooftops, my skillet was cool and my rounds of bread already dried through. I filled my basket for the day's supper just before a set of storm clouds sailed in on the wind, dark as the night and grumbling with an awful fury. When the rain came, it pounded the roof like a thousand angry fists, and I cowered in the corner against the peg wall. In the distance the rain fell so heavily a white veil blocked my view of the fields around me. When it passed, steam rose from the fields and rooftops, the leaf tips dripped of silver and the ground reflected the light on scattered puddles. The air was freshened, moist and cool on my cheeks. I looked to the fields again and could see no workers. Mr. Drax had led the gangs out of the punishing storm.

I covered my basket and hurried to the kitchen to make sure the breads were there when the meal was served. Mr. Drax nodded as I approached.

He had seen me, and my work was done. I was *elated*. My only trick now was to escape to the path without anyone seeing me go.

Oh, I was wise, very wise! I smiled sweetly at Timothee as he waited in line for his serving. And when most of the others were eating or tending their own cook fires, I casually walked to the woods as if to relieve myself.

By then dusk was near. I made sure no one was behind me, smoothed and tied my hair at my nape, and headed straight for the pathway to Plymouth. I found it, looking just as tempting and beckoning as it had when Timothee first showed it to me, though still dripping with rain and the path more mud than dirt. Still, to set my foot upon it was such a feeling I can hardly describe, a far cry from what I'd felt when I'd set on the path to Dingle where I'd first met Kade. I'd been so foolish then. Now I knew much more about the world and had a stronger hold than ever on my destiny. This step gave me power. I was not running away from something; I was taking things in hand, and I would begin to make things happen instead of things always happening to me. Wouldn't it be grand if Kade could see me now? I pushed away the pang of sorrow that threatened my happiness and fluttered down the hill as if wings propelled my feet.

The path was well worn and easy to follow from Timothee's rise down to the dense forest at the base of the hill. From there it seemed to branch out like a river delta or the crooked fingers of a crone's hand all reaching in different directions. I imagined a group of slaves running down the hill and then suddenly scattering to confuse someone who chased after them. Would the paths continue in different directions within the forest, or would they converge on a single destination? I examined all the options. The wrong choice could lead me away from my goal, but indecision was my true enemy. The longer I stayed in one place, the more likely I would be discovered. Then I saw my guiding sign: a footprint pressed well into the dirt, with distinct crescents where the toes had pushed forward. I stepped into the depression, only slightly larger than my own shoe, and moved on through thick brush and ropey vines that blocked the way so fiercely in some places I was forced to crawl beneath them.

The path spilled into a field where root and earth had been dug, scraped, and turned for replanting. It was soaked by the rain and smelled of rich soil and sour decay. Jug-size rocks had been gathered by a gang and piled along the edges. If I crossed through the middle I would be spotted by anyone looking down from the hill, for it was not yet fully dark. Over the treetops, chimney smoke assured me I moved in the proper direction, so I stayed to the edges of the field and kept the smoke in view.

It was there beyond the field that the trees began to change in shape, their branches lower to the earth and their trunks fat and twisted, the leaves more broad and waxy. Salt from the sea mingled in the air. Tall, spiky grasses reached my shoulders and over my head, and the ground around them was mushy and clogged with old roots. I had trouble finding any path at all, or any good purchase for my footing, fearing I would lose my shoes to the muck.

A strange bird burst from the grasses just before me, and had I not seen him as he screeched, I would have sworn someone had stabbed a wee babe with a dagger. So bristled was I from the sound that it was a moment or two before I heard the clacking, as if a hundred children were banging their little wooden spoons together over and over and without rhythm. As I pressed on, the sound grew stronger, and though I searched for the source of it as I moved, the fading light and shadows revealed nothing.

Things moved in the grasses behind me and on the ground before my feet, and knew not if they were wild animals or spirits pressing closer. The hair on my scalp bristled like a scrub brush, and my stomach knotted into a hard, fiery ball. What creatures surrounded me? Were these the horrors Timothee foretold? What would Aengus say of such a fearsome place? And where, dear St. Brendan, was the chimney smoke to guide me out?

Something crept about just ahead, and then the clacking grew so loud in my ears I could hear nothing else. Something tugged my skirt and I screamed—I could not help it—and jerked my skirt back lest I be drawn down into the mud and slime and eaten alive by whatever hunted me. I ran, and never will I know how my shoes stayed with me through such a wretched place. I stumbled and ran all the harder, sure this was hell itself and these creatures would sup upon my flesh.

An amber light flickered in the distance, and though it might have been the torch of a runaway slave hunter, I ran toward it, ready to welcome any horror that was different from this one. I pushed as hard as my knees would go until I hit a dense clump of grasses, and then clawed desperately until I tumbled through to the other side. I landed in a ditch but was now on solid ground. The clouds above parted and I could see slightly better, so I stayed where I fell trying to catch my breath and slow my terrified heart. I gathered my skirt about me and then felt something hard stuck to the hem. One of the horrible creatures had attached itself to my skirt. I reached frantically for a stick or a rock by which to kill the little monster.

I found something smooth and hard with sharp edges, and I pounded against my assailant, but the creature was like a cobblestone. I pounded and stabbed but could not kill it. Then suddenly it let go and skittered off to the swamp from where it had come. I had just enough light to make out its shape: I was about to be eaten by a crab, and perhaps a whole army of them. Horror shuddered up my spine and the backs of my arms and legs. I hauled up out of the ditch, ran along its edge to put good distance between me and that awful place, and tucked my weapon into my skirt pocket.

I followed the amber light until I could make out the shapes of rooftops and a ship's mast. The harbor. I had made it to Plymouth. The smoke that had been my beacon billowed light gray above a shingled roof, barely visible now above the blue-black sky. I crept along the ditch until my nose told me I had found the tavern: the familiar smells of putrid garbage, foul tobacco, stale beer and piss. All of it thrilled me until my journey was forgotten, my shoulders and arms were ablaze with goose pimples, and my legs could not carry me fast enough.

The plank door at the back swung open just as I approached. An old man stepped out, heaved the contents of a slop bucket into the ditch where I'd just been standing, and left the bucket by the door. Praise the darkness, he did not see me. I seized the bucket as if I'd emptied it myself and went inside.

The tavern was oddly quiet for a drinking establishment. But for the glow of a pipe illuminating someone's nose, I could see no other faces. Then a small turf fire near the front came into view, bronzing the profiles, heads, and caps of men pressing together in conference. I stayed to the shadowy edges and crouched low to conceal my stature. The longer I could go unnoticed the safer I would be.

"Here then, lass!" I heard someone call and felt as if a spear had run right through my heart. I turned slowly. A round fellow with a broad feathered hat motioned me over. I took one step closer.

"Trade yer bucket fer a pitcher o' grog an' get yer arse back to me table." He pressed a coin into my palm. His words were firm but his voice kind, and he smiled in a grandfatherly way, reminding me of old Mr. Fitzgibbon. I heard hardly another distinct voice, only soft murmurs all about, making me wonder what I had come upon. I went for the drink as if I'd worked there all my life, though my feet and legs ached from my travels.

I found my man near the back door, filling earthen pitchers as fast as the wooden keg would flow. I tossed the coin into a bowl at his feet. He gave me a nod, and I lifted two jugs.

When I turned I heard the single piercing cry of a horsehair bow drawn against a catgut string. *Music.* Blood bubbled up from my core and into my chest and shoulders until I thought I would burst from my skin with uncontainable glee. I had to clench my jaws together to keep from laughing out. The fiddler began with a fierce release of pent-up energy equal to my own.

I wanted to shove all the men aside and move to the fireside, to see his fingers frolic, to feel in my hands and feet the vibrations of every chord, note, and beat. I wanted to dance! I carried the jugs to the fat man's table, though my hands shook and the drink sloshed. My eyes must have blazed like a sizzling fire.

"Ah, then. Our maid loves the fiddle!" my customer said. "Take yerself a knee, darlin'!"

But it wasn't just the fiddle playing. Someone else took up the bodhran and pounded the tipper like the beat of my own heart. Another held a flute and hurled out high, insistent notes that pricked my skin and vibrated within my bones. My scalp tingled and my blood surged.

"Sit, lass!" He tugged my arm. I felt tears and laughter and explosive shouts of joy battle fiercely for attention against the trembling barrier of my teeth. His knee bounced merrily, lifting me with the music and slamming me back down again as his heel hit solid floor. His arm circled about my waist, tight and as thick as a tree limb, but I cared not. When had I last heard music? When had I even allowed myself the thought of it? Oh, how I had missed the sound and the pleasure of it rippling beneath my skin.

My gentleman stilled his knee only when a young man stood before the fire to play his flute solo. Starting softly at first, the notes sailed out like blue smoke into the crowd and settled into a fog; then the player lifted them, adding a haunting melody of lilts and valleys: it was the sea, beckoning, teasing, offering escape, pleasure, riches beyond imagination, and eternal doom. I felt it swarm about my head, encircle my shoulders and neck, and then, unexpected like the prick of a needle, force the tears to my eyes.

Then came the intruder to my reverie, a fat hand rising from my waist to my breast. I was startled and looked to my gentleman, who had launched his assault even though the tears of emotion brimmed in his own eyes. I jerked away from him before he had a chance to seal his grip.

"Ye'll be havin' none o' that sir!" I shouted. "Small though they be I've not been growin' 'em fer the likes o' you!" I slammed my fists against his chest so hard his chair tipped over backward, and he lay on his back staring up at me. The others at the table bellowed and guffawed. Another reached for my skirt and I slapped his hand away. The binding popped loose and my hair tumbled down around my shoulders. I bent to retrieve the grass braid, and then stood tall to repair my appearance as haughtily as I might. From the corner of my eye I saw a pipe being lit and instinctively glanced in that direction. The orange flame defined the face of my own master, who glared not at his glowing pipe, but at me.

I had no choice then, did I, but to run.

I burst through the tables and out the back door, hearing it slam on its leather hinges behind me. I ran along the edge of the ditch as fast as my legs would go, my heart pounding fiercely and my lungs aching for the want of air, but I did not stop until I'd reached a solid tree and fell to the ground behind it, heaving for breath. I peered around in the darkness, searching for any sign of someone following after me. I was alone but for the constant, eager clacking of the horrid little crabs. The very thought of them caused my throat to seize and my tears to flow uncontrollably. Then a fury, fierce and pure, boiled into my cheeks and burned as if someone held hot irons against them.

"What am I doing in this forbidding place?" I shrieked at the tree. "Such nasty creatures about me, and the one single night I find my countrymen, I am nearly eaten alive. I know one moment of joy as the music fills my ears, and then I am assaulted by a breast-groping stranger and spied by my master who most surely will sell me or hang me from a limb!"

I kicked and slapped at the gnarled trunk and then picked myself up again, leaving the offending tree and clambering up the hill along the roadside, pushing harder through the brush. I had to get back to my hut. If I could just get back, the master may not have recognized me or would not remember our encounter. The whole night could be forgotten.

But my journey was not finished. To avoid the swamp I had to follow the road back to Sharavogue. I had to claw my way through thickets and vines to avoid being seen. The first steep rise stole my breath away. I was grateful to recognize heaps of cane trash at the edge of a cane field where I might hide and rest a bit before pushing my way up the next hill. I stumbled through them, feeling my way through the darkness and the tall, dry stalks until I came to a clearing with a broad-trunked tree in the center. I threw myself against it, sorry I had cursed the last one I'd found.

I hugged my knees tight against my chest, my feet throbbing. For just a moment, I squeezed my eyelids closed against the night, as if I could wish away my circumstance. When I opened them again the world was brighter, lit by stars that had shed their cloudy robes. The tree was dead or nearly so, its leafless branches reaching out like dark, wretched bones. Then, just where I had passed, I recognized the shape of a man.

I yelped and hugged the tree for safety, but the man did not move toward me. His bare feet dangled just above the sand and his thin legs were still. He was naked, his arms hanging limp at his sides, and his ribs could be counted from where I sat. His face was turned upward, bathed in faint, silvery starlight as if he pleaded to the heavens for a mercy that could not be had. About his neck were heavy strands of twine that suspended him from the highest, thickest limb. His thickened tongue protruded from his lips, and his white eyes bulged against stretched, shiny lids.

Though the scene was horrid to look upon, I could not turn away. Something was familiar in the shape of his jaw, the side of his head, reminding me of the man who had laughed at me when I'd first come off the wagon at Sharavogue. I looked about frantically for signs of those who had done this to him, but we were alone. I was the solitary intruder at his secret rite, the unintended witness to his horrid disgrace. What had he done to deserve such an execution? I looked at his face, not peaceful in dying but anguished and confused. What had he wondered at that last moment, when life was choked from him and he knew there was no escape? A shudder shot up my spine and prickled beneath my scalp. Had he been a runaway from Sharavogue? Would the master do such a thing? Would he do it to me?

I hugged my tree all the harder, as if it could somehow protect me from such things, but a realization was dawning that I was truly in danger worse than anything I had experienced so far. Even before the moment I huddled at Cromwell's feet, I had always believed I was especial, because the faerie thorn had always been at my doorstep offering sanctuary. I had believed that bad things could go on all about me, but I alone was shielded. I was invincible. I had my destiny, and St. Brendan walked before me to see that it would be done.

But the eyes of this man told me he had believed the same, looking up to the heavens, pleading for the always-expected miracle. Why had he not been saved? And why, as close as I was to similar circumstances, should I expect the intervention that for this man had never come?

I was paralyzed for a long moment. All of my protectors—my father, Aengus, and even Kade—had been stripped away from me. My only friend at Sharavogue was Timothee, and he was not likely to protect me when I had lied to him and done what he'd warned me not to do. St. Brendan had always been my source and my solution, but it seemed he too was stripped away. I could rely only on myself now, to make sure I survived. Without survival there was no destiny, no return home, no justice for Ireland or even the dream of it, ever again. Without survival there was no Burke stronghold, no castle, no memory, *no future*.

I crept slowly away from the corpse, as if to run would be disrespectful. I reached the road and dared to walk upon it, hoping that in the nearness of dawn there would be few travelers, that all would be at their homes fast asleep.

The steepest hill was where the road narrowed through thick, dark brush until it delivered me at the gates of Sharavogue. Only then did I fall again to my knees to catch my breath. Only then, when my heaving began to still, did I realize the eerie quiet. And in that moment, when safety was minutes away, the darkness betrayed me.

"Do you know, lass," a voice said softly, "I should hang you for your insolence alone?"

I jerked around madly, for I could hear it but not see its source and could not determine from which direction it came, as if the Devil himself whispered down to me from the clouds.

"Did you follow the road to town?" the voice asked. His boots appeared then, outlined in moonlight against the silver sand before me. The rough shape of his horse appeared on the rise just beyond him. The master stepped closer, and goose pimples hardened on my forearms.

"Did anyone see you go?" he asked.

"No, sir. I stayed to the wood and the swamp."

He sighed deeply. "One is as dangerous as the other. I should hang you and toss you into the sea, and it would be a mercy. You know not where you venture. This is not a land of good neighbors and moral codes, religion or even family. We are far from the reach of England and her laws, and all the world's anarchy comes here to seek a fortune. You are but a piece of meat and this island will see you dead before you even discover where you are. I should kill you just to spare you, for you know no better.

Realize at least this: had my neighbor brought you to me as a runaway,

I'd have had no choice but to hang you in front of every other slave as a lesson and a warning. Do you understand?"

"Yes, sir." I said, but I did not. The only thing I understood about this insane place was my heart-pumping fear.

"The wood and swamp are plagued with lawlessness," he said. "The most heinous crimes of all the island take place in those dark corners. Things go on there that are worse than criminal, worse than deadly. What did you see? You must tell me."

My throat caught as if a piece of twine cinched about it, then slowly eased away. "Horrors that I fear to describe, sir."

High clouds must have passed, for the starlight revealed the shape of his head, and his face turn down as if he examined the dirt for a better explanation. "Even if our crimes do not condemn us, the ghouts and marshes are fraught with sickness and disease. The vapors alone are to your detriment. Do not go there again. Ever." He stepped closer. "You saw nothing more specific? No one who…?"

His voice trailed off, but I offered no response. How could I speak the unspeakable? He was close enough now that I smelt the whiskey on his breath and felt a heat and stillness between us as if everything else was shut away. I dared not move, my body tensed from shoulders to toes.

"It is a hanging offense to leave the plantation without permission. You are young and impetuous. You do not understand what I…" His soft-spoken words trailed off, and yet his speech was like a dagger to my gut. "Do not force me to such levels of discipline." He turned and retrieved his horse from the rise. "Climb on."

I dared not refuse him. I stood, shakily, and grabbed the horse's mane for balance. The master held my arm to lift me as I mounted, then walked the horse slowly through the gates and back down the road to the slave quarters, where the only sounds were soft snoring and the songs of the mourning dove. To my amazement, he stopped beside my tiny reed hut. He knew where I slept. I dismounted quickly, but he grasped my arm.

"Heed me, lass," he whispered gravely. "Let no one know what you have done, or that I have left you here. A word of it will bring your death."

He released me, turned and led the horse in the direction of the stables. I felt my lungs expand with a full breath of air, perhaps my first in many an hour. Darkness had begun to lift, yet I felt grateful for just a few moments of rest before the call of the horn to begin the day's work.

As I lay down my head, it occurred to me the day was Sunday, slave market day. I could hide myself away all day, and perhaps by the time work resumed the master would have forgotten all about me.

My heart settled down at the mere thought, allowing a faint smile to touch my lips. I was to be spared. I'd had my adventure and heard the music of Ireland. The next time I went to the tavern I would find someone who could take me back there. I squeezed my eyelids tighter, trying to envision the green hills of home, but the image of the hanged man won out, the bulging eyes turned up to the heavens.

It could not have been two hours passed before I heard a stick rattling against my hut. I peered through the reeds, grateful for the distraction. The silent girl had wrapped her hair in a blue scarf like Badu's. I crawled out into the dirt, feeling the heaviness in my legs and dizziness as the blood pumped and eddied in my head. She offered something tied up in a rag.

"What have you brought?" I whispered. I untied it to find a biscuit and a small piece of cheese. It was exactly what I needed. My stomach sprang to life at the mere sight of nourishment. I started to speak, but she touched my lips and nodded toward the road.

In the growing lavender mist I saw the outline of Badu's turban and a small wooden cart she pulled behind her. She was headed down the wagon trail that passed the slave quarters and turned out toward the cane fields. The silent girl beckoned me to follow.

17

Market Day

On Sunday they rest...but some of them who will make benefit of that day's liberty, go where the Mangrove trees grow, and gather the bark, of which they make ropes, which they truck away for other Commodities, as Shirts and Drawers."

~ Richard Ligon, 1657

The wheels on Badu's cart creaked past the cane fields until the trail narrowed to shallow ruts and high grasses. We continued on through the forest and then turned just beyond, where the way became rocky and uneven. My feet ached, remembering with their sore spots the journey finished only hours before. I stole a look at the silent girl and she smiled, her teeth gleaming in the dawn's amber light. I was too tired to speak, and though Badu's lips moved constantly, she spoke not a word to us, so we carried on in quiet procession. When we came to the last turn, I found my voice, or it found me.

"God's wounds!" I blurted. I saw before me the very tavern I had visited the night before, and the ditch I had crawled along to reach it.

Badu pulled her cart to a cleared area just a stone's throw from the tavern's door. This, I guessed, would be where the slaves' market would be. I had stumbled and struggled and crawled and cringed through the darkness along a path I could barely see; when all I had to do was follow this back trail to arrive at the same place. A hot fury splashed my cheeks, and I thought of Timothee, smiling in the queue as he waited for his supper.

Badu regarded me through narrowed eyes. "Our travels be harder when run by self-will," she said slowly. I stared at her, gaping as if she had just read my mind, but she turned to her cart, unpacking the necessities she'd brought. The silent girl arranged a frayed canvas on the grass and placed Badu's three-legged stool on one end. She laid a rough-edged board lengthwise beside it, and Badu began to hand her earthen jars and pots to set on its grayed surface. She poured something from a jug into a small gourd and passed it to the silent girl, who sipped and passed it to me. It was some kind of juice, sweet and sticky on my lips. Then Badu sat on the stool, her bare, calloused feet positioned squarely on the cloth before her.

The silent girl motioned to me to sit on the grass. I lost my balance and fell against her arm, causing us both to giggle until Badu silenced us with a cold stare. We sat up straight and attentive.

Badu lifted one of the jars, pinched out some kind of herb, whispered over it and then sprinkled the dried leaves on the cloth before her feet. From another jar she pulled a small black twig and dropped it behind her back. She gave us each another hard stare to command our obedience, but I was not about to move or speak. I was wary of her powers and eager to see what came next. Badu reared her head back until I could see white creases in her neck and the broad roundness of her nostrils. She began to speak in the blended syllables of a well-practiced chant. The silent girl closed her eyes as if in prayer, so I closed my own for a moment, hearing Badu more clearly though I could not decipher her words.

Soon I heard sounds that caused me to look about. Others were arriving in the clearing, choosing places to settle for the day and show what they had to trade. Some brought fruits or vegetables they had grown next to their slave huts, or portions of rum from their masters that they would rather trade for meat. Some brought things they had made from what they had, like mats woven from cane trash and rough garments fashioned from flax. There were seashells and colored stones, calabash bowls and wooden spoons, and other things I was anxious to discover. I had not yet left Badu's side when the wailing began.

Far away at first, it grew louder and more anguished as it approached. Then a procession appeared at the bend heading straight for Badu. A woman screamed and cried uncontrollably as she was led by others supporting her arms. It seemed she could barely walk, stumbling at times, her feet crossing and dragging until the others had to lift her up. Thick tufts of wooly black hair matted around a dark face swollen and streaked with tears, and her mouth was stretched so wide as if she could not make the opening big enough to release the pain she felt. She screamed sentences I could not understand, though I thought she spoke in English. Her cries grew louder and so intense I wished to cover my ears, but I dared not move; and then she fell on the canvas at Badu's feet. She cradled those feet in her dark, gnarled hands, pleading and whimpering until her teardrops stained the dust on Badu's skin.

All the others at the market stopped to watch, standing still and silent. Then, behind the crying woman the procession parted. A large bundle was laid on the ground and the cloth fell open. I saw a face I'd hoped never to see again, though I believed I might see it for the rest of my life.

The twine had been removed, but its marks remained about the neck and jaw. The rest they had left as they'd found it, so that the horror would not be lost on all the viewers. The tongue was as black and thick as I remembered it, and the eyes still bulged as if ready to pop from their sockets. In the morning light they were white as the clouds, and black flies darted and buzzed around them, eager for a magnificent feast. I felt as if a cold hand gripped the back of my neck, digging in with sharp, icy fingers. My legs begged to run as far from there as they could go, and I feared I would pee myself until the silent girl's warm hand touched mine and I wondered, did they know I'd been there? Did they know what I had seen?

Badu bent forward and gently placed her hand on the grieving woman's head. The woman bawled out her agonies anew and collapsed head and arms into Badu's ample lap. Badu stroked her hair until her sounds subsided. Then, from a pouch tied at her waist, Badu took a pebble and placed it on the woman's tongue. She moved the woman aside and Badu rose from her stool.

Everyone backed away from the spectacle, wanting to see but not be involved in the drama that was unfolding. Badu pulled away the shroud and exposed the corpse to the light, drawing gasps from the crowd and a loud tortured moan from the woman sucking on her stone. Badu knelt and pulled the lifeless head to her lap, lightly stroking the dirty, matted black hair. She ran her knuckle along the cheek and brow, and then moved down the length of the body, tracing her fingertips along chest, hip, thigh, and shin. The body was thin, but the stomach was bloating in death. The hands and feet were stiff, their surfaces like tallow. The privates were no longer exposed, but loosely wrapped in coarse linen, the same kind I used to drain the cassava. Icy fingers squeezed my heart. Was this who had stolen my cassava meal? Was I to blame, as Timothee had warned, because I'd put temptation before him?

Badu raised her arms to the sky and chanted a verse in deep, soulful tones so moving I began to cry, though I still could not understand her words. Then she scraped a handful of dirt from the ground beside her. She sprinkled half over the body and squeezed the other half into a tight clod. She hurled the clod at the chest, and it exploded in a shower of sand and soil.

"No!" People in the crowd shouted angrily, and the wailing woman gaped, as if frozen in horrified silence.

"He be a thief! He be lost to us!" Badu declared. She closed the shroud over the body and gestured into the air as if to push it away from her. She reached into her cart for something and then turned to the woman. "Anna, you bury him quick, and you put dis beside him." She gave the woman a small sack of seeds. "He don' come back from de dead until he plant and plant and plant dese seeds. And den, when he be buried, you sprinkle dis aroun' his grabe."

From an earthen jar she poured black sand into her palm and showed it to the crowd. "If he try to come back he cannot leave de grabe until he count every single grain ob sand. He be not welcome here."

Anna screamed madly and threw herself at Badu's feet. She pounded her fists on the ground, screaming until two other women came to her side and lifted her up. Badu backed away. The crowd began to murmur and whisper, and I heard a strange word, said softly at first as if even to say it demanded great caution. Then caution was abandoned.

"Jombee!" someone said.

"Jombee!" another cried.

Badu returned to her stool but sat with her back turned to the crowd. The grieving woman wailed Badu's name and broke free of her helpers. She ran around in front of Badu, clutching her own round belly and then stroking it, and I knew she was with child. Badu's back stiffened as Anna fell to her knees before her.

"Please, Badu. I mus' know somethin' from him or de babe be as dead as he. I mus' do..." She trailed off and wept, then raised her swollen face to Badu. "Jombee? De Jombee dance for de babe?" she whispered.

Badu shook her head slowly, her shoulders beginning to shudder as she lowered her chin to her chest. Badu the strong, Badu the powerful and mystical, was weeping silently. She took a deep breath and lifted her chin to the sky, exhaling to the clouds sweeping by above us.

"Too soon for de dance," I heard her say. "And de moon be not right. A fortnight, and we see." She stood up from her stool and faced the crowd. "We see when de dance be upon us, but it be not now," she said. "If de time will come, dere be much work to do. Dey mus' be a feast. We speak no more of dis until de time be right. Now go."

Anna seemed relieved. She ran to the shroud and hugged it, and the crowd closed in around her to lift the body and carry it away. Only a few dared to look back over their shoulders at Badu glaring down on them.

When they had gone, Badu returned to her cart and fiddled with jars, picking them up and examining them, then setting them back down. She grumbled softly to herself and clicked her tongue, then grumbled harshly and looked up to the heavens. After several moments she turned to the two of us, still sitting like statues in our places on the grass.

"Stealin' be a bad thing. It be not tolerated on de plantation, and it be not tolerated among our kind."

Did she mean our master hanged the man? Or was he hanged by slave gangs who condemned him? I'd have no answer, though I desperately wished to know. She spoke directly to the silent girl. "I would not do it, be it not for de babe." She reached for the girl, then stopped herself and turned back to the cart, shaking her head. "I would not do it."

Badu traded little that day, as if the sad procession had left a pall over us and to come too close was to risk some kind of doom. In the afternoon the silent girl visited the other traders, but I fell asleep in the grass and awoke to something sharp stabbing into my hip. It was my weapon used to fight the land crab. I had tucked it into my skirt the night before. When I pulled it out, it looked like a piece of pottery blackened by smoke and many coats of mud. Who knows how long it had been in the ditch or what kinds of weather or trampling had ruined it? With sand and pressure I slowly worked my way through the dark outer layers. I rubbed and cleaned until I saw a design painted into its surface: birds in flight. It was the other half of Badu's treasured saucer, the one I'd seen in her house.

Badu was brooding, separating seeds from long, flattened pods and all the while shaking her head. I was afraid to disturb her, but I thought the gift would mean something special to her and worth the risk. I knelt at her feet.

"Badu?" She looked up at me, clearly annoyed at the interruption.

"I owed you a debt for giving me the overlooker vine. I've brought you this." I handed her the painted shard.

She touched it gingerly at first, then laid it across her palm and ran her finger along the outlines of the birds. I held my breath, waiting for her response. When she looked up I felt all fear leave me, the way shape leaves a portion of lard as it melts in a pan. Tears rimmed her eyes, and a gentle smile lifted her lips.

"Child," she said. "Sweet, troubled child. Aren't you just de riddle?"

18

The Jombee Dance

They may dance a whole day, and never heat themselves; yet, now and then, one of the activest amongst them will leap bolt upright, and fall in his place again, but without cutting a caper.

~ Richard Ligon, 1657

Days passed and I did not see Badu or the silent girl. I focused on my breads, draining away the poisons that tainted the meal, wanting at least for a while to see no more of the horrors of Montserrat. I wanted no tragedies of life that distracted me from my own. No Jombee dance, whatever it might be, would bring me any closer to my voyage home, or to the House of Cromwell and the task that awaited me there.

I avoided Timothee as well, for showing me a treacherous slope when a good trail just beyond would have served me better. I withdrew from all around me but the work within my hand and the careful contemplation of my next venture to the tavern. I did not wish to defy the master, and I knew what risk I took, but I had almost managed to push away the vulnerability that had come over me. Youth wears its shiny armor and abhors the sharp points of reality. But each day I blunted them a little more until I convinced myself I was shielded from the hanged man's fate and would remain so because my destiny demanded it.

One night a harvest moon rose early, big and golden, painting dusky ochre over treetops and hedges, and every pathway and stepping-stone. A strange white veil shimmered behind it, pressing the orb so near I wondered if it might fall to earth. I heard the fear in the voices of others as they hurried to the shelter of their huts. It was yet another omen, lighting my way like a great amber lantern and frightening away others who might discover me.

I summoned my courage and crawled from my hut, but the silent girl was there waiting for me, her slender hands beckoning me toward the yard. I frowned and shook my head. I had my plans, and now that I had turned down the road I did not wish to change them. But she followed after me, grasped my wrist tightly, the light in her eyes pleading, and she pulled me behind her.

It was clear to me then there was nothing for it. I could not walk away from her, and I could not take her with me. In that moment my loneliness and curiosity overpowered my strongest intentions.

I followed her up the hill to Badu's house, and then along the narrow path where Badu collected her magical herbs. The shadows in the wood were black as pitch, reflections on leaves and branches pulsing forth at every turn, alive and curious. The night songs grew louder as high-pitched insect sentinels signaled approaching danger. Ahead of us a small light glowed and flickered—a yellow-flamed torch flaring larger as we descended into an earthy depression as broad as the main yard; a secret valley tucked within the forbidding wood. Shafts of moonlight slipped through the canopy of black branches and mingled like watery spirits among the unsuspecting slaves who gathered at the bottom.

Some of them I knew and many I didn't. They spoke in whispers and congregated near a long trestle table laden with food. And yet no one approached it. No one even went close except for one small boy who fanned away the flies. My own cassava breads were there, and big gourds heavy with drink. Trenchers of meat, fish, and boiled maize steamed into the night, causing my mouth to water and stomach growl.

Badu presided from her stool, her blue turban secure about her head and a long robe of the same color cascading to her ankles, making her all the more imposing. She did not look up but kept an odd focus at the space between the crowd and the table, as if she willed a barrier there and maintained it with the pressure of her stare.

We sat in the dirt at Badu's feet, for a long time doing nothing more than watching the people approach. Nearest to Badu was Anna, pregnant and unsteady, her eyes swollen and teeth clenched. Maestro was easy to spot, his head above most of the others, wandering among them but speaking to none. The two women from the curing house whose names I never knew wandered along the fringes. And nearest the table were some from the field gangs, looking wasted and eyeing the meat anxiously. We all waited, perhaps an hour, until Badu rose from her stool and raised her arms before the table. Every voice fell silent.

"Come now." Badu's voice was deep and strong. "De spirits dun take what dey wan'. We eat and we drink what dey leab for us, and den we begin."

"Begin what?" I asked the silent girl, but she only looked down at her hands folded neatly in her lap.

"Begin what?" I asked Badu when she returned to her stool.

"You go eat now. Dis be a sacred time. Don' be askin' me."

I followed the others to the table. I had not tasted roast pork for a very long time and longed to place a piece of it on my tongue before it was all gone. I felt nearly faint for all the wondrous sights and smells. There were berries of many kinds, and little fruits scattered around the table. The jugs were filled with juices and drinks made from special island plants. Someone had made sweet cakes, and I longed to sink my teeth into them. At the center of the table a large wooden trough was filled with some kind of stew.

"Dat be goat water," someone said as he scooped a measure into his calabash bowl. "For de Jombeeeee!"

I skirted around him, selecting the things I knew or could recognize and piling them onto a banana leaf. It was a feast just as Badu had said it would be so many weeks ago. Who had prepared it all? Where had so much food come from? We ate with our fingers and wiped our chins on our dirty sleeves.

With my hands still laden I returned to Badu, who was giving the silent girl a drink from a large calabash. She held the bottom, forcing the girl to drink more, and when she finished the girl wiped her mouth and looked up dutifully. Badu refilled the bowl and the girl drank again.

"What does she drink, Badu?"

"Bush tea, made of de forest."

"Why does she not eat?"

"Everyone do not eat as you do, child. Do not ask! Be silent. Be watchful. You will see."

To wash down my food I filled my gourd with this juice and that one, tasting each one for its flavor: one heavy and thick as syrup, another tart with bitter aftertaste, a third one earthy and sour, causing my lips to pucker and searing my throat as I swallowed. I began to feel warmth settle into my shoulders and belly, and my lips soon loosened to a comfortable smile.

Before long, three men rolled a log into the clearing and produced drums of various sizes, made from wood and skins. The largest could have covered a water barrel, and the smallest could have made an odd-looking hat. They sat on the log and began to beat these drums with their thumbs and the backs of their hands. The sound captured me instantly, as the oldest and youngest among us began to move in time with the rhythm.

Someone else brought hollow sticks as long as my arm and beat them with smaller sticks, adding a sharp, reedy sound. A piper's notes pierced through with a melody, lilting like a dragonfly over stones and fallen logs. Others joined the dance, stomping the earth until it shook beneath me and a strange echo filled our earthen valley—as if a thousand wolves had been sleeping beneath the ground and growled their fury at being awakened.

The air trembled with music and vibration. A woman began to sing, and I was so moved I got up to join her but fell back down again, dizzy and woozy. Badu smiled and shook her head.

"It be de rum, child. All de jugs hab it. Rum bring out de spirits, and you nebber know who dey might choose to tell der secrets. Maybe it be you dis time! Stan' up slow and you be all right. Der you be. Go on now, de bof of you."

I ran with the silent girl to the midst of the dancers. We swayed and shook our hands above our heads. People bucked and kicked and twisted until it seemed their backs might break. A jug was passed, and we drank and passed it on. When it was empty another appeared; we drank and the music grew louder. Even Badu danced, her long blue robe flowing about her in flutters and folds, and her turban holding its place though she reared back and chanted into the wind, weaving her voice around the drum beats as a shuttle moves yarn.

As the moon passed from one side of our gathering to the other, each dance grew more frenzied than the last. A man crazy with rum swaggered through the crowd, shaking his hands and hollering. "I be him!" he declared. "Don' you see how I be? I be him!" But the people kept dancing.

"What does he mean, Badu?"

She shook her head and frowned. "He say de Jombee come into him. Say de spirit ob de dead now speak through him. He wishes it so, but it don' be."

She ignored him, continuing her chants. She filled a cup from one of the jugs and tossed the liquid into the air above her. "Bring de Jombee down from de trees!" she shouted. Soon another did as she had done, and then another, until it seemed to rain the juice and bush tea potions, and the air all around us smelled of meat and sweat and rum.

"De maize!" she shouted, and women scattered dried corn kernels in a wide arc around the dancers. "Draw Jombee in!" Badu shouted. "Closer!"

They worked until the maize formed a double circle around us and golden speckles at our feet. Badu took cup and jug and cast the potion into the trees on every side of us. "Draw Jombee in!" she chanted over and over.

The music soared and the drums thundered and the dancers swirled into a frenzied blur until I was not sure I saw what was before me, as if I stood at the end of a long hallway, watching myself and others flail about. The silent girl danced, her feet barely touching the ground as she passed over it, floating, dipping and swaying but never falling. No longer silent, she twirled at the center and crooned and moaned. Badu danced in among the others until she was close to the girl, listening, her eyes wide as she motioned to the drummers to quicken their beat.

"Fowl!" she cried out.

From a crate beneath the table someone drew out a live squawking hen. Badu seized it by the throat and held it high near the torch where the girl could see it. "Ayeeeeeee!" Badu screeched.

The silent girl turned. Like a cat, she leapt for the hen and clenched it in her mouth, her white teeth gleaming of moon and firelight, her hands trembling high above her head. A woman screamed and the girl leapt at her, shaking the frightened hen violently like a mad dog. She carried it about, shaking it until she ripped off its head and let the blood spill across her chin and chest. She held the dead bird above her, its blood raining upon her hair and her face. The crowd moved away, but no one stepped beyond the ring of corn. Badu moved closer, cooing, soothing. The girl held the feathered carcass high and began to turn, turn, again and again, spinning, an arm above her and another stretched before her, spinning faster and faster until I thought I myself might lose my dinner. Badu waited until the girl slowed and her eyes bulged, white-rimmed and fierce. Then she moved in.

"Who be you? Tell us," Badu asked her.

The girl turned to Badu, her face streaked with tears and blood, her bloody tongue lolling from her lips. "Haaaaaah!" She hissed and ran around the circle until she came to Anna. She pressed the dead hen against Anna's chest, and Anna fell to the dirt, wailing as loudly as she had at the market.

The girl ran the circle once again and began to dance and twirl wildly.

"Tell!" Badu demanded. "Tell me now!"

The girl twirled to a stop, her chin thrust into the air as if a spear had passed through her mouth down to her heels, pinning her to the ground. Her body vibrated and jerked with the force of the impact. She spoke, but her voice was weak.

Anna came closer. "He be here? My mate?"

Badu held Anna behind her and repeated. "Who be you?"

"I be! I be!" The girl was free of her spear and twirled again, arms flailing and blood dripping from her mouth as though from a terrible cut. She crouched low and began to circle Badu like a fox closing in on a wounded dove.

"Where de bats dwell!" The girl spoke in a deep, hollow snarl.

"Where de bats dwell," Badu repeated.

" ...above de high garden," the girl rasped.

"Above..."

"Aaaaah!" The girl's shout sounded like the cry from an angry old man deep within a cave. "De riches! De riches!" She bucked and twirled, and then the invisible spear returned, bolting her to the ground with her spine stiff and chin extended. Her mouth stretched down in a grimace of agony and despair, white froth appearing at the corners of her lips mixing with the dark blood.

"Onc...by...one...it...mus'...be...done." She gurgled and the spittle increased at the corners of her mouth. She turned slowly, facing the people behind her. For a moment everyone stared and made no sound, not knowing what would come next and fearing it greatly.

"Only...one...by...one."

Tears brightened by the torchlight fell like jewels down her cheeks, and she turned back to Badu. Then her knees gave way and she collapsed in the dirt. Badu cleaned the blood from her chin with the long blue sleeve and rocked the girl against her breast. Anna crawled closer, and Badu gestured for me to come near.

"I take her and wash her. She be done now. Anna, you mus' go up de mountain. Child," she turned to me, "you go along and lead de others. Anna know de way and what mus' be done."

"But what's wrong with her? Is she dying? I want to stay and see that she's all right!"

Badu glared at me. "Do you not see she be with me? What you gon' do dat Badu can't do? Every hand be needed, one by one as de Jombee say."

The other dancers closed in around us, as curious as I was about what had taken over the silent girl and as shocked by her speech. The Jombee spirit had spoken through her. She could talk then, couldn't she? That could only mean that most of the time she just wouldn't. Badu had asked her questions, and now I had many more to ask, but Badu shoved my shoulder hard.

"Go now! While de moon light de way. Get dem all behin' you and go!

Anna stood trembling at the edge of the field, rubbing her heavy belly and staring fearfully back at me. I grabbed the first hand I could reach and led a wobbly man back toward her. Then I grabbed another and another until I had eight people in a row. After that it was as if I was the dog and they the sheep, falling into step behind the others. Anna nodded and climbed the slope, ascending into the woods. I looked back, but Badu and the silent girl were gone. Only the stool remained.

We emerged from the trees behind the big house like an eel navigating among jagged rocks. To the north the dark and toothy Chance Mountain rose from the hillside. I ran ahead to be near Anna, climbing the steep path. Though she clutched often at her belly, she moved relentlessly forward, and I had to work hard to keep up.

"Anna, where are we going?" I whispered as loud as I dared, so that she would hear me but I would not arouse whatever lurked in the trees and shrubs around us.

"Hush! De Jombee say where to go, and we mus' go. We be at de high garden before long, and den you see."

"What's the high garden?"

She continued on the trail but answered patiently. "It be high above de plantation, wif yam and maize and fruits growin'. De master see it be planted and take us dere when de Caribs come. Sometime dey be angry, want to kill us all, but de master take us up de mountain and keep us hid until de Carib go away. If dey come up de mountain after us, de master, he shoot dem down again."

The path narrowed around a jutting rock, and I felt my way around it behind her. The moonlight made following easier, but the path was unfamiliar and treacherous in some places. I peered over my shoulder at the others, maybe twenty or more, following steadily behind me. It was a good master who planted a garden to feed his people and protect them from savages. How could he be the same man who had also tried to rape me?

And who kept us all as slaves, no matter how well treated? I was not sure what to think of him.

"Anna, will the girl live?" I waited for her answer, but it did not come.

"Anna?"

She sighed and took a deep breath. "She be in a state for a while. De Jombee can mash some folk all up. Dey speak through her. Dey can be bad, cause troubles. Jombee choose her mos' ob de time, close to death as she be. Badu take care ob her. She be all right with Badu."

"But why is she close to death? Is she sick?"

"Oh no, she not sick. She strong. Master try to kill her, but she don' die. Some be skeered ob her 'cause dey think she part Jombee herself, but she don' hurt nobody."

Something like hot iron pierced my stomach, and I stopped as if a stone wall had sprung up between us. "The master tried to kill her?"

Anna turned to look at me. The whites of her eyes glowed, and I saw the tender movement of her hand across her belly. Her shoulders slumped. "He wasn't but a child, all upset, mebbe didn't know no better. He try to drown her in de pond. Mebbe jus' wanted to see what she do. He ain' nebber seen no baby before. Some folks say when she scream he got scared and run off, and dat's why she didn't die, she just float to de edge an' somebody fish her out. Other folk say he drown her for sure, das why she can't talk, and de debil fish her out. Dey say de debil bring her back to life, make a hell right here for de master. Only time she talk be when de debil or de Jombee talk through her."

I shuddered. How could it be true? She'd been nothing but kind to me. "What do people call her?"

Anna laughed a little, and then the laugh turned into a grunt as she climbed higher. "Folks don' call her nothin'. It be up to de master to name her, like he name ebery baby. He don' gib her no name, and even if he had, folks be 'fraid to speak it." Anna groaned as she climbed over a fallen log.

"Hol' on now, be sure everybody still comin'. We got one more rise to go and de garden be dere."

"Anna?"

She sighed loudly. "What is it now?"

"Was it really him? Was it truly your man speaking through her?"

She stopped and I saw her shoulders rise and stiffen. "Nobody know for sure, not de girl, not eben Badu. But I felt him dere, sure as I feel you standin' behin' me. And, fact is, it ain' 'bout knowin'. It be 'bout believin' and trustin'."

The path turned sharply just behind a rock ledge jutting through tangled vines—a fine place for someone to hold a musket against intruders. Beyond the ledge, the path opened onto a grassy, gentle slope edged by trees and thick underbrush. A kitchen garden stretched before me, bright with moonlight and comfortingly familiar. I wanted to stop and rest, to look at the maize stalks bending like dancers in the wind, and the bean vines and the yam leaves like adoring faeries genuflecting at their feet. But Anna didn't stop; and beyond, the shadows grew darker still.

19

The High Garden

It was harder to ignore the Carib Indians, who sometimes traded cordially with the English and sometimes shot at them with poisoned arrows.

~ Richard S. Dunn, 1972

Anna crossed the garden toward a cascade of rocks, where a thin stream of water glinted and trickled over its edges and down the mountain. She climbed over it and passed beyond my sight. I had to follow quickly that I did not lose her, and watch behind as well to make sure the others were still coming.

Should the Caribs find the garden, they would have yet another search to find the people they would slaughter. The cave was a further climb, and the opening nothing more than a shadow behind a tree. Anna disappeared into it like a spirit, disturbing the roosting bats that screamed and charged us. I ducked to keep them from tangling in my hair, and someone behind me yelped and nearly fell on the rocks. I followed Anna into the cave, lit only by tiny slivers of golden moonlight streaming through the branches at the opening. As my vision adjusted I could make out Anna's knee where she crouched. The stench assaulted me then, sour and heavy, eating up all the air. Anna held the hem of her skirt over her nose and mouth, so I did the same. She waved an arm toward the cave wall and pulled something toward us. I was not sure what it was until I touched it, but then I could smell its pungent scent mixed in with the bat excrement.

"Red cedar," Anna whispered. "De masters keep dis for demselves, for buildin' and makin' things. It be de bes' wood on de island, and fetch a fine price. It be a hangin' offense for a slave to eben touch it, but my man wanna buy his freedom, and me and de babe's. He hang for his stealin' sure enough, but not for any ob dis. Nobody know 'bout dis 'cept me, and I nebber know where he hid it.

"He gots other things, too, ober dere—de silver tankard and de pewter. We got to take it back, all back to de master before de Carib come and de master fin' out, or before he see it missin'. And we got to do it all tonight, afore dawn, jus' as de Jombee say. Elsewise, me and my babe be sure to die for it."

I held the cedar to my nose to smell its tart sweetness and felt its rough edges against my fingertips. My eyes adjusted and I began to see the wood pieces, most of them cut to the length of a shinbone. They were not meant for framing a structure or erecting walls, but for finer crafts, like carved balusters, corbels, stair brackets or gable ornaments. The pieces were many, stacked to the top of the cave and as far as I could see into the darkness. Tucked among the wood were other small treasures wrapped in linen or cane trash.

"Anna! It goes forever! How can we possibly..."

"One by one," Anna said. "It be de way he brought it up. Don' know why he think to hide it here, but dis where my man keep it, and we mus' take it back right now, before de next sun rise."

The cut cedar felt heavy and awkward against my chest, and was certain to slow our progress descending the mountain. We had to get the wood and all the other stolen things back before dawn, before the master could see us carrying it, and before Mr. Drax came for us, ready to drive his work gangs to the cane fields. How could we do it with so far to come and go?

Anna pushed me on the shoulder, just as Badu had done. "Pass!"

I passed my piece of cedar to another slave waiting at the opening. No sooner were my hands empty than Anna forced another piece into them. I passed it to the next one. We worked without speaking until the last slave's arms were loaded and they headed down the mountain.

"Keep them coming, Anna. I'll stack them at the turn of the path before the garden. People can move faster if they don't have to climb across the rocks."

I carried the wood from the cave to the garden path until my knees ached from the climbing, my arms felt like twisted ropes, and my hands were scraped and stabbed with splinters. When the last slave had carried a load away, we cleared the cave of every remaining treasure and waited at the trail for them to return and help us finish. But time passed and no one came up the mountain. I watched the sky, willing the moon to hold its place, though I knew our time was short. Anna lay back on the ground, cradling the babe in her womb. We waited in silence until I swore I would load every last treasure on my back and carry it down the mountain by myself. But I knew I would never make it; I would fall and be killed—or worse, be discovered with arms full of the master's treasures. My head would sit on a pike in Plymouth's square, a warning to every slave in Montserrat who dared to steal, or I'd be hanged in the swamp where the land crabs could sup on my feet.

Anna began crying as the first streaks of pale light colored the vast horizon. My gut twisted, and a panic climbed the rungs of my ribs to settle in my throat, its weight heavy and its scales sharp and cold. And then at last I heard them. Thanks be to St. Brendan, they were back.

The second climb up the mountain had taken too long. I loaded each pair of outstretched arms as swiftly as my own arms could work. Anna sat on the ground, rocking back and forth, weeping as the darkness steadily faded. Maestro was last in the line. Without a word he took everything that was left save one last piece of cedar for me, and turned back down the mountain.

"Anna, we can go now. Hurry!" I helped her stand, but the weeping had found purchase and she could not stop. It drew on her strength, and I feared at every step she would tumble and kill herself and the babe at once. I hugged the cedar against me with one arm and held her steady with the other as we slowly descended. By the time we reached the plantation it was full light, and Mr. Drax waited for us at the gate, the whip and bill fastened at his waist.

"Where hab you gone when dere is work to be done?" He glared at us, and I glared back equally harsh. I was tired and frustrated that the night's work had taken so long. I was frightened and angry at having been caught. Mr. Drax looked us over from head to toe, glanced up the mountain path behind us, and then fastened his eyes on the parcel I held so tightly.

He came at me fast, like a hawk swooping on prey. His face was inches from mine as he jerked the wood from my grasp. "Dis be de wors' ob your troubles yet. Dis mus' be punish!"

He turned to Anna, who was still weeping and barely able to stand. "Go!" he shouted at her. She wailed and ran off without a backward glance.

Mr. Drax clenched my wrist and pulled me past the big house toward a shed, well behind the kitchen and a stand of trees. Inside the shed, red cedar was stacked evenly and neatly, its tangy scent sharp on the morning wind. He placed my wood on a stack that seemed to be waiting for a last piece to make it even. He grunted, perhaps disappointed to find that the wood was all there, that I had not stolen the rest of it. He dragged me back toward the kitchen, his rough fingers squeezing back the blood.

"*Stand*," he ordered, and shoved me against the rails of a fence. He stopped, took a long deep breath, and turned his face to the heavens as I'd seen him do before. His eyes were closed and his lips barely moved, but I knew he was praying, and in my veins my blood began to course and toss like the stormy sea and my insides to twist and churn. He lowered his chin slowly and glared into my eyes, then jerked the whip from his waist and held it up. "Turn to de post and lean to it. Lift your skirt."

I shrieked in horror. He put his hand to my face and shoved me back around to the fence post, then jerked my skirt up above my knees. "Hol' de skirt dere or I whip you eben harder about de face and neck," he shouted.

I held it. He grunted behind me like a wild hog, and I shut my eyes against what would come next, my heart no longer beating, only fluttering like a dying bird in my chest. I heard the whip before I felt it: singing through the air until the crisp snap of its frayed leather bit the skin of my legs. The pain exploded and shot from my calves to the back of my neck in a half-breath's time. But there was no breathing, for the next blow struck near the first one, and I clenched my teeth and held on bitterly, bracing against a third. It came, higher this time, on tender skin behind the knees that split open at the impact. Then came more sharp stings across my calves, my ankles, my thighs. I lost track after that, my body full aflame with pain and fury. I made my fists like iron, and I held the wooden post, willing myself to die standing if I must rather than let him see me fall. I came near fainting until I realized I had to breathe, and I sucked in air only to force it out with a cry when the next blow landed. By St. Brendan's balls I stood my ground, but I could not keep the tears from streaming. I heard a shout, and the blows stopped. Mr. Drax wound the whip and fastened it to his sash.

"Get to de cassaba house and start your breads. You be late." His voice was high and gravelly. I waited for him to walk away. If I had to look at him, sure I would have stolen the strength from the heavens to leap at him and rip his throat out with my teeth. It was the gory vision of the hanged man once again stopping me; and there was one thing more: I heard Kade whisper in my ear, "Keep your head about you, Elvy. *The game is not over*."

I was not dead, though I felt near to it. I dropped my skirt to cover my bleeding legs and turned slowly. Not a soul was in the yard, no one about to see. I thought a shadow moved in an upstairs window of the big house, but it was gone so quickly I could not be sure. I fell to the ground and cried until I could cry no more, then felt the screaming pain again as I hauled myself up and tried to walk.

The cassava house was bright with sun by the time I got there. My legs swelled so that I could not bend, and every movement caused explosive pain that registered in my head, my fingertips, the backs of my eyes. I swore every oath I could recall, and I made my breads, every damn stinking one of them. When the last one was dry I hurled it just as hard as I could over the treetops, caring not where it landed or what became of it.

I delivered the rest to the kitchen and went to my hut without food. I wished to be alone, to face no one, and to hear no words from those who had not come to my aid. I knew a hate for Mr. Drax that nearly reached the heights of what I felt for Oliver Cromwell, but not quite. Mr. Drax acted as he thought he was expected to do. He held no real power. He held a whip, a bill, and the master's confidence to manage the labor of his plantation. But Cromwell acted out of pure cruelty. I had suffered, and every slave on Montserrat had suffered because of him.

No matter. What had happened to me changed nothing except to strengthen my resolve, to set me squarely on track to get back to Ireland or wherever Cromwell was by now. I would kill him, sure enough. I would torture him slowly, ensure his pain, and kill him with a furious glee. And I restated my oath that he would see it in my face at the moment he died.

When darkness fell I tried for sleep that would be my only escape from pain. Instead I heard a soft thump against the side of my hut. I crawled, awakening the soreness with every move, and found a bundle wrapped in a rag just at the opening. I lifted it, and then I smelled a horse and heard the creak of a wagon in the darkness.

"Put de aloe on your cuts. Eat de bread, den chew de leaves I gib you. Dey ease de pain." It was Badu, speaking low and soft, just above a whisper. My childish heart fluttered, and I wished I could but run to her to cry into her lap. But I stayed.

The wagon creaked again as she climbed into the back, and then it began to move away. It might have been Timothee, but in the dim evening light I could have sworn it was the master himself holding the reins.

The bundle held a tiny pot of sticky butter. I smoothed the salve gingerly over the welts and cuts on my legs. The bread was stale, but the leaves newly sprouted, sweet and tender. I gnawed them until my face tingled, and then I spat a bitter paste.

20

The Governor of Montserrat

A pleasant and fruitful land [Montserrat], very rockie but a sandy soyle; the ways uneven and in some parts dangerous.

~ Christopher Jeaffreson, 1676

On the first day I could walk without pain, I waited impatiently for night to fall. If I'd had any belongings to gather I'd have taken them, for I never intended to return to Sharavogue. I set out on the dirt trail for Plymouth with nothing but a searing resentment and ironclad determination.

The high crescent moon brought with it no wind. Insects flitted about my face and neck. My skirt was a sight worse off than the last time I'd come to town, but there was nothing I could do for it short of stealing something from the laundry. The filth on my face and hands, though, would surely label me a slave rather than a barmaid. I crossed a narrow ditch to a small pond where I might make myself a bit more presentable.

As soon as I knelt the gnats descended in a cloud about my head, splitting even my lashes and stinging my scalp. I splashed and scrubbed my face quickly and rushed back to the road to escape the worst of them. The firelights in the town calmed me and I inhaled deeply of the smoky air as I moved along the ditch to the back door of the tavern where I could slip in unnoticed. I meant to find the fat man who had favored me once before. If he'd forgiven me for overturning him in his chair, he might help me. I had little enough to bargain with, but I was fierce ready to offer it up.

In the dim amber light he was easy to recognize. The broad feathered hat was as before, and he lifted his tankard until the bottom was the top, allowing the ale to flow down his whiskers. The place was not as crowded, but the barman was still filling the mugs as fast as he could. I grabbed two and carried them to the fat man's table.

My gentleman looked up with no surprise, as if I'd stood before him just moments ago. "There ye are now darlin', and it's late as well for I'm parched as a feather on the wind!" He pulled me to his knee and the ale sloshed onto my skirt. He carried on as if my presence was well accustomed, boasting and bantering with the others at his table.

"If it's governin' ye need in these parts, I'm yer man. Sir Anthony Briskett himself, now he was a giant amongst us, there be no doubt, and may he rest in peace. But the one they be givin' us now? I'll do as well or better and with a bit less thievin' on the side!"

"Mind yer tongue, Mr. White," a fellow remarked from the shadows. "Word is Osborne brings an iron fist and takes unkindly to criticism. Know ye that he keeps his spies about!"

"Pah! I'm too old fer panderin' to pups. Anaways, 'tis nothin' but the truth I'm speakin'. Word is the man's not satisfied with Briskett's job alone, nor his own estate, though it be finer than most. Nay, he'll be peerin' o'er the fence where he sees the pasture greener. Lest ye be thinkin' peerin' o' the sort is hardly criminal, it's his own sweet sister be livin' there, sadly widowed and fortunate to find a new husband to protect her lands and her child."

"Sure, ye're not sayin' the governor would confiscate his own sister's lands!" someone else queried.

"I know what I know, that's all I be settin' about. Best he not venture near me, hear ye? I'll be teachin' him some respect when he comes around to my little corner of the island." Mr. White fell silent when the big wooden door swung open and four men in fine jerkins pushed inside toward a table. My ample fellow stiffened and chattered no more but watched the newcomers from over the rim of his tankard. I paid them little attention, seeing the interruption as my opportunity.

"Sir," I leaned close enough to see the hairs sprouting from the rim of his lobe, and whispered into his ear. "Be there a ship due into the harbor, fine sir?"

"A ship," said Mr. White, still watching the newcomers take their seats.

"Yes, sir, mayhap to collect its goods and head home to Ireland?"

I suppose word of home captured his attention, for he turned to look upon my face. "Home, is it? And tell me now, if there were such a ship, would ye find yerself on it?"

"I would, sir. I'm needed in Ireland, and it's of great importance."

Mr. White nodded. "So it is, so it is," he muttered, and then he turned back toward the others at the table. "And ye'd leave our lovely isle of Montserrat to carry on without yer female graces? It cannot be! Isn't it so, lads? Do we not need to keep our ladies here, fer they be in such short supply?"

"Aye, there's the truth!" someone responded.

"Yer bein' such a young one, we've much to do with ye. Beside that, passage be costly, lass, and dangerous fer travelin' alone," Mr. White continued.

"Might we go together then?" I whispered, surprising myself with the words, and even more so by my own bold gesture. I reached out a stealthy hand for his and placed it just under my breast, where he might feel a warm bulge pressing against his knuckle. His eyes narrowed, and I knew my meaning was clear. Just then a high, gruff voice broke through the din.

"Barman! I believe I'll be sampling a bit of what Mr. White's having this evening." The powerful voice came from a man who'd come in behind the other four. He wore a long wig of cascading curls, an embroidered cloak that reached to his knees, and heavy buckled boots. In his left hand he carried a walking cane with a silver handle.

"It's himself, Governor Osborne, sir. A fine evenin' to ye," the barman called out.

The men at the table burst into a cautious laughter, and Mr. White pushed me away. "Go then, lass! Bring us all another round. And more ale, less froth! Serve our governor first, as it's clear he's a thirsty man."

I stood, suddenly awash with fear, my heart beating a panic in my chest. *The governor*. Just steps away from me, and calling me to his table. How could it be true? I had longed for an opportunity to meet the governor but had not even considered it at this time, or in this place. I had reached such a desperate state I was completely unprepared, my speech for him all but forgotten. And the figure of him in his finery was far more intimidating than I'd expected. I wanted Mr. White's help now, for he seemed a far lesser threat. I served tankards quickly at the governor's table and turned away, but I was stopped short by the governor, whose fist grasped the folds of my skirt.

"I said I'd have what *Mr. White* was having." He spoke softly but a little highly pitched. I'd heard such a tone before, and feared it. He drew me backwards until I found myself perched on his thigh. The others at the table watched and then turned away, making their pretense at being preoccupied, as if whatever the governor was doing was not the most important thing in the room.

"No covering for your hair, lass? And what a fine copper lot of it you have. You must be a wild, lusty one." He swiped his hand to my breast so quickly I could not stop him, and nuzzled my hair as a man might bury his face in a bucket of cool water. Then just as quickly he shoved me away, and I hit the floor hard on my buttocks, sending a tremor up my spine.

"Christ in heaven! You look like a rose and should smell as such, but instead you smell like a horse's arse. Where have you been? Did Mr. White dig you up from the bog? Be gone from me with your soil and your foul stench."

I would have run away then, but it was already too late, for as I tried to stand someone put a boot to my behind and sent me careening toward the next table, and someone there grabbed my hair, made a loud retching sound, and shoved me back to Mr. White, who by now would have naught to do with me. I'd become the sport of drinking men, and of lesser value than an empty jar to kick about. I was shoved and tossed and kicked and slung against the wall, my hair jerked and my skirt lifted while men gasped in horror and feigned nausea, until the barman himself lifted me from the floor by my waist and heaved me out the door from whence I'd come.

As if my treatment was not yet a great enough horror, I landed sure enough in a pile of horse dung. My sore legs throbbed with pain as I crawled around the side of the building, hauled to my knees, and leaned against the boards to gather my breath. There in the shadows I waited, weeping silently as I tried to pull myself back together, but still hoping I might overhear them as they left for the night, chattering in their drunkenness. Any word, any word at all, I prayed. Let me hear about the ships due in the harbor. But they stumbled out by ones and twos and offered up none of what I longed to hear. How I hated them all for it. I hated them just for breathing. A cold stone pressed against my heart, and sent rueful thoughts into my head. Suppose I never got home again? Suppose all my schemes and plans were just foolishness, as Timothee said, and I was doomed to die as nothing more than a filthy slave snagged forever on the jagged teeth of Montserrat?

My spine stiffened and my empty stomach twisted into a hard knot. "I will not die," I whispered into the night. "And when I control my kingdom once again, I will fight you all until you beg to kiss the bottom of my dung-smeared slipper!"

But then, as quickly as it had arrived the strength in my spine faltered and my shoulders sagged. The truth was I'd been weakened by their cruelty. The cold stone had made its bruise, and I was numbed. As dawn approached I had to draw myself up and climb the road back to the plantation, my legs searing and my head aching from the futility of it all. By the time I reached my hut, I was near delirious, and the workday yet ahead.

For days I am sure I cooked, ate, drank, and slept, but I recall not a moment of it. Then one morning I awoke with my head aching so severely I could not bear to lift it. Soon after I reckoned with this, a monstrous pain seized the backs of my legs where I had been whipped, but deeper still into the very muscles and bone. I could not move nor cry out. I heard the others leaving for the fields or the big house but could not go after them. I told myself it would pass, just a momentary punishment for having gone without rest. But it did not pass. Instead it worsened, and then I began to shiver against a cold so profound it seemed an ice blanket enrobed me. I had no shawl, no fire, no cloak, nor even the slightest rag to clench against it. I covered myself with straw and trembled beneath it with a violence that would not cease, as if the Devil held me in his fist and shook me like a charm against the angels. For hours the fit commanded me, until the reeds of my hut rattled and clattered as if they might soon fall down around me.

And then as quickly as the ice blanket had enclosed me it was ripped away, replaced with something new—a fever hot as a turf fire. I welcomed it at first, a comforting delirium that would carry me into a careless sleep, but then it pressed down upon me until I could barely draw breath, and I longed desperately for a cool drink I knew was not forthcoming. I saw no light of day, but huge torches blazing before a dark castle and my father's head on a pike before it, his lips mouthing words I could not understand. I saw Kevin Harrington swaggering, laughing, and then his head falling away from his shoulders. I saw Aengus, eyes full of terror, reaching for me beneath the faerie thorn, his hands and fingers bleeding and I not able to go to him with my limbs all entangled in the roots. And then St. Brendan came to me, his hair aflame. He reached for me and lifted me free, for I weighed nothing at all, and carried me to the alabaster castle. I lay on the backs of white sheep whilst an angel above cooled my brow with her breath like snow. Then I drifted away as the foam on the ocean, until the sky opened up and Timothee reached through to retrieve me, and I heaved into the bowl he held for me. I looked into his tender eyes and all went black.

"Eet's the tertian ague," I heard Timothee say. "Her symptoms are clear as any I've seen, and you know, sir, I've seen them aplenty. She was eento the swamp, breathing of the vapors. Eet leaves little question een my mind what has happened. She's still young, but she's not yet gained her strength back full from the treatment of Mr. Drax. The disease found her easy prey, I suspect."

"She *will* survive," the master declared.

"Eet's to be seen, sir. The fever must run eets course, and she's full up with eet now."

I wished to argue, but felt as if my body was piled high with hot stones. I could not move nor escape the raging heat that engulfed me. And I thirsted. For a sip of cool water I would give my *soul*. But I hadn't even a whisper to offer.

"She's to stay in the big house, then, until it passes. Give her water. Keep her cool. If it worsens, we'll bring up the doctor from Plymouth. In the meantime, have her hut burned in case this sickness lives within it. I'll not be sacrificing any more slaves to this island!"

My hut. As sad and tiny and lonely as it was, it was still the only thing that was mine, and he was burning it. Where would I live? Where would I sleep? Or did he already assume I would die? I could not die. I needed more time. I needed my freedom. I willed myself with all of my spirit to stand up and slay these men at my bedside and leave Montserrat forever. But even with my last measure of strength I could do nothing, as if I was dead already. I must have cried then, for I felt the touch of a soft cloth at the corner of my eye.

I do not know what passed after that. I drifted up toward the light and down into the blackest darkness, and back again in both directions. Was it hours? Days? Weeks? I only know my fire raged on for so long I should have burned to nothing a thousand times, and yet I remained. This was hell then, as the priests described, to burn eternally but never rest. I felt a finger at my cheek, another pulling open the lid of my eye. Someone lifted my hand.

"Her pulse ees even weaker now, sir." Timothee said. "The doctor's ministrations have made no difference. If she's to survive I suggest we all pray."

I heard nothing more, though I tried for the sound of my own heart beating. Then there was a screech, the wood of a chair leg scraping the floor, and heavy footsteps walking away.

"Incompetent fool of a doctor. I should not have bothered. I only hope I've not waited too long. Let Badu take her," the master said.

21

Army of Souls

A spider bruised in a cloth, spread upon linen and applied to the forehead or temples.

~ Cure for 'tertian ague,' Leonard Sowerby, 1652

The next thing I remember is the grip of strong hands about my arms and legs. I opened my eyes with some difficulty and recognized the dark wood of crude rafters brushed by the pale light of pith candles. Soft murmurs from many voices floated like dust particles, and the slow, regular beat of a drum encouraged the weak rhythm of my heart. The heavy scent of fresh crushed herbs descended like a fog and mixed with something else, familiar and yet alarming: sweet, dried maize...and rum.

I recalled these scents from only one occurrence, the Jombee dance for the hanged man. It had so thrilled me and confused me, and then led to my troubles with Mr. Drax. I wanted to leap from wherever I was and bolt out the door, run like the wind to escape; but the fever still raged and I could not move nor even lift my head, which, I suddenly realized, was cradled in someone's hands. I forced my eyes to open.

Badu looked down on me with sweet kindness. When she saw I had awakened, the expression disappeared. Her eyes widened and slowly filled with fire. She drew back her lips like a fierce cur to reveal jagged teeth. Her rounded jaw clenched as if to restrain the desire to kill.

Two fingers pressed above my eyes, forcing them closed. I could not resist any more than I could keep the sweat from trickling from my temples as if to tease the parched passage of my throat. Would that I might capture that droplet with the tip of my tongue. But then I tasted something sweet that coated my lips and burned as I swallowed. Was it mead, or was it rum sweetened with some kind of juice? I could not trust my own sense of taste, but my body fell to its powers, my tensions melting in its syrupy glow.

Badu uttered strange words that came from her depths like bats awakened from endless black crevices. I heard commotion, as if their wings beat against the walls that held them. Then slowly the sound took clearer form, and I thought a hundred dancers did circle the place where I lay, matching the drum's beat, their feet pounding the plank floor as distant thunder pounds the heavens. Someone began a high-pitched chant that others joined, and the drumbeat grew louder. I wanted to sleep, to feel the thunder in my bones and be comforted. But strong fingers gripped my limbs again, and stripped away my coverings.

I tried to curl inward to hide myself, but I was too weak against them and fell back as four women washed my skin with cool cloths that smelled of urine, and then sang as they painted my thighs, arms, and stomach with strange shapes using sticks that scratched my skin. Badu offered the drink once more, and I went for it eagerly; but instead of the rum mixture or even ale or water, it was a thick, bitter brew of herbs and bark smelling more like dirt.

"Swallow," she commanded, and then forced more between my lips. Only when she was satisfied I had drunk enough did she release me, settling my head on a cloth pillow.

Her potions worked their magic, making my limbs immovable as ancient tree limbs and my body a trunk of iron. I succumbed, my impulses dissolving in the dark waves, and yet my mind aware.

One woman released a screeching wail, and the thunder of drum and feet intensified so that my pallet began to tremble. Then Badu gave a scream so low and horrible it must have come up through her feet from the very bowels of the earth. She wailed from high above me and then slowly descended. The people around me dropped to their knees. The drum ceased. The chanting ceased. No one moved nor seemed to breathe.

"Now it be time," Badu said in a voice that echoed across my mind. "Now we have come! Steady in purpose, strong in resolve, de army of souls."

"Army of souls!" the chanters whispered.

"Army of souls so bound in brotherhood, so quiet in spirit, step from de wood unheard, unnoticed, yet terrible in dey power."

"Terrible!" some of the chanters responded. The drumbeat returned, softly and rhythmically, a reminder of the passing of time.

"*Silent.* Silent now," Badu continued. "Creep from your hiding place, sweet army, low and slow like great iguana, down to de water's edge where de dark ripples reach for your feet. See de big canoes waiting on de shore. See de wild river, flowing red with blood, churning, rushing, rumbling. Mighty river, beckoning. Do not listen. Do not let it touch you. Side by side you run. Slip into de canoes and away."

The drumbeat quickened but remained soft like the footsteps of soldiers stealing through the woods, then settled.

"De canoe, she rock, but you pay no mind. Dip and pull. Your oar moves you forward. Dip and pull. Dip and pull." Badu kept on, and the drum sounded like the oars breaking the river's surface. "Do not look at de rippling water. Do not see de blood. All about you de monkeys swing in de trees, de night bird calls. Do not heed. Stay your course, see you de fortress in de distance. Faster now."

The drumbeat quickened still more, and my heart pounded with it. I floated high above like a child watching a battle from a tree on a distant hillside. My skin burned. My body trembled. Badu moaned and sighed.

"She see you now, hear de sound of your boat, hear de cry ob de river tellin' Mabouya your army draw near. She know you come, she know why, she know not when or how. She try to steal away a soul from de army. She lonely. She want her child by her side. But de child belong to de army now. You keep on, keep on, steady in purpose, strong in resolve, army of souls."

"Army of souls," the chanters responded.

"Army of souls, *beware*," Badu cried, and the pith candles were doused, the room plunged into darkness. "She try to hide, she test your courage. She send de storm clouds to threaten you and make a curtain to block your way. But you be not distracted, you be not scared, you carry on. You know where de river go. De river flow to Mabouya's door."

"To Mabouya's door."

"Mabouya, far up de red river from where all babies come. Dip and pull. Dip and pull. Dip and...Ayeeeah! Hear de boat as she scrape de shore." The drum pounded quick and hard, then stopped. "She waits," Badu whispered. "She know she cain't keep a soul from de army, but sometime she cheat. Sometime she try to hide one or take one back dat she like. Mabouya be powerfull, pull many tricks, but the army be strong and fearless. Slip from de canoe onto de shore, away from de river of blood.

Follow de path. Though it be dark, it be not far. *Soft*, don' let her hear you."

The floor began to rumble with soft thunder, and the drum joined in, slowly at first and then faster, faster, faster...and as Badu clapped her hands above my head, a single candlelight returned. "See de light now, army of souls. She wait in her stone castle. She wait for you. Go."

The drum kept its pace and I heard around me the panting of the chanters as if they truly ran up a treacherous path. The drum ceased.

"She hear you now, but she not see you. You be deep in her chamber. She sit in a great chair with a golden back that tower over her head. Her feet rest on de back ob a gret turtle. Fire burn on her hearth. Dogs moan and quiver in slumber. Move closer. See de bright feathers in her hair. Her long locks flow wild about her face, red like de river of blood. Her eyes burn like de fire."

And I did see her. The strangest sensation came over me and I was transported. Though I knew my body lay sick and fevered on Badu's floor, I was wide awake and soaring above the army as it entered the castle and the alabaster chamber where Mabouya waited. I looked down and saw the woman in her golden chair, its tall back intricately carved with exotic animals and strange patterns. Her hair was of copper like mine only far brighter, like the flames of a well-fueled fire, alive and wild, adorned with the striped tail feathers of a hawk, the blue-green wing feathers of the gallinule, and the white crest feathers of the night heron.

Her eyes were blue flame, and when she lowered her lashes to look at the babe in her arms, the light still streamed from beneath her lashes and from her hair to illuminate everything around her, an aura of light too beautiful to be mortal, too frightening to penetrate, and far too bright to offer any shadow or shield from her gaze. And though I knew I was a grown woman in Badu's care, I knew as well I was the babe in the grasp of the sorceress, the malevolent queen whose power was strong and fierce beyond my reckoning. I was in danger but I feared for the army as they crept ever closer. I felt Badu's hand turn cold and quiver at my cheek.

"Hide! Low down. Don' let her see you," Badu cried. "Ah, dat's right, powerful army of souls. Wise army of souls. Surround her. Wait for her weakness. Wait until she shows it to you..."

I heard not a breath nor a whisper, but waited for Badu's next call, my skin tense and alive in anticipation.

"Wait now. She drift. She know you be dere, but she don't see you. She be sleepy. She loll her head so heavy, so weary. Your prize be in her lap, small like a kitten. Mabouya drift, her eyes be closing, her hands weaken. Get ready to grab. Her head be dropping. Dere she go, and NOW!"

The chanters were on their feet, no longer chanters but dancers again, pounding and stomping the floor until it seemed the house might collapse around us. I felt my pallet lift and wobble in their hands, higher, higher. Badu's voice was beneath me now but *Mabouya's* eyes snapped open, her lips parted in surprise and our eyes met for an instant, then the blue light blinded me and a burning pain seared up from the tail of my spine and exploded at the base of my skull.

"RUN!" Badu shouted. "To de river! Hurry. Leave no one behind. Run!" And the floor thundered and the air filled with whoops and screams. Badu raised her arms over my head once more and brought them down. My pallet returned to its place. All those about me knelt on the floor.

"Now pull! Pull. Pull. Dip and pull. Dip and pull. Row your baby's soul back home. Row it. Row it!"

The room began to sway, and the chanting returned low and fast. I felt dizzy, queasy. The drum beat fast and hard as if to pound on the top of my skull.

"And now we reach de shore again," Badu said. "We thank de river of blood for sparing our lives. We return de canoes, and thank dem, too. Dey serve us well. We come back home now, our journey done, our prize won. Mabouya cannot follow. We are safe but we hab not finish our task." A woman approached me with a wide wooden bowl, and Badu stood beside me, her hand on my chest. "Back away now, make room for de soul's return."

I must have opened my eyes, for the shadows about me grew taller but the sounds more faint. Badu dipped her hand into the bowl, and it came out glistening in the candlelight. She placed it on my stomach, dark and hot and stinking of blood. She smeared it from my breasts to my privates, back and forth, back and forth, as if plowing a rut, back and forth. She called out, "We gib thanks to Mabouya for returning dis soul!"

The crowd thundered and cried, and the drum beat fast and hard, rising, rising, louder and faster, and Badu held her hand high over me, shaking it, her eyes wide and wild. A woman screamed, and Badu's hand crashed down into my belly as if to wrench out my very core, and then pressing, pressing, filling and filling, rubbing the rut she had created.

Just as I thought I could not stand another second of it, she jumped back, her hands waving high over her head.

"De evil be torn away, de blessed soul returned!"

"De soul returned!" the crowd chanted.

Badu's eyes bulged, her breast heaved. She fell against me and then collapsed on the floor. If she fainted, I do not know, for I slipped into my own pit of darkness.

I awoke—was it days later, or weeks? Consciousness seemed to rise like the rim of a brilliant sun after a night's storm, and in time I became aware of familiar things: The heat of the master's kitchen, the bustle of work, the smell of human sweat and roasting meat, the low voices of men, and the talk of war.

22

Supper for the Governor

It seems to me the Europeans do not well who coming from a cold Country, continue here to Cloth themselves after the same manner in England, whereas all Inhabitants between the Tropics go even almost naked...

~ Dr. Hans Sloane, 1687

"And so tell me, Governor Osborne. More than four years have passed since he beheaded our anointed king. What do you hear of the bold General Cromwell? Has he taken to wearing the crown?"

I shuddered at the sound of Cromwell's name. From the great room where the supper table had been set, the master's voice was dry in tone, as if he did not really care about the answer to his question, or knew it already. Cook pulled a crisp white apron about my waist and tied it with a snap. I wore a clean skirt and shift, a new bodice, and my hair was bound beneath a stiff linen cap.

"Ye're still thin as a pike," Cook whispered, "but ye're strong enough now to handle a bit o' work, and fer my mind ye're long overdue. Keep yer eyes down and hands to yer skirts unless yer servin'. The shoes can't be helped. Pray the man does not give ye much notice."

If she'd had a name before coming to Sharavogue I would not know it, for everyone in the household called her Cook. She was long faced and gray headed, eyes beady and black, and a dark whisker or two curled out from beneath her pointy chin. I wanted to be near her as a chick stays near the hen. She gave my behind a smart, motherly whack.

"Mind yerself tonight, dearie. It's the governor hisself who honors our table. Embarrass the master and ye'll be served up on a platter like the rest o' the livestock. Ye're a bit of a raw egg, but so be it. We'll turn ye into Tart de Bry. Just carry the bread to the dinin' table, then stand aside."

"The…the governor is here? Here?" It was just dawning on me that the master had assigned me to the kitchen and now I'd be serving the very man I'd sought from the day we set sail from Ireland. But since our encounter in Plymouth, I feared him as much as I longed to speak with him. I assured myself he would have forgotten me. Perhaps I could approach him now, as a member of the Sharavogue household rather than a dirty bar girl. I cursed, for I had no letter to present; but surely with my new status he would hear me out. I held my head high as I carried the wooden bowl of fresh cassava bread to the table. Who had made it, if not me? I wondered, then dismissed the thought altogether as I took in the sight of the two men before me.

The master's thick brown hair was combed straight back, making his whiskers and unruly eyebrows more severe. His curls splayed over the lace collar, but his shirt lay open at the throat. White lace sleeves nearly covered his hands, which rested casually on the arms of his chair. He looked regal, as if there wasn't a soul on earth who might trouble him at his own table—not even a governor. And this was quite a feat, considering the extravagant spectacle of the man.

Buttoned to the broad chin in a stiff-collared shirt, the governor's burgundy brocade vest strained across his belly. Curls from his brown wig tumbled to his breast, and a bit of sweat did drip from his temple thereabouts. Voluminous breeches gathered at his knee above gold-colored stockings and beribboned ankle boots. When I dared glance at his face I was astonished, for his small black eyes hungered as if I was raw meat prepared for the roasting. His lip curled up on one side, revealing a yellowed incisor. His brows arched, the combed hairs reaching for shelter beneath that sweaty wig.

I placed the bread bowl on the table as silently as possible and stepped back toward the wall. I wasn't sufficiently armored for the scrutiny I now felt, relieved only when their attention returned to the conversation.

The governor reared back his head to empty his wine glass. He wiped his lips with his fingertips. "Oliver Cromwell," he growled, "is a blathering, arrogant goat. What does he know of the needs of commerce? His answer to everything is war."

The master smirked, forming three fine crescents at his cheek. "It's what he knows, sir. Some say it's all he knows. Many before him have seen war as a grand stairway to power. Cromwell makes a show of collecting money for his precious army, and the masses believe he is their great protector."

"Stop, please, before my ample appetite withers like a rotting pear. You know, do you, that the title of 'Protector' has been circulated as an alternative to crowning him king? This, the man who beheaded King Charles and shook the foundations of every monarchy in Europe?" He spat loudly on the master's clean floor. I searched about me, but there were no rags with which I might lift the foul mess. The governor eyed me expectantly. I dropped to the floor, intending to use my skirt hem, but it was new and I dared not soil it. I removed my linen cap, and a section of hair tumbled about my shoulders. He captured a hank of it between his fingers and pulled it as I worked.

"If he insists on capturing Hispaniola, he'll be an embarrassed protector," the master said. "The island is too well defended and he'll send his soldiers to their graves. I'd wager he'll discover this soon enough and then try for Jamaica. But his captains are poorly organized, and it will be a bloody sacrifice for a dubious political victory. Jamaica is a pit of disease."

"Bother, I say. There are things of far greater interest at our feet, do you not agree, Tempest?"

"Things of interest, yes...Roger." The master grumbled and scraped his chair closer to the table. "The Navigation Act is more than a bother and is not likely to disappear because we ignore it. Let Cromwell have his tribute for herring caught near England, and let his ships have salutes from foreign ships passing in the English Channel. And if he wants to own more islands in these seas, let him. What do we care? But the Navigation Act cuts us to the bone. All goods imported to England must be carried on English ships? When the Dutch are our lifeblood? God's wounds!"

The master waved me away and I hurried back to my place by the sideboard, shoving my soiled cap into my skirt pocket and trying desperately to recapture my hair without it.

"It's true," the governor replied. "The Dutch serve these islands well, with ships more frequent and swift. The merchants are mostly trustworthy, I daresay, but there are those who warn...well, we mustn't let them get the better of English trade now. There's a new corner of the world ripening, and rather nicely..." He glared at my bodice. The master glared also, but at my eyes. While my cheeks burned from embarrassment, I feared his seared with fury, and I prayed I might not face another whipping.

A warm hand grabbed my elbow and pulled me back toward the kitchen as two young slave girls carried in a tray of roasted lamb with sweet potatoes swimming in fat. I lost the gentlemen's attention.

"Talk of a Dutch war brings me to the heart of my business with you this eventide, Tempest." The governor lifted his knife and eyed the platter as if to slice off a morsel of fat before the meat was served. He set it back down as Cook bustled in with a long carving knife and began to cut thick slices.

"Ah, so we have business in addition to a social call," the master said.

"In time, my good sir, for the business at hand is causing my mouth to water and want." He took a large bite of fat and meat and chewed noisily, smacking his lips and groaning. "Would that my sister's cook was as talented."

"Yes, governor," the master said. "I was crushed by the news of Elizabeth's passing. She was young yet, and not long married to Mister Waad. Such a hardship on your family I dare not imagine."

"Yes, my family. I suppose we shall miss her. My sister did well in her first marriage to Anthony Briskett—a fine governor before me. She was a sad widow after his passing. As for her second choice, I believe she acted in desperation and haste. I warned her repeatedly that the man was not her equal. Perhaps she succumbed to her fever as a means to escape the untenable situation in which she found herself. Samuel Waad is a fop."

"You truly do not like Samuel? I've found him to be most polite and pleasant."

"I think your vision is clouded, but only because he did not marry *your* sister. Now she is gone and he has taken control of an estate that exceeds the quality of any on Montserrat. He lives as a king in his stone house, richly furnished with thirty servants to attend him. He has seventy cattle or more, five hundred sheep, and better than fifty slaves to toil in his fields. He dresses in silks and struts about Plymouth, tapping its streets with his cane as if he owns them. It is another case of the Dutch carving off the best for themselves—a shameful twist of fate that begs a remedy. And more so, for there's my sister's young son in need of guidance. I cannot leave him to Waad's attentions. I must consider what is in my power to do—I daresay is my duty to do."

My master sipped his wine, nodding slowly. "You are both still feeling your grief. Given time, I'm sure you and Waad will come to terms."

The governor drew back and looked away. "Terms." He began to dab at his cheek and forehead. "'Tis a hearty meal, and a man must eat well, yet I feel I might swoon in such heat. Do you mind, sir?" He lifted his wig slightly. The master nodded, and the governor removed his wig and placed it gently in the chair beside him. His own darkened hair was sweat-plastered to his head. He dabbed at his face and behind his neck and then gulped more wine.

"Cook!" the master shouted. "We must cool our guest, Governor Osborne." And as if she had already sensed his needs, she shoved a palm frond in my hand and sent a slave boy to the opposite side of the room with another. "Stir the air for the gentlemen," she commanded.

"Ah, there's an improvement," the governor said. "Now, Wingfield, you can understand, of course, that our Lord Cromwell means to take from the Spanish in this realm, as well as the Dutch. He calls for men to take up arms in the cause. As governor, I am dutifully bound to respond."

"So you are. We shall provide food, water, and tobacco to the war ships that stop here."

"And men. We are asked for soldiers."

"Call up the militia. Those able to leave their plantations can join the expedition, although I would advise against it. The war is ill-fated, from a man who knows infantry but nothing of ships and navy."

"Surely you realize I cannot spare the militia. Who will protect our citizens if there be an attack from our warring enemies, or from the Caribs? Both pose an equal threat."

"It is so. Well then, Cromwell's admirals must seek their men in St. Christopher."

The governor shifted in his chair, recrossing his legs. "I had thought we should send slaves as a show of support. Your Maestro, for example, would make a formidable…"

"Governor, Maestro is critical to my processing operation. I believe you know that. He will not be joining Lord Cromwell's soldiers—not he nor any other from Sharavogue."

The governor shifted again and speared a potato for his trencher. He sliced it open and popped half into his mouth, tapping the edge of his trencher thoughtfully. "Wingfield, you realize in the realm of his responsibilities a governor must support the leadership of his country. He must assess the resources, having a true account of the holdings throughout the lands over which he presides."

"Must he now?" The master replied. He ate slowly and selectively, watching his guest.

"Aye, well. It falls to me to answer to the king—had we a king. If we cannot support the expedition with manpower, then there are the taxes and tariffs to be paid, and only by understanding the true values of our properties and productivity can I accurately represent to London. And more so, only then can I do my best to retain as much wealth as possible here, for our own."

The master pressed back against his chair. "I see. General Cromwell is not the only fellow who sees himself in the role of protector."

The governor's cheeks reddened, and he drained the wine from his glass. "It's my role to keep us all in business, sir. We have built a decent settlement. I would see it grow and prosper."

"Of course."

The governor mopped his brow again. "I will need, in fulfilling the obligations of my office, to carry out some examinations. In some cases these may be extensive, and in others only perfunctory. The results of these will be recorded in a book for my eyes only, so that I may have a full accounting of the health, wealth, and value of every estate on Montserrat."

"Every planter knows his value and production, sir. You need only to ask, as it is within your power to do. Certainly this would save the time and expense of these...examinations to which you refer."

"Yes, yes, it is true, and I would hardly suggest that your own accounting would be anything less than honest. A gentleman of your stature would do only as his honor commands. But you must realize there are some who lack the same, shall we call it—character? And I can hardly be expected to put my own position and estate at risk for the sake of a scoundrel."

The master leaned toward the governor and placed his hand flat on the table between them. "There'll be no examinations at Sharavogue, Governor Osborne. You shall have your accounting and nothing more. If it is scoundrels that concern you, take your examinations to them."

"We could certainly negotiate, Tempest. For certain considerations a perfunctory visit would be more than satisfactory."

The master's back stiffened. His Adam's apple dipped and returned. "There will be no examinations at Sharavogue."

The two men stared at each other in silence for what seemed like several minutes, though it must have been only seconds. The air stilled, though we waved our palm fronds through it. At last the governor lifted his fork and speared another slice of lamb from the platter. "There remains the matter of the Dutch."

"Meaning?"

"I can hardly be expected to risk my head for the executioner without reasonable incentive. If I am to report to the Exchequer and to Parliament that we have no business with the Dutch, while their ships sail in and out of Plymouth fully loaded, there must be ample compensation. Do you take me for a fool?"

The smirk returned to the master's lips, and he shrugged. "I take you for a governor and a businessman, sir. I'm sure we can work out a reasonable percentage so that you find yourself busy at the leeward side when certain ships call in our port."

"I have my own family to support, my sister's son who needs my care and..."

"Yes, Roger. More wine?"

"I will, yes, and if I might excuse myself to relieve my aching bladder?"

The master nodded and gestured toward the door. As the governor rose from his chair, I dropped the palm frond and ran into the kitchen.

"The master needs more wine!" I spoke quickly to Cook. "I must go...I fear I might be sick!" Cook nodded as I ran out the back door, and though my stomach churned, it was not with sickness but with anxiety that my opportunity had come to speak to the governor alone. I ran to the corner of the house where I might peer at the copse of trees where men typically purged their water, and waited for him to emerge. I felt the spring's warm wind swirl about my neck as I planned what I might say—my station, my situation. That I now knew his disdain for Cromwell only strengthened my belief that he would help me.

Then I felt my sash jerked rudely at my back, and my apron fell about my feet. A large hand grasped my hair and shoved my face and breasts against the stone foundation of the house. Hot breath burned the top of my ear and smelled of meat. My skirts were being tugged and jerked up from the hem.

"So you've come for me, lass? You desire me, so?" The governor's unmistakable voice was higher than my master's, but harsher. I tried to squirm away. "I *knew*," he said. "I saw the heat of desire in your eyes, the lovely beads of perspiration on your lip as you worked." He slipped an arm about my ribs and squeezed my breast. "You saw I could take you places, aye? Do things for you no man has ever done before. You could see the great bulge in my breeches that wants your nubile mound, to feast upon that peak that hides within your folds of flesh. I shall ram my cock deep within your corridor until you scream with pleasure and I harvest that sweet young seed." His hand plunged between my legs and grabbed my private parts. "I will sample what I will on every estate, starting with this wild little morsel!" He pressed me all the harder and I felt the brush of his bow-tied shoe on my ankle as he kicked my legs apart. He thrust his knee between my thighs as his fingers groped and probed. I yelped and jerked, but his hand left my breast and pressed my throat, with his chest and belly crushing against me. I could not breathe enough to scream, barely managing a faint squeal. He laughed in a deep, guttural way and bit the top of my ear. I was done for, trapped by a monster with a hunger for flesh.

And then came a loud cough, clear as cannon fire, only inches from my head.

"Is this your examination, Governor Osborne? For she certainly is my property." My master leaned against the foundation beside us, his cheeks blazing as he glared at the governor.

The governor froze, pressing his hardness against the back of my skirt. He turned his head slowly toward my master and cleared his throat. "An untimely interruption, Tempest."

"Yes, I see that. You will release her."

The governor stepped back and I fell to the ground, my hair and skirts all about me. "Simply a temptation I could not resist. That is all. A ripe plum to be sucked. You understand these things. I'm sure you've had her yourself."

The master shifted, revealing a pistol in one hand. "I understand completely, Roger. I believe my percentage for trade with the Dutch now has been paid. Shall we call for your carriage and driver?"

I scrambled to my feet and ran into the kitchen where I might hide among the pots, catch my breath, and compose myself again. Cook looked me over, touched her hand to my wrist, and said nothing but went about her business. I began to weep silently, the tears wetting my cheeks, my chin, my shift, my hair. I continued until I heard the shout at the horses, the crack of the whip, and the wheels of the governor's carriage on sand and stone.

"It's our lot, lass," Cook said. "Nothin' fer it but to be grateful ye're alive.

Here now, on yer feet, and take this in to the master." It was a dish of fruit soaked in brandy. The master waited in his chair as before, his cheeks dark and his raging brows obscuring his eyes. I placed the dish before him, next to his rusted pistol, and stood aside.

After a moment, he spoke softly. "Where is my spoon?"

I ran to the sideboard to fetch one and placed it by his bowl, wanting to kick myself for such stupidity.

"Thank you." He did not begin to eat but continued to stare at the bowl. Then he looked up at me and I wondered if he thought, as I did, of our first night together. "Elvy..."

It startled me to hear him speak my name. "Sir?" I responded with a quick curtsey.

He regarded me, lips parted as if to say more, but then he closed them and looked away. "You may go."

23

In the Master's Household

For rest we will nott, untell we have done some thinges worthy of ourselves, or dye in the attempt.

~ Sir Henry Colt, 1631

In time I grew more comfortable with my duties in the big house. With the dawn of each day I trudged the wide stairway slowly, carrying fresh towels for the master's morning ablutions. So often I had dreamed of the stairs in my own castle, the polished alabaster steps winding upward to my chambers, how cool and smooth they would feel beneath my pampered bare feet. But never had I imagined the warmth of polished wood, a comfort even to my sore and callused soles, or the clean, rich scent of it surrounding me so. I closed my eyes and pretended, imagining myself entering my own chambers as I tapped on the master's door.

"Enter," he shouted, and my brief vision was shattered.

The swollen edges of the door stuck, but I pushed hard and it gave way, opening to a large room bathed in sunlight. On the far side, two windows faced southeast for a view across the cane fields and the rolling landscape between the Soufriere Hills and St. George's Hill.

The washstand was to my left. I placed the towels beside the bowl and took the pitcher to fill with water, trying not to look at him as I turned. He sat on a carved wooden bench at the foot of the bed, and from the corner of my eye I saw he wore riding pants and was preparing to pull on his boots. He was not yet fully dressed and used no manservant to assist him. The early sun cast a soft golden glow across his bare shoulders. I wanted to look but I dared not. Under his gaze, my shame over the encounter with the governor was renewed. I bowed my head, hugged the pitcher to my chest and I moved quickly toward the door.

"God's *wounds*," the master bellowed. "Why is it with the day's beginning I must be subjected to such a scowl on your face as you serve me?"

"Your pardon, sir," I said.

"Nay, Elvy. No pardon. I'm asking what burden you carry, for clearly its weight is heavy beyond that of a porcelain pitcher. Are you not glad to be a house servant? Are you not grateful to be elevated from the fields and the cassava house? What troubles you so?"

I was astonished. Could he not see? Could he not imagine? I glared back at him, though I knew it was impertinent. "I am grateful, sir, to work within the household instead of the field, and I am grateful for your...interruption, I should say, of the governor's advances." I curtseyed stiffly and he nodded in return. "But still, sir, I am imprisoned. And I..."

He returned my astonishment. "Imprisoned? You are working out the terms of your indenture. You must know the difference between this and living as a prisoner."

"I do, sir. Yet I am kept from my home," I replied, "and in this way it is the same as being chained, for I am kept from my destiny." I knew I sounded foolish to his ears, but I had not realized it until I heard my own words pass my lips that I had come to think of things this way. It was an offense against God, anything that kept me from my intentions for Cromwell, from my plan to live and die for Ireland as my father had. Thanks to Badu I had survived the fever, but it made me all the more certain that I was saved for this reason and my time could be short. I knew the frustration and despair had begun to show on my face since the whipping at the hands of Mr. Drax. After my encounter with the governor, I seemed to be edging toward a precipice between desperation and hopelessness.

"Destiny," Master Wingfield said, pulling on his shirt. "An interesting word. I suppose one seldom thinks of slaves and indentured servants as having a destiny other than to serve. A rather arrogant viewpoint, I now realize, but somewhat ingrained. Forgive me, and please...what is this destiny that awaits?"

"I should not burden you, sir. Please excuse me." I stepped closer to the door.

"Please. This interests me." He gestured for me to sit in the side chair by the washstand, leaned forward and folded his hands between his knees.

I approached warily, not sure if it was honest interest or merely a morning's entertainment that attracted him. The side chair was carved from mahogany and finely upholstered, smooth and cool to the palm of my hand. So close to the master, I recognized the scent of the launderer's soap in his shirt, and beneath that something more earthy and animal that I took to be his own—his skin, his sweat, his oil that caused a light sheen on his nose and the dome of his forehead. I remembered the scent bodily, the way hunger responds at the scent of a meal, but my mind flashed to the dark night far beyond that of our first encounter, to a night by the fireside at my father's knee. A dense longing curled and constricted around my throat and windpipe, thick and sticky-hot as the molasses at the bottom of the cook pots. My eyes began to fill, and I prayed the master would not see. Was I to tell this man the true nature of my resentment, the true goal of my heart? This man whose veins most surely ran with Irish blood but whose livelihood depended on the good graces of the English crown? I had crossed so many boundaries already, but to reveal my deepest sorrow? My murderous core?

I remembered then my father's admonishments: *Here now lass, ye're a princess, castle or no. And what becomes of a princess? She becomes a queen.* A queen who has nothing to fear. I pressed my shoulders against the chair back and lifted my chin, sitting taller than before. I cradled the water pitcher in my lap and looked boldly into the master's eyes.

"Once I was to be the mistress of a great castle, to reign over lands rich and vast, even more so than these at Sharavogue. The power of my family goes back hundreds of years. My destiny is to regain our lands, so that I may return to my castle and maintain it for my children and all those who come after me." I felt proud of my words, but the master dismissed them with a wave of his hand.

"There is not a man or woman on this island who does not have a similar story to tell. I myself long for an estate near Wexford that my father lost to the English. The fact is, most who come here will never leave. Many brood and cry over what might have been or should have been. But you? Your eyes burn and your features sharpen at strange times, as if you are a predator sensing something near, or willing it to be so. Something different drives you, Elvy. That is what I wish to know."

I don't know why, but I wanted to tell him. He could have me killed for it. He could hang me from a tree or cast me into the sea where I might join Kade as food for the sharks. I trusted him, or mayhap it was just my pride and defiance, no less dangerous to me now than they were when I first confronted Cromwell. I wanted to tell my master everything. I wanted to speak it all out loud again, to give it life.

"It is Cromwell, sir. I cursed him once, right squarely to his face, and swore I would kill him for his mean work in Ireland. I intend to go to England and do exactly so, and then return to Ireland as her hero."

He simply stared, for enough time that a gourd of milk could have curdled, or so it seemed to me, and then he burst into laughter so deep and so robust I felt my hand curl tightly around the pitcher, and I rose up as if I might shatter it against his head. My cheeks seared. He stopped his laughter abruptly and considered me.

"Elvy, I must apologize. You are quite serious. It's my arrogance again. Do forgive me. Please. Sit back down. I want to talk with you."

"I will not! Servant or no, I will not be laughed at in such a way. The murder of Cromwell is no joke to me, nor will it be to the filthy scoundrel when at last I return to do the deed!" But I was still a servant. I stopped short of storming from the room as my feet so badly wished to do. The master stood and touched my hand as if he had read those very desires in my eyes.

"I cannot blame you," he said gently. "You've revealed to me something intensely personal and for which you clearly have great passion. Though you may not forgive me just yet, I beg you please sit with me for a while. If you speak of this a bit more, perhaps I can help you and thereby make amends for my rudeness before. You wouldn't know this, but I've no love for Cromwell myself."

His fingers lingered upon my hand, and the manner of his words gave me pause. He honored me, and yet I feared the more he knew of my life the less of it was mine. His eyes seemed attentive and true. And the fact is, I had carried this story inside for so long, to speak of it brought me renewal and a grand relief. Except for Timothee who would no longer hear of it, I had told no one since I'd confided in Kade on the *Jackdaw*. By the stars in the heavens, that had been years ago, and all the while the fire within me still burned as strong.

"My father was killed early in the rebellion," I began, feeling the warmth of the master's hand still resting on mine. "Cromwell came to Ireland to crush us all, not for what the rebels had done, but in truth because it was a fine excuse to wipe the island clean of us and take our lands. I saw Cromwell himself strike down the most beloved young boy of our village.

I cursed him and he sent his soldiers chasing after me, but I escaped. He is evil and cruel, and he must be killed. I vow to do so with my own hand unless another brave soul already has beaten me to it."

The master nodded slowly, considering me from head to toe. "The Protector is quite alive, I assure you, though I venture there are many who would see his head on a pike if chance allowed. His little war in these parts is failing. His men are dying as his admirals squabble amongst themselves. He will fail in Hispaniola, and if he comes away with Jamaica, it will be nothing short of a bloody miracle."

He rubbed his eyes and then considered me once again. "Even if you were to board a ship to England, how would you find him? I believe he has long since left others to carry out the—resettlements—in Ireland, and I'm told he moves frequently between palaces and estates." He spoke softly, all traces of laughter now gone.

"I do not know, but he is famous and everyone speaks of him, so find him I will."

"He leads an army and is surrounded by guards and parliamentary advisors. How will you kill him?"

"I do not know, but I will trust St. Brendan the Navigator to guide me; and if I am fortunate, I will find Cromwell sleeping and will lay open his throat before he can wake."

He shook his head. "It is an angry girl's dream of revenge. Elvy, you are thousands of miles away, and even if you were free to go, the obstacles that block your path to Cromwell are insurmountable. To continue to feed such a dream will only result in a festering sore that eventually will kill *you*, rather than Cromwell."

But I refused to heed. "I will kill him. And when I do you will hear all of Ireland rejoice. The governor...I must...He is an Irishman. If I could just make him hear my story...mayhap he would set me aboard a ship and..." I stopped, going too far.

"You of all people should know by now the governor is a scorpion. Have you ever seen a scorpion?"

"No, sir."

"It is a hideous insect akin to the spider, but with claws like a lobster. The end of its segmented tail it is equipped with a long black barb, sharp and lethal. While its victims are occupied trying to free themselves from it horrid claws, it whips its tail around and stabs to the heart to deliver its quick and deadly poison. Your man Osborne is a poison against which few can defend themselves. It's rumored that some have died trying. You are a young woman without the slightest defense and...I believe you've already seen what the governor would do for you."

My cheeks burned once again. Damn my Irish complexion that displayed my feelings as bright as a painted house. "But if I could get a formal audience, if I could get him to listen..."

He stared at me for a moment, and then dropped his gaze to the boards at our feet, his lips turning to a frown. "There was a time when I wished to kill my father, Elvy. I wished this as if it was far more important than even the air that I breathed. I shamed him with my behavior. I criticized him publicly, and for my youthful indiscretions I was sorely punished. He caught the fever and died before I could kill him, leaving me alone in this wretched place to live out a dream that was never my own. Even now I nurture a hatred that consumes me and can never be relieved. It is what I deserve, Elvy, but it is not worthy of you."

I bit into my lip where it trembled, and willed myself not to cry.

The master shook his head. "You are young, Elvy. To the governor you are but a morsel from which he would gnaw away the best and cast your bones aside. Go now. Let us not speak of this again for a little while. You may trust that I hold your words in confidence."

I rose from the chair, dismissed. "I'll bring your water, sir." I closed the door behind me and started down the stairs, feeling lighter than I could scarcely remember for having released my secret, but feeling also a quiet dread for laying myself so bare before him. My desire was unresolved, and yet, despite his kind warnings my heart pounded out its urgency. T*empest Wingfield*, I said to myself. My Lord Tempest Wingfield.

The silent girl was climbing the stairs, carrying a stack of clean bed linens for the master, a feather duster tucked beneath her arm. I was grateful to see her, to be distracted from the warring emotions inside. Just as we met on a step I looked into her black eyes staring into mine. She seemed scared as a cornered church mouse, the feather duster trembling against her side. She was as fearful as I, and yet she smiled. I started to speak, and as I opened my mouth we heard from behind the master's door the most horrible explosion of the bowels. Sure, there was no mistaking the sound, but it was flatulence of such power, worse than the bellowing of a cow. I would have sworn the windows did shake.

The poor girl must have seen my eyes nearly pop from my head, and we collapsed together, straining to hold in the laughter and failing. My eyes ran with tears, and the poor girl was shaking, this time from mirth, but we could not calm ourselves before the master yanked open his chamber door.

"What have we here?" he shouted, his face truly reddened. "Is there a problem?" He had pulled on a dark red robe over his shirt and pants, and I noticed for the first time that his hair stood on end at the back of his head from his slumber. He was in danger of setting us to laughing all the harder.

"Nay, nay, sir, I dropped the duster, is all. We've got it just here," and I raised her feather duster over my head. "I'll be fetching your water and breakfast." I stood, smoothing my hair back and trying to look neat.

The silent girl placed the linens on a bureau outside his chambers. The door closed behind him, echoing in the stairway, and we hurried downstairs to the kitchen. I took her hand and squeezed it until our giggling began to subside. "What's your name, lass?" I asked her. "The people must call you something. Please. In all this time I've never heard it spoken."

Her smile began to fade, and she looked down at her bare feet. "Girl," was all she said. At last, she had spoken just to me. I could not tell from her face if she was twelve or twenty-five. Had no one bothered to give her a proper name of her own, not even in secret? I felt a flame catch in me to light a hundred candles.

"Girl!" I shouted and had to stop myself before stirring up the household once again. "Girl. *That's* what you're given?"

She simply nodded, the white kerchief about her hair bobbing gently.

"You deserve a better name than that one, and you're to have one." Though I knew it was another rule I was breaking, I sat on a stool of woven rushes to think about the right name for her. She was so silent, and yet she had been my true ally in such a strange place. Lucky I was to have such a store of old stories from my dear Aengus O'Daly. I closed my eyes to let my thoughts come forward in answer to a need, and they did not disappoint.

"Nessa," I told her, tucking a frayed corner of her kerchief. "There now. That's a fine name for one such as you. Nessa was a king's wife and daughter of a magician. I myself am a princess. Now you can be a noble too, and when I have my rightful lands returned to me, you can come to live there with a fine home of your own. We will be friends forever and ever."

Nessa smiled, but her eyes didn't shine with the laughter we had shared. "Ness-ah," she repeated. "It is mine?"

I could not answer, distracted by the pounding of horse's hooves nearing the big house.

24

Witness to an Execution

Who is he that cann live long in quiett in these parts? For all men are heer made subject to the power of this Infernall Spiritt. And fight they must, although it be with ther owne frends.

~ Sir Henry Colt, 1631

The horseman arrived in a cloud of dust and dismounted so quickly he stumbled and fell to his knees, then scrambled back to his feet. The master watched from the steps of the big house. Nessa and I peered through the doorway behind him. The arrival caused such a commotion even the workers watched from the yard, the boiling house, and the curing house.

"I bring n-news sir. From Plymouth and from Samuel Waad's residence." The rider dusted off his breeches. He was tall and exceedingly thin, with pimply cheeks and sparse, spiky hair. His voice cracked, unable to find its timbre.

"Bring water!" The master shouted without turning to us. Nessa ran to the kitchen, but I stayed where I was, not willing to miss any news that might be helpful. The young man trembled and fell to his knees again.

The master stepped closer. "What is it, lad? Are you ill?"

Nessa brought a tankard from around the side of the house, and the fellow gulped, spilling water down the front of his tunic.

"The war, s-sir. The English c-came a month ago, calling for volunteers and..."

"Yes, yes, I know. They were sorely disappointed in the lack of response. What is it, lad?"

He coughed and stuttered. "My uncle, Thomas Hurst, s-stayed on as a g-guest of Mister Waad."

"Ah. So you are the nephew of the notorious English gentleman who beat his tailor with a cane down in Plymouth. Is that it?"

"It is so, sir, yes. Ap-p-ologies sir. Th-the guh..." The boy looked down at his dusty boots and took a deep breath. "The governor had him arrested and committed to prison, sir."

"Gleefully, I'm sure," the master replied. "Yes, I have heard of this fulsome incident. And I have heard also that Samuel has been unsuccessful at retrieving Mister Hurst. I'm afraid I'm unable to lend a hand in this one, boy. It is an uneasy dance between Mister Waad and the governor. Waad's honor has been breached with his guest receiving such treatment, and Governor Osborne intends further injury. They trade insults until all the island speaks of it. Until Waad opens his purse and pays a hefty fee, I doubt the governor will be of a mind to relinquish his charge. Give Mister Waad my best, and I thank you for the message delivery. You needn't have rushed so." The master started toward the house again, but the boy lurched forward.

"My p-pardon, my Lord Wingfield, if you please."

"Yes? What is it now?"

"It is Mr. Waad, sir." The boy cleared his throat, and I could see now his hands trembled at his sides, and his eyes began to fill. "He...has written a letter."

The master stopped. "What is your name, boy?"

"William, s-s-sir."

"Now then, Will, please continue. About the letter."

"Yes, s-sir. Apologies, sir. It...it was a terrible letter with all sorts of accusations, sir! It m-m-made the governor fierce angry. Mister Waad was to go to court over the incident, but he was collected on S-Saturday and..."

"Collected, you say?"

"Sir, h-he...he was held two days' time. He's to face court-martial. To-today."

The master stood silent, still, considering the information. "Then the war has found our door, and we fight without honor the Dutchmen among us." He turned, walking swiftly. Nessa and I had to jump out of his way. He grabbed a large bell that was stored just inside the door and started ringing it loudly.

"Where is he being held?" He shouted to the boy over the noise.

"Near St. Anthony's Church. I can take you to them, sir."

Timothee ran toward the house in answer to the bell. Several slaves followed him.

"The horse and wagon, Timothee. At once."

"Sir." Timothee nodded and ran to the barn and stable. The master paced before us, one hand rubbing the other, then both hands at his temples, combing through his hair from ear to nape as he pondered.

"I see what Osborne has done. If Waad was to face trial for his words, it should have been dispensed with in general court, in open session. But because it is wartime and everyone is militia, Governor Osborne...*Of course*. He's sprung his trap, hasn't he! He made it a secret session. He's calling it treason, and a matter of military security, no doubt. With his men backing all that he says or requires, he may do as he pleases."

"A-And...and Captain Matthew F-Ffoyer, when he d-did protest on my uncle's and Mr. Waad's behalf, the governor put him in i-irons."

"In irons! Ffoyer deserves no such treatment. It is an outrage!" The master was pacing faster, the fall of his boots thundering across wooden planks and causing the steps to shudder. "Cook. My musket and powder!"

I had not realized Cook had come up behind us, but she nearly knocked me over with the swish of her skirts and ran to get the master's gun. The horse snorted and huffed as Timothee brought the wagon around to the front of the house and waited as the master stowed his musket under the canvas behind the seat. The wagon screeched and jostled as he climbed in beside Timothee. He hesitated and then turned to me.

"Elvy, run to my chambers and fetch my sword from its pegs above the bureau. Hurry!"

I gathered my own skirt and dashed up the stairs without thinking, anxious only to retrieve for the master what he had requested. I found the sword swiftly enough, the morning sun still glinting on its silver hilt. I had seen it there before, a weapon of such finery I could hardly imagine it a tool for killing, and I dared not touch it. But the master waited, so I lifted it from its wooden peg mounting, feeling the brush of the silk sash slip across my forearm. The sword was bright and lighter than I expected, its scabbard touching the ground as I hurried down the stairs. I reached the wagon's side and Cook lifted the sword and tucked it beneath the canvas with the musket. The master regarded me there, out of breath, my apron askew. Nessa stepped up beside me.

"Warrior-child," he said, a sad smile creasing his cheek. "Since your own experience has not been sufficient, would you like to see the kind of governor from whom you seek a formal audience?"

I nodded vigorously.

"Then get in. Both of you."

Nessa and I clambered breathlessly into the back of the wagon, and it jerked forward as Timothee snapped the reins. The boy swung back onto his horse and led us down the mountain.

As the wheels rattled and bumped over rocks in the road, Nessa touched my nose to gain my attention and pointed upward. I realized we had our heads tucked beneath the seat, just below the backsides of Timothee and the master. We began to giggle, Nessa shaking silently and me struggling mightily to hold it in. Timothee's hand shot behind him and brushed our shoulders, warning us to silence. He was right, this was not a time for laughter; but I was divided between the severity of our mission and the joy of looking into Nessa's eyes, as if for the first time I had a best friend or even a sister.

Above me was the master, stern and volatile with a tender heart, and above Nessa was Timothee, scolding us like a protective mother. I felt the beginnings of something warm and fleshy, small like a pumpkin seed forming a core where I had felt nothing but gaping emptiness for all the days since I'd left Aengus. At the same time, my arms recalled the weight of the master's sword that lay on the boards near our heads, and the power it contained. I longed for the feel of it. Had I grown stronger from the time I was a child fetching the broadsword for me Da? I closed my eyes and saw myself gripping the sword easily, wielding it in a broad arc and slicing through the air.

As the wheels creaked and turned beneath us, the master grunted, cleared his throat, and spat into the dirt. "So tell me, Timothee. What do you hear? What has been the tenor surrounding Waad's situation and the letter?"

"Sir, I do not..."

"Oh, pah! Timothee, do not waste my time with your charades. Believe me, I am well aware of your secret doings and your network across the island. Why do you think I allow you to do it? You must divulge to me at once what you know if I am to be of any service at all to Waad."

Timothee remained silent as the wagon rolled on, perhaps thinking carefully before responding. Then he spoke plainly. "Master, most of the planters would stand with him, for none have been spared the governor's purse-pecking and many fear him. But the letter cannot be denied. Even the Irish een the governor's service say eet ees treasonous. To stand with him ees to face great risk. I believe eet will be Waad's undoing."

"You should have come to me earlier, Timothee." We rode without speaking, the master ruminating and Timothee, Nessa, and me leaving him to it.

When we arrived in front of the church, the boy dismounted and came to the master. "It's just there, the house behind and just a bit farther, with the iron gate."

"Yes, I see it. I have been there before to meet with the militia," the master said.

The streets were quiet, all but deserted, and even the yard of the house to which they pointed was closed and silent as if all within still slept. "His men are all there?"

"I do not know, sir. Likely there are Irish militia guards."

"Yes. That scoundrel Nathaniel Read and his fellows, I'd wager. Tell me what Mister Waad wrote in his letter."

"Oh, sir, Mister Waad was in s-such a state he could not rest until he wrote it. I myself delivered it, though I wish I'd c-cut off my h-hand instead. It demanded release of my uncle and charged that the governor kept felons and murderers in his service. It even ch-charged that the governor ruled not by the laws b-but by his own exorbitant will and ladies' fancy." The boy's face reddened. "I heard it all myself, for the g...governor read it aloud as I awaited his dismissal."

The master cleared his throat and glanced in my direction. "His dalliances are well known on the island. The letter was true, but unwise. No doubt Osborne wanted all to witness the letter's accusations. What did the governor then do?"

The boy swallowed, his Adam's apple bobbing. "Sir, I..." He looked to his boots.

"Tell me all, boy, if you want help. Hold nothing back."

"I swear by all the angels, sir, I did see him bow his head, and then a smile gathered one c-corner of his mouth and held there. He turned to the wall so his face could not be seen, but his shoulders rose and fell with what ap...ap-peared to be l-laughter, and then became deep breaths. When he t-turned toward me again, the smile had become a horrible grimace, and his eyes did blaze with ha-hatred. He bade me go in harsh voice, and I heard orders being shouted behind me as I rode away."

"What kind of orders?"

"H-he would ha-have the s-s-stockade prep-pared, sir. And he called for men of the m-militia to report to him."

The master turned and looked up at gray clouds threatening over the harbor. "So," he said softly, "Osborne wasted no time. Waad is in grave danger." He turned back toward the iron gate. "All the planters are militia. I must wonder why I was not summoned with the others. As a planter I cannot be seen to be aiding a treasonous prisoner, and no doubt they have labeled him so by this hour. But as militia, it is my duty to assist. If I am not too late, I will speak to the governor and try to bring Waad out. Pull the wagon up to the gate, Timothee. If I am successful, we'll needs be at the ready to carry him away." The master peered over his shoulder at Nessa and me. "I should not have brought you to this. There is too much danger. Cover yourselves with the canvas and make not a sound."

Timothee snapped the leather and the horse lurched. Nessa's head bumped against the boards and she winced, rubbing it lightly. I peered out, expecting to find townspeople going about their business, but not a soul could be seen, not even at the farthest edge of my vision. I felt the gravity of the situation then, my feet and hands suddenly cold as if they had plunged into an icy stream. All my earlier joy was replaced by a gnarl within my stomach, tightening with each breath and straining the skin rigid at the back of my neck.

We did as the master asked, and then I heard the clink of the iron gate. I squeezed my eyes closed so I would not see the master pass through it. Then there came a bang on the wooden door so firm I thought the rough planks shook and the house trembled at his assault. There came no response, and the master pounded again, this time bellowing his demands.

"Open this door. I am militia, reporting now, sir. I require access at once!"

I heard the click of the door's hardware. No doubt the whole town heard it, for there was not even a small bird to sing. I could not bear it another moment and pulled the canvas away that I might see through the space between the seat and the sideboards. The door creaked slowly open, just wide enough for a narrow face. The man responding was shorter than the master, and at first seemed agreeable-looking, but something was wrong. His hair was a rich gold but sparse and greasy at the top and hung to his shoulders, a forelock curving like the tail of a lizard toward his ear. His eyes seemed friendly enough, but one was smaller, tucked beneath a scarred, misshapen brow. The hand that gripped the edge of the door was small like a woman's, and dirty.

"Major Read. I expected as much," the master said.

The man smirked. "As did I, Wingfield. What took you so long to insert yourself where your presence is not desired?"

"It is *Lieutenant Colonel* Wingfield, as you well know. Why was I not summoned? Are all of the officers present?"

The smirk turned to a half-smile, revealing yellowed teeth and a dark hole where one was missing. "Some. But you were not summoned because the governor has no need for you. What is your business here?"

The master stepped back slightly, regarding the man. "You know, Read, each time we meet I am startled that the people of Barbados would have asked you to leave. Shocked, really. And now the people of Montserrat must enjoy your...countenance. Where is Governor Osborne? Open up and stand down. I should like a word with him."

Read's smile turned to a snarl. "He is engaged, Lieutenant Colonel. I am under his direct orders to allow entry to no one. Were he not engaged, I see no reason the governor would bother with you."

"And pray, why is that, Major?"

Read looked down and cleared his throat, perhaps rethinking the confrontation of a superior officer. "He is engaged, as I said sir, with matters of defense and security. I assure you your support is not needed at this time."

"Stand aside, Read. I must speak with him at once. It is a critical matter!"

Read's look turned cold. "My, how our precious, privileged gentry seem to believe all doors must open at the whisper of their command. Kind sir, the governor is busy with critical matters of his own. If you must see him, you are required to wait." He slammed the door and did not return, though the master pounded and shouted for Governor Osborne. He pounded on closed shutters and on walls at the side of the house, but still to no avail. He returned to the wagon.

"Pull around to the side, Timothee. If they'll not grant me entry, at least they will know of my presence. It may cause them to hesitate if they are looking to harm Waad. Beyond that, as Read has said, we will have to wait."

The boy led his horse behind as the wagon came to a stop beside the house. The stockade fence enclosed the back yard, but from a small rise we could see most of the grounds. The master sat in silence for a moment, and then stood beside the wagon. Will joined him there.

"Will, Samuel Waad is a good, honest man," the master said. "He was dishonored by your uncle's treatment, that a guest in his house should be handled so by local authorities. But he has felt dishonored for some time by Governor Osborne's behavior, both personal and professional. If indeed he is in there, Samuel stands for many of us, you understand?"

"Y-yes sir," Will answered.

"Honor is a..." The master ran his hands through his hair and then jammed them into his pockets. "Honor is the thing to which all men must aspire, Will, but it is demanding and has many costs. Worse yet, it is out of fashion on an island distant from the rigors of the English court. With no king, England itself spins in confusion, like a rudderless ship in a monster storm. Cromwell's republic threatens to capsize, while each man stabs the next in hopes of gaining a stronger foothold. Here the sea separates us from even the lowest level of statesmanship, and the only rulers are greed and power. We try to maintain a sense of order with our traditions and customary routines, but truly how does a man find his way amongst such treachery?"

Will said nothing, waiting. The master began to pace, flexing his fist. His boots disturbed the dust and sent the motes swirling in a frenzy about him.

"Why was I not called? Why was I not notified at once when Waad was taken?"

"I'm bitterly sorry, sir. I came as soon as..."

"No, no, boy. By the *militia*. I should be in there now. That I might hear the charges, that I might be a voice of equal stature with the governor to fend off what is surely a one-sided tirade against Waad. Osborne will have brought in those he controls and those who harbor no feelings for the prisoner but see a chance for profit. I can guarantee you none others sit at the governor's elbow. Waad is at best defenseless, and I cannot gain entry without storming the walls. And even if I should, what help have I against troops, with one gun, one boy, a priest, and..."

"We can fight them!" I popped up from behind the seat. "We can tear them apart, by St. Brendan's eyetooth, I swear we can!" Blood rushed to my cheeks and burned at my throat. I lifted the hilt of the sword high enough that they could see it near my face, though the awkward strain of holding it caused me to drop it back to the canvas.

Nessa stared at me wide-eyed. The master and Will stared too, shocked by the outburst and no doubt shocked that I, a weak young woman and a servant, should brazenly interfere in the affairs of men.

"Down, lass," Timothee whispered.

The master looked saddened, then turned away. It was enough rebuke to silence me, and I could only watch the shape of his back and the form of his shoulders as he conversed with Will and morning became afternoon.

"I only wish…," the master continued. "Will, I despised my father for most of my life. So many things he did to draw such hatred, not the least of which was coming to this wretched island that most assuredly caused my mother's early death. My father was as inaccessible to me as the governor is now, though I sat at his very knee. He has been in the ground for many years, and with the time and distance I can begin to appreciate what things he did impart. No man makes every right decision, he would say. Honor is not about always being right. It is about having the courage to admit when you are wrong and then stand down. And it is about having the courage when you are right to stand up, in the face of whatever assails you. I believe that is what Samuel Waad does today, God be with him. In the face of evil, a man might wonder, what does it matter? Devil take your fee and leave me to my quiet comforts. But evil is never satisfied, and a man of honor knows to concede only opens the gates to greater demands and places the gentleman behind you—or the boy, in this case—at even higher risk. To stand up is to risk everything, even life itself, and the honorable man knows such a choice may someday come.

"I fear for him, Will. Governor Osborne's honor was bought with his office. If he orders an execution today, it will not be for defense of honor, but for control of a plum estate. And there is no honor in killing he who is at your mercy."

From within the house we began to hear boot steps against floorboards, the scrape of chairs, the banging of a door against a wall. The master ran to the gate with Will and Timothee behind him. Nessa and I took the reins, huddled together on the wagon seat, and waited.

From the back door men emerged one by one in a line, each carrying a musket, and began to fill one side of the yard. Most wore work clothes: loose linen shirts and breeches, tunic or doublet, dingy stockings and dusty boots, suggesting they were summoned with haste and allowed no time to apply the garments appropriate for an assembled militia. A few others stepped out in black cloaks and broad hats and stood near a table and chairs that had been set outside the door. One man noticed us watching and shouted an order.

"It is Lieutenant Dabram," the master reckoned. "If it could be said of a man, then he is surely worse than Major Read." Upon Dabram's orders two from the lineup came near the gate and stood before it as a second barrier to us, their muskets at ready. I saw the master's back stiffen. I started for the musket and sword, but Timothee glanced over his shoulder at us, shaking his head and frowning.

We waited longer, the sun burning our shoulders, until a shout of attention stilled the yard and the very air about us, and a man in manacles was marched from the house by two guards. They positioned him at the far end of the enclosure, then removed the manacles. The man turned and we could see him clearly, dark hair in sweat-dampened spikes about his face, mouth swollen and sagging, fine clothes rumpled and filthy, and yet his eyes were bright.

"Samuel!" The master called, but it was as if no one heard him. Waad did not so much as blink in our direction. A second order issued, and Governor Osborne emerged from the house in full finery, his lace collar eliminating his neck, the black curls of his wig reaching nearly to his waist, his face pale and taut, his lips pursed like a thin black scar above his chin. He sat at the table and read something none of us could hear.

"He's reading a verdict. Samuel! Governor Osborne!" the master called again, but there was no response, no recognition. It was as if we were not there. Will began to cry.

A third shout of orders jolted me like a knife to the back, and six men stepped out from the line, marched to the center of the yard, and turned to face Samuel Waad.

"Water. Please." Waad called out. He appeared frail, as if his knees might give way beneath him. He spread his legs farther apart to steady his stance. The governor nodded, and Waad was given drink.

"Now, what say you?" The governor called.

Waad stood tall then, squared his shoulders, and lifted his face to the sun. "If I die today, Governor, it is with good conscience and for my country's laws."

"Governor Osborne, I implore you! Open this gate! This must stop at once!" The master shouted, banging furiously against the gate. The guards leveled their muskets at him even as the six men before Samuel Waad leveled theirs.

The governor did not turn from his intended victim. "Fire," he said simply. The muskets exploded.

"NO!" the master leaped against the fence posts. Without thinking, I rang the sword from its scabbard and ran to him, but it was too late. Through the fading thunder and billowing smoke, we saw Waad fall to the ground.

I turned away. The Plymouth rooftops paled in the glowering sun. No ships bobbed in the harbor. No messengers were at hand who might witness the day and carry news to the next harbor. No higher authority would come to change what had happened, and no wind blew but a gentle leeward breeze that would by afternoon carry only the season's rains. The Irish governor had killed the Dutch gentleman. The Irish were no different, after all, than the English. Cruelty reigned. We were without justice, without recourse. We were without hope.

Night came to Sharavogue, as heavy, dark, and reasonless as the first night I was there. Just as he had that night, the master retired to his chambers and began a binge of drinking so loud and so violent that all the house servants left him alone there, lest he pull his pistols on whomever might offend him. But I stayed in the dark corners of the lower floor, my back against the stones, and listened. The more he raged, the more I cried, as if his rage was a blade that allowed my festered wounds to bleed.

In the morning Nessa came, and together we gave him Badu's potions to ease his sickness. We pressed cool cloths upon his brow. We emptied his chamber pot and brought him watered wine. We watched him sleep, and when Nessa went away, I lifted his sword and returned it to the pegs upon the wall. I polished the scabbard until it shined there as a brilliant ornament, no battle fought and no lives saved. I found a place beside the master's bed, reached out and grasped his hand.

25

The Master's Birthday

There is little that can withstand a man who can conquer himself.

~ Louis XIV, King of France

We measured time by harvests amid the ceaseless rhythm of labor: the swinging bills, the cutting of the cane, the droning turn of the oxen at the mill, Maestro's timed and methodical orchestration of the cook pots, the day, the night, the tides, the persistent washing of the ocean against the island's steep cliffs. Though the flowers bloomed on the hillsides and the winds brought the scents of mountain and sea, Sharavogue seemed as flat and colorless as the linens I pressed and folded every day and delivered to the master's chamber.

My arms and legs moved without complaint, my hands produced the work that was required, my eyes saw all the movements around me that carried on life as before, but somehow a veil had fallen between these workings and my senses. I ate but did not taste. I slept but did not rest. And each day was nothing more than a passing sparrow, and each day was the same.

The only change I noticed was that of my own body. My breasts had grown fuller, until I could cup them in the palms of my hands, and the bony angles of my hips had softened. When I peered into the master's looking glass, I saw less of the wild, dirt-smeared urchin with out-thrust chin and challenging eyes. My lips were fuller, my brow defined, my cheekbones forming the structure of my face.

I did have my friend Nessa. I had my place to sleep near the big house that was sheltered from rain and wind. I knew what was expected of me and from where each meal would come, and apart from these comforts my interest in other people and events waned. Even Plymouth lost its appeal as I slowly released hope of finding anyone among the taverns' customers who would help me. I do not believe I had grown complacent, but a veil obscured my horizons and I no longer felt I could reach beyond my own gaze. It was the slave mentality settling in, a vacant existence from which even the longing for something lost has sailed away. But after a time the visions began, terrifying and violent.

The first was so real I felt the blood splattering across my breast. I was not asleep. It was not a dream. It was Kevin Harrington standing before me. The blood gushed forth from his neck in quantities he never could have possessed, and yet he talked as calmly as if asking for a portion of bread, speaking words I could not understand. And then as suddenly as he came he was gone. I saw only Cook at the washbasin and shadows in the corners, gray and indistinct. I pushed the vision from my mind. Years had passed, though I knew not how many, since Kevin was long gone. I dismissed it as a freakish incident never to return.

But then the next vision came, more demanding than the first. Cromwell's face loomed before me so near I could count the hairs that sprouted from his moles and note the very texture of his pockmarked cheeks. He bore down on me, eyes blazing like a madman, and revealed his teeth, sharpened and yellowed as a wolf's. I felt Cook's firm hand shaking me and realized I was screaming.

I stayed outside more after that, believing the blazing sun would burn away these apparitions. As I gathered the linens that dried in the breeze, the third vision came as the others, but more brightly colored and sharply defined. Cromwell returned, this time in full battle armor. He slashed his sword through the air so swiftly I could not see its path. Then he dropped it, and I felt a horrible pain in my gut as he reached in and withdrew the heads of Aengus and my father. I doubled over in pain and for two days suffered a dysentery that kept me from my work.

Badu came to me then. She waited for me as I crossed the yard from the privy, her eyes ablaze with intention, but not unkind. She pressed a small bundle of leaves into my hand.

"Prepare a tea twice a day, child. It will ease your body. De torments of your mind are your own. What must you do?"

It brought tears to my eyes. I had told no one of my visions. I did not know what I must do. In the kitchen I found Timothee at the worktable, a broad wooden spoon in his hand and an enormous mixing bowl before him. A fine white dust had settled like a halo around the bowl, and some of it powdered his tunic. He glanced up at me and raised an eyebrow. Cook was bustling about, grumbling to herself, so I said nothing and went straight to my corner to begin sorting rags.

"Tell me, Cook," Timothee said. "What has become of our little princess with the very big destiny? Has she left us already, and does blood flow on the English Island? What word have you? I cannot say I miss the atrocious singing, but I do believe there was something een that naïve defiance that gave a body hope. A pinch of salt, *si vous plait*?"

Cook complied, shaking her head. "We are all born to a station, priest. Idle dreamin' won't change it, and the sooner a person accepts things as they are, the easier life will be. Does the master know ye're usin' his goods fer this fool concoction o' yours?"

Station. I thought about it as I pulled a clean rag from a pile and began to fold. Station. Da always said I was born to one, but sure he never imagined the one I filled at present. I remembered his tales, but I did not believe them anymore. And what did it matter, to live as a servant or a princess in a castle? Even the master, in his high station, was as miserable as any slave.

"Eet ees for his birthday, and don't you go telling him. Eet shall be a surprise, and he will not be angry. Now bring the sugar. Not the brown, the white."

"The white! It's the master's reserve. No, no, I cannot let you use it!"

"Bring eet, Cook. Hurry, now! And then get the butter and eggs."

Cook looked doubtful but stepped into the pantry and brought out a hard cone of white sugar, shaped like the pots where it was cured. Timothee used a paring knife to shave portions from its edges. "I do not understand this. What in the world is it ye make?" Cook asked.

"Eet will be a cake! A beautiful birthday cake with a delicious confection all around eet. And no, you do not understand because eet ees *French*. Made only for the wealthiest at court. And today, eef you are fortunate, you will taste Heaven. Oh yes, and fetch me a portion of rum. He'll like that best!"

Cook stood her ground, glowering at Timothee, who was making a proper mess all across the table. She placed the butter and eggs before him and then pressed both palms firmly on her hips. "Fetch, did ye say?"

Unwilling to breach the question further, both turned to me. "Elvy, you know where eet be kept. Bring me a portion of rum. And, mind you, don't spill or he'll smell eet and spoil the surprise," Timothee said.

I nodded. The rum was just in the next room, but those two might quarrel for hours over who would go for it. To keep them from bickering I brought the jug to the table and returned to my rags. Then I realized the kitchen had gone quiet, and both Timothee and Cook stared at me.

"Did you see that, Cook? Not a word. Not a protest."

"She's gone daft. Possibly a bit o' sunstroke. Child, drink some ale or a bit o' juice! It'll help season the blood. Aye, blood. Maybe it's the bleedin' what she needs."

"She ees like a sick kitten, ees she not? Cowering een her corner?"

I watched the two of them, feeling small. *Station*. Timothee gave Cook a wink and finished mixing his batter. "Now, that package just there, Cook. Will you, please?"

Cook lifted a brown sack to the table and it made a soft clanging sound. Timothee untied the bindings and revealed a strange metal hoop—something like my bread hoops but larger and solid on one side. He set it flat on the table, rubbed it with lard, and then dusted the lard with cassava flour. He poured his batter neatly into this contraption, and it settled out in ripples like a pond. As Cook and I watched, Timothee scraped the batter clean from the bowl but for one thick glob sticking to the wooden spoon. He held the spoon toward me.

"Here, leetle princess. Put your tongue to this. I can promise you have never tasted the like. Eet will cure what ails you, or eef nothing else, eet will bring you pleasure."

I stood slowly and reached for the spoon. A drop of yellow, sticky batter fell from it, but I caught it in my hand. I tasted that droplet first, not willing to make the commitment of putting the spoon to my lips. It settled on my tongue like butter, but sweeter, with a creamy texture. I cast off my hesitation and put the spoon to my mouth The batter blanketed the surface of my tongue, cool and gentle like an unexpected breeze, then melted to the sides of my mouth where the sweetness caused my cheeks to tingle and the back of my mind to quake. I had tasted honey before, straight from the bees, and I had savored the honey cakes made by the village women back in Skebreen to celebrate Samhain before the onset of winter. No matter that I could not remember the last time my tongue had known such pleasure; this was something different. My eyes popped wide and I looked to Timothee, whose lips were parted, awaiting my response.

"More?"he asked.

I nodded vigorously. Laughter burst from his throat and he grabbed the spoon away. "That's my leetle bird! Of course there will be more, but you must wait. The waiting makes eet even more delightful, and the taste when cooked cannot be surpassed."

"But what is it? Why do you put it in this hoop?"

"In this way eet ees done in France, my dear. For the king himself. This ees but a small hoop. Cakes for the king are prepared larger and with such splendor I dare not even imagine. When he gathers his courtiers around and they are in his favor, he serves them such delights decorated with thick sugar confection and fruits and flowers, sometimes even jewels to color the presentation and feed the eye. From such splendor a king gets some of his power, my dear. Wait, and you shall be richly rewarded."

I licked my lips and returned to my work just as Timothee and Cook returned to their banter. But my work was quickly done, and though there were other tasks that wanted doing, I resisted leaving the kitchen with all its heat and tantalizing scents. Of all tasks, waiting was most difficult.

At suppertime, the master arrived at his dining table with a dark cast to his cheeks and a frown tugging his lips. He smelled of liquor, though he'd come in from the fields less than an hour before. Anxious for his arrival, I had set the table with the best silver instead of pewter, and though a bright dusk lingered, I lit extra candles on the sideboard to make the room more cheerful. Timothee hummed in the kitchen, putting his finishing touches on the cake, and Cook tended to her roasted chicken that smelled so delicious it caused my stomach to grumble and cramp.

For his birthday there should have been guests to dine, friends to share his cake and rum, but none arrived and none were expected. More frequently the master dined alone. I poured his wine. He emptied the glass and I poured again. He ate in silence, glancing out the window to the twilight, away from the flickering candles. Timothee and Cook watched from the kitchen as he picked at his food and then pushed his plate away.

Cook shook her head, clicking her tongue. "A sad state, that is."

Timothee straightened. "Sir," he said, approaching the master's table.

The master turned. "Timothee. You are not at your cabin with your books. Is something wrong?"

"Quite the opposite, sir. Do you not remember that today ees your birthday?"

The master turned back to the window. "Tell Cook the chicken was delightful."

Timothee gestured for Cook to bring the cake. "Eet ought not be ignored, sir, when there ees much to celebrate. The harvest, at the very least, and your own good health. Ees eet not worthy of acknowledgment?"

"As you say, Timothee."

Cook bustled in with all the energy of a strong gust of wind and planted the platter before him with a flourish. "There ye be, sir! I'd say ye've got a cake alone worth celebratin'!"

The cake was round as a wagon wheel, covered from top to bottom with a pale yellow confection of pure sugar and butter, flavored with juice. On top were thin slices of mango and papaya arranged like the spokes of a wheel, and at the center the bright pink blossoms of bougainvillea. It was the most beautiful thing I had ever seen. I could scarcely imagine cutting it open to eat it, and yet I could hardly wait.

As the master eyed the cake, a half-smile came to his lips. He turned the platter around that he might see the cake from all sides. Cook brought in a large knife and a small plate. "Shall I serve you, sir?" She beamed.

"No, wait!" I blurted. All eyes turned to me, and I found myself mumbling out my explanation. "It…it's just that me Da always allowed there be a wish on one's birthday. Shouldn't we start with that?"

"Oh, yes!" Cook affirmed.

The master looked at me, and the smile seemed to falter; then he took a quick breath and recovered it. "Well, let's see now. I could wish for a fine harvest, but we've had it, have we not? I could wish for health, but as you say, Timothee, we're all back about our business. I would wish for great goods and surprises to come on the next ship. But then little comes that we don't fiercely demand months in advance. What then? I can think of nothing else."

Cook stood with the knife in her hand trembling slightly, as she was unsure of which way to turn. Timothee responded.

"Well, sir, why don't you think on eet. Cook will serve the cake, and suddenly an inspiration will come."

The master looked away as Cook began, but I watched her knife sink deeply into the butter-colored icing, disappearing into the soft depths and coming out again, pushing tiny bunches of crumbs to the surface. With the second cut she lifted a wedge and settled it upright on the plate so that the master could see the bits of fruit within that matched what lay on top.

The delicate flowers beckoned. Had it been presented to me, I would have sunk my spoon into it without a second breath. But the master hesitated. He stared at the cake, glancing up at Timothee, then at Cook, and finally at me. The half-smile was gone. He took a bite of cake. For the briefest instant, like the light of a shooting star, I saw a boyish glow cross his face and quickly fade.

"It is remarkable, Timothee. As fine as any cake King Louis eats today, I'd wager, and finer than I deserve. Thank you."

"Eet ees only my pleasure, sir." Timothee replied.

Cook beamed. "I'll bring ye some port, sir." She disappeared into the kitchen.

Then, without taking another bite, the master pushed his plate away. He reared his head back, and his cheeks turned ruddy. When he leaned forward again, his eyes were bright and fierce, his cheeks dark.

"Would that the day of my birth were truly worth celebrating, Timothee. My mother would have said so, but she left me far too soon. And my father? His interests were varied, were they not? And I've spent most of my years despising him for who he was, who he was not, and the things he did that appalled me. Today it stands without dispute that I have failed completely in that thing I'd hoped to achieve above all others: To be nothing like him. I am, in fact, his mirror image in face and in deed."

"Sir? Why would you say..."

"Because I have failed, Timothee! A fine man is dead because I failed to intervene quickly and with the right force. Sharavogue does not thrive but needs investment I am not able to make, and so we struggle on each day. I've no wife and no son to carry on from what little I have built upon my father's dream." He looked up at me and then quickly away. "And when I am alone and ache for...no, lust for something even within my reach, I cannot give what..."

We heard a soft tapping, and Nessa was at the dining room door, holding a package draped with fresh cut flowers, a birthday gift for the master. She stepped forward, but the master glared at her and stood, the backs of his legs forcing his chair to screech on the floorboards. Nessa stopped.

"And when I lust," the master said too loudly, "I am like my father most of all. The single difference is in his ability to conceive, so that I am even less a man than he!"

He picked up the plate of cake Cook had served him and shattered it against the wall, then stared at each of us as if daring us to speak a word, though my hand was firmly across my mouth. Then, as if this act was not enough to relieve his fury, he lifted the entire cake Timothee had prepared for him and hurled it squarely against the wall. In pieces it fell—first the wooden platter, slamming to the floor and then bouncing and clattering as it settled; the cake's top stuck to the wall; the bottom slipped away and broke into chunks as it fell. Then the top began to slide and crumble and drop away until what remained on the wall were the crushed petals of pink flowers smeared among the yellow icing and golden crumbs.

The master stood before me. "Wishes are what you want? Wishes consume you and bear no fruit. I'll tell you my wish," he said harshly. "That a great storm arises from the sea and washes this island clean away. The world will be far better for it!"

He moved toward Nessa. She dropped her gift and ran from the house. The master followed behind her but climbed the stairs to his chambers. We listened for it and were rewarded with the solid whump of his slamming door.

"Well!" Cook declared. "His bloody cake can rot where it lay, fer all I care." Her cheeks blazed and her eyes glistened. She turned on her heel and left the house.

The room went ghastly quiet then, as if a great spirit had touched its lips to the window and withdrawn all the air. I stared into Timothee's eyes, where tears had begun to well. He wiped them with the heels of his hands. "I suppose we must clean this up. Before the ants come for eet."

I crawled on my hands and knees to where the cake lay in pieces, reached up to the wall and dug a finger into the icing, then put it between my lips. It melted on my tongue until all my mouth was watering with pleasure, conjuring something long ago forgotten, a sensation of honeyed milk droplets tasted from my mother's fingertips, though I could not be sure if such a thing ever happened. "It is delicious."

Timothee smiled sadly. He went to the sideboard and withdrew two silver forks, reserved only for the most special guests. He handed one to me, sat down beside me on the floor, and we began to eat. I speared a chunk of cake heavy with icing and fruit and popped it into my mouth. The cake was so delicate it melded with the icing and gave it substance, so that the pleasure lasted longer and settled into my belly like a magic elixir. We delighted in it, though the master now raged overhead.

"Timothee" I sat back, licking my fork. "What did the master mean, about lust? Is he in love with Nessa?"

He snorted and shook his head. "Eet's not that, my dear. Eet ees of much greater history than that. Nessa was born on this plantation before old Master Wingfield passed away. Her mother died in childbirth, and Badu took her in. Nessa ees the master's half-sister."

A cold realization washed over me, and a number of things tumbled into place. The master's father had sired Nessa with an African slave woman, and the master resented her deeply. "That's why he never named her," I said. "He was angry that she was born. And it's why he tried to drown her all those years ago. It's why she is always here but never speaks, as if she wants to be near but does not wish to offend him by her existence. She must fear him, and yet I know she adores him."

"He's not a bad man, Elvy. You know that. He's tormented, and far too often engages his demons."

"Why does he not free himself, then? He has the power. He could simply leave."

Timothee slowly selected a particular chunk of cake, larger than most and abundant with icing. He held it just near his lips. "One day the master will cast out his demons, and he will make this plantation very profitable, a great place from which all other planters will learn. He ees so close to eet he does not see, but I know eet, and een his heart he knows as well. Some men fear their own success, so eet may be he discounts it. But when it is revealed, then the other planters who barely survive on their low-grade tobacco will see him as a hero, and they will come to him. They will make their investments een sugar as others have done on Barbados and Saint Christopher. This entire island will prosper, with Tempest Wingfield leading the way. Eet seems that every great deed requires struggle and doubt."

I returned to my cake, pondering. The master and Nessa were a family. Sharavogue belonged to them. One day it would be a great plantation for all the island to see. My belly was nearly full, and yet I ate. "King Louis eats such things?"

"He does. Daily. I have eet on the best authority and was sent the recipe by my dear cousin who served the king at court. Louis was but four years old when he inherited the crown. Now he ees very close to your own age."

Timothee stuck a stout index finger into a large glob of icing that remained on the wall, then pointed at me with the laden appendage. I pressed my finger against the same spot and came away with an equally inviting morsel. We savored them together, and I closed my eyes for an instant just to carve the experience into my memory forever. My heart swelled and I felt my own tears begin to rise.

"You know what, Timothee? Something just happened."

"Ah. And what ees that?"

"I've remembered who I am."

"Well, thanks be to God and all his angels! Tell me."

I shrugged, savoring the last bit of icing lingering on my lips. "I am your student, Timothee. Will you teach me something?"

"I am your servant, mademoiselle."

26

What Swords Could Never Slay

Without a sign his sword the brave man draws,
And asks no omen but his country's cause.

~ Alexander Pope, English poet

I met Timothee at the rum house while the master still slept off his rages from the night before. Timothee sat alone in the morning mist, blunting the tip of a cane stalk longer than my arm. He wrapped cane trash around the opposite end, then cut a length from a branch and secured it crossways to the cane. "This," he said, offering me his creation, "ees your sword."

I was at once disappointed. "We cannot use a true sword? The master has a..."

"I am well aware of all things the master has. And, of course, you see, eet ees a hanging offense to..."

"I see, yes." I glanced up at the big house, the dew still glistening on the rooftop, the windows glaring down blankly. I wished the master had kept his usual routine and gone early to town or to the field. Then I might have crept into his bedchamber and touched that sword again that hung on his wall. The stalk of cane did not convey the same feeling that had come from the sword. I longed to feel such power again.

"Hold eet thusly." Timothee positioned my right hand. "This crosspiece ees called the quillons, meant to protect your hand. Bring your forefinger just so, across the top of the quillons and around to secure your hold. There now. Stand up straight, your shoulders back, your stomach pulled toward the spine."

He looked me over, shaking his head. "Hardly the figure of a fencing master, but since you are royalty and have a duty assigned by St. Brendan himself, I will teach you what I can."

I tightened my fingers around the cane and tried to quell my smile. I leapt across the yard, thrust high to pierce the neck of a giant, and jabbed low to dispatch any who might attack me from the bush. Pleased with myself, I returned to him, my cheeks hot with exertion and limbs tingling with excitement.

"There now, Timothee. Do you see how my abilities are coming to me just as the instinct to hunt comes to the wolf? My lessons will be easy."

"*Ah!* Narcissus spies himself een the water and ees pleased. On the contrary, leetle bird. I see many lessons more to be taught than I first had anticipated. The first, as always with you, humility. Now, return the sword to me and we'll begin."

Timothee cradled the makeshift sword across his palms reverently, as if offering up a gift. "Your body ees your castle. The sword ees your army, your defense and your offense, your honor and your power. Stand solidly, your knees like those of a jackal, ready at all times to spring. Feel the center of your body, the straight line from your crown, down to your heart, and then along your breastbone to your gut. Feel the strength een your thighs and your feet touching the ground. Een this you find your balance. Without eet your castle will topple. Like the elephant of the Orient, feet as solid as trees, balancing the castle perfectly on eets back, advancing fearlessly. This ees your first stance.

"Next, hold out your hands." He placed the makeshift sword in my palms and adjusted them until they reached straight out from my shoulders. "There now. Slowly bend your knees as eef to sit een a chair."

I did so easily and then straightened up again.

"Fine, leetle bird. Now continue."

"Continue?"

"As before. Yes. Until I say to stop."

I continued holding out the sword and squating until my arms trembled with exhaustion and my knees ached. Sweat rolled from my scalp down the sides of my face and neck. I welcomed a cool breeze from the west, where a dark squall raged on the horizon. "Shall we expect a storm, Timothee?" He glanced out to sea. I paused my torturous exercise the instant he turned his head.

He looked west, then back toward the east. "I believe the squall ees far enough out that eet will pass us by, unless the master's birthday wish ees to be granted. Then, eet will gather strength and turn at the last instant to destroy us. Some ships een eets path seek safe harbor. Two approach. I can just define the outlines of their sails."

I dropped the cane sword. "I cannot do it a moment longer, Timothee!"

He shook his head again. "What kind of queen will you be, who whines at the first sign of pain? You've suffered worse, have you not?"

"I have," I said, not wishing to remember. I continued, feeling the argument of muscles.

"Here. Some lunges now. I will help you." Timothee stood beside me and took up the same stance; then as we stepped and stretched forward, he began to sing. "*Ay-nee-nee, ay-nee-nee…*"

I laughed. "Timothee! What are you doing? You hate that…"

"Sing! Eet helps to distract you from the pain."

"Ay-nee-nee, ay-nee-nee," I began. But before we reached the second verse, Timothee stopped, gazing toward the horizon and the ships moving fast in favorable wind, bearing down on our tiny island.

"One of them ees Portuguese," he said. "I have not seen such a ship here for some time. What news do they bring? I wonder, but my gut warns me to beware."

By afternoon a cold wind swept the island like a dragon's tail, pushing the ships into harbor. For three days a gale shook the tree limbs and howled about the windows, lusting for a prey huddled just out of reach. Had the main storm hit the island, the master's wish would have been at hand, but its sharpest teeth fed best on the blood-warm waters at sea. Destruction would take another form entirely.

Days after the storm had passed, as the master finished his breakfast, a messenger boy brought a letter and then disappeared quickly down the hill back toward town. I delivered the missive, wondering what news it held. The master gazed out the window absently, unsealing the page with one hand. At the reading, Cook and I watched his face lose color and his body shudder. "Fever spreads in Plymouth," he told us. "A Portuguese sailor has died. Many have shuttered their homes against his disease yet it finds new victims daily."

Cook held her breath, as did I, and she spoke for us both. "Is it the plague, sir?"

He turned to us, eyes blazing. "I do not know. Elvy, go to Badu. Tell her she is not to go. I cannot spare her from the plantation, and if she were to take ill I..." He wiped the corners of his mouth with the linen napkin and set it on the table's edge, but it fluttered to the floor. "Tell her she must not go."

I looked at the letter on the table, and master's hand resting upon it. Such a small thing to bear news of such weight. Of course! If Badu was to go to Plymouth, who would care for the sick at Sharavogue? Worse still, what if Badu was to sicken? Who would care for Badu? The master was wise to think of her first. I hurried out the kitchen door and down the hill to Badu's cabin.

The door was open when I approached, and sunlight sliced between the boards that made her walls, casting yellow lines across her floor. I peered inside, but she was not there. Nessa stood in a corner, surrounded by dark twigs and cuttings, and jars in disarray. She turned slowly toward me, the rims of her eyes glistening.

I took a deep breath. "The master said Badu must not go." I spoke, but my words held no strength.

"She must not," Nessa whispered.

Badu did not return that night, or the next. The master insisted no one should go after her until he heard that the fever had run its course. When a third night passed and she did not return, the master summoned his wagon before breakfast and drove it down the mountain alone. It was dusk before he returned. We heard the sounds we had listened for the entire day, the calling of the birds and the crush of rock beneath wooden wheels.

Timothee took the reins and helped the master step down. Nessa and I ran to the back of the wagon and the bundle of coverings that cradled Badu. Her face glistened. Her lips were bluish gray. The fever held her in its grasp, already reducing her size and strength.

"Badu!" I cried. "This cannot be!"

The master's voice was harsh. "I found her in one of the houses, nursing a kitchen slave. We'll carry her to the downstairs chamber, Timothee." And to Nessa and me he shouted. "Bring water, clean blankets. Have Cook prepare that bush concoction she gives to others. Hurry. We must break this fever at once."

Nessa and I ran like wild children to fetch anything that might help. Nessa brought all sorts of herbs from Badu's house, her garden, and the forest behind: cat's claw and buttercup for colds, gum bush leaves and pom cooly seeds to cool and purify the blood, bat root for the ague, and elder leaves to calm and relax. She carried them to Cook, and together they began to brew a bush tea. I bathed Badu's face and neck with rags soaked in cool water. Timothee gave her sweet rum. The master paced the floor outside her door and on the boards above us that creaked and protested every step.

At dawn the following morning, I held Badu's hand as she slept. It was hot and damp with sweat, the skin tough, the fingers still plump; but bones had begun to show, and the knuckles were larger than I had remembered, the long fingers beginning to take an unnatural curve and the fingertips cracked with wear. Nessa curled and slumbered at Badu's feet, though the master had demanded we both stay away. As I watched Badu's gentle breathing, she squeezed my hand. I looked into her eyes, red rimmed and dark with pain, but still the kind eyes I had come to love. She smiled weakly. I started to pull away.

"I'll get the master," I whispered.

But Badu held tightly to my hand and shook her head.

"Then I must wake Nessa."

Badu squeezed my hand again, and weak though she was, she pulled me to her. I leaned close to her lips. "What is it, Badu?"

She stared into my eyes as if to bore a hollow in my mind in which to store her words. "In fever, times come when de veil fall away and I see de ages. I see you now, child. You are searching, as he searches. De two must meet." She coughed shallowly. Nessa stirred but did not wake, and Badu continued. "I see de spirits dat carry you. You will succeed if you heed dem."

"Badu, is it so important when you are sick? You must..."

Badu shook her head weakly and squeezed my hand with greater force. I chastised myself for arguing with her when she had so little strength.

"I do not know how to hear them, Badu. What must I do?"

"What you wish to become, you are. What you seek is within your grasp. When you go, press against your breast dat which brought you here." Badu started to rise, her eyes fierce. "You must do dis. Remember!"

"Badu, please." I held her down. "All right, I promise I will remember. If you will rest, I promise I will," though I had no thought of what I agreed to do. My cheeks grew hot and tears spilled. "Badu, you are very sick, and yet you think about me and about so many others. Please, how can I help you?"

Badu smiled peacefully and settled into her pillow. "Wake Nessa now."

I reached down and shook Nessa's shoulder gently. She pressed her hand against mine and sat up. She looked into Badu's eyes, and they gazed at each other for a time, communicating without words in a language I would never know. Then Nessa kissed Badu's cheek and nodded.

"Go," Badu told me. "See to de others in de slave village. Many are sick. Some will die. Nessa is here to care for me. Go. Take de bush brew. Hold dere hands as you have held mine. Do not fear de fever. Give dem comfort."

I nodded and hurried to Cook's kitchen, where the smells were strange and pungent. She looked as if she had a fever herself, the sweat dripping from her chin as she boiled a huge pot of Nessa's herbal brew and strained the brown juice through cloth into calabash gourds waiting on the table. I knew then this was not the first time Sharavogue had fought disease, and I stepped in to help Cook where I might not impede her organized process.

We loaded a yoke with as many gourds as my shoulders could carry, and I balanced them, still steaming, carefully down the hill toward the slave village. They clattered and sloshed with each step. A crow dived toward my head and swooped away on a sharp arc. The day's sun had never brightened to gold but left its reflections pale gray and shrouded its face with haze as if it cared not to look at the troubles our little island now faced.

The slave village was silent as a churchyard save for the buzz of an insect on the wind. I passed no one, and it occurred to me that in Plymouth they might have sealed people in their homes and painted their doors as they would for a plague. But this was not plague, and in this little village the residents had no doors except for makeshift coverings woven from sticks and palm, cane trash and calalu leaves.

Then I heard a deep, phlegmy cough and a clearing throat as fierce as a wolf's growl. My gut warned me to run as any child would run from the sound of a wolf in the forest, but the sound came from the largest hut. Maestro's hut. And inside, his two wives cowered against the far wall, one of them cradling an infant to her breast. I went first to the infant, but its dark skin was cool as it suckled, and it looked healthy and well tended, its high forehead smooth and shining.

The sight of Maestro on his pallet curled into a shivering ball chased away my own wolves, and I rushed to him with my largest gourd; but then I knew it would not be enough. Without thinking, I turned to the wife who had no child. "Run to the big house. Bring rum, blankets, and clean rags, as many as you can carry. Tell Cook I sent you. Now go!"

She bolted from the hut, and the other carried the infant outside, leaving me alone with Maestro. I rolled him onto his back and managed to raise his head enough to allow him to drink some of the bush brew. It streamed down his chin as dark as blood, but he swallowed. I held his hand, spotted pink with burns, and pressed myself against his side to afford a measure of warmth. Any other time he might have swatted me away like a fly, but he was sick past the point of knowing or caring.

Thanks be to St. Brendan the woman was swift and Cook generous. I wiped Maestro's head and chest with the rags and covered him with a blanket, then mixed a hefty dose of rum with his bush brew and forced him to drink. He looked at me gratefully. I stayed with him a while longer, until the shivering eased and he slept.

At the next hut I was less fortunate. A gang worker lay on his back, his eyes open and pestered by flies. No one cared for him, no one comforted him. No brew would ease his suffering now. I waved the flies away and covered his face with a rag. It could have been me, had not Badu and Nessa come to save me. The thought drove me on to the next hut and the next, holding the hands of the ones who might yet live and saying a prayer for those beyond saving. By the end of the day, I had found four dead, six hanging on to life by the fragile shreds of a blanket, and a dozen more hiding in their huts from the fever's relentless march.

Mr. Drax himself was not to be found, and in the yard the cut cane and cane juice were spoiling, the boiling house fires growing cold. The curved bills of the field gangs were at rest, and the uncut cane reveled and swayed in a knowing wind.

27

A Fever's Toll

Intermitting fevers of all kinds, were very epidemic all over the islands when I was there, so that the third part of mankind were taken ill of them, from children at the breast to old aged people.

~ Hans Sloane, 1707

In the frightful days that followed, Nessa was at Badu's bedside day and night, sometimes chanting as the dark candle flickered, sometimes humming softly as a mother to an infant, sometimes bathing her in scented water and crowning her head with fragrant flowers, sometimes only weeping oily tears at her breast. Twice she bade me to help her collect vines and colored stones to place beneath Badu's bed, to distract the jealous spirits and keep them away. When Badu slept so deeply she would not wake, we sprinkled black sand in a thick forbidding line around her bed.

"If Jombee come, he count every grain of sand before he take her," Nessa whispered. "He count and he count."

The fever broke for a time so that our shoulders settled down and we breathed the cooler air, and then it returned like a raging fire so that our muscles coiled and braced and we grasped desperately at any remedy we could conspire. And then, when a white cloak of fetid heat settled over the island, Badu began to improve. She opened her eyes. Nessa brought fresh pillows that raised her higher in the bed. She peered at us with pink-rimmed eyes and sipped Cook's steaming broth. With a single faint word to Nessa she asked after the others in the village. Nessa squeezed my hand, and we prayed that this time the fever had passed from her entirely.

In the afternoons while Nessa and Badu slept, I carried more bush brew and broth to the slave village. The sickness continued on its heartless path, and while I rejoiced to see Maestro rise weakly from his bed, two little children in the next hut had died, their bodies shrouded in tattered linens, awaiting the customary rituals that Badu could not bring. The master searched for help and medicines in Plymouth, but none could be had, and since the Portuguese ship had come and gone, no other merchant ship's sails pierced our horizon bringing needed supplies.

I was tired but could not sleep. When darkness came I took my cane sword and practiced in the yard behind the big house. I imagined the fever was a dragon, and over and over I cut off its head and disemboweled it, and yet it reassembled to fight again. I fought until I could raise my arms no more, and then slept sitting up, resting my head on Cook's kitchen table. In the dawn's gray light, Cook shook my shoulder and whispered in my ear.

"Rise, child. Time to work." I looked into her eyes and she smiled. "Badu wishes to eat."

I wanted to run to Badu, but Cook caught my arm. "Slow yerself; there's a tray needs carryin'! Give her plenty and let her eat what she wants; don't force or she'll not be holdin' it down. There's broth, bread, a porridge, and a cup o' watered wine. And this." She added a bowl of sliced fruits to the tray. "Nessa's favorites."

Nessa was working a wide-toothed wooden comb through the ends of Badu's hair when I set the tray on the bed. Badu's face had lost its pain; her cheeks were glowing like silver in the pale light, her eyes were bright and filled with peace. She nodded, reaching for the wine.

"Nessa has much to do dis day. Your work be not done either, child." Her voice trickled like water over smooth stone.

"What can I do for you, Badu?"

"Not for me. See to de master."

"The master has gone to town. He..."

"De master be at de boilin' house, thinkin' he save de harvest. Go."

I shook my head. How could she know such things? But I dared not question that she did. I ran through the big front doors and down the hill to the boiling house. In the yard two slaves worked slowly, feeding fresh-cut cane from a small pile into the press to squeeze out what juice they could. It trickled to the cistern, and there Timothee checked it and gathered up a bucket half-full. He lifted his face to me and I saw his sunken eyes, his cheeks white as goat's milk and stubble of beard darkening his jaw.

"Best not go een, leetle bird. I cannot get the master to..."

I froze for an instant, as if icy water splashed my face. I suppose I had not believed Badu, but now I realized it was true—the master was trying to save the harvest himself. I stepped inside to see his bare, sweating back, much narrower than Maestro's but every bit as muscled, stirring and ladling a boiling pot as one small boy fed the fire below with dry, black sticks. But for the two of them the boiling house was empty, and they toiled in a process that normally required a team of several men in constant motion.

"Master Wingfield?"

He turned slowly. Nothing could have prepared me for what I saw. With the white steam roiling around him, his rich dark hair plastered his skull like black tar. Sweat poured from his jaw and chest, and veins pulsed at his neck like purple vines trying to strangle him. His eyes were black and fierce at their core, and yet his face held no color and no thickness of skin against bone. It was a death mask with burning cinder eyes and a bare-toothed grimace of hysteria and agony.

I ran to him, and Timothee came behind me. I touched his arm and knew at once it was not the steam's heat that gripped him. It was the fever.

"Master!" I shouted. "You must..."

"Leave me!" He roared with such monstrous fury Timothee and I stepped back and the boy ran from the house in terror; but then something crossed his face that robbed the spark from those cinder eyes. The ladle fell from his hand, and his knees gave way. His eyes rolled back, and he fell to the floor before us.

"Take his legs!" Timothee cried. He lifted the master's shoulders, heaved him up and carried him as best we could to the big house, and up the stairs to his chambers. By the time we reached his bed, the master's skin had begun to cool, and then he began to shiver, his lips turning the same bluish gray I had first seen on Badu. Cook ran in behind us.

"No! Not the master. If he dies we'll all be lost!" she bellowed.

"Cook!" I halted her. "The bush brew. Bring it."

"And warm watered rum with honey. He likes that." Timothee said.

"And stones. We'll heat some stones by the fire to warm his bed."

"I'll get them," Timothee said. "Sit with him here, and eef he tries to rise..."

"I'll not allow it." I declared.

Timothee looked down sadly at the master's trembling form. "Good, my lady. May God be praised eef the powers of a princess can shield us from such disaster."

I took the master's hand in mine. If he was aware of it he did not care, and when he quaked with the fever, he squeezed my knuckles with the force that might come from a drowning man being pulled from a raging sea. He held fast, my master, and when Timothee came with warmed stones, I shoved them among the bedclothes with haste, lest the chills find a vulnerability and surge into that rare breach.

Timothee touched my shoulder tenderly, and I could not hold out longer, as if his gesture released a gate latch allowing hot tears and mangled cries to spill forth. My breath squeezed from my lungs and then dragged back in again through clenched throat and strained chords.

Through the night and next day I would not leave the master, though Timothee and Cook swore to stand my vigil. We swaddled him like a babe as we rolled him to one side and then the other to change his soaking bedclothes. His eyes barely fluttered at the disturbance, his lips remained slack. The fever waxed and waned, chilled and seared the master with such a fury I thought his mind could not withstand it, let alone his tortured body. And yet his breathing came and went in shallow gasps and deep, anguished moans.

On the third morning Cook demanded that I eat. "Ye canna save the master if ye're dead yerself. Now it matters not to me if ye taste it, just shovel it in and swallow!" She handed me a bowl of gruel, but the scent and the look of it put my belly into a spin, and then my gut as well. A sweat popped out on my brow and there was nothing for it. I left Cook in the master's chamber as I ran for the privy outside.

"It'll be nothin' but dry heaves!" Cook hollered after me.

And right she was, as my body tried to void but could do no more than cramp and twist, punishing me for neglect. When the turmoil eased a bit, I sat on the stone wall near the woodshed, even the hot air feeling cool against my sweating scalp. A rain squall played toward us on the horizon, but still no ships approached. How I had hated being aboard the *Jackdaw* so long ago, and how strange that now my heart would leap at the sight of it and I would gladly throw myself on the captain's mercy to take me back home again. I was tired of heat, tired of the seasons that were all one on this jagged little island, and tired of the constant effort required just to keep the rain, the wind, and the forest from reclaiming every inch of ground. I was tired of the planters and their games of politics that shattered people's lives and treated workers like rubbish, tired of the insects that nagged and stung me night and day, tired of the storms and sicknesses and struggle, always struggle, and for what? What did my struggle bring me? Did it yet get me one step closer to my home or my destiny? I was sick and tired and had nothing to show for my years of toil in this place. And now there was nothing but sickness, fever, and death wherever I turned. I'd have fared better if it had been me over the ship's rail as we reached Barbados instead of Kade. My hands trembled as I remembered that, my crime, and I remained until I could hold them steady before I chanced again the stairs to the master's chamber.

At the top of the stairs Cook stood in the chamber doorway, shadows falling dark about her skirts and her thick, toughened fingers pressed against her lips. A shudder raced up my back and I bounded up the rest of the steps and into the room. My throat caught on the still air, and in the dim light the bedclothes looked gray and flattened. The master had rolled from his side onto his back. His hair fell across the pillow, black and sweat-soaked. His lips were blue, his eyes slits of white, and I saw no rise or fall from that noble, bristled chest.

"Timothee!" I screamed with every force I could muster, my dry throat searing. I scrambled down the stairs and found him coming toward me. My face was enough to inform him, and he pushed past me, thundering up the stairs; and then I ran to the downstairs chamber for Badu. Only she had the powers to save him now if there was any chance at all. I stopped short when I reached the open doorway to her room.

Against the fading light of day, the heavy shutters were closed. Bars of pale light came through the slats to mark the floor. A candle burned steadily in each corner of the room, one at the head of the bed, another at the foot, causing figures like spirits to dance and flicker above Badu, who lay silent and uncovered on the bed, her legs straight and bare, her hands crossed neatly over her ribs, her cheeks flaccid, her face serene. The rich scent of honey mingled with jasmine and wild hyacinth. Nessa knelt on the floor, a pan of water beside her, a towel in her hand. A cry escaped my lips, and Nessa held up her hand to stop me.

My voice caught. My eyes filled. "Nessa, she was recovering..."

"No. She was not." Nessa turned her head from side to side, her gaze hard and purposeful. "She know death comin'. She prepare. She tell me things to do. She gone already, but she come back jus' to let go. You will see. Her pyre be made ready even now in de hollow."

"But I..." There was nothing I could say then. Nothing that would change anything. I felt as if the blunt end of a club had been rammed into my gut. I feared the fever. I feared my own death. But I did not realize until that moment that I would have died a hundred times rather than face the death of those I'd come to love. Badu was my mother, my protector, my wisdom, and my holy spirit. *She could not die*. And yet she lay, and a fury flared within my veins that I had no strength to tamp.

"Why did you not tell me?" I screamed at Nessa. Anger sparked the bile in my gut, and I screamed yet again from the deepest core of my being. Nessa stared, her own eyes bright with tears.

I have no pride in what I did next. In the very instant I should have run to Badu and cradled her lifeless body in my arms, should have shared my tears with Nessa and stood beside her to prepare Badu's body for the pyre, should have run upstairs to help Timothee and Cook with the body of our master, I ran.

Like a foolish, selfish child, I cast off all the courage I had gained, all the trust Nessa and Cook and Timothee must have had in me, and ran as fast as I could away from the big house, away from the slave village and the boiling house, the carriage house and the rum house, through the front gates of Sharavogue and down the rugged mountain. I ran for a long time before my legs collapsed and I lay, heaped in a ditch until my breath returned. It was only then that I realized where I was going.

I could not face the sickness that was so close to me, hovering like a heavy cloud in that house, ready to consume us all. Without my master, without Badu, there were no pillars to hold up our fragile existence, no strong arms to shield us from the doom that tumbled down like stones from the mountain; and I could not die, could not expire on this forsaken island, a black and empty expanse of sea between me and my rich green earth and the sparkling gray stones that would be my castle, and the people who waited for my return. I had to live. *To live*.

I had no choice now, and but one dark opportunity. I needed the help of one man. However perilous it might be, I was going to the governor. I was going to get myself free of Montserrat at any cost.

28

The Governor's Bargain

'Tis a very strange thing to see in how short a time a Plantation formerly clear'd of Trees and Shrubs, will grow foul...

~ Dr. Hans Sloane, 1687

The dusk had faded to a starry evening by the time I found the governor's plantation. I'd not been there, but everyone on the island knew where it was, and I knew how to reach it by road and partly by crossing the cane fields. A fire burned brightly in a far section of field, filling the air with its eerie orange light and sour, sickening stench of the burning dead.

My gut begged me turn away and drown myself in the sea before approaching this place, but I kept on, refusing to heed. When the house appeared before me, I saw it was not like Sharavogue, sitting high on its stone foundation with window eyes glaring down. The governor's house was low and massive, shaped like a crab with its high center set back from low gabled wings outstretched like eager claws. I looked about warily but saw no one in the yard, so I ran for the double doors in the center, opened wide onto a polished stone floor. One lantern burned on a table in the entry, casting a jaundiced glow over a red cedar carving: a field slave, bent to his work with a long curved bill.

Down the hall, dim light from an open door painted the walls an unsavory ochre. No one was about, no one to stop a slave girl from entering a gentleman's home. All was silent but for the wind whistling its high alarm on the mountainside. I walked softly toward the light and peered into the room.

The governor himself was there, a single candle burning on his desk and a bottle of port before him. I knew it was he from the same wooly brow I had seen before, and the blunt, brutal chin. His chair was turned toward the window, and he seemed to be watching the last strip of silver sink below the horizon into night. The room smelled of cedar, sweat, and putrid smoke, and I thought perhaps wine mingled there also, heavy, sickly sweet, and dark as blood.

The governor looked up and turned to see me standing in his doorway. He lifted a glass and drank the last of its contents. One corner of his lips creased his cheek, not with a smile but with a smug acknowledgment of something long expected.

"Ah, timely providence. Come closer, my dear."

"Your pardon, Governor, sir. Your servants were not..."

"Bah! I have sent them all away until they can come back without their whining and their fever. I've not the time nor patience. Let me to my house alone for a while. And now..."

"Governor, sir, I..."

"Stand here, in the light."

He gestured to the floor just next to him. He was not as I'd seen him before, dressed in his wig and fineries. His head was bare, and his white shirt lay open at his chest. As I rounded the corner of the desk, I realized he wore nothing more, cooling his near-naked body with faint breezes from the window. I started to turn away, but his hand shot out and grabbed my wrist.

"Now, let me see you." He slid the candle across the desk toward me. I swallowed hard and straightened my shoulders.

"Governor, sir. I am Elvy Burke of Skebreen, from your own province of Munster. I came to these islands with a letter of introduction from Lord Condon. It was taken from me so I've nothing to show you, but I ask for your help as my countryman. I'm high born, asking only for return to Ireland to take up my lands as are rightful to me."

"Turn around," the governor ordered. Confused, but not wishing to offend, I turned. He placed a hand on my hip, the heat of his palm searing through my skirt, but I held my tongue and peered over my shoulder.

"Unless you are a Stuart, which would likely only get you beheaded in these times, your level of birth is of no consequence." He spoke slowly, drawling out words like thick molasses. "You are chattel. You belong to

Tempest Wingfield, as well I remember where I first saw you." He smirked and ran his hand down the curve of my hip to my thigh. "It is one of life's little ironies that you, with a body meant only to please a man, should become the property of one whose loins are useless."

Hot blood flared to my cheeks and turned to face him. "I am not..."

"And yet perhaps the providence be yours, my dear. You've found the fellow whose loins are proper functioning and have caused many a maid to squeal in her pleasure." I backed away, but he held fast to my skirt. With his other hand he began to stroke his own privates. "Ah, there now. I'll prepare what you've come for in very little time. Lift your skirt high and give my hound the scent of his prey."

"Governor! I came to ask your help. As an Irishman you must understand. I cannot stay here. Will you see me home?"

He lifted his gaze from my breasts to my eyes and held there, sharp and penetrating. "So, it's a bargain you're after, is it?"

He tightened his hold on my hip, and the reality of what I was doing began to dig its claws deep into my belly. I knew not whether the choice I was making meant honor or defeat, but I had sealed it when I ran away from Sharavogue. If it would keep me alive, and if it would get me home, my maidenhead was but little sacrifice. "It is," I responded.

He dipped his chin, but his gaze held. "A girl who comes on the recommendation of Lord Condon is worthy of special consideration. A merchant ship is due on tomorrow's eventide. Please me well and I'll see you on it." He pulled me toward him, but I pushed back.

"As a passenger, not as a slave."

His grin returned and he nodded once again. "By my letter and seal." He stroked himself with greater vigor, and I could see the flesh growing in his hand. "Now, my little Irish lass, lift...your...skirt."

He released his hold, and the queasiness grew wild within my stomach, but I'd gone too far to back down. "First the letter, and coin for my passage."

He frowned, his thick brow furrowed. "You do not trust the governor of this region? You test me, girl, and I am not a man of patience. If not for the wine that has made me pliant..." He reached for his pen and blotter and pulled paper from his desk drawer. He dipped his pen, and the quick scratchings against the page comforted me a little while my legs threatened to give out beneath me. He finished, blotted the ink, and set it aside to dry. From another drawer he removed a carved wooden box, dipped inside, and showered his desk with a handful of silver coins.

"All that you ask is given. You may proffer the letter to anyone in authority and they will see to you." He pushed away from the desk and hiked his shirt over his rounded belly, fully exposing the dark patch at his crotch and the flesh there that he then began to tease and twist. "The time has come for your part of the bargain, lass. And do not keep me longer from it."

My heart began to flutter wildly in my chest, like a raven in a too-small cage beating frantic wings against the confines. I slowly bent forward to grasp my skirt at the knees, and as I did his hand shot down my bodice to roughly squeeze my breast. With the other hand he grabbed my waist, lifted me off my feet, and carried me squirming toward a chaise beneath an open window. He dropped me there and collapsed on top of me, his sour breath rasping against my temple. I pushed against his shoulders with as much effect as a fly against a boar's hide. He jerked my skirt up over my chest and eagerly probed fat fingers into my sex. He gasped and then pressed his lips against my ear. "An intact maiden! Delightful. I'll get you captain's quarters for this morsel."

In an instant his hand was away and his hips slammed between my legs. I screeched as my thighs were forced apart and I felt a sudden searing thrust, pushing, piercing, grunting in my ear, and then an explosion of pain like liquid fire blasting from my privates through my abdomen and radiating upward to my chest and downward along my aching thighs.

Tears streamed from my eyes and soaked the hair at my temples, and the throbbing began as if a giant hammer beat out a tin bowl from within. I turned my face to the window and saw the distant smoke rising in black vapory fingers, long as knives and swirling with gleeful avarice. I could not breathe with the pain and the weight of him, and then the governor grunted and heaved upward on his elbows.

"Now then, the first act of business is concluded. Let's get to the rest of it."

He stood over me with some effort, grunting and creaking at the knee, and jerked me up by the waist. He turned me away from him and forced me forward over his desk, my cheek slapped against the cold coins that littered the surface. I felt the butt of his leathery hand pressed firmly between my shoulder blades, holding me down. He forced my thighs apart with his knees, gripped my hip bone like a handle and thrust his way inside me, pounding and grunting, his barbed pike skewering my softest flesh, my organs, those smooth tender walls scraped and bruised and torn, those precious parts but rare and bleeding meat to his carrion crow. He pounded on, growling like a wolf, and I heard myself screaming until my breath no longer filled my lungs and I thought to die in fever must be mercy, for I was sure my life did bleed out of me like water. Then with one last excruciating thrust he cried out and fell across my back, sweating and gasping until his breath began to return. He pushed away from me at last, and sat down on the floor at my feet.

He coughed and cleared his throat. I began to push away from the desktop as he reached up for his glass of port and took a drink. He exhaled heavily, pulled his shirt off over his head and used it to wipe his privates. Then, seeing the bloodstains, he heaved the garment into the cold hearth.

He staggered naked back to his chair; returned heavily to where I had first found him and reared back, returning his gaze toward the window.

"Now get out," he said. "Be gone from here."

I raised my head and pushed myself up from the desk with great effort.

I pressed one palm against my aching abdomen and straightened my skirt with the other. "Governor Osborne…"

"You've soiled my chaise. I had it shipped from France, you know, upholstered with fine brocade, and now it is ruined. I'll have to have it burned on the morrow." He opened the center drawer of his desk, scraped the coins into it, and slammed it shut. "Get out, I said."

"Governor, you promised me passage. My thighs and belly still throb and swell with the price I paid for it."

The governor grunted once again and huffed out his breath. "You did not please me. You were inexperienced and soiled my blouse as well. I should hang you for that alone."

"I will not go without my coin! I told you Lord Condon recommended me! You have written the letter you promised. Give me the money for passage and then I will gladly be gone."

"I know of no Lord Condon, and if I did I would give you no passage. You are the property of another planter and not mine to free. Nor would I do so and risk the wrath of my lord Cromwell, by whose pleasure I serve as governor here."

"Cromwell!" My anger burst higher than a wildfire's flame, and my hated enemy's visage burned my eyes. "Cromwell does not rule here!" I shouted.

The governor turned his head slowly, the candlelight flickering in his black eyes and his face without emotion. "Quite right. Cromwell rules England, and the better part of the world. But still, I rule here. And as such, I tire of you. Be gone before I run you through and have you pitched into the fever pyre."

I pushed the letter before him. "Seal it." My guts quaked. I do not know from where such effrontery surfaced. But he pulled the letter to him. He folded it, withdrew the burning candle from its holder, and dripped the wax. He pressed an initial ring into the congealing puddle, then smiled broadly and pushed it toward me.

"Sail on, little slave girl. You have been used and cast aside, as appropriate to your value. Small loss to Tempest Wingfield, I should say. Sail on now, to your doom." He stood, the dark night outlining his naked form, his skin reddened by the candle's glow.

"Thomas!" he hollered gruffly. "My pistol! Fetch my pistol!" From somewhere nearby I heard the quick slap of bare feet crossing the polished floor. Fear washed through me like a rogue wave.

I took up the letter, grabbed my skirts around me, and ran from him. In the entry I saw the cedar carving again, and I grabbed it. I don't know why, except to extract one last thing of value that might be traded for ship passage, or to save the slave figure from its terrible existence in such a wicked household. I bolted for the door and ran until I was well past the plantation's horrid gates.

I stayed on the main road this time, so great was my fury that I believed I might chew the very head from any who might dare confront me, or beat them senseless with the carving. I ran until my lungs burned, and then I ran more. I ran until my feet and legs seared in painful protest, but welcomed the distraction from the throbbing in my womb. I ran on, and this time I knew not my destination, only that it must be as far as I could possibly go from the governor and his stinking, disgusting ways. I ran where the road narrowed to a sloping path and rejoiced that it made my progress so fast my legs could barely keep up. Then the path seemed vaguely familiar, like a vivid dream long forgotten and suddenly recalled, triggered by an unexpected vision. I was there, on the path where I had first seen Badu in her turban, her followers around her, washing the body of the slave woman who had lived in my hut.

There was the lip of the silver pond, lapping gently against the stony bank. I knew at once St. Brendan had sent this to me, to cleanse me of the demon that had possessed me. I set my letter and the carving safely among the branches of a nearby bush and then slipped out of my clothing and into the warm, caressing water. With sand from the bottom I scrubbed my skin nearly raw where he had touched me. I had to remove any trace of his touch, his odor. And when I could wash no more, I cried, and hoped the tears would wash from my mind every vision of the experience. Even if the pond possessed the magical powers Badu said it did, I knew though I might wash away the man's physical presence, a part of me could never be restored. Tears dripped from my chin to make their tiny ripples in the water's surface. I looked up at the sealed letter, glowing in the starlight and out of place among the dark, waxy leaves. I wondered, would it purchase my freedom or instead seal my fate?

As the water held me, I began to feel something else, though I may have imagined it, as if a tender hand played over my crown and warm fingers brushed against my cheek. And I heard a voice, so soft and distant, and yet distinct in my ears. "*Child.*"

Sorrow surged from my chest to my throat; my eyes filled and my nose swelled. Badu. I loved and needed her so, and now she needed me. How selfish and stupid I had been. How cold and thoughtless. I meant to play the game of the masters to get myself free, and instead I had only succeeded in deserting the ones who needed me most, betraying my own being for the hope of something so shadowy and untouchable, so vaporous a dream that with every moment it drifted farther and farther from my grasp. It was complete folly just as the master had warned. Now I wondered if the thing I was meant to do was not across the sea at all, but right here before me, and I had ruined it.

I rose up from the water, reached for my clothes, and saw a faint orange halo among the trees on the hillside just west of Sharavogue—the hollow where Nessa would have taken Badu.

I quickly pressed my feet into my shoes and stuffed my letter against my breast. I grabbed up the carving and cradled it to my ribs. If I hurried I could be with them soon. There might still be some way I could help. But as I ascended the narrow path, I saw two more lights on the far west horizon, glowing an amber made only by fire.

29

Funeral for Badu

For when he flies away he finds the spirits dancing on the mountains and so he learns the spirit songs.

~ Elias, Akawaio shaman of the Carib culture

The darkness settled in firmly, and though I feared I could not find my way without Nessa as my guide, the ceremony for Badu drew slaves and servants from all over the island, and I followed the torches like a trail of fat fireflies that encircled the rim of a faerie ring. This was where I first learned of the strange Jombee dance, and where I first heard Nessa speak. It was where I first felt like a daughter to Badu. And though I had known loss before, this was the first place I felt its wolf tongue lick the casing of my heart.

I descended the narrow trail into the bottom, focusing first on the funeral pyre at the center, where torches on pikes burned fiercely. Constructed of scavenged wood and cane trash, Badu's final bed was cushioned with banana leaves and a thick layer of bright, tender flowers. She lay still upon it, her indigo turban and robe in perfect place, her feet bound in white cloth. Her hands held the tools of her ministry: herbs, vines, white flowers, and even a sprig of cane, bound together in filmy white ribbon.

Women circled the pyre, now and again placing fruits and trinkets into her bed, crying and wailing like the mourners of a keening. Just beyond, a fire burned low, ready to fuel the pyre, its smoke undulating to the heavens in a twisted dance.

On the crude tables before her an array of gourds and trenchers were filled, but not with food for the serving. The only feast this night would be for the flames. There were gourds of black sand from the foothills and baskets of dried maize to be scattered in an unbroken line around the pyre, so that Badu would rest and not return. Colored stones and pottery served as gifts from other slaves who had little to offer. Mountains of sweet fruits filled long trenchers, their juices dripping away, their rich scent mingling with the rum—a golden elixir for the rising spirit, to send her on her way and to share with her attendants should she feel so generous. Candle lanterns flickered, shedding a thin yellow light on the untouched offerings.

Nessa organized each container on the table. She saw me approaching, set down her work, and came to me. My tears burst forth when I looked into her eyes. She took my hands, looked at my skirt, my body, my hair, as if in an instant she understood what I had done. She kissed my brow, and we dropped to our knees together, crying as one until the worst of it had passed. Then she raised me up. A slow drumbeat filled the hollow like the steady thud of a constant heart, and the crowd moved together near the pyre, waiting.

"Badu is ready now." Nessa led me to the pyre and stepped up on a board that allowed her to reach Badu's side. She placed her hand on Badu's forehead and began to speak in that private tongue, soft as a mother whispering her babe to sleep. And when she was done, she placed a number of trinkets at Badu's side, things that had meaning only between them, gifts for the afterlife. She stepped down and nodded to me, my time to say good-bye.

The closer I came to Badu, the more my anxious stomach writhed in protest, but as I reached out and lay my hand on her shoulder, a calm settled over me and warmed me like a peat fire in a hearth. Her face was more beautiful than ever I had seen it, and she seemed to smile as if she had seen what worlds lay before her and was pleased. I bowed my head.

"I have nothing to give, Badu, when you have given me so much. Had I known I could lose you so soon, I would have stayed by your side instead of always seeking my escape. I would have been a better daughter to you. I have been so..." Foolish, I wanted to say, but no more words would come, and I knew even if I spoke them they didn't matter now. As I stepped down I remembered the cedar woodcarving. It seemed fitting that she should have something of value to take on her journey, and that perhaps her funeral fire could free the slave captured in the wood. I placed the carving against her hip and touched her hand one last time. Though it was cold, it was still the firm, powerful hand of my mother. I thought I could hear her voice whispering softly to my heart. *I know you are here where you belong, and I will remember.* A warm breeze caressed my neck, and my pulse surged.

Nessa handed me one of the gourds. I followed her, spreading my fine black sand in a narrow trail around the pyre. Others joined us, and we worked as the torches raged and the candles burned low. When we had finished, Nessa stepped forward one last time to remove Badu's turban. Badu's hair was combed, oiled and gleaming in the raucous firelight.

"I cannot bear to watch her burn, Nessa," I said softly. "I cannot stand to see it, and then tomorrow bury the master as well."

She took my hand and squeezed it. "Badu has asked for dis, and at de end of it her spirit will be free. It be a great gift, freedom. She ask dis of me, but not of you. Go to de master. He be very sick, but he live."

"He lives?" I felt my heart flip as a fish caught, desperately gasping for that bit of air just offered. "But, Nessa, I saw..."

"He lose his breath. Timothee force it back into him. Badu say it be not de master's time, but he mus' fight."

Nessa's eyes were bright and clear. She released my hand. I kissed her and ran for the path that would take me home to Sharavogue, to sit at the bedside of my master. The trudge up the hill was painless, so light was my heart that he lived. At the top of the hollow I looked back over my shoulder where the torches cast giant shadows under the trees. The people had begun to assemble in the center, encircling Badu, their shoulders nearly touching as if they filled the pews of a church. Then two men brought one of the big carved chairs I recognized from its usual place at the master's dining table. Nessa lifted a burning branch and set it to the bottom of Badu's pyre. A flame licked tenuously at the dry wood and then found the papery-light cane trash more to its pleasure. Flames leapt like dogs to their meat, casting bits of debris into the air in frenzied orange sparks and black smoke, and then breaking up like a flock of rust-colored wrens surging quickly through the lattice of wood and fiber beneath Badu's bed.

Nessa sat in the chair facing the burning pyre. Her back was rigid, expectant. And before I turned to leave, I saw two slave women come from behind her to place the indigo turban on her head. I heard the rich cries of joy amidst the sorrowful wailing, and then I climbed above the ridge where the leeward fires painted the skies in titian fury.

30

The Master Rises

So violent and spreading a fire this is, and such a noise it makes, as if two Armies, with a thousand shot of either side, were continually giving fire, every knot of cane giving as great a report as a Pistol.

~ Richard Ligon, 1657

The big house reared back against the coal-black mountain, all but abandoned as the approaching dawn sent faint tendrils against the windowpanes to test the climate of her arrival. The heavy front doors groaned as I passed through. A single candle flickered beside the stairway.

I carried it with me to the top of the stairs, where a sliver of light beckoned beneath the master's chamber door. I pushed through to find him in his bed almost as I had left him. The room smelled of wild herbs, melting wax, and heavy, sour sweat. Though the candlelight was dim, I could see his chest rise and fall, and with greater ease. Timothee stood at the window, hands cupping his elbows within the loose sleeves of his shirt. He turned and offered a weak smile, then an arm to wrap around me in welcome.

"He recovers, but slowly. We must give him all the time he needs. The harvest ees lost now anyway. We'll make the best of what we have when again he ees well."

"You gave him breath, Nessa said."

"I learned a technique long ago, to breathe into someone whose air has been knocked out. I had no idea eet would succeed for the master. A lucky fate has he."

"And a very faithful servant." I touched my palm to the master's head. It still burned with fever, but his face had softened and it seemed a more natural countenance. I left him to his sleep and returned to Timothee's side. From the high viewpoint the fires to the west seemed larger, and thick gray plumes rose like fists to pound away the waning night.

"Timothee, are they fever pyres?"

"No, they are too great. More likely they are planters' houses burning. Could be there ees a slave uprising, but I have heard no rumor of rebellion. I think we are visited by Caribs from St. Christopher. They favor surprise and would have landed their canoes on the leeward side during the night."

"Caribs!" Fear renewed its hold on my chest, though I was exhausted and longed only to sit in silence by my master's bedside. "But why, Timothee? Why would they come now?"

"Who knows what forces drive them. At times they are eager to trade and at times want only to retake their former dominion for the gods. I do not know what fuel ignited them this night, but the fever has spread far and eats at their loved ones too. When a Carib ees sick, his family does not go to him, believing they will only make him sicker. And when the sick die, the survivors strike out. Turning helplessness and grief into rage ees not an uncommon human phenomenon." He shot me a meaningful look, then turned back to the fires. I stiffened.

"Well, they dare not come to Sharavogue! Too many are sick. We cannot move them to the mountain. We have no time to deal with such an invasion."

Timothee smiled and shook his head. "No time? Always the princess, you think the savages should consult your calendar before engineering an attack. What better time to strike than een our weakness?"

I sighed. Of course he was right. "But what could make them go away? What do they want?"

He pondered, as if he'd not thought of it before. "I suppose there was a time when they wanted only their places back unbothered, to hunt and fish and camp. But their hopes for that must have been lost early, eef not when the lands were cleared for cane, at least after the massacre."

"Massacre?"

"Not here, but in the settlement on St. Christopher, years ago. One of few times the English and French had a meeting of the minds, and bloody eet was. Together in the deep of night they crept into the Carib camp and slaughtered the savages as they slept een their hammocks. Men, women, children, all were treated equally under their guns and knives. Were I a Carib, I'd see in my mind the blood of my brothers and dream only of seeing French and English blood in equal measure—or in far greater proportions until all the islands were wiped clean of us."

I felt a tingle at the back of my neck creep forward across my scalp and settle over my brow. I'd heard such talk before, hadn't I? From the Barrys around my father's hearth, and from the men in Skebreen at Aengus's tavern, who dreamed of wiping Ireland clean of the English. And sure it burned deep in my own heart, the vision of Cromwell's life bleeding out of him and me standing over him with my dagger dripping blood. I had been the victim, my father killed and my homeland stolen from beneath me. But now I was among the aggressors, within the big house—the very symbol of the planter's power over the slaves and the natives. And now we were facing those who would eat the very hearts out of us.

Light from the eastern sky grew strong enough to illuminate Timothee's face, always robust and merry, now drawn and shadowed with fatigue.

"Timothee, I am here now and will stay with the master. Cook will be up soon. Go and rest. If the Caribs come this far, we will need your wise head and strong arms."

"Oui, I will go at dawn. I should enjoy a bit of ale, some bread and cheese. Then I will find my sleep at Cook's hearth. But I wish to see the sun's glory before I go, and perchance see it rouse the master."

I left him gazing at the horizon and pulled the side chair closer to the bed, feeling beneath the bedclothes for the stones I had placed there, smooth and solid against the palms of my hands. I would have Cook reheat them if the master's chills returned. For the moment, I watched his breathing and allowed my eyes to scan the curve of his chin, the broad warrior bone of his cheek, and the ridge of his brow so often furrowed. Though he looked very thin, he still retained the presence of a man of great power. I wondered now of that face, once pressed down upon me just as the governor had done a few hours before. I wondered, if the master had been successful that night when I first arrived at Sharavogue, would he have handled me in the same way, and would I still have been able to love him as I did now?

The letter I had stuffed to my breast chafed against my skin, and I pulled it out hesitantly, looking at the mark of the governor's ring pressed crudely into the sealing wax. I ran my finger beneath the folded page to break the seal. The script was slanted and extravagant, with hard edges and heavy, commanding flourishes. They filled me with foreboding and returned the throb to my womb.

"Timothee," I asked softly. "I have learned my letters but still have trouble reading the cursive. Will you read something for me?"

"What could it be?" Timothee stood behind me, lifting the candle from the master's bedside. "Let me see."

He held the letter before his eyes, the candle flickering wildly. He frowned. "Eet says, to the person this letter ees presented, the bearer ees an escaped slave and should be apprehended at once, presented to the authorities and hanged. Eet ees signed by the governor. How did you get this? How did you..." His voice trailed away and he looked into my eyes. I looked away. He dropped the letter to the floor. When I looked at him again his eyes were rimmed with tears.

"You go too far, leetle bird. Of course he has betrayed you. He knows nothing else. May God have mercy on you, restore you, and bring you consolation." He whispered a prayer just as the sun's golden halo pierced the horizon. The master slept on, and I felt Timothee's warm hand on my shoulder. "We will speak more of this in a while. You will call me eef..."

"Yes. Thank you." I listened to the sound of his footsteps growing fainter on the stairs. When I heard them no more I allowed myself to weep.

The morning grew hot as the sun climbed higher. The master moved his head and muttered, as if attempting to shout orders at someone, though his voice remained too weak. I went to the window hoping for cooler air and saw Mr. Drax alone in a field just below the house, dressed in his long tunic. He leaned his staff against his hip and removed his broad-brimmed hat, lifting his face to the heavens. He was praying as I had seen him do so often, just before he beat a slave with his whip. In that he served the master, I knew I had to accept him, but I knew as well I would always despise him.

He dipped his chin and replaced his hat, then gripped his staff firmly beside him as he surveyed the field. Was he deciding the contents of the workday, or contemplating the team he would assemble? Or was he merely awaiting instructions from his god? Suddenly he straightened, his shoulders reared back. He dropped to his knees, his hat fell to the ground behind him and then, as if a hand gently drew him down, fell on his side.

For a second I simply stared. He is dead, I thought, and how grand would the changes be that would come in his absence. A part of me wanted to stay silent, to make sure whatever had caused his fall would fully succeed, and then my silence was overridden by a high, primal scream out of the depths of my gut. I shouted at the slaves I saw coming up from the village; then I heard other screams from the yard. Behind me the master raised up from his pillow.

"What is it?" His voice was gruff with phlegm.

"Mr. Drax has fallen." I went to the bedside, but already the master was attempting to rise. "No. Please, Master, you must stay. Timothee will see to him. Please do not rise!"

He pushed me away with more force than I expected and started up anyway, but then he swooned, the blood rushing to his head and making him collapse, cough and gasp for air. "Leave me. Go to the window and be my eyes. What has happened?"

I grasped the windowsill and looked to the field. "No one has reached Mr. Drax yet, but slaves from the A-gang are running toward him. Some of the African slaves are coming up from the village, a band of a dozen or more, men and women among them. They carry some kind of bundle, but they are moving in such a tight group I cannot see what it is. They move swiftly, sir, at a trot, as if of one animal. They are nearing the front of the house now. I'll go down to them," I said.

"No. We do not know what other dangers are about. Let me see what they carry." He pushed himself up from his pillows and swung a leg down from the bed until his toes brushed the floor. He had no balance and began to fall forward even before his other leg came down. I caught him before he toppled.

"You must stay in bed..."

But he waved me off with a growl and planted both feet solidly, then pushed against my shoulders to stand. He swayed on his feet, and then leaned an arm across my shoulder. Together we walked together to the window. His scent was so strong I wondered did he sweat his very life's blood. Sweat beaded on his forehead and above his lip, and I felt his fevered heat against my side. Yet he moved on until we reached the window and looked down upon the slave band in the yard and two men from the field approaching with Mr. Drax. Timothee stood on the bricks below, and then Nessa joined him, her turban gone and her hair free about her face. The slaves laid Mr. Drax at her feet.

"Go to her," Tempest whispered.

I brought the side chair to him that he might sit and then ran down the stairs so quickly my feet hardly touched the boards. I found Timothee standing just as before and Nessa crouched at Mr. Drax's side. His body was rigid and without breath, a crude arrow protruding from his back.

"Carib," Timothy said. "Likely 'twas not the cut that kilt him, but the poisoned blade. I do not know where they have gone, but they have given us this warning, and they will be back."

Nessa shook her head slowly and began to mumble a chant of some sort. I touched Mr. Drax's shoulder and realized my hand was shaking mightily. Above us Tempest waited.

"Mr. Drax has been kilt by a Carib arrow," I called to him.

The master looked across the yard and toward the sea. His face was so pale I feared he would collapse right then. He heaved a great sigh.

"Timothee, see to his swift burial," he said firmly. "Find as many of the slaves as you can and bring them to the storehouse. More Caribs will come tonight. We must prepare. Elvy, find Cook and bring her to me with a list of our stores."

But then the pack of slaves pulled tightly together, knelt as one at Nessa's feet, and presented their bundle of woven grass mats. Words passed between Nessa and two of the slaves. She opened the bundle slowly and tenderly. Inside, a tiny infant the color of molasses shook tight little fists at the sky. I knew at once it was Maestro's child, presented to the master for protection.

Nessa stood slowly and looked up at the master. Their eyes met and held for a long moment. I did not know what passed between them, my master and his unnamed slave, my friend ever silent to her master. When she turned to me I knew our mission had changed. I felt the looming pressure of the mountain at my back, and the impenetrable sanctuary that waited at the end of that steep and treacherous path.

I nodded, knowing without asking what must be done. I hurried to the kitchen where Cook, as solid as a castle wall, was entering a riotous panic. A basket filled to the brim with sweet potatoes tipped from the table, scattering tubers across the floor like stones on a river bottom. And baskets were everywhere, Cook turning to this one and then to that one, muttering in high pitch. "The dried peas could...Oh, what have I done with them? And the maize? Have we eaten it all when summer's yet before us?" She let out a screech. "The chickens! Someone collect the chickens. And where did I just put my hogshead of flour!"

"Cook!" I shouted to demand her attention. "The master wakes. He calls for you."

"I canna come now. The Caribs! What will become..." I grabbed her arm. Her nose was swelling to a fierce red, foretelling the tears that would flow. Together we ascended the stairs to the master's chambers, and just outside his door she stopped sobbing, took a deep breath, straightened her skirts, and wiped the tears from her cheeks.

But the side chair by the window was empty, and so was the master's bed. He had collapsed on the floor beside it. "Here, Cook! Help me."

We gripped him beneath his arms and together raised him up to the bed, lifted his legs and covered him with the bedclothes again. It was purpose enough to set Cook square on her footing.

"As if we are not in enough of a dither without yerself clamorin' fer attention," Cook scolded the master. "Will ye rob the savages o' the fun o' killin' ye?"

The master lay back on his pillow. "Ah yes, here you are and now I recall the reason for my desperate desire to live."

"And so yer sarcasm returns, and now ye're off to blatherin', sir. What is it ye want with us?"

"Have you brought the list of stores? We must prepare for..."

"Och! Am I a fool now?" Cook responded. "We're after packin' fer the trek to the caves and don't ye be botherin' yerself with it until we come fer ye with a stretcher."

"No. No stretcher."

"Well, ye're not about to walk, sir. We're to carry ye up..."

"Take the slaves and the infant and go as soon as you've gathered them. Take everything you can carry. Elvy is to lead. Take care of the children and those who still burn with fever. Timothee will follow with the horses."

I broke in. "So we'll just leave you here to be burned alive in the house? No! It will not be such. Cook will lead. Timothee and I will fetch you in the wagon."

"And how will you carry the fevered? And the stores of food? No, I will not go while others have need. I will have my pistols and I will fight them, but I will not leave. There is little time to argue and I am still master here. Now go."

A tight knot in my stomach broke, and its energy surged into my bones. "No. I will not permit it." I stood over the bed, fists on my hips, and spoke directly into his face. "If it offends you then you can hang me when your health returns. The Devil take the savages, for I care not what they do. I'll not leave your side, and there isn't a power on this island that can remove me."

Cook stood back from me, astonished, and I do believe a giggle escaped her lips. "Well there ye be, sir. She's a force, is she not?"

The master tried to rise, but the morning's exertion had taken its toll. His cheeks lost color, and profuse sweat dampened his lips, his neck, and his hands. He collapsed against his pillow.

"You see? You have no choice in the matter." I went to the window. Timothee and the two slaves had collected Mr. Drax's body and were heading for the tiny graveyard just north of the storehouse. "Cook, when Timothee returns we'll load the wagon with food and get it as far as the trail head. From there it must be carried by hand. Then he can return for the sick ones in the village. But Nessa should go now with the babe and the other slave children. We must get them to safety first."

I turned back to the master. "Sir, where will I find your pistols? I must make them ready." He looked up, his eyes growing bright as the fever surged. He opened his mouth but hesitated. To intentionally arm a slave was a considerable breach of law, but these were unusual times. He nodded toward the armoire that held his clothes. "Bottom drawer. The key is among my stockings."

I found the key swiftly and unlocked the drawer, removing a large wooden box with a brass lock. Inside, nestled in a bed of deep green velvet, were two flintlock pistols, their wooden stocks molded and their actions rusted and stiff. I knew nothing of guns, but it was clear these would never serve us now. I turned to speak to him, but the master's eyes were closed and his chin trembled with the chills. I set the box back in its drawer.

"Cook, we must warm the stones for him. Go back to your packing, and I will bring them down to the hearth. If you should see Anna, please send her to me. We must prepare the house."

While the master groaned in protest, I extracted the stones from his bedding, piling them into the apron of my skirt. It did not occur to me until I stood, the weight of the stones bearing me down, that I'd been without food or sleep for some time. My vision was hazy and my arms weak. I approached the stairs with stones clacking and clattering together, suddenly feeling dizzy and fearful that I might stumble and fall. I used my hip to brace myself going down. Anna waited near the bottom, her face shining with perspiration and her eyes casting about wildly. I remembered she had never been inside the big house. She was fearful of being where she did not belong, and at the same time wondrously curious.

"If the house survives, Anna, you will see every inch of it, I promise. For now you must help me. Go to the wood behind Badu's house and look for a vine with white flowers, the overlooker vine. Get as much as you can carry and bring it to me. It is strong, so you may have to rip it from its roots, but I need no less than four full strands. Can you do that, Anna? Please?"

"I mus' climb de mountain. My baby girl be wif Nessa, she take de children up and I mus' help her with dem now. Caribs come, missy. Caribs. Can't go down to de village now."

"Anna, please! Badu would want you to do this. It is for the master. I would go myself but the master is sick and I can't leave him." The stones were growing heavier, my arms beginning to ache. Anna backed away.

"Nessa and my girl need me now. Cain' go back to de village. Cain' go back." She backed away from me until she was against the stone wall, and then she turned and ran out the door toward the kitchen. She was the only one I knew of who might have understood, and now I had no one to call on. The edge of my skirt slipped through my fingers, and the stones pounded the floor like gunfire.

31

May 1658
Fire at Sharavogue

Ants, or Pismires...are but of a small size, but great in industry; and that which gives them means to attain their ends, is they have all one soul.

~ Richard Ligon, 1657

Like a caged wolf I paced. I busied myself, binding my hair with a strip of white linen, replacing all the candles in the holders, dabbing the sweat that beaded on the master's brow, though my own sweat trickled between my breasts and down my spine. The smell of smoke grew stronger, and a haze of gray had settled across the horizon.

"Sleep now," I told the master. "I'll wake you if they come."

He smirked at me—sure it was the Caribs who'd be doing the waking, and their arrival was not in question, only the hour of it. Though I know he struggled to remain alert, the fever still ruled him. His eyelids fluttered and soon I heard the soft, even breathing of slumber. I looked through the open window at a smoke plume rising in the west, from a plantation that by now was a smoldering ruin. The darkness had not yet conquered the day, and I lit the candle at the bedside more for comfort than for light.

We were alone at Sharavogue. Timothee and Cook had taken the last of the supplies in the wagon and were probably just now reaching the crest of the hidden garden. Nessa had been gone for hours and surely was in the cave with the children and the rest of the slaves. Mr. Drax was dead and buried, no one to mourn for him. I was glad they were all away and glad to be at the master's side, but there would be no one to help us when the Caribs came. The militia would not come, and if there was anyone else on the island that might, I was sure they already were engaged elsewhere.

I clung to the thin light of dusk and prayed that something might distract the Caribs or tire them of their rampage long before they reached us. It was my foolishness once again; for even as I thought it, I realized though the other fires smoldered, there was fire burning anew—and much closer. The scent of it was rising on the wind, sweet at first, like one of Timothee's cakes coming out of the oven, but then turning sour and pungent as tar.

"It is the governor's storehouse, most likely. That's the scent of burning molasses." The master rose up slightly in the bed, turning toward me. "He will have militia there to defend it, and they'll put out the blaze if they're able, not to worry."

I scoffed. "Why would I worry for the governor's storehouse? It is the shorter distance between us that concerns me. If the militia runs them off, would not the Caribs come here next?"

He shrugged. "It is still a considerable uphill trek, and there are other sites between that could detain them. Plymouth itself is downhill and offers finer targets in a tighter package."

"Mayhap, but more risk of people loading muskets. The Caribs no longer have surprise for an ally."

He inhaled deeply. "Right you are, m'lady. A palpable terror precedes them now."

He slurred, almost delirious, and his face grew pale. His thickened eyelids began to droop, but when he could no longer hold his head up the drop startled him awake.

"My pistols are ready?"

"They are beneath the bed, sir," I lied. It was enough to satisfy him, and he dropped back into a fitful sleep. A shudder traveled my spine like a mouse bolting for its nest hole. If the Caribs came, better he should sleep.

I settled into my chair to wait, my shoulders high and my back stiff. I had been here before, hadn't I? Defenseless as a kitten while a crushing and brutal force approached with bad intent. If I had a bridge before me, again I would tear it down, if only to slow the inevitable. But there was no bridge, nor any certain way by which they might come.

They hit the cassava house first. From the window I saw dark smoke curling above it and then violent flames engulfing one side as quickly as the spark of a flint. I wanted to scream, but my sound would only call them to us. I squeezed my throat, exhaling in thin, tight gasps.

In a few moments I heard them. They were quiet, to be sure, but to my heightened senses they were loud as a swarm of locusts settling over our grounds in the rustle of cane trash, in the absence of birds, and in the odd change of character of the very air that surrounded us. They were coming for us, sure as the night.

From beneath the window came the slightest crack of a twig and what sounded like a deep-throated grunt. A rushing tide of panic filled my veins. What could I do? What could I do? I was a fine shot with a good rock. I ran to the bed and gently removed the stones Cook had warmed, now cold and ready for a new use. I lined them up at the master's feet, my handy arsenal; but there against the linens they seemed forlorn and insignificant. Even if my aim were flawless it would not be enough to stop the Caribs with their poison darts. I scanned the room again and spotted Nessa's feather duster, forgotten on the washstand. I seized it, ripped feathers from their binding, loosed my hair jammed them into the locks about my face, mayhap to scare them or confuse them if only for an instant. Still, I knew it would not be enough. I searched frantically for a better weapon until my eyes settled where the setting sun painted a bronze glow above the bureau. There, shining like the last gold crescent of hope, was the master's sword.

I brought it down from the wall easily, grasped the hilt, and hooked my finger over the quillons as I'd been taught. The blade scraped only a little as I pulled it from its scabbard, and then I held the cold steel in my hands. The feel of it set my arm and shoulder tingling with power. The sword and whatever skill I could bring to it would have to be enough, for there was nothing more to be had. I positioned the point before me and took my stance—legs wide like a man's—between the open door and the bed.

What had Timothee said of these savages? They once captured an entire crew of Spanish sailors, castrated them, and roasted them like pigs for a feast—though the Spanish had raided Carib settlements for slaves. The Caribs murdered their victims with poison-dipped arrows and darts blown from a tube—though the English and French had slaughtered them with guns and swords.

I shook off these thoughts. I could entertain no sympathy when they were coming for our very lives. I knew when they arrived, for their scent filled the house: dirt, smoke, blood and sweat, spoiled meat, and the strange odor that must come from a diet of red peppers or the dye they extracted to stain their skin. I heard their short, angry puffs, the clatter of wooden bow and spear, the close rub of human flesh.

The master snorted in his sleep, and I glanced at him. When I turned back, two Caribs filled the doorway, and behind them came the dark silhouettes of several others.

The first was tall, his black hair long and loose over his shoulders, cut short and straight across his brow. His reddened skin glowed with the last amber of sunset. A woven grass garment covered his shins. But for that he was naked, and though I wished to I dared not look away. His fierce black eyes regarded me as I did him, and I felt a chill shoot up the back of my neck and expand at the base of my skull.

The second, even more horrifying, stepped toward me. He was shorter, redder than the other, with a huge green stone pendant hanging from his neck. His hair was cut as the other across the brow, but the back and sides were cut bluntly into odd shapes and stuck out wildly in all directions. He regarded me like a predator, his mouth opened to reveal sharp, pointed teeth. My heart was near exploding and my throat cramped into a hard stone. He blocked the door and I was cornered, with the master helpless behind me.

The taller one raised a bow over his head and gripped a black bill from the cane fields as if he might lay open my gut and cut my legs from beneath me. Something shifted inside me then, bursting like a flame. I squeezed the hilt and felt a fierce vibration rippling up my wrist until my shoulders and chest tingled with force. I heaved the sword and made my body like iron. "Ye'll not pass! Be gone," I hissed with all the hate I could muster from the deepest core of my gut. They hesitated, and then the smaller one advanced.

I screamed, "I am queen here. Do you hear? *QUEEN*. And right mighty I be. Ye'll not pass further or yer head will ride the tip o' my sword on its way through yon window!"

The taller one glanced at the other, and they moved in a little more. My scalp grew rigid and felt as if it might tear open. Without thinking, I raised the sword high and gave my head a vicious shake so that my hair fanned out in all directions and the feathers flew.

"BE GONE!" I screamed. With the setting sun behind me my hair must have looked like a blaze, for the smaller Carib's shoulders reared back and his eyes widened. He gestured as if to push at me with painted palms. I raised the sword even higher and hissed like a mad cat.

"*Mabouya*..." the tall one uttered.

I knew the name. Only Badu had dared speak it, but I was mad with fear and I seized it. "MABOUYA." I screamed without mercy to my lungs and scraping throat. I brought the sword level with their eyes and stepped toward them. The small one screeched and my blood raged with fire. He lunged and I thrust instinctively. The sword sliced through his throat and a fountain of blood pulsed and splattered. His round eyes bulged with surprise. I pulled back, and he fell to the floor in a clatter and slap of limbs and bare flesh, his lips working, his legs jerking. The shadowy figures behind him froze. The tall one stumbled back, then gathered his senses and raised the bill like an ax to cut me down.

"*MABOUYA*," I shouted again, hoping to summon from the depths of my soul the blazing blue of her eyes, and then a great explosion rang through the room, deafening me. I watched the tall one's mouth fall open exposing his few teeth, and the black hole that opened his chest fumed with smoke. He dropped to his knees, his lips oozing crimson from the sides. His head began to sag, and he looked up at me, confused and sad as a beaten puppy. He fell forward to the floor and did not move. I turned to see Tempest's hand raised from the bedclothes, holding a pistol I had not seen before.

The sword grew heavy, and my arm weakened. I dropped it with a great thud and went for the stones, solid and sure in my grip. With all my might I pelted the shadowy figures beyond the door. My aim was true, and cries of pain, rage, and surprise burst forth until the last of the Caribs thundered down the stairs. There was shouting in front of the big house, and I believed they would fire the house and we'd be burned within it.

But then someone shrieked far off. I heard gunfire nearby and thought I heard the Caribs running through the cane. Then I heard only the crackle of flames as the cassava house was quickly reduced to ashes. I sank to my knees beside the bed and waited for their return, my heart unwilling to ease its furious pounding. I stared in horror at the blood seeping from the lifeless bodies on the floor. The silence gradually returned, and I could hear the master's breathing and smell the sulfurous gunpowder.

We waited as the darkness settled, listening, until a coppery glow from the south brightened the walls. I peered over the windowsill at a grand orange blaze that colored the sky over the next rise.

"They've gone to the next plantation. They're burning it!" I thought I was whispering, but it came as a shout.

"Galways plantation. It will be a great loss," the master said. I touched his forehead.

"Elvy. I'm all right."

I sank to my knees beside him and my shoulders began to tremble as if the Jombee had taken over and was shaking my body like a fist. I felt the tears then, and my lips pulled back in a grimace I was glad no one could see. I watched through a tearful blur the terrible beauty of amber light expanding and brightening as the burning plantation fell to ruin, wanting never to know of the horrors experienced there. I wailed and sobbed and shook uncontrollably, and when I could wail no more I felt the master's warm fingers touch my head.

"Rise up, Elvy. Sit here beside me."

I did so, wiping away the streams on my cheeks. "Where did you get the pistol?"

"From beneath my pillows, loaded and ready as always."

"The pistols from your drawer. I didn't bring them…the rust was…"

"I know. You should have brought them. Everything rusts in this God-forsaken place, but it doesn't render them useless if you know your weapon. The mere sight of them can be a hindrance."

"I am sorry, master."

"For what? We are alive. You have defended me and saved Sharavogue from the torch. May God preserve that wild red hair of yours. They must have thought you were their devil, the one who brings the thunder and great storms." He tousled my hair and began to chuckle; and then I laughed with him, laughed and cried, at last releasing the high tension that had gripped us throughout the day. Afterwards, exhausted, we listened to the sounds of the night around us, the return of the cicada, the soft wind sifting through the brush, the occasional creak of wood or shutter that is natural to a house. The master took in a slow, deep breath.

"Listen now, there's something I've wanted to tell you." His voice was gentle, his face tinged with bronze from the distant fires. "Yesterday when Cook brought my bread, I could not eat it but dropped it to the floor. The birds came for it, through my open window. First to arrive was a little brown warbler, awkward and inelegant, a juvenile with white tufts about her neck and shoulders. She pecked gratefully at the crust until two bullfinches, looking quite smart in their black cloaks and russet tunics, strutted, flapped their wings, and then dove at her maliciously."

I smiled at him, wiping again at damp cheeks. "Very mean, those two."

"Yes, and our little warbler was no match for them, so off she went, leaving the bullfinches to peck at their spoils. Before long they became greedy, the one stabbing at the other to have the entire bounty to himself. They fought and fluttered, and seemed to forget all about the bread until they settled down again to pick it apart. But our little warbler was not to be forgotten. She returned, this time with a bravery they hadn't known she possessed. She landed on her feet beside them, spread her little brown wings and screeched, and the two startled bullfinches flew off. The little warbler returned to where she had started and began again to eat. A scrappy little thing, wouldn't you say?"

I thought I had finished my weeping, but the tears streamed once again down my cheeks. I sniffed and nodded. "Quite," was the only word I could speak.

"I'm not a great believer in such things, but I thought it might be an omen." The master smiled, then reached into a drawer in his bedside table and pulled out a folded parchment. He handed it to me. "So, I decided I must act on it."

"What is this?"

He pushed himself up a little higher in the bed. "Elvy, from the moment you arrived on Montserrat you've wanted nothing more than to return to Ireland and kill the man who caused you to be here. I thought it was folly. If the armies of Scotland, Ireland, and the Catholic Church could not defeat Oliver Cromwell, what could a little sylph do against such power? But time has passed, and much has changed. Cromwell rules with an iron fist, but beyond his army context he does not know how to lead, and he does not own the hearts of his people. They want to dance and sing again. They long to return to the old ways, where at least they could know pleasure without disdain.

"I believed it even before tonight, but after seeing you stand against those Caribs, I believe it fervently. Should you by some miracle actually confront the man again, I think the Lord Protector will get exactly what he deserves."

I looked down at the parchment, still not understanding.

"Go," my master said at last. "I shall never know my own heart's desire, but will take some comfort by helping you toward yours. Your period of indenture has nearly been fulfilled, and to see it through to the end serves no purpose. Take this letter to the House of Cromwell. It will get you a position among his servants. If the hate still simmers in your blood, go there and see what you need to see. Confront him if you must. Like the little warbler, take back what is yours in some way. Only do not give up your life for him. Make peace, Elvy. Then go home. Go home to Ireland."

For several seconds my mind searched but was dumbfounded. I was laced with gratitude and confusion. But soon my voice returned. "I had thought I should finally give up that mission, to stay now with you, sir," I told him. "You need me to look after you."

He shook his head sadly. "This fever will pass, as always it does. Yea, I believe it passes even now. One day it may ruin my heart, but that is for the future. And I have others who will look after me, as always."

"I don't know if I..."

He stopped me, squeezing my hand, and continued. "So many years ago, I should have listened to my father. I should have married when he urged me to. I might have had at least one child before the sickness made its home in my veins. Even one child, if it survived, would be enough to..." He shook his head. "I was rebellious. I wanted nothing of what was expected of me. I wanted freedom, adventure. I feared responsibility. I feared I might rule my child as I had been ruled, with intimidation and humiliation, and call that love. I wanted no part.

"And when the sickness came, my choice was torn away, leaving me with too much sorrow. How I have longed for that one instant, to touch the fineness of my child's hair, to look into eyes that reflected my own and see recognition, see that wide-eyed look of trust and hope. I would have given up anything and everything for that."

He looked down at the rumpled sheets that covered his hips, and when he looked up I saw in his eyes something new. Tenderness, yes, but something even more than that.

"Don't let your hatred be your sickness, Elvy," he said gently. "Families are all that matter, and the things you would hope to achieve in one generation, though they be not realized now, may see the light of day in the next or the next. I don't know where it all leads or why it matters, but it does. Someone must carry the sword and the lamp to eternity."

Tempest reached into his bedside table again and pulled out a purse heavy with coin. He opened my trembling hand and placed it in my palm. "Go," he said. "You are free of obligation to me, and you have a different destiny. Yet it burns. Ah yes, and let me not forget." He withdrew something from the drawer and handed it to me. I held it up and knew in an instant it was the angel—Kade's golden coin.

"Plucked from the sand at your feet on the day you arrived. It's been in safe keeping all this while. A very special coin, is it not? I suggest you use it wisely."

I was stunned. There in my hands were the three keys to my freedom. I had more than enough coin for my passage across the sea, and a letter of introduction to get me right into Oliver Cromwell's house. I could see him dead at long, long last. If I were meant to suffer in hell for Kade's murder, surely St. Brendan himself would intervene for me after Cromwell's.

The third key, the angel, was cradled in my palm. I could not return it to its rightful owner, but still it had come back to me. I did not know its purpose, but I would treasure it for as long as I could.

A thunder of footsteps broke the quiet, and I lunged for the sword; but it was Timothee who appeared. We gaped at each other, both gasping for breath, until he surveyed the two bodies in a heap before him. He nodded, looking from me to the master to verify our safety.

"Timothee, the others. How do they fare?" The master asked.

"They are well, sir. And except for the cassava house all of Sharavogue is spared."

"A strange and bittersweet victory, to enjoy the preservation of that which for so long has been hated."

Timothee smiled. "Hated as the schoolboy hates his school but will throttle the first who would dare to speak against it."

"Just so," the master nodded.

"We had some welcome assistance, sir."

From behind Timothee, Will Hurst stepped forward carrying a musket. "I c-came up from Plymouth. I hoped I would be of s-service to you, sir. I fired some shots."

The master smiled. "Will, I believe they were brilliantly timed. For that we are grateful."

I heard the stair creak once more, and this time it was Nessa who appeared in the doorway.

"Nessa!" I cried out. She glanced quickly at the master, then nodded at me and smiled. She looked down at the dead Caribs, but simply stepped over them to get to the bedside. She touched the master's forehead and neck.

"Nessa." the master whispered. It was the first time I had ever heard him speak her name, the name I had given her that now the entire village used.

She took his hand and squeezed it. "I am here."

"I have freed her," he told Nessa. I have freed our girl. She can..."

But the master could not finish. Violent coughing seized him, and when it stopped his reddened face streamed with sweat and his breath was shallow and wheezing.

I grabbed Nessa's arm. "I cannot go. He needs me. He will die if I leave him now."

Nessa touched my hand but shook her head. Her eyes were as gentle as when first we met. "He want you to go. It be right. But you mus' go without fear. He will not die. I be here for him."

And now it was I shaking my head. "Oh Nessa, I always thought, if I were to leave Sharavogue, you would come with me. I could not bear to think of you as a slave for your whole life."

Nessa smiled, and in her eyes I saw something I'd never seen before, something indistinct and far away, an ageless wisdom of the nature of things that I knew I could never gain. She looked down at the master. "I live in Badu's house. I tek up her work. I be not a slave here, Elvy. Dis be my home." She looked up at me. "My mother was a slave. But Tempest and me, we be free."

As she spoke his name I stared at her and lost my breath. I understood at once how much had transpired between the two of them. How could so much hate and so much love travel the same corridor? I did not know the answer but saw very clearly that it could. I knew as well that a different battle had taken place that day, and that hate had been defeated. I began to cry again. I could not stop myself. Nessa leaned over and kissed my cheek.

"You mus' go, jus' as he say, and go now. It be dangerous to go into Plymouth, but a merchant ship hide jus' beyond the cliffs north. De merchant offer passage for ones who wish to leave de island. Pay him well for your safety, but do not show him your purse."

I nodded silently, my tears streaming.

"Go to de blue pool, Elvy. Follow de little path dat lead beyond it. A pinnace will take you to de ship dat take you away. Go now!"

I stood, knowing I had to leave but unable to move my feet. I looked at the master's face. His eyes were only narrow slits, but he nodded at me, and I saw just the hint of a smile touch his lips. Then Timothee squeezed my elbow.

"You must hurry, leetle bird. The pinnace will set out soon, and eef the militia arrives you will not be allowed to leave the grounds."

"Timothee!" I hugged his neck. "My friend, my teacher. I'd not have survived here but for you."

He laughed. "Do not be silly. You barely survived een spite of me. At least your swordplay has been for profit. And I will be going away as well, a fortnight from now when the missionary ship arrives. The master has purchased my passage to China. I am freed as you are, to pursue my dream. You must sail away and not look back, Elvy. All occurs for a reason, and we are all enriched by each experience een ways only God can imagine. Now *go*."

I left then, running down the stairs with all the swiftness I could muster, though I do not know to this day how I found the strength. I ran through the yard and the gates, straight to the blue pool and beyond, where the pinnace waited just as Nessa said. Others were there also, and by midnight the ship sailed with sixteen passengers. I looked back for a long time until in the darkness I could barely see the black outline of the island against the blue-black sky, and a tiny orange glow where the Galways fires still burned. Just above it on the dark hillside, there were tiny yellow lights and I knew Sharavogue was safe.

We sailed through the straits between St. Christopher and Antigua, then north on the northeast trade winds to catch the prevailing westerlies. Of the crossing I remember little, for I cried almost incessantly. I cried for Badu, my only mother, and for Nessa, my lost friend. I cried for Kade, my partner, my shame and my sorrow. How beautiful he had been, and how cruel and stupid I had been. I cried for Aengus, and for Timothee. Both had tried so hard to protect me when I had been nothing but foolish. I cried for Tempest Wingfield, who granted my freedom but would never have his own. I cried for all the years I had spent there on Montserrat, wanting only to return home to Ireland. Now Montserrat seemed like home and Ireland just a strange and cold place barely remembered.

And at last, I cried for my father. I had never, ever allowed myself to cry for him. But now that I knew I would never see my master again, a flood of tears gushed forth for the one I'd missed for so long.

I cried and moped for five weeks, and in the last week as we neared the shores of England, I stopped my crying and fed my fires of purpose. I was approaching Cromwell, and with each day I felt the surging determination return to my shoulders, my arms, my gut. Very soon I could well see him dead, though it might bring with it my own end. Tempest's words of advice did not sway me, for I believed with all my heart I could not begin a new life until Cromwell's was extinguished forever.

32

The House of Cromwell

And I saw and felt a waft of death go forth against him, that he looked like a dead man.

~ George Fox, 1658

Along the quay in London, the wagon drivers congregated amidst the stench of dead fish, hot tar, seaweed and horse droppings. The calls of seagulls could barely be heard above the shouts of merchants, seamen and streetside vendors, the clatter of horses' hooves, the slap of water against the wharf, the wind singing through the lines of tall ships.

The master had written "Whitehall Palace" across the folded parchment he had given me, and the mere mention of it brought a nod from any of the drivers. I begged a ride from a gray-bearded fellow named Wain who swore he was bound straight for Whitehall's kitchens.

The road was narrow and bumpy in places, and crowds were constant as the wagon creaked along. My gaze played over the jagged, soot-blackened rooftops and my thoughts found rest in the steady plodding of the horses. The gilded August light awakened my senses. Damp air moistened my skin and breaks of golden sun settled into my bones like warm milk soaks a crust of bread. How different from Sharavogue, where I'd stopped noticing the changing seasons, and all seasons seemed the same.

When we stopped along the way, I washed as best I could, working a comb through my hair until it could be smoothed, braided and tucked beneath a new linen cap. With another coin from Master Wingfield's purse I purchased a thin carrot soup from an innkeeper, to give me better color when I presented myself for work. Thus I prepared my appearance and my stomach, but I had no way to prepare my eyes for the damning spectacle of Whitehall.

What had I envisioned? Across the years, the vast ocean, the rugged roads, did I think Oliver Cromwell would reside in a gray stone castle like those in ruins I had known in Ireland, or the gleaming towers I had conjured in my dreams, his daughters tip-toeing on narrow stair and huddling for warmth by a great-room hearth? If my murderous spirit had lost any of its steam during my indenture, the boil surged anew as the enormity and grandeur of Whitehall swelled before me.

"Holbein Gate, they calls it," Wain exclaimed, his face alight with pride. "It be the biggest gate into the palace, methinks, but they be three others, all of 'em with gardens, ye see."

Dragon scales of red and yellow brick rose before me and surrounded me in all directions, as if the monster coiled and waited for its prey, the entrance yawning wide to swallow us in. Beneath the limestone arch four tall men could stand on each other's shoulders and still not touch the apex. On either side of the gate were guardhouses, dark and forbidding, and castle guards in russet coats with muskets black and ready. Above the arch, three stories with tall narrow windows peered down on all who entered but prevented any view inside. The brick battlements reached so high into the heavens God himself might reach down to place the guards, just as a child arranges toy soldiers.

So confident were the palace guards, they merely nodded at my driver, not bothering to question the nature of his cargo or the intentions of the plotting assassin who fumed beside him. The team drew us beneath the arch, the groan and creak of leather and wood all the louder within the enclosed space. Beyond the gate, the walls stretched in every direction far beyond my view. Directly before us a garden sprawled: asters and angel's trumpets studded a labyrinth of thick foliage, and oversized human sculptures presided over secluded benches and private walks. Yet there was no human life to be seen, no living, breathing person that might call hello or beckon the driver on.

"This be the Spring Garden. In the old days, ye'd see a fellow chasin' a skirt round the bush here and there, and hear a giggle rise from one o' the young maids. It were a meetin' place, and some say the courtiers under old King Charles used to meet their favorite ladies here. Spring, ye see? When everyone goes a-courtin'. But the Lord Protector closed it down to such traffickin'. Not fond o' such goin's on, is he. No public allowed in at all, and the courtiers dare not be seen here lest the rumors start or the Protector be displeased. Naught but the gardener be seen here today."

I stared in wonder, such beauty and lush extravagance that none could enjoy because of Cromwell and his nature to despise and deprive. How I hated him. And now I was sure many others hated him as well.

Behind the garden, the brick of the gate continued in a huge, imposing building, its walls rising above us with a balustrade walk about the rooftop. Its enormous gabled windows overlooked looked the carriage park and its own narrow guardhouses. My back stiffened and my stomach began to seize and curl within.

"The palace. The residence. We are here," I sputtered. Wain laughed so hard the spittle flew and showered his beard.

"Not at all, child. It be the banquetin' house. Designed by the great architect Inigo Jones 'imself. It be where the kings have their parties, is all. The ladies and gallants arrive in their carriages yon, and tiptoe up these stairs in their finery. They wander about those upper floors in their embroidered slippers, peer out the windows o'er the boats on the river, and all fer the privilege o' bein' served and entertained by the Lord Protector hisself.

"Those stairs, mind, and the gallery beyond, are the very same where King Charles passed afore bein' brought to the scaffold for his beheading, at the behest of our Lord Cromwell. I'd wager the fact be not lost on any guest arrivin', whose footsteps o'er they pass. A chillin' thought, eh? And in the cellars, I hear there's a grotto and a privy drinkin' den fer the menfolk, built by King James and now a spot fer the Lord Protector and his cronies. But ye want tell of the residence, ye say. And so I'm to show ye. Look now, down the road here as far as ye can. And then, look down here to yer right, as far as ye can. See now?"

"I see buildings and houses all joined together, of brick and limestone and wood and glass."

"Aye, and within be a splendor and magnificence the like of which you and I will never know." He chuckled, and then slapped his knee. "Whitehall Palace, and welcome to ye. Two thousand rooms, girlie. Acres and acres of it, a-sprawlin' along the river front to put the fear o' God in the heart of any foreigner dares sail up the Thames."

I gazed about in awe and disbelief, but all the while the fire in my belly began to spread, and I felt it burn beneath the skin of my thighs and my arms, my scalp, my breasts, my fingertips, my eyelids, and even my tongue. He lived and breathed within my midst, and in splendor and magnificence. Because of him, beloved people in my village were long dead. Because of him, I'd spent seven years of my life so far from my home I could barely remember it. He lived in luxury, leaving my people in starvation and squalor, filth, and blood; leaving his own subjects in poverty and oppression, unable to enjoy the simple pleasures of flowers in a park. He does not call himself king, and yet he places himself in opulent, exalted surroundings and decides the fates of all who breathe of the air.

Now more than ever, I longed to sink my blade into his flesh. Now more than ever my hate channeled into a roiling stream and bound my bones and muscles in a mighty current of need.

"So now, dearie," my driver said. "We have kitchens by the dozen. Which kitchen was it ye're a-wantin'?"

"The main one," I said. "The one that serves the Lord Protector his breakfast."

The first time I climbed to Cromwell's bedchamber I followed Sarah up the narrow back stairs, her hips brushing either side of the wall as her ample bottom shifted and swayed. Sarah was the chambermaid with the most seniority and also, I found, the most information. I could not see beyond her then to gauge the steep, dark tunnel I would soon come to know.

"The missus, she had this passage built when she first come to Whitehall, ye know. She and the Lord Protector lived at first in the Cockpit next to the Spring Garden, whilst their chambers was bein' readied. O'course, it weren't no real cockpit with cocks fightin' and all, not since old King Henry; but they still calls it such. And whilst they was buildin' the new chambers, the missus says she does better lookin' o'er the servants than lookin' o'er the politics at the banquet table, so she wants some corridors fer duckin' in and out. And then once they is built, she wants us servants usin' 'em so the guests don't see us at all, as if their fine linens and wines and trenchers o' food show up magically before 'em, untouched by hands the likes o' these."

She turned and waved her stubby fingers in my face, then gave me a wink. "The Protectoress, she come from noble blood, but the truth is she weren't nothin' but a farmer's wife for most of her years. That's what the Protector did, ye know. When he weren't leadin' the army, he were leadin' the cows to pasture." She tittered like a starling in a pile of good seed.

Near the top of the stair she pointed to a sconce. "The candle here is always burnin', so it's to be changed every three hours, and don't be late or the missus will howl." She turned to look at me, nodding. "Ye've come at the best time, otherwise there might not ha' been a job to be had. The Protector's favorite, his daughter Elizabeth, passed away just a month back. He was poorly even then, but since Bettie's death he's gone worse and worse. We're all busy seein' to his needs and keepin' the rest of the house in order besides. And it's lucky you had your letter of introduction. The missus say she don't remember any Tempest Wingfield, but our Lord Protector remember 'im just fine and his father as well. God-fearin' people, he say, with good conscience. If not for that ye'd be back on the street, fer they've not been in a mood for hirin' folks since the assassination attempt."

My stomach lurched. "Assassination?"

"Ah, well, if ye've not heard of it ye're among a rare few. Sure, it's been two year past, but the man's name was on everyone's lips at the time: Miles Sindercombe. He were a surgeon's assistant, and went by the name o' Fish. I seen 'im around sometimes. A cranky wisp of a fellow. Anyhow, he were hired by folk who wished a king back to the throne. Prince Charles, the king's heir, is exiled to France, ye know, and drunk as a sot, some say.

"So this Fish fellow thought he would shoot my Lord Protector in his carriage as he rode to Hampton Court fer the weekend. Only my Lord decided not to go, and so the plot failed. Then the fellow planned to burn my Lord in a fire as he sat in church. Church, mind ye! But fool that he was, he botched the whole thing. Guards found the fire starter and Fish was arrested, and then, just before he was to be hanged, he poisoned hisself. Somebody sent 'im a letter coated with arsenic, and he rubbed it on his face and nose and hands, knowin' it would save 'im from a traitor's death. They buried 'im under the highway anyway. Could be ye passed right o'er 'im on yer way into the city."

"I feared something like this might happen," I muttered more to myself than to Sarah. "I might have been too late. I'm glad he failed."

"Well, of course, we all are. I do believe the Protector hardly knew such commotion was goin' on, and once he learned of it he merely chuckled. 'Little fiddlin' things,' he called it, as if he were pure untouchable, ne'er to fear. It was all a frightful scare fer the rest of us, mind. A nasty business that, but some ha' never forgiven our Lord Cromwell fer the execution o' King Charles—unholy, they call it, and place all the blame fer it on my Lord.

The civil war ended years ago, but we're as divided as e'er on most counts, I dare say." Sarah was nearly out of breath as she reached the top landing. She inhaled deeply and turned.

"There now, when ye reach the top, polish the door handle and oil the hinges, but ne'er enter the room unless the missus herself tells you so or gives you a sign. We do not e'er wish to disturb our Lord Protector. These days he rests little enough, what with the steady stream o' physicians and visitors. Some o' these courtiers think he's sure to pass away and want their moment to gain a last bit o' favor. But the Lord Protector's been as sick many a time and always gets back on his feet, ne'er you mind."

She crooked her finger, beckoning me closer. "I'm the only one knows o' this, but it might come in handy if ye're to mind this door." She ran her thumb along a narrow line that looked like a darkened vein in the wood, but in fact was a crack barely wide enough for the edge of a coin.

"Ye mus' be at the right level and angle to see, but if needs ye can tell if the room be empty or full. Saved me many a trip down the stairs and up again. Just make sure the Protectoress don't find out about this crack or she'll have those carpenters whipped fer such a flaw."

"Of course," I nodded. I peered through the crack and felt a chill seize the back of my neck and scalp. I could see the posts and curtains of Cromwell's bed, the embroidered upholstery of the armchair beside it, the dim paneled walls and the archway leading to the anteroom, the rich silk carpets, and the carvings on the drawers of the bureau. I could see the Protectoress, her shoulders sagging in her voluminous brown gown with its puffed sleeves and white lace collar. Men's voices muttered softly, and someone was weeping though it resembled muffled laughter. "Sarah," I asked cautiously, "about that Sindercombe fellow."

"Oh, 'im," she replied.

"What would have been his fate? What is a traitor's death?"

"My goodness, ye have been a far piece from this side o' the world not to know what every soul in England has known since childhood. 'Tis an 'orrible thing to witness, and yet the gallows be packed with the crowds whene'er it be done. Ye've seen a hangin', sure enough, eh?"

I nodded. I had not seen the man hanged, but his bulging eyes and thick tongue had left such wounds on my memory I knew they would never be healed.

"Fer a traitor, hangin' alone is too kind," she continued. "They hang 'im all right, but then bring 'im down from the gallows just before he dies, lay 'im out and cut 'im open, pull out his bowels to show 'im and all the world. He'll die soon enough, and then his head's chopped off and stuck on the palace gate fer every passer-by to see. His body is quartered like any side o' beef, and each piece skewered and displayed about the city, a rottin', stinkin' mess to warn anyone what might try the same crime. And then finally he's buried under the highway where no one can grieve fer 'im. Many a soul in the Tower o' London has died tryin' to escape such a spectacle. If he's already dead, there's no show fer the public, ye see."

"Yes, I see."

It is one thing to nurture a hatred year upon year and to envision your enemy's painful death. And it is another thing entirely to envision your own, bloodier and far more brutal than anything you might have perpetrated or even imagined. The burning in my stomach flared anew. Within my gut—which would be displayed and hated for eternity—the Devil pressed his sharpened fingernail and stirred my entrails about.

"Please excuse me, Sarah."

I ran for the privy. Though the air was cool enough I sweated until my scalp was soaked, my gut cramping and twisting like a dishrag to squeeze out all that it held. I cried of the pain, but also of the place I had come to. There was no retreat now, was there, from what I was destined to do? I thought I had been given a destiny that would make me cherished and exalted, and instead I would be damned forever. Still, it was my path to walk and mine alone. If I would be damned for doing the deed, would I be equally damned for not doing it? Where was the honor here, and where defeat? I had stood at the very threshold. And every three hours would take me there again. I knew with absolute certainty I had to act on the morrow, or I would forever lose my courage.

So resolved and exhausted, I slept that night like a newborn babe in my narrow attic cot. Before dawn the clatter of arriving carriages raised every servant from bed to attend to the early visitors. I hurried to replace the candle in the corridor and peered through the crack in the door for a glimpse at the morning's circumstances. The Protectoress was there, dressed in black velvet, her shoulders hunched forward, her hands cradling Cromwell's. A few other visitors in dark robes stood nearby, some of whom I was beginning to recognize. Doctor George Bate had arrived. He swept back his black physician's cloak and began to examine his patient, while behind him stood Charles Harvey, the groom of the bedchamber, who leaned close and whispered into the doctor's ear. Harvey's forehead was deeply furrowed between his wiry brows. I heard a faint moan and a cough, assuring me the Protector still lived.

I hurried downstairs to join the other servants, carrying breads, boiled eggs, sausages, fruits, and watered wine to those gathered at the breakfast table. They were courtiers of some rank I could not determine and all wore their Puritan black. Sarah said they were important: members of a privy council Cromwell himself had appointed. Each of them seemed to believe the Protector would die, for their talk focused entirely on succession.

"The Lord Protector must name his successor today, this morning." The first councilor slapped his palm on the table. "If he is lucid at all he must speak a name, or at least point a finger at one amongst a written list."

"It is so," said another. "What a cruel irony if the Protector should pass away—he who fought with such vigor to reunite the nation after the war—and then by his death shatter it once again into so many factions wrangling for control. The Royalists are but one, and are of far less concern to me than the rivals within Cromwell's own family."

"It must surely be young Henry Cromwell to follow Oliver," the first one returned. "No other knows the Protector's strategies, and his skills with an army are firmly commanded. It's this that keeps the regime steadily in place, even as the Royalists most assuredly are plotting."

"No. It will be Henry's brother Richard," a third man declared. "He knows less of army machinations, of course, but he is a scholar—the Lord Protector himself selected his reading matter—and he is steeped in politics and court life. Our Lord Protector will choose him as a means of shoring up the support of the nobles. For the Royalists, he makes a more palatable alternative to Charles Stuart."

"Richard is weak, as any man can see plainly in his dull eyes and timid expression. Howsomever, any choice at this late hour will surpass none at all," the first replied. "I fear a great turmoil that threatens to topple each of us, and the country besides, into a dark abyss."

"We must pray about it," the second fellow offered.

"Enough prayer!" the third man shouted. "An entire day was given to prayer just yesterday, and yet the Protector writhes in his bed, and yet we have no successor named. It is time to *act*."

The rustle of silk beneath her heavy velvet skirts signaled the entrance of the Protectoress, her thin lips pinched together and her pale jowls streaked with tears. "The Lord Protector has awakened," came her voice, bitter and trembling. She plucked at the cameo pinned between her breasts. "He will not break his fast, so you may see him now. Go quietly, and do not tire him or Dr. Bate will have you out." She stepped back from the doorway, revealing the grand staircase that led to the Protector's bedchamber. She lifted her chin to look down the length of her nose at each privy councilor, making the deep caverns about her eyes seem even more sunken. Then she turned her face away.

Though the urgency had burned in their voices before, confronted by the stricken vision of the Protectoress they hesitated, nervously wiping their fingers on starched napkins. After a long moment it seemed even the air did not stir, and then the first to speak pushed back his chair, and one by one the privy councilors started up the stairs.

Sarah helped the Protectoress to a chair at the table. I backed away silently and ducked into the kitchen. I had spotted the cook's fruit knife, well sharpened with a length of blade worthy of my task, but small enough to be secreted in the sleeve of my blouse. Pressed to the pad of my thumb the blade quickly drew blood, and I knew I was equipped and ready. I sucked the wound and tucked the knife away, then filled my apron pockets with fresh tapers for the sconce.

"I'll see to the candle, then," I announced to the cook so that no one would look for me. My skin began to tingle and my blood flowed as a cool stream rushes to the sea. My hour approached. I did not know when my moment would come but was certain there would be only one.

Heavy draperies closed out the light of day, but within the bedchamber the candles burned brightly as Doctor Bate, looking like an ancient wizard in his broad velvet hat, presided over the Protector's bed. The doctor was in his finest element now, the man to whom all turned for answers, the man who ruled the medical care for the man who ruled much of the world.

"Stand back! I must have more room," he demanded. The councilors took one step back, but no more. Doctor Bate moved around the bed to retrieve one of his instruments, and at last I could see Cromwell himself, his body nearly flattened, his head resting awkwardly on thick pillows, his crown covered by an embroidered, cream-colored cap that slipped down to touch his brow. His eyes were closed. His bony hands clutched, released, and clutched again the twisted bedclothes across his chest.

One of the councilors spoke up. "Clearly he suffers pain, doctor. Can you not..."

"I have administered the appropriate medicines," the doctor said. "I will not be second-guessed by the layman. If you wish to stay, confine your remarks to your own business."

A heavy silence followed. Someone came near and stood in front of the door, blocking my view so that I had only the sounds of rustling fabric, soft footfalls, and low murmurs to inform me of what was taking place.

Then there was a burst of noise and my view was restored. Cromwell had pushed himself up in bed, his face alight with passion.

"It is a terrible thing!" he said, his voice raw and high. "A terrible thing to fall into the hands of the living God!" He fell back in the bed and the doctor checked him once again. It was the first time I had heard the man's voice in seven years, yet I would recognize it, having the same fervor when he shouted out the scriptures as when he'd shouted across the River Ilen.

"He has lost consciousness. You must now leave him to his rest," the doctor said.

"But, he must be awakened! Please, Dr. Bate! He must speak to us. We *must* have his answer."

"Did you not hear, sir? He is in conference with God. Leave him be."

Charles Harvey ushered the men out. "I will stay with him," he assured them. "I will send for you when he rouses."

I pressed against the door. If only he and the doctor would leave as well, my task would be done. But they crowded up near him, watching, waiting. I replaced one candle, and then another, sweating in the close confines of the narrow stairs and the tight constraints of my bodice.

By late afternoon the councilmen returned again and tried to stir Cromwell to consciousness, tapping his cheek, pressing his shoulder. He did not open his eyes nor lift his head, yet he spoke.

"...A single covenant...before the foundation of the world," Cromwell murmured. "It is holy and true. It is *holy and true*." And then he fell away again into that dark world of dreams.

As the disappointed men descended once again for their supper, I grew restless. I feared, as they did, that the man would die in his bed before my business was concluded. And then what would I do? What would become of my long-sought destiny? And yet again, what if I left him to his natural death and instead he lived? My muscles jumped and twitched beneath my skin. I wished to run like a madwoman among the palace parks, sucking the fresh air deep into my lungs. My throat longed to scream and shout with all the fury I felt inside, rising to a shining pinnacle, to a spire so sharp it scraped the sky. But I could do none of these things. Perhaps I was going mad, and Cromwell would have his final victory over me. I was not a princess. Though I had climbed the steps of this palace, I was still just a maid on a stairway. I could not kill. I could do nothing but change the burning candle.

As night fell the councilmen returned, this time more agitated than before. Five of them gathered around Cromwell's bed, forcing Doctor Bate and Charles Harvey to the hallway. They called to him firmly, sending the Protector into a fit of sorts. He thrashed his thin arms on the bed and turned his head this way and that. He raised his eyes only as slits, as would a drowsy or drunken man, and though they shouted commands at him he seemed incapable of responding. At last they quieted, as if they had given up their task, and then one of the councilmen sat on Cromwell's bed.

"Will it be Richard?" the man asked, his voice loud as a minister at his pulpit. He obtained no answer. "My Lord Protector, please! Will it be Richard?"

Cromwell seemed to give a faint nod, though it might have only been a tilt of his head in sleep, and the councilman pressed his ear close to Cromwell's lips.

"Yes!" the councilman shouted, rising up from the bed. "Yes! I heard him whisper! You all saw, you all are witness. *Richard* Cromwell is named successor to Oliver."

The councilors looked at one another, seeming a little uncertain, but mayhap were relieved to have some kind of answer, any kind. The councilmen bowed at the sick man and, their need fulfilled, left the bedchamber. In came the doctor then, and Mr. Harvey. And in walked the Protectoress. She bent and kissed her husband tenderly, and he roused enough to take her hand. Though his eyes were half closed as before, he spoke this time with brief and lucid strength.

"You physicians think I shall die. I tell you I shall *not* die this hour, I am sure on it!"

After such exertion he sank back into the pillows. I heard the soft murmurs of the Protectoress and the press of her skirts against the bed linens. I watched her retreating sway as she took the doctor's arm and they left the bedchamber. Mr. Harvey approached the bed and touched the Protector's hand. "Your work is done, my lord, and your body is cold. I will stoke the fire. You must rest now, for the journey ahead."

And Cromwell spoke once again. "Truly God is good, indeed he is. He will not…"

"Leave you?" Mr. Harvey finished. "No, good sir, God will not leave you. Nor will I. Now sleep."

My heart sunk to my gut as I watched Harvey bring the fire to flame and take a chair next to it. He pulled a small leather journal from his doublet and began to write. Of course he would stand vigil to Cromwell. Of course! I should have known they would never leave such a powerful man alone on his deathbed. But why wouldn't they? How much longer could I wait?

My chance came only moments later, for Harvey put down his pen. He slipped low into his chair, and in a moment his leather journal fell to the floor with a soft thud. He drifted quickly into a deep sleep, his raucous snoring providing me greatest comfort. I pushed open the door.

I crept toward the bed on my knees, my skirts hiked up to my thighs and the warm wooden grip of the carving knife clutched firmly in my hand. I rose up.

The great Oliver Crowell lay on his bed, his emaciated form barely lifting the bedclothes but for his toes, his knees, and the flaccid fat of the old man's belly. Just an old man with sagging face and strings of dull hair. Even in this state, he was to me an awesome sight; the embroidered night-cap might well have been a royal crown encrusted with jewels. He was the leader of an empire, the general of a brutal, killing army, the heartless murderer of thousands of my countrymen. The bile rose up from my gut, reminding me of all the terror and destruction this man had caused, giving me strength.

I moved closer, prepared for the stench of him. Seven kitchen maids had been tasked with collecting roses from the garden to perfume the fetid air of his illness, yet with each exhale came a weak wind laden with disease and decay. But illness would not be the source of his demise now that I was at his bedside. Just as hanging was too kind for the traitor, disease was too kind for the Protector. How great would be his surprise to know that, after all these years, he would yet pay for his crimes? How great would be the despair of the people I had seen today, to find Cromwell's life spilled out in a thick red pool among the bedclothes? How piercing would be his lady's mournful cry?

I sat on his bed and lifted the knife silently, though my blood rushed against my eardrums. Wasting no time, I touched the blade to his neck, just below his ear where I would begin to lay open his throat. I pressed, but drew no blood.

Was the man dead already, or was he some kind of supernatural creature who did not bleed? I needed better leverage to make my cut felt. I rose up on my knees and knelt on the bed beside him. Instead of the throat, I decided to bury my knife deep into his heart. I touched his chest carefully to find the breastbone, and then placed the blade's tip just under it. When I sank the blade it would open Cromwell's heart and spill his wretched life into the cavity of his chest. I applied pressure, his nightgown puckering against the blade's point. Cromwell's eyes fluttered, the lids flew open, his pupils boring into my own. His mouth fell open.

"Bettie?" He whispered so faintly, as if in a dream.

I stared, shocked and frightened. My arms froze. Bettie! He mistook me for his dead daughter.

"Bettie, sweet. I prayed you might come back to me, though I knew it sinful to hope. And yet my God delivers me, does he not? Bettie? I must still be beloved of God."

He must not think I am she! He must understand why I would murder him. "I am Elvy Burke, of Skebreen," I whispered harshly. Mr. Harvey's snores carried on, undisturbed.

"Hurt? Yes, I feel great pain, my love, but your presence comforts me and I find peace in your eyes, though my heart is troubled. You must tell me, you who have already touched the face of God. Is it possible to fall from grace?"

I hesitated, confused by his question. "To fall from grace. I…No! I am not Bettie," I recovered, "I am Elvy. I am of Ireland." I made my voice as fervent as whisper would allow.

"No. Thank you, Bettie. I had prayed it be so. Because of what transpired in Ireland, yes. You warned me, didn't you, sweet child, that Ireland would bring me ill. I had grace before that. I led my men to victory in civil war. I united the country. I had grace under God and he gave me good counsel.

"But then Ireland. So much blood. So many fallen on both sides. Thousands killed on my order, Bettie, but it was right that they should die for the safety of English people. It was God's righteous judgment! Wasn't it,

Bettie? Was I right and true, or was that the moment of my demise?"

I reared back, and it was all I could do to maintain a whisper and not to shout. "That was the moment I became your mortal enemy! That was the moment you deserved to die by my hand. That moment my destiny was born." I gave more pressure to the tip of my blade, but I could not push it in while he still spoke, while it was not me he recognized, but some beloved ghost.

"It has plagued my life, Bettie, for that is when I first took to bed with the ague, the torturous fevers of that blasted Irish swamp. And the fever torments me year after year—the cold shivers, then burning and sweating as if my very body might melt away; it is a punishment, Ireland, like the recurring whip of a higher judge. Has this been my eternal hell, Bettie?"

The ague! I did not know he suffered from it. Such justice that, to pick up disease in a country where he himself had spread like a deadly plague across our lands.

"Or did it begin on that cold, bleak January," Cromwell rambled on, "the moment King Charles was executed? It was cruel necessity, Bettie. And it was *my* necessity, for Charles could never have been trusted. But was it *God's* necessity, as I so fervently believed? Or was that when the stone began to grow in my gut? Tell me, Bettie. I beg of you."

Stone! A fever rages in his blood and a stone grows within his organs. Was it a stone like those, round and heavy, I had cast at the shins of Aengus or at the heads of the Caribs fleeing my wrath? With this weapon I had always excelled, but I had raised no hand here. This stone was cast by another. Long ago I had vowed he would die in agony, and now it be so. Cromwell's tears seeped from the outer corners of his eyes and soaked into the linens on his pillow.

"Please, Bettie. Tell me, for there is one more thing that haunts me, and I must feel your gentle hand to give me peace." He pushed up slightly so that his face caught all the glow of the candlelight and I could see it for all its warts and crevices, the piercing hateful eyes now dark and empty, like deep tunnels as he slipped into the far, unreachable end. "Near the last of my progress there, Bettie, in the westernmost of Munster, there was a boy. And when he died, a girl who...So young, Bettie, her hair blazing red, her eyes wild with fury.

"I should never have…Truly, I did not want…" He began to drift off. Mr. Harvey snorted loudly, and I thought he might wake, but he settled back into his grinding snore.

"Bettie, I never realized...so much raging after that dreadful march... the boy so young and my rage gotthe better of me...and then I sent my soldiers after the girl. She cursed me. She was quick-witted like you, but I wouldn't have...I only meant to bring her back, not to...I only hoped somehow..."

"What? What is it? You must hurry!" I knew my time was running out.

"Sweet daughter. It is not my design to linger, but it is my design to make what haste I can to be gone. My dear, that girl—I only hoped she would somehow find her way home."

I stared into those bottomless eyes and stopped my breath in my throat. Had I been that girl? Could this treacherous soul be believed, that he had not intended my death? And if that be so, might I have stayed all these years, and might I have had a grace of my own to live among my countrymen?

He collapsed back on his pillow and his eyes returned to those narrow sunken slits. He had not died, but I knew his time would come soon. I breathed at last, and felt the iron fist that held my blade soften into bone and flesh. I exhaled slowly, withdrew the sharp point from its lodging in Cromwell's gown and slipped the blade back into my sleeve. I heard my father's question and I straightened my back. *Honor, or defeat?* There could be no honor in killing he who was all but dead, I would answer. But neither was there defeat in retracting, for Cromwell writhes on a devil's spit forged of his own deeds, and there to stay through all eternity with no salvation coming and none of his beloved sons grieving at his bedside. And then I heard the voice of Tempest Wingfield: *There be no honor in killing he who is at your mercy.*

Cromwell was but a last gasp from oblivion, and I need not bear the burden of his killing upon my soul, nor face a horrid traitor's execution. Yet I wondered at Cromwell's confession: if he was evil, could evil also be merciful? And if it could, would evil as itself then survive?

Just as I heard a rousing snort from Charles Harvey, I leapt to the bedside and stood, calmly as my heart would allow, replacing the taper that burned there. I turned to the bleary-eyed groom, offered a bleak smile and a curtsey, and disappeared into my stairway.

From there I ran down the stairs, through the hall, and outside into the fresh, perfumed garden, into the brisk night air that heralded the change of season, and into the bright September starlight.

33

Confessions

Now go we in content; To liberty, and not to banishment.

~ William Shakespeare

I was returning to Skebreen. It would not be as I had planned. I would not return to Ireland as the hero, the rebel-assassin who had rid the world of a long-hated oppressor. I was merely a messenger now: "Oliver Cromwell is dead," I would tell everyone. "Pray for the return of Charles Stuart, the rightful king."

Dr. Bate would later examine Cromwell's body and claim the cause of death was overcharged vessels in the brain and foul oil in his spleen. Some would accuse the doctor of harboring royalist sympathies and poisoning Cromwell himself. No one would ever notice the cut beneath Cromwell's ear, or the other beneath the breastbone, or if they did they dismissed such wounds as mistake, perhaps a slip of the doctor's own blade. None of it mattered anymore. Not to me.

I had left Whitehall Palace with nothing—not even a wrap to warm my shoulders—and though Kade's golden angel mostly had been forgotten for all the time it lay tucked against my breast, it burned as I considered what I needed to do. Badu had warned me to press against my breast that which had brought me to Montserrat. I had thought she referred to my destiny, but now I knew she could only have meant the angel, the very one Master Wingfield had told me to use wisely. There was nothing left for me but to return home to Ireland, and the angel was all I had to buy my passage.

I bargained with a shopkeeper for a proper exchange. I did not know the coin's true worth, but I argued its value until I had shillings enough to pay for my travels and some food. Even if I arrived penniless, if I could just get back to my own village I knew I would be all right. Still, I felt a sore vacancy where the angel so long had rested, and an even greater vacancy in my core, where my hate had lived.

I had done what I believed was my true purpose. All those years, the people I had met and loved, the dangers faced, the distances traveled across the wide open sea—all had prepared me for one task, and it could only be by God's hand that I found my way to Cromwell and into his very bedchamber. In the end, though I was willing, assassination was not required of me. So then, what did it all mean? What was the journey for? And now that it was over, I suppose I no longer had purpose. I was, after all, never going to be either a princess or queen with lands and castle, nor would I fight like a rebel warrior. I was returning to my tiny village as nothing more than I was when I left: a peasant girl, an ordinary person of little value. It was a hard thing, to let go of the burning hate that had driven me all of my life, but perhaps more difficult still to relinquish importance.

I do not recall the details of those next days, or with what load of cargo I arrived in Wexford, but it was a hay wagon that carried me west along the coast road toward Munster. From Kinsale the road bumped along ever so slowly, undulating along high bluffs of shaggy grass and low muddy bogs, and each green hill rolling into the next to become endless patchwork of green and gray, jogging my mind with memories of times before Cromwell, when my world was safe and small.

Somewhere along this road the empty hole began to fill again, with hopes that I would find the River Ilen and follow it until I found Skebreen. And if I found the river I'd find the tiny white flowers that grew along its banks. And finding those, then also I could find the old path to my father's hearthstone, and see if the faery thorn still grew beside it. Those things would bring me comfort as the past receded. The past was just a story now. What would I find in the village I once knew, and who would remain among the faces I'd long remembered? Would anyone welcome me home? Had things changed so in my absence that it might no longer be home to me at all? And most important, would I find my Uncle Aengus? Hopes bubbled forth the longer I traveled, but none of them really mattered, because Skebreen is where I would go and where I would stay. I was twenty and four years, too old to expect a happy marriage and children, or to ever find love.

Kade had offered the only taste of romance I'd ever had, and I'd destroyed it. And yet he still owned all the empty places in my heart, even more so than my father had. The best future I could hope for was a comfortable existence as a spinster. Perhaps I would use my lessons from Timothee to bake sweets fit for royalty. And even if it meant I lived in poverty I would give them away to all the children in the village, and sell the rest to the adults who had money to pay. If I were at least to find Aengus alive, it would be enough to soothe my aching soul.

On a wagon much like this one I had traveled with Kade, long ago before our fortunes changed direction. How I wished he were beside me now, to speak with reason and calm my heart, or at least make me laugh just a little. I would show him what I was now beginning to recognize as my own: the rise and fall of Munster's wave-washed coastline, the very breath of the ocean rising in the wind, and the welcoming breast of the green inland hill. I filled my lungs with the sweet salt air, and knew as intimately as my own tender flesh the shape and color of the moss on those solid, eternal rocks. I knew the low trees crooked and bent by the wind, the scent of the dense black turf and the tender permanence of the blue-gray sky. The old wooden wheels creaked so loudly I thought at any moment one might fall off—an omen perhaps, heralding change.

Overhead the seabirds quarreled and then I thought I heard the distant clop of horse hooves coming toward us at a trot. My back stiffened as I looked behind us, my view of the rider blocked by the hip of the last great hill. A horseman on a path conjured for me only the frightful expectation of threat and loss. Instinctively I buried myself beneath the blanket of hay and peered from beneath my covering to see who was closing in.

The horse was right smart, a proud head lifted to the wind. He carried a lone rider, and the clouded sky allowed no sun to illuminate his dress or the shape of his face. I relaxed a bit. If the man meant trouble, then sure between the old farmer and me we might do him the greater harm. It was just a gentleman traveler. I was home now, and no one sought me.

"Here we be, lassie," the farmer said, touching my shoulder. "The town's but a stone's throw fer a man with a fine arm. Keep watchin' just ahead and we'll see the old church steeple only a heart's flutter away. We'll be wetting our throats soon as well." I peered around the farmer to see smoke rising from somewhere among the trees. Behind us the clopping drew near, the rider's cloak tails flapping in the wind. I caught a scent on the air as rich and beloved as my own father's beard: the fresh breeze blowing in from Baltimore, the sweet-spiced aroma of earth, oak, fire and sea. *Home.*

The rider approached, his velvet garment deep red, with a golden plume blowing hither; his cloak stormy gray with black embroidery and a silver brooch; his breeches butter-colored and his stockings white as milk. A fair rich man, so he was.

"G'day," he said, arriving beside us, and the farmer grunted in return. Dark curls clung at the man's neck. I noticed the strong curve of his jaw, and then his face turned and I saw the crease of a clever grin.

I flailed about to get a better look as the trot changed to canter around the bend ahead of us. The gentleman had a fair resemblance to Kade. If only it could be Kade, I would gladly swallow my own tongue if it meant I could reach him faster. But it could not be Kade. Could it?

Without waiting for the wagon to come to a stop I jumped free of it and tumbled to the road like a birdling from the nest, falling flat on my back so to knock out my wind, but scrambled to my feet again and began to run at such a pace I left the old farmer and his plodding horse behind. I turned just to blow him a kiss and ran around the bend. There before me was our old stone bridge.

They'd rebuilt it, hadn't they? The planks across the top were heavy and worn, and the stone sides where pieced together but hardly engineered. My heart rejoiced at the ramshackle sight of it. Who would have known the terrible tragedy that had taken place there, or the beginning of a long and fateful journey for a frightened and foolish young girl? I could not think of it, nor stop to remember the day, the blood that was shed, the lives forever changed. I crossed the very spot where Oliver Cromwell had once stood, and chased after the rider with the feathered hat.

Beneath the bridge the Ilen swirled happily against the stones and the afternoon sun painted her long tresses gold and white. A new inn had been built just at the far riverbank, its boards still clean and raw. I lost sight of the rider as he turned behind the yellow daub walls of the next structure. I stumbled into a puddle, soiling my skirts from hip to hem. I struggled up again, but my breath was nearly gone. When I heard the old creaky wagon catching up to me, a second burst of energy flowed into my veins and I soared, a flooding stream, a hawk diving from the highest treetop, slicing through the air. And then I stopped.

The gentleman had reined his horse before a tavern. He tamped his boots against a stone, removed his hat and shook it to dislodge the dust, and stretched his arms high above his head. He was not nearly as thin as Kade had been, but had the breadth of shoulders, the shape of his head, the casual stance with one knee bent, one hip below the other. My heart leapt like a dancer. Like ten dancers. Like ten thousand doves in frenzied flight.

I stepped forward but hesitated, remembering my muddied skirt, my filthy hands, my hair whipped about my face in a tangled, horrid mass. Even with the help of all the saints and faeries combined, there was no way to I could repair my appearance.

He turned and I ran to him—no stopping me, for I'd lost my head. I aimed for his doublet, meaning to throw my arms about him, but we fell together against the rough tavern wall. I was breathless and had knocked him senseless besides. For a moment we could only stare into each other's eyes, but then the corner of his lip curled and he found the means to speak.

"I've come lookin' for a princess," he said lightly. "Do you happen to know if there be one about?"

"Kade! You are here. You're alive!" I blathered the obvious, so much to say but unable to gather words of any meaning.

"So it would seem," he replied.

"But I pushed you into the sea myself. The captain said you were eaten by the sharks."

"Ah, and, of course, the captain was known for his honesty. Did you not see the ship that sailed just behind the *Jackdaw*? Did you not see them haul me in? That ship was bound for Jamaica, an island of a thousand opportunities for the man willing to see them."

"You…were not indentured? You were not a slave?"

He fingered the broach at his shoulder. "At first, aboard the ship. But the captain took a liking to me, and it seems my particular skills are highly valued in Jamaica. Have you seen many slaves thus attired, my lady?"

I stepped back to look at his clothes. I was so elated to see him, and yet I felt the twinge of envy that my path had been so different. I had tried to kill him, and he had found a better life. I had tried to save myself and had found brutality, disease, and loss. How strange the twists of fate.

"I searched for you, Elvy. As soon as opportunity allowed I traveled the islands to find you. First I returned to Barbados, but you were not there, nor in St. Christopher, nor Antigua. It took some time, but when I found a ship bound for Montserrat I met a planter in a tavern who said he knew you, and you had gone home."

Tears sprang to my eyes. "Were they all right, Kade? When I left the… island was under attack by the Caribs."

"I saw no sign of it. The town of Plymouth remains prosperous."

I heaved a sigh of relief. "And so you came here?"

"I had to find you. There is something I must return." His cheeks turned dark crimson, but he looked into my eyes.

"To me?" I asked, still babbling like a fool.

"I took something from you and thereby may have done you great harm. When we were together on the *Jackdaw* I…I had no one else in the whole God-forsaken world. I thought if you had your letter we'd be separated and I'd not see you again. So I took it. Rather a joke now, isn't it?"

"Jaysus, Kade! What on earth?"

He looked down as if examining the toes of his shoes. "Your letter of introduction to the governor. And when you shoved me overboard at Barbados, it was in my pocket." He produced a paper, folded several times into a small square, filthy and frayed on all edges. I unfolded it carefully, though the fragile page was torn along one fold. At last I held the tattered thing before me. The ink had been watered until words were mere scratches among the stains.

"It is completely unreadable." I smiled.

"I am not a thief, Elvy. I needed you to know that."

"You are not a thief," I conceded. Then my jaw dropped as my mind raced through the years past. If I'd had the letter, I might have been spared my indenture and escaped the beating at the hands of Mr. Drax. I might have avoided the great fever that shook my bones and nearly killed me. From the first, I might have been taken freely into the household of the governor, that thieving, murdering, conniving devil, and then never, ever have been free again. I would never have met Tempest Wingfield or Nessa, Badu or Timothee. I would never have survived to stare into the face of Cromwell himself.

"You are not a thief, Kade, and I am not a murderer." He looked at me, not understanding the tears that streamed down my cheeks, his eyes looking painfully uncertain. "Kade McEown, St. Brendan himself may never know the horrors you prevented by your deed, but no matter now. Thanks be to God you're alive and you're here, and I'm standing before you."

His smile returned, but at the very sight of it my chest tightened and my thoughts clouded, for I had my own confession to make.

"I must ask for your forgiveness, Kade."

He cocked his head. "Aye?"

"For pushing you overboard. I was foolish and impulsive and should never have done it. You gave me your lucky gold coin to keep for you.

I lost it once but then I got it back, and I knew I had to keep it for something important, but ended up spending it selfishly to buy my passage home. I should have kept it. I should have found another way. But now I've no coin left to give you."

Kade frowned, tapping an index finger against his chin. "I remember now. To be sure, it was a special coin, that angel. But then it served its purpose, didn't it? You are here, exactly where I hoped I'd find you." His eyebrows lifted as an idea seemed to come to him. "Stand here, Elvy. Do not move, I have something to show you." He retrieved a bag from his saddle. "Now then, hold out your skirt as if I were to fill it with grain."

I did so, and he emptied the contents of the bag—coins, handfuls of them, heavy, clinking, clanking, shining coins, gold as the sunset, gold as the leaves on the asters, gold as the flecks of color in his eyes that seized my fascination and would not let loose their hold.

"I always thought I'd save one for luck and set it amongst the stones of my hearth once I found my bride," he said. "There are two more for my eyes, and two for hers, when we pass away to Heaven." He took my face in his hands and held me there, his lips just an inch from mine. "May that day be a long time in coming. As to the rest of them, I am sure we'll figure out their purpose as we go. For I've no intention of leaving you, Elvy Burke."

I swallowed hard to make sure I could get out my answer. "I've no intention of letting you."

There came a great squeal of swollen wood against a door jamb, and a bent, gray-headed barkeep stepped out of the tavern, a bucket in one hand and a well-worn broom in the other.

"What be the trouble out here?" he demanded. His back straightened then, and his thin neck stretched high. His eyes were obscured behind thick round lenses, the last of the sun glinting off the glass. He stared in our direction for a moment, but seemed confused and I was not sure if he could see anything at all. Then his chin leveled, his shoulders squared and he dropped the bucket and broom into the dirt at his feet. "Ailbhe," he whispered. His two palms clapped his whiskered cheeks.

"Gentlemen!" he hollered. "Lads! Come out and see what's come to us. Come out! It's a miracle, it is. T'anks be to God and all the spirits above and beneath us," Aengus cried out. "'Tis our own sweet daughter, at last. Our Elvy's grown up and come home."

Author's Note

As you reach this page, I hope you have enjoyed *The Snow Path to Dingle* and the ups and downs of Elvy's adventure. The process of writing it was an experience full of discovery and expansion.

All of the main characters in Sharavogue are invented, including Elvy, Aengus, Kade, and everyone on the plantation. Historical figures including Oliver Cromwell and his family, Governor Osborne and Samuel Waad are faithful representations based on my research, and sometimes including in their dialogue actual words or statements recorded in letters or journals. Waad's execution is covered in several books and documents. It may be of interest that Waad's family submitted a complaint to Oliver Cromwell, but Crowell referred the issue back to his deputy in the West Indies, and from there it seems it was never addressed. Doctor Bate, Charles Harvey and Miles Sindercombe were actual people in Cromwell's history. The historical facts of the time are woven in as accurately as possible, as they contributed to the story.

It was my good fortune to visit Skibbereen, County Cork, when I was about 19 years old. The memory of it lodged in my heart and there was no question that it must be Elvy's home. I have used the old spelling, Skebreen, that is used on 17th century maps. There was skepticism from one reviewer as to whether Cromwell actually traveled so far west, however I discovered an historical map confirming his route not only to Skibbereen but beyond, past Bantry to the Glengariff River.

In my readings I came across a legend that, upon learning of Cromwell's approach, townspeople had dismantled a bridge in hopes of keeping him away. The location of this bridge was not clear, but I was fascinated by the idea and have used a bit of creative license to include it in the first chapter and to place it in Skibbereen.

The island of Montserrat in the West Indies was chosen as the location for the sugar plantation, Sharavogue, because a colony of Irish planters developed there—it being one of the last islands that still had land not claimed by the English, Spanish or Dutch. The plantations did require slave labor, and the islands in those areas did experience the raids of Carib tribes. There are some interesting books on the plantation development of these islands that are included in my list of sources. In the 17th century, many planters and slaves died from malaria or yellow fever, which would not be controlled effectively until the 20th century.

Readers have found the production of bread from cassava of interest. The production process was likely of greater difficulty than described here, where Elvy works alone; by most modern descriptions, a team of workers form an assembly line to carry out the steps required. Cassava flour is gaining some popularity because it is gluten free and grain free. Tapioca flour is made from the same root, but processed somewhat differently.

The Jombee dance described in Chapter Eighteen may seem very fanciful, but the ritual is well documented by Jay Dobbin in his book, included in my source list. I have used it here because it is site-specific, and adapted it somewhat for the story and time period.

The death of Cromwell is also well documented, and I have used some of his own words in Chapter Thirty-two. Except for his sentence about not intending to linger, the delirious deathbed conversation with his daughter Bettie is fictional.

The quotations at the beginnings of each chapter I have collected from various sources during my research. Most are from adventurers who traveled to the West Indies in the time period and recorded their observations in letters or journals. I owe the greatest debt to Richard Ligon for his colorful descriptions of Barbados. Prior to Chapter One is a poem, *On the Sea* by John Keats, published in the 18th century. The poem addresses the power of the ocean, of God, and of human emotion. I felt it appropriate to Elvy's experiences.

Thank you for reading this book. You may also enjoy the prequel to Sharavogue, The Prince of Glencurragh, which is about Elvy's father and mother. If you have other questions about the content, please contact me via my website, ***www.nancyblanton.com***. While there, please subscribe to my newsletter to receive updates on signing events and new books.

And, if you like what you've read, please consider posting a review on Amazon, Barnes and Noble, or Goodreads. Reviews are very helpful to other readers and to authors.

Selected Sources

The Arcanum: The Extraordinary True Story. Janet Gleeson, 1998. Warner Books Inc., New York.

A Brief and True Remonstrance of the Illegal Proceedings of Roger Osburn (an Irish man born), Governor of MountSerrat, March, 1654.

Cromwell. Antonia Fraser, 1973. Grove Press, New York.

Cromwell in Ireland: A History of Cromwell's Irish Campaign. Rev. Denis Murphy, S.J., (year). M.H. Gill & Son, Ltd. Dublin.

Fire from Heaven: Life in an English Town in the Seventeenth Century. David Underdown, 1992. Yale University Press.

God's Executioner: Oliver Cromwell and the Conquest of Ireland. Micheal O'Siochru. 2008. Faber and Faber Limited, London.

A History of St. Kitts: The Sweet Trade. Vincent K. Hubbard, 2002. Macmillan Publishers Limited, Oxford.

If the Irish Ran the World: Montserrat, 1630—1730. Donald Harma Akenson. McGill-Queen's University Press, Montreal & Kingston, London, Buffalo.

Montserrat, Emerald Isle of the Caribbean. Howard A. Fergus, 1989 (second ed.). The Macmillan Press, Ltd., London and Basingstoke.

Oliver Cromwell. Helen Litton, 2000. Wolfhound Press, Ltd., Dublin, Ireland.

Sugar & Slaves: The Rise of the Planter Class in the English West Indies, 1624—1713. Richard S. Dunn, 1972. University of North Carolina Press, Chapel Hill.

The Jombee Dance of Montserrat: A Study of Trance Ritual in the West Indies. Jay D. Dobbin, 1986. Ohio State University Press.

The King and the Gentleman: Charles Stuart and Oliver Cromwell 1599-1649. Derek Wilson, 1999. St. Martin's Press, New York.

The Rise and Fall of the Plantation Complex: Essays in Atlantic History. Philip D. Curtin, 1990, 1998. Cambridge University Press, New York.

Traits and Stories of the Irish Peasantry, Vol. 2. William Carleton, 1842 (1990); Colin Smythe Ltd., Gerrards Cross, Buckinghamshire; B&N, Maryland. Back Bay Books, Little, Brown & Company, New York.

Wars of the Irish Kings: A thousand years of struggle, from the age of myth through the reign of Queen Elizabeth I. David Willis McCullough, 2000. Crown Publishers, New York.

Whitehall Palace: an architectural history of the royal apartments, 1240-1698. Simon Thurley, with contributions by Alan Cook, 1999. New Haven: Yale University Press in association with Historic Royal Palaces.

About the Author

Nancy Blanton's passion for Ireland's history comes from her father, who treasured his Irish heritage and loved everything about the people, the land, the pubs, the stories, the songs, and most especially the horses.

Her novels about 17th century Ireland have garnered enthusiastic readership and two of Florida's prestigious Royal Palm Literary Awards for historical fiction.

Her blog, *My Lady's Closet*, focuses on writing, books, history, personal branding, historical fiction, research, and travel. Readers can subscribe by visiting her website at www.nancyblanton.com.

As author, journalist, magazine editor, and corporate communications leader, Nancy has won numerous awards for products and professional leadership. She has a bachelor's degree in journalism, and a master's degree in mass communications. She lives in Florida.

Connect with Nancy:

Blog: https://www.nancyblanton.com/blog
Facebook: Nancy Blanton.Author
Twitter: @nancy_blanton
Instagram: blantonn17c

Printed in Poland
by Amazon Fulfillment
Poland Sp. z o.o., Wrocław

31786895R00163